Lady

of the

House

Lady
of the
House

LYNN BRAXTON

SOUTHERN STAR PRESS
An Independent Publisher

Lady of the House

This work of fiction is solely the product of the author's imagination. Any similarities to actual persons, living or deceased, places, names, characterizations, recorded events, or incidents are unintentional. Named cities are used to geographically set the story.

First Publication Date: April 2014
ISBN: 978-0-9914663-5-1

Published by Southern Star Press, LLC
Monticello, Florida

www.LynnLBraxton.com

Cover Design by Kimberly Killion
The Killion Group, Inc.
www.theKillionGroupInc.com
www.HOTDAMNdesigns.com

Printed in the United States of America

This book is dedicated
to all
the ladies of my house.

Acknowledgements

Creating a book can be a rewarding, yet sometimes lonely journey. Having friends along to encourage and support the effort makes it all the better. My deepest gratitude to those who have traveled with LADY from the beginning . . .

Members of the Wednesday Night Writers of Tallahassee, Florida
Adrian Fogelin, Noanne Gwynn, Leigh Muller, Gina Edwards, Leslee Horner, and Richard Dempsey

Special thanks

To my editor and friend,
Gina Hogan Edwards
who searched
for and found the errors when
I could no longer see the page.
www.AroundTheWritersTable.com

-and-

Award-winning author, Donna Meredith
The Glass Madonna
The Color of Lies
Wet Work
for invaluable advice and technical assistance
throughout the initial launch of
this book.
www.donnameredith.com

Lady of the House

A Novel by

Lynn Braxton

The Main Characters
1828 – 1843

The City of Charleston
Swan House
Lily Perrault
Kate Perrault
Captain Ezra Swan (deceased)
Georgette LeBlanc
Thaddeus Parks
Jack Faro
Fiona O'Flarety
Franklin Miller
Xavier
Micha & Joseph
Polly
Sauchie
Mohab

The DuPres
Adelaide (Beauchamp) DuPre
Doctor Gaston DuPre (deceased)
Doctor Paul DuPre
Constance Dupre (Wellington)
David (Davy) Wellington DuPre
Caleb
Tilde

The Claibornes
Judge Nathan Claiborne
Honora (Beauchamp) Claiborne
Simon
Hester

The Flynns
The Reverend Stephen Flynn
Grace (Pickering) Flynn

Ginny Flynn
John Davis
Cassie

The Armstrongs
Brewster Armstrong
Minerva Armstrong
Sarah Armstrong
Linus
Bernice

Others in the City
Auctioneer Sam Gunnells
Enos Kemp, Gunnells's right-hand man
Doctor Hadley Baker
Dressmaker Madame Gerow
Ferryman Grady Forbes
Esperanza Piero, boarding house proprietor

The River Road Leading to Charleston

The Turnbulls, Three Fountains Plantation
Thurston Turnbull
Margaret Turnbull
Percival (Percy) Turnbull
Marylove Turnbull (Tredaway)
Johnny Tredaway

The Edens, Eden's Gate Plantation
Victor Eden
Augusta (Flynn) Eden
Charles Eden
Grier Taylor
Colombo
Zina
Juno

Pansy
Rameses
Pearl

The Wellingtons, Cottonwood Plantation
Daniel Wellington
Emma Wellington (DuPre) (deceased)
Iretta Wellington
Maybelle Wellington
Elzy Parrish
Walter

The City of New Orleans

The Cruz Family, The House on Rue Royale
Andre and Lizette Cruz (deceased)
Celine Cruz
Etienne Cruz
Phillipe Cruz
Catherine (Perry) Cruz (deceased)
Odette
Emil

The deFonvilles
Louis deFonville
Estelle deFonville

The Convent
Sister Agatha
Sister Mathilde

The Charity Hospital
Doctor Phineas Bannon

The Boarding House
Elvira Suggs

Prologue

Charleston, South Carolina
May 1, 1828

The house at the furthermost end of Battery Row stood silent in the pre-dawn stillness. Only the soft rustle of wind through the trees relieved the heaviness that enveloped the four-storied structure. Lanterns used to mark the shell-packed avenue leading from the main gate were without light for the first time in more than twenty years. Inside, servants hurried to cover mirrors in the ballroom with yards of black crepe before daylight slipped across the widow's walk atop the roof and penetrated the house through the windows facing east.

On the second floor, four mourners kept their vigil in the main bedchamber and spoke in inaudible tones. As daylight began to settle among the trees and dapple the avenue, a tall rangy figure emerged onto the upper outside gallery. Thaddeus Parks scrubbed wearily at his swarthy features and heaved a deep sigh.

The most notorious woman in all of Charleston had died at half past midnight. Even now, word of Kate Perrault's passing was being whispered by stealthy messengers to other households throughout the city. The gentlemen who frequented her magnificent gaming palace would awaken to a sense of inexplicable loss; their ladies would sigh with relief and prepare for afternoon social calls with unusual anticipation. But none would present themselves at Swan House to offer condolences or at Saint Bartholomew's Church to pray for her soul.

Kate had fled from New Orleans twenty-two years before, arriving in Charleston under the protection of one of its most infamous citizens, Captain Ezra Swan. When the aging sea captain fell ill and died within a year, the society who had shunned him since his youth was aghast to learn he had left his fortune, and Swan House, to his beautiful young paramour.

With a cynicism premature for her years, Kate had defiantly transformed Ezra Swan's house into the grandest gaming palace east of the Mississippi River. And, for the next two decades, she set about relieving Charleston's gentry of a sizable portion of their considerable wealth.

It was this legacy—and the hidden secret concealed beneath the very foundation of Swan House—that would pass to her only daughter, if Lily Perrault could be found.

A jeweled box beside Kate's bed was said to contain an unsigned letter confirming the child's death during a fever epidemic that ravaged New Orleans a year after Kate fled the city. Cruel in its brevity, the document offered no clues to the whereabouts of her daughter's final resting place. It was said that Kate read the worn parchment before retiring to her silken bed at dawn each day. Those who claimed to have seen the letter declared it was the reason Kate never returned to New Orleans. Yet, as she drew her last labored breaths, she had feebly clutched at Thaddeus's sleeve and gasped, "My Lily, she's alive!" Her eyes blazed with a flash of joy before her fingers slipped from his arm.

Thaddeus stood helplessly by as her best friend, Georgette LeBlanc, pressed Kate's withered hand to her cheek and wept with unrestrained grief as the light disappeared from her eyes forever. What had happened in those final seconds of her life to convince Kate that she had been the victim of a monstrous hoax for all of those tormented and lonely years?

"It's the truth, what Miz Kate said 'bout her girl. She seen her, she did."

Thaddeus didn't bother to turn, nor was he surprised that Kate's maidservant had slipped up behind him unheard. Polly had been part of the Swan household from the very beginning. Ezra Swan had given her over to Kate when he first brought her here. And no one knew Kate Perrault better than the mulatto.

"We got no protection now that Miz Kate's gone," she whispered nervously. "You got to find that girl, Mistah Thad, and bring her home to her mam's house."

He turned slowly and folded his arms across his chest in weary defiance. His dark eyes challenged her. "And how the hell am I to do that?" he protested softly. "None of us know for certain who Kate Perrault *really* was before she came to Charleston, or why she left her daughter in New Orleans in the first place. If the girl is alive, she'll be a woman grown now. Maybe with a family of her own. And even if I am able to find her, what makes you think she will agree to accompany a stranger half-way across the dadblamed country?"

"She got no family 'cept Miz Kate. You just trust her mam. She come, she will."

He watched her walk back into the room and help Franklin Miller lift Georgette to her feet. Polly guided her toward the door. It would be hours before they emerged from the cellar below. Not even death could interfere with their mission. As the lock clicked softly behind the two women, Kate's banker sank to his knees beside the bed and lifted her hand to his lips, his shoulders shaking with silent sobs.

Thaddeus frowned and turned back to grip the railing. Polly had placed the responsibility of finding Kate's daughter squarely on his shoulders. To her way of thinking, the matter was settled. He could ignore her demand to search for the girl, but they both knew his conscience wouldn't let him.

It had been fifteen years since a pair of gunmen had ambushed him on a back street in Savannah. Crippled lawmen weren't worth 'two fer a penny' but he had been lucky. Georgette had been the first to recognize the worth of the drifter who cleaned their stables and slept in the loft above the stalls. She had persuaded Kate to move him into the big house and entrust him with the protection of her household. As the years passed, they came to understand one another. He had no choice but to seek out the truth. If Lily Perrault was alive, he would find her and bring her home to Charleston.

Three weeks later, on May 22, 1828, Thaddeus Parks boarded a ship bound for Louisiana.

One

The night was swallowed up in a wind-driven mist that concealed a crumbling wall ahead. Thaddeus Parks urged his spavined mount through a dense tangle of vines and briars. A night creature scuttled across his path, chattering angrily at the intrusion. He slapped irritably at the tendrils of Spanish moss that trailed from the branches of an ancient oak, sorely tempted to turn back to town and avail himself of the first saloon he came upon.

He had arrived in New Orleans two weeks earlier to discover that the city abounded with cemeteries, the marbled crypts of the rich standing in stark contrast to the desperate barrenness of the potter's field. He had searched each one and found no trace of Lily Perrault.

Finally, forced to rely upon his instincts as a lawman, he strapped on his weapon and worked his way south, traveling through swamplands and bayous, seeking out remote settlements and plantations beyond the city's boundaries. Two days into his journey, he doubled back and headed for New Orleans. He was convinced he would never find the woman he was looking for when he spied a clearing through a thicket of trees and undergrowth. A barely discernible path led him past the charred ruins of a house toward a walled enclosure in the distance. He dismounted and approached a sagging gate of rotted planks and rusted wire. It creaked eerily on its broken hinges in the steamy silence. The cypress grave markers beyond the gate were all but hidden beneath a thick matting of brambles. Most of the single names carved into the lichen-covered wood were no longer legible. He judged it to be the final resting place of the household slaves who had once served the ruin he had just ridden past.

But the smallest of the graves was different. It was set apart from the others and looked as if it did not belong there. He knelt and traced his fingers across the markings chiseled into the clay dome and squinted at the crudely formed letters.

L I Y

1806 – 1807

His heart hammered against his ribs. Could this be what he was looking for? There was only one way to know for sure. Thaddeus pushed himself to his feet and hurried toward his mount. There was a settlement nearby where he could purchase the supplies he needed. But he would have to return when it was dark and there was no chance anyone would be about to witness what he meant to do.

Later that night

In the distance, a bull gator bellowed across the water followed by another closer by. Thaddeus dismounted and loosened the tools wrapped in a leather blanket tied to his saddle. He leaned a small hand pick against his leg, disengaged a lantern from the pommel, and retrieved a lucifer from his vest pocket. The flame sputtered and settled into a soft glow in the glass dome he held aloft. A gust of wind rustled the leaves overhead. A shiver rippled across the back of his neck.

He pushed aside the gate and made for the mound of stone and mortar at the far corner of the enclosure. If this was the grave of Kate's daughter, the poor waif had marked a brief passage through life and remained forgotten for more than twenty years. He set the lantern on the ground and shoved the edge of the pick through a crack in the dome. It broke with surprising ease, caving in upon itself. He knelt, pushed the lantern close to the opening, and raked away the pieces. His eyes narrowed. A muscle twitched in his jaw. No small body had ever lain in this godforsaken place.

The fog-shrouded streets were deserted by the time he rode back into town. He guided his mount toward the livery stable. A lantern over the door cast its reflection upon the wet cobblestones. The old leg wounds were paining him badly, and he groaned as he swung down from the saddle. He rubbed a scarred hand across the stubble on his narrow cot and flung the contents about the floor. "Ain't nothing here, Harry."

"Check the mattress, you idiot!"

The youth drew a blade from his boot and stabbed at the rough ticking. Suddenly, the door crashed inward, slamming against the wall.

"That's me bedding, you pig swill." Elvira Suggs braced the ancient weapon against the doorframe and strangled the trigger.

"Christ!" The younger emitted a shrill yelp as the blast splintered the shutters from their hinges. The two robbers dove for the open window.

"What the hell's going on here?" The boarder from across the hall burst from his room, forgetting he was stark naked.

"Robbers!" she shrieked. "They attacked Mister Parks. Lordy, he's dead! Somebody fetch Doctor Bannon. Lizzie, bring towels. Mister Jensen, cover yourself!"

The long hall lay in shadows. Whether the day was beginning or ending, Thaddeus could not tell. He grimaced fiercely as a bitter concoction trickled down his throat. Hooded specters wavered above him, murmuring unintelligibly. Soft and gentle hands brushed his face. He sensed the nearness of an angel. Another voice penetrated the peaceful oblivion that began to settle over him. The touch was not as gentle, but probing and sure.

"Mister Parks?" The voice grew more insistent. "If you can hear me, sir, open your eyes."

Thaddeus squinted, scarcely able to make out the face above him. The features were neither youthful nor old in spite of the silver that prematurely faded a crown of disheveled brown hair. There was strength enough in the man's arms to lift another with ease. He was a giant with kind and compassionate eyes.

"Ah, good, good." A sound of triumph. Again the pincers probed. Thaddeus cried out, and miraculously, the angel touched him again.

"Looks like he's coming around." The doctor glanced across the bed at the young novice and reached for the strips of clean linen she placed within easy reach across their patient's chest. He made quick work of the bandage and tossed the soiled rags into a basin which she carried away.

"Open your eyes, Mister Parks. Come along, now."

Thaddeus struggled to bring the wavering features into focus once more. "Who are you? Where am I?" he whispered.

"Doctor Phineas Bannon, at your service, sir. You had us worried for a while."

"Doctor?"

"You were brought here several days ago. It seems you were set upon by two ruffians intent upon relieving you of your possessions."

"Possessions?" *The boarding house!* Panic flashed in Thaddeus's eyes.

"Lay back, man. The indomitable Miz Suggs routed the louts from the premises and saved your belongings. All of your things are here in safekeeping, less a small compensation the good woman felt was her due."

He sank back upon the pillow clearly relieved. The doctor stepped away from the bedside. "I have other patients to attend to. Get some rest. I'll come around later and see how you're progressing. In the meantime, I leave you in good hands."

"Much obliged, doctor." Thaddeus closed his eyes and felt himself drifting into a natural sleep. When he awoke, the hall was dark but for the soft glow of oil lamps at either end of the room. He watched a slender figure take up a lighted candle and make her way quietly between the double rows of beds, stopping to adjust a blanket, offer a soft word of comfort, and satisfy a feverish thirst. He felt himself drifting off again, rousing when she approached his bed.

"Is there anything that I can do for you, Mister Parks?" Her whisper was as sweet as an angel's harp.

He opened his eyes slightly. Framed in a white veil, the face of a young Kate Perrault gazed down at him behind a pair of ill-fitting spectacles. She drew back at the sound of his startled gasp. He stared up at her for the longest time. She ventured a shy smile.

"Yes ma'am," he whispered hoarsely. "I think maybe there is."

Two

August 1, 1828

Lily opened the shutters of her cubicle to the sounds of the city awakening beyond the convent walls. In the distance, a group of young postulants hurried along an open corridor to begin their daily chores at the charity hospital nearby. Ordinarily, she accompanied them, but today she was leaving the order and the only way of life she had ever known.

It had been more than twenty years since the Ursulines had discovered her abandoned on their doorstep. She had few memories of the first years spent in their care, but secrets about her shrouded past had suddenly been revealed by the arrival of the stranger from Charleston.

Thaddeus Parks had been released from the hospital a week earlier and appeared at the convent asking for her the same day. At first, no one believed his shocking claim until he produced a miniature of a lady he identified as Kate Perrault, herself a citizen lately of Charleston. Although years separated them, Lily's startling resemblance to the portrait in his possession convinced Thaddeus Parks that she was indeed Kate Perrault's missing daughter and heir to an establishment he referred to only as 'the Swan.'

Her first impulse had been to refuse his request to accompany him to Charleston. Yet his persistence had unleashed a secret yearning buried deep within her heart. Although the woman Thaddeus declared to be her mother was dead, there remained a chance, however slight, that the journey into Kate's past could lead her to her father.

Once she agreed to the voyage, the days sped past in a flurry of preparations for her departure. She had never ventured outside the city of New Orleans. To sail across a vast ocean promised to be an adventure that could scarcely be imagined. She turned from the window and looked about the small room feeling a lump gather in her throat. A scarred medicine box rested on a table near her bed. Phineas Bannon had given it to her when she began to accompany the older nuns to the docks to treat the ailments of the derelicts and consumptive coughs of the street whores.

She had surrendered her robes and veil to the Novice Mistress the night before and been allowed to select a few traveling garments from a barrel of clothing donated for the poor. She fingered the faded brown cloth of the dress she was wearing and felt oddly exposed. A straw bonnet with a frayed grosgrain ribbon lay on the bed next to a battered satchel. She sighed. At least her brogans were her own, scuffed as they were. She turned at the sound of a knock on her door.

"Sister Mathilde."

"Lily, Sister Agatha sent me to fetch you," The young novice whispered urgently.

Without a word, Lily brushed past her friend and hurried down the long hallway. Sister Agatha had pleaded fatigue and excused herself from the evening meal the night before. All the years Lily had been in the Ursuline's care, it was Sister Agatha who had supervised her lessons, taught her stitchery, and watched with a keen eye when she took instructions from the other sisters. Concern for the frail little nun caused Lily to quicken her steps.

She struggled to hide her dismay when she entered a room scarcely larger than her own. The figure on the bed appeared shrunken and childlike. Wisps of thin white hair escaped from beneath the old woman's sleeping cap. Lily blinked back the tears that welled up in her eyes. She rushed toward the bed and knelt, gathering Sister's gnarled hands in her own.

"I was afraid I would not have a chance to say goodbye."

"Oh, I could never permit you to go without seeing you one last time," Sister Agatha whispered, pulling her hands from Lily's grasp. She pointed to a plain wooden chest at the foot of her bed. "There's something in there that belongs to you. You should take it with you."

Lily turned and carefully lifted the lid and reached into the chest.

The fringed magenta silk was creased and felt cold to the touch in spite of the warmth of the room.

"You were much too young to remember, but it was during the time of the great fever that we found you lying in a basket at our door. You were wrapped in that shawl." Sister Agatha drew a labored breath. Her fingers trembled as she pointed to a faintly smudged blemish.

"Look closely there. You can still make out the partial imprint of a name in the corner. Most of it has long since faded away. We took your name, Lily, from it."

"Do you think it belonged to my mother?" Lily whispered in awe. Her fingers traced the fine appliqués. Although the colors were faded, it was obvious that it had been a very fine garment once, one that a lady would have worn. As a young child, she had hidden behind Sister Agatha's robes and peered intently at the ladies who served as patronesses of the orphanage when they came to visit. She had always hoped a pair of loving arms would reach for her. But none ever had.

"Perhaps. But when no one came for you, we all agreed that whoever left you with us must have perished during the epidemic. So many died that terrible summer."

Lily clutched the shawl to her and reached for Sister Agatha's hand once again. "Mister Parks says Swan House is of good size. Several people live there now. A boarding house will require hard work, but you have taught me well." Lily blinked rapidly.

Suddenly, a bell jangled in the distance signaling a caller at the gate. "That will be Mister Parks."

"Oh, I shall miss you all so." Panic edged Lily's voice as tears slipped down her burning cheeks. "I could sell the house and return. I am sure to receive offers for it," she blurted impulsively.

Sister Agatha reached to stroke the golden curl that had come loose from the girl's knitted snood and shook her head wearily. "No, child. I think you're intended for this journey. Now, hurry along. You do not want to keep the gentleman waiting."

Thaddeus pretended not to notice the anguish in Lily's eyes as she pushed her way through a throng of well-wishers and hurried toward him. He heaved her valise up to the driver he had hired to take them to the docks and turned to hand her up into the carriage.

As the team lurched forward, her carefully set features began to crumple. Thaddeus quickly snatched a handkerchief from his vest pocket and pressed it into her hand. His senses quickened as the driver urged the team to a faster pace. His protection of Kate's daughter had begun in earnest. He had said little to her about the future that awaited her. And to be sure, there *was* a reckoning coming.

Three

The *Harlequin* appeared trifling small alongside other vessels that crowded the harbor. Thaddeus had paid a fair amount of gold to arrange private sleeping quarters for his charge. The cramped cabin boasted only a narrow bunk and a washstand bolted to the floor, but Lily was accustomed to spartan conditions and appeared to find no fault with it. An hour after he left her to settle in, she made her way back up on deck.

From the rail, they surveyed the bustling scene on the dock below. Flanked by a mountainous wall of crates and casks, a parade of conveyances continued to arrive, discharging passengers in a rush of last-minute farewells.

Lily ventured a nervous smile. "I never imagined I would leave New Orleans."

"Don't expect you had much reason to." Thaddeus frowned, quickly dismissing the images of Georgette and Franklin that flashed through his mind.

He straightened and watched a mule-driven wagon lumber across the wooden dock and come to a stop directly beneath the *Harlequin's* berth. The lone passenger flicked dust from his green velvet lapel and grimaced at a ruffled cuff soiled by the iron manacles that spanned his wrists. An astonishing thatch of red hair curled against his collar; a frown settled beneath a moustache of the same hue.

One of the guards dismounted from the driver's seat and motioned to the prisoner to follow. The second guard shouldered his weapon and trailed behind. As the strange procession gained the *Harlequin's* deck, the shackled man sighed, thrust out his wrists, and craned his neck for a look at Thaddeus and Lily.

"G'day to ye, folks. Faro's the name. Jack Faro."

Thaddeus tugged at the brim of his hat. "Thaddeus Parks," he gave a curt nod in Lily's direction, "and Miss Lily Perrault." His suspicious glare bore into the newcomer. Swan House was well known to men of Faro's obvious inclinations. If the gambler had ever chanced to pass through Charleston, he would instantly figure out that Lily was somehow related to the richest woman in the city. Thaddeus exhaled slowly when no sign of recognition registered on Jack Faro's features.

Instead, the gambler ignored his guards and managed an awkward bow in Lily's direction. "Ma'am."

Behind the specs perched on her nose, her startling blue eyes struck Faro with the force of a thunderclap. He grinned inwardly at her flushed response to his frank appraisal.

The manacles clattered to the deck. He rubbed his wrists and winced as one of the guards dropped his valise at his feet. Everything he possessed had been hurriedly stuffed into that receptacle, including three bottles of fine Irish whiskey.

"Farewell, gentlemen. It's been a pleasure to share your company."

The two men laughed as they descended the plank. Faro was not a bad sort. But, to be discovered in the boudoir of the constable's niece had earned the fool a one-way passage out of New Orleans on the first available vessel.

Jack retrieved a coin from his vest pocket and tossed it to a passing crewman. "Here, fellow. Stow me things below. I'll be sharing quarters with another gentleman." He heard Thaddeus groan audibly.

"Ah, don't ye fret, Mister Parks. I do not snore. In fact, I sleep as peaceful as a babe." Jack positioned himself on the opposite side of Lily and surveyed his traveling companions with a practiced eye. Judging from Thaddeus Parks's attire, he was not a gentleman of means. And the girl was garbed no better than a steerage passenger. If no one else boarded the *Harlequin* before she sailed on the morning tide, he would arrive in the city of Charleston virtually penniless.

For more than a week, the *Harlequin* forged a southeasterly course across the open Gulf. Jack chafed at the endless solitude. Any hopes he had of luring his dour cabin-mate into a game of chance had quickly been dashed.

He sank onto a makeshift deck bench next to Lily, folded his arms across his chest and yawned. "I've scarcely had a wink o' sleep since we left New Orleans."

It was true. Thaddeus's thunderous snores reverberated through their cabin nightly. Jack's frown turned to a sheepish grin at the sound of Lily's shy laughter. A comfortable sense of familiarity had begun to develop between the two of them.

He watched Thaddeus ease himself away from a pallet of crates with a painful grimace.

Lily swiftly gathered up her stitchery. "Come, Mister Parks. You should rest." She paused to give Jack a quick smile. "You will excuse us, Jack?"

He nodded and watched them go, a puzzled frown creasing his brow. Before they reached Charleston, he intended to find out all there was to know about Lily Perrault and that sullen old barnacle attached to her side.

From the bridge, the captain watched their progress toward the passageway then trained his glass upon a wall of angry looking thunderheads building on the horizon. There was no reason to alarm the two of them, or the gambler, but the *Harlequin* would almost surely be overtaken by the approaching storm by midnight.

Later that night

Jack sat alone in the galley and struggled to focus on the cards spread out before him. Overhead, the lantern swung a shaft of light in a widening arc across the table. As the hours passed, he felt a growing sense of unease. The captain had warned that passage through the straits would be the most treacherous part of the voyage, but there was no need to worry. The *Harlequin* had navigated it countless times without mishap. But the crew's activities had become more harried as darkness descended, and this damn scow was bucking like a mule.

He flung the cards aside and fumbled inside his coat for his flask. He belonged in the glittering salon of a riverboat with a beautiful woman at his side and a winning hand spread out before him. Instead, he seemed destined to end his twenty-seven years in a deep and murky hell of storm-tossed seas. Only the day before, he had sheepishly confessed to Lily that he had never learned to swim a stroke. A wave of self-pity washed over him. If only she was here to comfort him now, not closeted in their cabin nursing Parks's mysterious malady. He raised the flask in a mock salute.

"To Lily," he mumbled and drained the last of the fiery brew down his throat. "Sweet Lil—" He slumped across the table. The flask dropped from his fingers with a dull thud.

Lily jolted awake as the ship heaved into a mountainous swell and plunged downward with jarring force. She could hear the howling winds and the faint shouts of the crew struggling to hold their course. She flung aside the bedcovers and lurched from her cabin toward the one occupied by Thaddeus and Jack. Thaddeus's chest rose and fell with a reassuring rhythm from the laudanum she had administered earlier. But the upper bunk was empty. Where was Jack? She had to find him!

A flash of lightning illuminated the passageway. She forced her way up the steps only to be driven to her knees as she reached the deck. Another streak of lightning danced across the rigging. Battered by the howling winds, the mizzenmast wavered dangerously. The falling timber sent an explosion of debris skyward as it crashed into the railing, and blackness claimed her.

By first light, the storm was spent. Jack lifted his head from the galley floor and struggled to pull himself back onto the bench. His body felt as if he had been put to torture, and his head pounded with the thunder of a hundred anvils.

"Jesu . . ." he groaned.

"Faro, Lily's missing!"

Waves of agony reverberated through his skull as Thaddeus grabbed the front of his coat and jerked him to his feet.

"Unhand me, ye bastard!" he croaked.

Thaddeus threw up his hands as a glimmer of reason returned.

Jack clung to the edge of the table gasping for breath. "What do ye mean, she's missing?" he croaked.

"She's not in her cabin. There's no sign of her." Thaddeus gestured angrily.

A cry of alarm from above sent the two men racing for the littered deck. Several of the crew were furiously tearing at a heap of torn canvas to rescue the person beneath it. Thaddeus shouldered his way through the crowd. Lily cried out in pain as he swept her up in his arms.

Jack braced himself against the open doorway of Lily's cabin and fixed Thaddeus with a baleful stare. "What's between y'self and the girl, man?"

Thaddeus awkwardly adjusted the bedcovers about her shoulders. Fatigue traced every line of his features. He sank on his haunches beside the bed and let his hands drop wearily between his knees. For weeks, he had scoured the city of New Orleans and every cemetery within its boundaries and beyond. He had desecrated a child's grave and would probably be sent to perdition for it even though the good sisters had assured him otherwise. He had been attacked and almost killed for a few dollars in gold. Then he had found Kate's daughter in a convent. In less than a fortnight, he would deliver her into Georgette's and Franklin Miller's hands, and her transformation from a young innocent to a woman of wealth and power would begin. Soon there would be no need for secrets. He glanced up at Jack.

"Her ma died a few months back and left her some property. I went to New Orleans to fetch her back to Charleston."

Jack drew a deep breath, scarcely able to hold back a foolish grin. How could he have imagined Thaddeus's interest in Lily could be anything more than a business matter?

Thaddeus noted Jack's obvious relief and sighed inwardly. If he had a grain of horse sense in his head he would have left Kate's girl where he found her, hidden away in a place where she would be safe. Instead, young Lily was about to be thrust into a role no amount of explaining could have prepared her for.

Four

The *Harlequin's* bow rose upon the gentle swells and descended in a laborious tribute toward the city in the distance. Overhead, seagulls circled lazily in the morning sun, their raucous cries interspersed with the faint tolling of steeple bells. By midday, the vessel reached its long-awaited destination, and messengers were dispatched to deliver the news of its arrival to addresses throughout the city.

For more than an hour, Thaddeus scanned the crowded dock for sight of a familiar coach and driver. When the polished brougham approached at a brisk clip and the coachman expertly guided the team within a few feet of the plank, he reached for Lily's arm and propelled her forward. "There's Xavier. Come along. Watch your step." His voice lacked any hint of enthusiasm.

She noted his stern features with dismay. Thaddeus's humor had taken a decided turn for the worse when she announced that Jack would be staying at Swan House until he could find suitable accommodations elsewhere in the city. She glanced back at Jack and sighed.

As they sped along the tree-shaded streets a short time later, pedestrians stared with undisguised curiosity at the familiar conveyance with a brace of golden swans emblazoned on each of its doors.

Jack stroked the soft leather cushion thoughtfully. Kate Perrault's coach boasted unexpected luxury, and those four thoroughbreds were as fine a team of matched animals as money could buy. As for that Xavier fellow, his eyes had all but leapt from their sockets when he clapped them on Lily. Whatever the coachman might have expected, she was not it. When she ignored his gloved hand and climbed unassisted into the coach, he scowled at Thaddeus with a condemning glare guaranteed to intimidate most men. Thaddeus had returned the unspoken censure in kind, dismissing the driver's silent rebuke.

After several turns past imposing mansions and townhouses, Xavier slowed the coach to a noisy clatter on the cobbled street and brought it to a halt. Jack leaned forward to peer out of the window and gave an involuntary gasp.

Two stone pillars supported a pair of ornate iron gates. Positioned atop each one, a marble nymph cradled an alabaster swan to her ample bare breasts. If those shameless pieces of statuary were any indication, the owner's taste had surpassed ostentation and lent itself to outright vulgarity. Jack shot a questioning glance at Thaddeus, who scowled an unspoken warning in return.

"Micah, Joseph! Git them gates open. Don't keep yore new mistress waitin' if you know whut's good for you," Xavier bawled from the driver's seat.

The two boys, as coal black as their sire, laughed at their father's empty threat and pushed against the gates, revealing an avenue sheltered by a canopy of oaks. As Xavier guided the coach through the gates, the two youngsters sprinted toward the house, their cries piercing the air.

"They come, they come. Mist' Thad and the lady come home!"

Thaddeus's eyes narrowed. He edged forward on the seat, frowning at the signs of neglect. Flowerbeds were choked with weeds, the reflecting pool was green with algae, and the fountain was still. In only a few weeks, Swan House had gone to hell. With a houseful of females and more than twenty servants, there was no excuse. Kate had to be spinning in her grave.

Xavier guided the brougham to the front steps. Nothing stirred on the upper gallery. No one was on the verandah. The draperies were closed tight against the noonday sun. The household still slept. Thaddeus clamped his jaw shut and wrenched open the door before Xavier could climb down to assist.

Lily crouched in the doorway. Her incredulous gaze swept the length of the house and up four floors to the top of the massive brick structure. Eight columns supported an upper gallery on the second story, which sheltered the verandah below. Moss-draped oaks concealed the subtle ravages that had begun to advance upon it, but to the unwitting eye, it was magnificent. Jack emerged from the coach as Thaddeus led Lily across the verandah.

"Welcome back, Mistah Thaddeus. Welcome." The old servant grinned hugely as he flung the door open. "Shore surprised to see you, sir. Just couldn't believe it when that messenger come to say you was back already."

"Mohab!" For the first time since they had disembarked, Thaddeus's relief was evident. Kate's majordomo was immaculate down to the pressed ruffles on his shirt, brushed coat and trousers, and polished boots. Somehow, Mohab had managed to isolate himself from the neglect that surrounded him.

"Where's Miz Georgette?" Thaddeus whispered.

Mohab chuckled. "Oh, still restin'. I didn't tell her you was back. Knowed you'd want to s'prise her. She shore gonna be glad to see you, yes, sir."

Thaddeus rolled his eyes and emitted a sound akin to a groan. He stepped aside to allow the servant a full view of Lily and Jack. "Mohab, say good day to Miz Kate's daughter, Miss Lily Perrault." He frowned. "And meet Mister Jack Faro. He will be staying on here for a spell."

The servant gave a pained bow from the waist, never taking his eyes off the pair. "Welcome, ma'am. Shore good to have Miz Kate's own kin heah to see after things. And good day to you, sir."

Jack nodded and followed Thaddeus and Lily across the vestibule. A niggling suspicion suddenly exploded into indisputable certainty. Yes, there they were! A half dozen gaming tables stood partially hidden behind a gold velvet drapery.

"Jesu!" he whispered and felt his senses quicken in anticipation. Sweet Lily had inherited a gold mine, and he could very well remain at Swan House for a long time indeed.

Lily advanced into the cavernous room ahead of the men. She struggled to take in the enormity of it all—the crimson damask settees, gilt mirrors, mahogany tables, and two crystal chandeliers suspended from a frescoed ceiling. A fireplace of Italian marble dominated the far end of the room. Brass banisters swept up either side of a central staircase and a dozen doors marched across an open gallery on the second floor, six on either side of the stairs. Swan House was a heady testament to Kate Perrault's astonishing wealth and a shrieking declaration as to how she had acquired it.

Lily moved stiffly across the floor to the foot of the staircase. Directly above the landing, a life-size portrait of Kate Perrault appeared to survey her domain with eyes that had seen too much of life and liked little of it. But for the shocking cut of her red velvet gown and a magnificent collar of diamonds about her throat, the likeness of Kate could have been of Lily herself. She felt the strength drain from her limbs and clung to the banister for support.

"Mister Parks," she whispered hoarsely, "what is this place?"

He hurried to position himself between Lily and her view of the portrait. "The others—that is, Kate's best friend, Georgette, and the banker, Franklin Miller—didn't think I ought to tell you anything until we got to Charleston. I was just supposed to find you and—"

A piercing shriek halted his protest. Doors flew open along both sides of the upper gallery. A pair of pudgy, dimpled knees flashed across the landing, and a figure in a blue silk dressing gown launched herself at Thaddeus. He spun around just in time to capture the woman hurtling toward him, as ten others clattered down the stairs on her heels.

"Thaddeus, you're back, you're back!"

Another shriek suspended their wild discourse. A mop of jet black curls and kohl smudged eyes ascended over his shoulder, and fixed on a tired straw bonnet with frayed ribbons.

"Thaddeus," Georgette hissed into her lover's ear, "your letter said that you found Kate's girl. But, who are *those* people?"

He disengaged her arms and stepped aside to permit Kate's best friend an unimpeded look at the travel-weary pair standing behind him. There was an ominous silence as they all surveyed one another. Those standing nearest to Lily attempted to conceal what bare flesh they could with their skimpy garments.

"Bessie, Jane, Louelle, Fanny, Mavis, and the rest of you, meet Mister Jack Faro."

Jack gave a sweeping bow in their direction. "Gentleman Jack Faro, at your service, ladies." A smile tugged at his lips.

The gambler's audience surveyed him with approving eyes, noting the fine cut of his coat and the irrepressible twinkle in his eyes. An appreciative giggle slithered up the stairs.

Thaddeus sucked in his breath. "And, *this* is Miss Lily Perrault, the new owner of this establishment."

Lily gave a nervous push to the spectacles balanced on her nose.

Georgette swayed. One hand clutched the banister while the other frantically tugged at her own revealing bodice. "My God!" she wheezed. "Kate's daughter in homespun!"

Thaddeus shrugged helplessly. At that moment, he would have welcomed it if a bolt of lightning had shot from the sky and blasted the floor from beneath him.

"Mistah Thad, Micah and Joseph bringing in the lady's and the gennleman's belongings." Mohab hobbled across the room toward them.

Lily spun around. "No!" A note of hysteria crept into her voice. "I . . . we won't be staying." She swayed, and felt her knees buckle. From a great distance, she heard Thaddeus shout her name. His arms captured her before she struck the floor. Georgette scrambled after him as he took the steps two at a time.

"Polly, Polly!" she shrilled. "Turn back Miz Kate's bed. Fetch salts and brandy. Hurry, hurry."

"Lordy, would you look at them brogans? My ma used to have a pair just like 'em."

"Shut up, Mavis, and bring that basin closer," Georgette snapped. "No, no, you're dripping water all over Kate's counterpane." She dabbed furiously at the damp stain. Lily coughed as the acrid smell of salts brought eleven anxious faces into focus above her.

"How are you feeling, sugar?" Georgette searched her pale features. "My stars, but you gave us a fright."

"Jack?" Lily attempted to rise only to find herself pushed back onto the pillows.

"He and Thaddeus are right outside the door, honey. Now, you just lay back and rest for a spell. It was a mighty long trip and bound to wear on a body." The girl did look fatigued and more than a little done in. What she needed was rest, and what Georgette needed was an explanation from Mister Thaddeus Parks.

"Please, I want to see Jack."

Georgette shot a warning glance at the others and nodded. She followed as they filed quickly from the room, remembering to smile at the stony-faced pair stationed on the other side of the door. She motioned to Jack to enter and grabbed Thaddeus by the arm, dragging him along the gallery to her own room.

Thaddeus watched as she lurched toward her dressing table and poured a hefty shot of bourbon into a glass, gulped it down, closed her eyes, and drew a deep shuddering breath. Georgette could be as volatile as Kate had been cool and remote. And the signs did not bode well.

"Thaddeus." Snapping black eyes raked him over. "From the looks of that girl, I would be willing to bet the house's take tonight that she's never known a man. In fact, she looks like she belongs in a convent."

His reasons for omitting any reference to the order in his letter had seemed prudent at the time. Now, he could only manage a guilty smile.

"Oh, no!" Georgette reached for the whiskey again.

Jack stepped hesitantly inside the door and gave a start. Kate's chamber rivaled the opulence of a queen's private rooms.

"Jack!" Lily sprang up from the pillows and reached for his outstretched hands. "Jack, we have to leave here, now."

His heart gave a sudden leap when she allowed his arms to close protectively about her. "There, now, don't carry on so, lass. You're tired, and you've had a bit of a shock. Come morning, if you're still of a mind to go, I'll take ye away from all this."

She pulled away and stared up at him, her eyes glistening with tears. "I didn't know. I swear I didn't."

He snatched a handkerchief from his vest pocket and lifted her specs, gently dabbing at her eyes. "Of course ye didn't." he soothed, drawing her into his arms again. "Jesu!" he exclaimed as a figure materialized out of the shadows. "Who are you?"

"Polly, sir." The amazon glided across the room as silently as a cat. Her stoic expression was unreadable. "I was Miz Kate's personal maidservant. Miz Georgette say I stay with the young miss." Soft light from the globed candles played against the angular planes of her face. Her burnished features appeared ageless, but her eyes were ancient. They bore through him as coldly as a sovereign might regard a servant of no particular consequence.

Lily turned. Her startled expression mirrored Jack's astonishment.

"Uh, Lily, Thaddeus says Kate's banker, Franklin Miller, is coming here first thing tomorrow morning. He thinks ye should at least hear what the man has to say."

"That's right." Polly nodded. "Mistah Franklin always come by on Fridays. He and Miz Kate took care of business on that day. Don't expect it to be no different now that Miss Lily come to see after her mam's place."

Lily's eyes widened. "Jack and I won't be staying."

"I take care of you just like I took care of yore mam. Right now, Alice is fixin' you up somethin' to eat and then you gonna take yoreself a nap. Ladies always naps afternoons. I 'spect the gennelman be a mite hungry, too." She fixed Jack with a knowing look. "He can visit later." She nodded in the direction of the door.

"Well, I suppose, that is, Polly's right, Lily. I'll find Thaddeus, and we'll get by just fine." Impulsively, he kissed her cheek and rushed toward the door, sagging against the frame as it closed decisively behind him. Georgette and Thaddeus heard the door slam and rushed down the gallery toward him.

"Well?" Georgette searched Jack's features for reassurance.

"She'll stay if that titan who's holding her hostage has anything to say about it."

Georgette gave an abrupt laugh. "Polly does have a way about her. The only one who could stand her down was Kate. And if that girl is anything like her ma, she will have the upper hand in no time."

Jack cast a doubtful look in Thaddeus's direction. "Begging your pardon, Miz Georgette, but I wouldn't place a poor man's wager on that happening. I warn ye both, Lily's of a mind to leave tomorrow, right on Miller's heels if I don't misjudge."

Georgette forced a practiced smile and locked her hands into the crook of the gambler's arm, pulling him toward the stairs. "Well then, we can only hope Franklin will be able to persuade our Lily to reconsider. Swan House is a very profitable enterprise, Mister Faro. Perhaps you would like to look around and judge for yourself? A man of your experience can surely appreciate the possibilities." She shot Thaddeus a warning look. They were going to need all the help they could muster, and Kate's girl seemed to put a lot of store in this fellow Faro.

Jack allowed himself to be propelled along. The gaming tables beckoned below.

Five

Lily sighed and burrowed deeper into the soft bed. A gentle breeze stirred the lace curtains at the windows. Across the room, a dressing table supported a vase of freshly cut flowers. The blossoms gave off a seductive scent that penetrated the veil of sleep that enveloped her. Suddenly, her eyes flew open. She sprang up from the pillows, pulling the bedcovers to her chin.

Polly glided silently across the thick rug bearing a silver tray and deposited her burden on a table near the bed. "You sleep good, Miss Lily." It was not a question, but a statement that invited no response. She moved to the foot of the bed and folded her hands across her belly. A crisp white pinafore relieved the stark plainness of her deep blue gown. A red scarf covered her head.

Lily managed an uncertain smile and nodded.

"Time for you to git up now and drink yore tea." The servant reached for the dressing gown she had placed across the bed earlier. "Miz Kate always took tea before going downstairs every morning."

Lily pushed back the silk coverlet and eased off the bed, painfully conscious of her threadbare shift. Polly swept the gown about her and tied the single ribbon at her waist.

"Where are my clothes?"

"Took 'em downstairs while you was sleeping last night. The laundress gonna wash and pack 'em away. Now, you just sit down and I fix you a cup of tea." Polly poured the steaming brew into a cup and added a measure of sugar and cream without asking Lily's preference. "It was yore mam's favorite, and I 'spect you gonna like it, too."

"I want my things."

"You don't need them rags." Polly walked to an armoire across the room and flung open the doors. "You and Miz Kate be 'bout the same size before she took sick. Nobody had finer clothes in all of Charleston than yore mam."

Lily's eyes widened at the array of elegant gowns displayed in the massive wardrobe.

Polly selected one of blue watered silk and walked toward the bed. "Miz Kate always say fine clothes make a lady feel right good 'bout herself. Hurry along now and drink yore tea while I get yore bath ready. You don't want to keep Mistah Franklin a'waitin'."

A few minutes later, Lily slipped out of the dressing gown and stepped behind a curtained screen. Thick towels lay within reach of an ornate brass tub. Jars of oils and scented soap had been placed on a rosewood table nearby. At the convent, bathing had been limited to a chipped basin of cold water and a worn cloth. She started to remove her shift and hesitated. When Polly made no move to leave the room, she let it drop to the floor and stepped into the steaming water.

Sunlight pierced the space between a pair of velvet draperies and inched its way across the two figures lying beneath the tumbled bedcovers. Jack stirred, conscious of the soft warm flesh pressed against him and the supple legs entangled with his own. A stray curl teased the corner of his lips. His smile deepened. He turned and gathered his companion close, burying his face in the mass of curls about her neck.

"Sweet Lily," he sighed and then froze. "Lily? Damnation!" He bounded from the bed, his disbelieving eyes following the trail of abandoned garments to the door. The nymph rose from the pillows stretching sleek and catlike, almost purring from the sound of it.

"Mornin', Sugar." Fanny brushed the hair back from her face, leveled a sleep-sated smile upon him, and watched him scramble to gather his belongings. Coins and bills spilled from the pockets of his coat and trousers. It was more money than he had seen in weeks. Where had it come from? He scrubbed at his eyes and struggled to remember. *The gaming tables!* It appeared that he had acquitted himself nobly with the rakes and gamblers of Charleston the night before. It was Georgette, that sly witch, who had set him up and entrapped him in the bed of one of Kate's doxies. Or were they Lily's doxies? He gave a bark of incredulous laughter. Oh, hell, he couldn't think.

He smacked his forehead and groaned. God curse him for the heartless bastard he was. He hadn't given a thought to Lily all the while. He had deserted her, left her to the mercy of that harridan who had ejected him from her room.

"Jack, what's the matter?"

He gaped numbly as Fanny flung aside the bedcovers revealing altogether too much delectable flesh. Her arms curved about his neck, and her lips teased his.

"I have to see Lily."

She chuckled, a rich and deep sound. "Whatever for?" Her breath was warm against his cheek. Her tongue circled the soft lobe of his ear.

"She needs me," he groaned.

"I hear tell Miss Lily has mighty important business with Franklin Miller this morning. He's going to tell her how rich she is. And Jack, honey," she whispered, "she's very, very rich." Her fingers trailed across his chest to the muscled flesh of his belly.

He groaned again. He had promised to take Lily away from this place after she met with the banker, and here he was, buck naked, just a few doors away from her. To his dismay, he felt his traitorous flesh responding to his partner's ministrations. "Jesu!" His breath quickened. "But she's waiting for me," he rasped.

Fanny tossed her thick chestnut mane and laughed. "Oh, la, honey. You really don't understand, do you?"

"Understand what?" He couldn't imagine what prompted another burst of laughter.

"The richest woman in Charleston doesn't wait for anybody. From now on, we are all going to be awaiting Miss Lily Perrault's pleasure. Just like we did for her mama."

"Lily's not like Kate."

"They are all the same when it comes to money."

He emitted a ragged sigh and surrendered to her assault. What the hell. He was only human. He seized her about the waist and hauled her onto the rumpled bed, dragging the bedcovers over them, smothering her helpless giggles.

Polly surveyed her handiwork, hoping her nervousness did not betray her misgivings about the meeting that was about to take place between Kate's daughter and Franklin Miller. She frowned at the faded gown Lily had insisted she retrieve from the laundry shed. She should have thrown it into the firepit as soon as the girl undressed and reached for her nightrail the night before.

"Mistah Franklin *shore* gonna be surprised when he see you, child." And it was true. But for that wretched garment and ill-fitting specs, Lily Perrault was the image of her mother. Franklin Miller had fallen in love with Kate Perrault the first time he had clapped eyes on her. The resemblance between Kate and her daughter was bound to weigh heavily upon his grieving heart.

Polly hurried her charge along the gallery toward the staircase, mindful of each door that closed softly as they passed. She shook her head, her lips compressed into a tight line. Kate Perrault had ruled her household with unquestioned authority. Those lazy trollops would not accord the girl the respect her mother had commanded. Georgette would have to look beyond her own grief and rein them in hard if she ever hoped to persuade Lily to stay at Swan House.

They descended the stairs in silence and crossed the ballroom to a hallway leading to the back of the house. Polly stopped at the last door and knocked.

"Mistah Franklin? Miss Lily's heah." She turned and beckoned Lily into the room and closed the door after her.

Unlike the rest of the house, the study was richly paneled and free of trappings, almost masculine in its severity.

Franklin Miller rose from behind the desk and motioned Lily closer. He was not tall by a man's measure, but there was a sense of strength and authority about him. Kate's banker was accustomed to power and possessed the will to use it, ruthlessly, if need be. Silently, he indicated a chair directly in front of the desk. He had purposely placed it there so that he might appraise her more thoroughly.

Franklin felt perspiration bead his brow as Lily crossed the room. Georgette had not exaggerated. The girl's features and the way she carried herself were Kate all over again, but, he instantly recognized their differences. From the very beginning, Kate had been fire and fury, while this timid slip of a girl was innocence and fear. He cleared his throat. "Forgive me if I appear surprised, Lily—may I call you Lily? I did not expect that you would look so much like your mother."

He indicated the chair meant for her and seated himself behind
the desk once more pretending not to notice the frayed cuffs on her
sleeves or that she tucked her scuffed shoes beneath the hem of her
skirt as she took the chair he offered.

"I have prepared a detailed accounting of Kate's assets. Her estate
is a considerable one." He pushed a stack of papers toward her. "We'll
begin with these. I'm sorry, but you do read, don't you?" She nodded,
and he breathed an inward sigh of relief.

"As her financial advisor and banker for more than twenty years, I
can answer any questions you may have regarding her business affairs."

The chiming of the mantle clock marked the first hour that passed,
and then another. There were accounts in Charleston, Philadelphia,
and as far away as London; mining in the west, ship building in the
east, textiles and iron manufacturing in the north, agricultural interests in the south, and Swan House.

"There's so much." Lily glanced up from the pile of papers that
littered the desk.

Franklin's eyes narrowed. A frown worked beneath his mustache.
Kate would have danced with glee at such a revelation. She understood the absolute power of money and the utter futility of respect-
able poverty. But her daughter was untrained in the most rudimentary
principles of business, and he suspected that she possessed none of
the personal accomplishments she would need to assume Kate's role
as mistress of this house. Yet, he was struck by the startling clarity of
her eyes, honest and forthright. Had Kate ever been so innocent, so
vulnerable? In spite of himself, his gaze softened.

"As Kate's only heir you have inherited all of it." Franklin leaned
back in his chair and attempted to gauge her reaction.

"I have no need of all of this, Mister Miller." She appeared to draw
back, distancing herself from the wealth represented by the documents
spread out in front of her.

His eyes narrowed suspiciously. "What are you saying, Lily?"

"It's just that I had hoped that I was coming home."

"But you are home, my dear. All of this is yours."

"I know what Swan House is, sir," she replied softly.

Franklin cleared his throat and reached inside his coat for the handkerchief in his vest pocket. "Indeed." Subtlety had never been one of Kate's virtues. It was that very brazenness that afforded Georgette and her collaborators the protection necessary to carry on their dangerous work. He hoped Lily didn't notice that his hand trembled slightly as he mopped his brow and returned the handkerchief to his pocket.

"Should you renounce your claim to the estate, Lily, everything we have covered, including Swan House, will be liquidated and the proceeds disbursed according to Kate's original will. Closing this establishment would be a reason for great rejoicing among her enemies—and your mother had enemies, make no mistake. She wielded a great deal of influence in this city. She always insisted upon anonymity in local transactions. Some of the gentlemen listed among her debtors represent Charleston's most prominent families. Their womenfolk will be among the first to denounce you for no good reason other than you are Kate's daughter, not realizing they maintain their positions by the grace of her generosity."

"If I choose to return to New Orleans, what will happen to Mister Parks and the others?"

"Thaddeus and Georgette will each receive a settlement. Georgette has been with Kate from the beginning. She would be compensated more generously, of course. As for the servants," he shook his head, "they are chattel and considered part of the estate. They could be sold to other households hereabouts, or sent to Savannah or New Orleans."

"The boys that met us at the gate, Micah and Joseph, could they be sold apart from one another?" she whispered.

Franklin shrugged. "It's possible they could be separated; almost a certainty they would be taken from Xavier, their father."

"Mister Miller," she hesitated and unconsciously gripped the arms of her chair, "did my mother ever tell you and Georgette who my father is, or where he might be found?"

He was taken aback by the unexpected question regarding her own past. He sighed. "Kate kept few secrets from the two of us, but she never spoke about the gentleman to either of us. I am sorry that I cannot provide you with that information. I would have no reason to withhold his name from you."

Lily gave a dejected sigh.

"Lily, a part of your mother will always be here. Do you really want to sever that last fragile tie? In time, Georgette and Thaddeus, and I would hope myself as well, can become your family just as we were Kate's. If you decide not to stay, everything will be lost to you." He dared to use one last desperate bit of leverage. "And think what it could mean to young Micah and Joseph if you go."

She clasped her hands tightly to still their trembling. "I am very tired, sir. I need to be alone for a while. There's so much to think about. Can we talk later?"

"Of course, my dear." He rose, alarmed at the sudden pallor in her face. She had endured much over the past weeks, and it was obvious she did not possess the inner strength that bolstered Kate during her darkest hours.

"Good day." Lily turned and hurried through the door, but not before Franklin saw her brush the tears from her eyes.

"Mohab."

"Yes, sir, Mistah Franklin?"

"Ask Miz Georgette to come down."

"Is the young lady gonna stay, sir?"

Franklin Miller's features were grim and weary.

The majordomo sighed and hobbled off to do his bidding.

The banker turned back toward the window and stared out at the rose garden. He and Kate had forged an empire in this room, the extent of which would astonish most speculators. But the end had finally come. Or had it? If the girl agreed to stay, she had much to learn.

"Franklin?"

"Georgette." He motioned her toward the chair Lily had vacated minutes earlier. Gone were any traces of the flighty bawd. Her face was stripped of the false wiles that so cleverly concealed a cunning as shrewd as Kate's. There was apprehension in her eyes and a tension about her that charged the room. He leveled a stern gaze upon her. "She has not agreed to stay."

Georgette closed her eyes. "I was afraid of it as soon as Thaddeus told me about the convent. Who could ever have imagined Kate's girl in such a place? Oh, Franklin, maybe we should tell her everything. Maybe she will understand and want to stay."

"Georgette, Stephen Flynn is committed to his cause, but we know nothing about this girl. She could be his greatest danger, or he could be hers." He shook his head. "Stephen and I grew up together. No finer man ever drew breath, but he's obsessed. Lately, he has become reckless, taking risks he would never have chanced a few years ago. I do not wish to lose a friend, not Stephen or you."

"Thank you, Franklin," she whispered, "and if Lily does agree to stay, I promise you I will send her away if she is ever in danger. It's the least I can do for Kate." Franklin's eyes were sad, and oddly defenseless. She reached across the desk and grasped his hand. "She's not Kate, my friend. It's only the physical resemblance that troubles you. Nothing more."

"Perhaps you are right. But have a care, Georgette. These are dangerous times."

Six

Acoach-and-four traveled at a brisk pace in the direction of the *Hannah Blue*, a three-masted barque set to depart for San Francisco on the morning tide. The coachman dismounted from the seat above as three able crewmen hurried down the plank to collect the passenger's trunks. Doctor Paul DuPre's expression was grim as he surveyed the ship that would take him as far as Charleston.

Jean-Claude Beauchamp grasped the golden head of his cane and searched his nephew's haunted eyes. When Paul's young wife died in childbirth more than a year before, the lad had fled to Boston and embarked upon a private journey to hell. Only a recent letter from his sister had miraculously halted the young man's mindless progression through the saloons and gaming halls of the city.

Enough of this nonsense! Constance had written. Their mother was desperate for his return. His infant son was thankfully too young to realize that he had been orphaned twice; first, by the tragic death of his mother and then by the selfish desertion of his father.

"Uncle Jean." Paul grasped the older man's hand.

"Convey my affections to your mother and Constance." Jean-Claude gave a resigned sigh. "And to Honora as well."

A wry smile touched Paul's lips. His uncle always referred to Aunt Honey by her proper name. While his mother's marriage at sixteen to the Creole doctor, Gaston DuPre, had met with Jean-Claude's enthusiastic approval, her twin sister had earned their older brother's everlasting disdain by wedding the English-born solicitor, Nathan Claiborne, six months later.

Honey Claiborne cared not a fig for either of her siblings' disapproval. At least, she had once challenged in a fit of pique, her Nathan would have an Englishman's good sense to die in his own bed, unlike Gaston, who had committed the unpardonable sin of expiring between the silk sheets of that whore, Kate Perrault.

Jean-Claude refused to acknowledge his nephew's reaction and instead pressed a leather-bound packet into his hand. "These documents will explain the additions to the ladies' investment accounts," Jean-Claude said, referring to the dowry trusts old Pierre Beauchamp had established for his daughters at birth. Their father's generosity had assured Adelaide's and Honora's social prominence in their adopted city of Charleston and handsomely elevated their husbands' positions as well.

"Mother and Aunt Honey will be pleased with your efforts on their behalf, Uncle."

"*Au revoir*, and Godspeed, my boy." Jean-Claude watched Paul exit the coach and advance up the plank without a backward glance.

September 2, 1828, two days out of Charleston
Paul thrashed helplessly in his sleep as the ghostly specter ran toward him, begging him to save her. Instead, he backed away and watched in horror as his wife stumbled, and death drew her down into a pool of her own blood. It was the same nightmare that turned his nights into a terrifying hell.

"Emma!" he shouted her name, awakening in a sweat and struggling to drag breath into his paralyzed lungs. He pushed himself to his feet and gripped the washstand, waiting for the wild hammering of his heart to subside. His shadowed reflection in the mirror was the face of a stranger with disheveled black hair and dark eyes filled with self-loathing. He turned abruptly and jerked on his breeches and snatched his shirt from a peg by the door.

The wind slammed into his body as he reached the deck and lurched toward the rail. Damn Constance and her cursed meddling, ordering him home like an errant schoolboy! Yet what right had he to be angry with her? His sister and Dan Wellington had installed his son in their empty nursery at Cottonwood when he had fled to Boston. They had nursed his colic and watched him take his first faltering steps. In scarcely more than a year since his birth, his best friend had become his son's father.

Constance and Emma Wellington had just begun to suffer the first tempestuous pangs of womanhood when he had left home to study medicine in Edinburgh. Four years later, as the first winter chill blanketed the land, he returned home to the unexpected news that his sister had recently married his best friend. When he rode through the gates of Cottonwood days later, Dan bounded from the house with a glad shout and propelled him toward the steps. Constance rushed through the door and flung herself into his arms. Laughing, the three of them hurried into the vestibule to escape the bitter cold.

He had come to an abrupt stop when Emma suddenly appeared at the top of the stairs. She smiled into his eyes and he knew in that instant that his heart was lost. *I waited for you*, she would tell him later, and he had no doubt that she had.

In the spring, he had taken Emma Wellington to be his wife at Cottonwood, in a garden filled with azaleas and wisteria. He had promised to cherish and protect her, but he had killed her instead.

Now, he was returning to the empty house they had shared in the city, and a lonely grave at Saint Bartholomew's. And there was the son he had been determined to put from his mind. It was better to end it all here before he reached Charleston. No one would suspect his disappearance had been anything more than a tragic accident. And he would be free of this wretched torment. He loosened his hold upon the rail and faltered as the image of his mother penetrated the madness that taunted him to take his own life. *Coward!* His conscience mocked him.

Charleston, September 4, 1828

"Miz Addie, Miz Addie! The ship bringin' Doctah Paul home done come. I'll fetch the carriage 'round." Adelaide DuPre's coachman scurried up the walkway as the messenger from the docks climbed into the battered trap and set off to deliver the news of other arrivals across town.

"He's home!" Adelaide rushed toward the vestibule with a joyful cry and whirled about. "Tilde, fetch my bonnet and my parasol. Constance, come quickly. Your brother's home!"

Connie started down the stairs and paused, her smile fading to uncertainty. "You go along, Mama. I'll wait here with Davy."

"But, dear, you must come," her mother protested. "Paul will be so disappointed if you're not there to welcome him."

She shook her head. If only she dared tell her mother about that horrid letter she had written. Paul wouldn't be disappointed. He would be furious. Oh, why hadn't she returned to the Wellington townhouse with Dan that morning instead of prolonging her visit with her mother?

Tilde thrust the parasol and bonnet into her mistress's hands and pushed her toward the door. "You hurry 'long, Miz Addie. You and Caleb bring that boy home quick as you can."

Connie watched from the window as Adelaide flew down the steps in a flurry of muslin and petticoats. Her mother was still picture-pretty. Her slender form belied her forty-five years. Hardly a hint of silver marked the ebony curls that peeped from beneath her flowered bonnet. Many found it surprising that she had not taken a husband from among the legion of suitors to seek her hand in the fifteen years since their father had died, but Adelaide DuPre's children were her heart, all that she needed to make her life complete. And her son had finally come home, no matter the reason.

Adelaide felt her heart quicken as her carriage clattered along the dock a short time later. She clamped a determined hold on her bonnet and urged her coachman to a faster pace. A bit of lace fluttered in her hand when she spied her son at the rail.

"Paul, darling!"

She gasped softly as he descended the plank. He looked older than his twenty-six years, hardened and wary. When he approached, she could tell by the pain in his eyes that his grief had hardly lessened.

As the carriage drew up before the DuPre house an hour later, Paul felt a suspicious tightening in his chest. He had put the place out of his mind those months he had been away. Now, suddenly, he realized how much he had missed it. Built of brick, its solid strength was relieved by intricately patterned ironwork that formed the balustrades and dressed the columns of the upper and lower galleries. Eight paned-glass doors stood open on each floor to capture the gentle breeze from the sea.

He stepped down, and reached to settle his mother gently to the ground beside him. When he turned, his eyes locked on the slender figure in a pale yellow gown standing at the top of the steps. Sunlight lent fire to the copper-colored braids that crowned her head. From that distance, he could only imagine the sprinkle of freckles that danced lightly across his sister's nose.

He tucked Adelaide's hand in the crook of his arm and started up the brick walkway, never taking his eyes off of Connie. Her tightly clasped hands betrayed her nervousness. A few feet from the steps, he stopped, struck by the beginning of a wistful smile that tore through his fierce resolve. Slowly, he disengaged his mother's hand and opened his arms.

"No greeting for the prodigal, moppet?" A slow grin transformed the harsh set of his features. With a glad cry, Connie sailed down the steps into his arms.

"Please, please don't ever leave us again, Paul." Her tearful whisper pierced his heart. He had always been her mainstay, her champion, and he had left her to suffer her pain and grief alone.

"Never," he muttered fiercely and meant it with all his heart.

Adelaide pressed her handkerchief to her lips, her eyes brimming as the two parted only to clasp each other close once more.

Connie clutched his hand and led the way inside. Anticipation sparkled in her eyes as they climbed the stairs and entered the nursery. As Paul drew near the small bed he felt his courage fail. The night his son was born he had begged God to take the child and let Emma live. The infant's weak cries had followed him as he fled from the house and wandered about the city streets, crazed with grief.

Connie reached out and brushed a dark curl from her nephew's brow. "He's an angel, Paul. Dan and I love him as if he was our very own, and Mother, la, but she spoils him shamefully." She smiled indulgently as her mother reached for her grandson.

Paul stared down at the sleepy child in his mother's arms. It was not Emma's likeness that was so evident in their son's features, but his own. Shaking his head in denial, he backed away and bolted from the room, ignoring Adelaide's astonished cry.

"Paul!"

A door crashed shut below.

Connie laid a restraining hand on her mother's arm. "Mother, wait. Maybe he just needs a little time."

Downstairs in the study, Paul sagged against the door, sick with shame. Until he gazed down at his son, he did not realize how little thought he had given to the child in the year that had passed.

When Connie joined him in the study later, he searched her face and found compassion. Perhaps it was too soon. He felt curiously humbled, grateful for her understanding, yet guilty that she must do what he could not. In time, she promised, he and his son would make a life together. He wondered if it could be true. How could he make her understand that young David Wellington DuPre evoked an irrational sense of fear in his father's heart?

Seven

Paul stood at the drawing room window, listening to the distant sound of thunder follow an evening rainstorm toward the sea. In a few weeks, summer would give way to the pristine beauty of fall and then to the gray bitterness of a Carolina winter. Even now, plantation families were preparing for the seasonal migration back to the country. Come spring, the exodus would reverse itself, and they would return to the city to an endless round of socials and summer weddings in townhouse rose gardens.

Adelaide eyed her knitting suspiciously and counted her stitches. With a sigh, she let the scarf drop into her lap. Paul had been unusually quiet at dinner, retreating into that dark place that invited no intrusion. She laid her needles aside and rose from the settee.

"I think I'll retire."

He turned as she touched his arm. "I apologize, Mother. I haven't been good company for you tonight."

"It's all right, dear. We are all weary. There have been so many callers since you returned." Her eyes misted as he enfolded her in a tender embrace. "It's so good to have you home again, son."

He watched until she reached the top of the stairs, then he turned and walked out onto the gallery.

Upstairs, Adelaide settled back against her pillows. "You know, Tilde, what my son needs is a wife and a mother for Davy. And there will surely be other children one day." She dimpled prettily. "I should like very much to have a granddaughter."

"Doctah Paul still hurtin' mighty bad, Miz Addie." Tilde closed the door of the armoire. "It might be best just to let things be for a spell."

"Marylove Turnbull might catch his fancy, and there's Angela Pickering. The Pickerings are an excellent family. Or perhaps Clarissa Pardee. No, no that would never do. La, with four daughters of marriageable age, Fennemore Pardee will be hard pressed to match the dowry Thurston Turnbull can provide for Marylove."

Tilde rolled her eyes.

Three days later, Paul stalked into the study and sank into the chair behind his desk. The frown that had marked his features throughout the afternoon had deepened into a menacing scowl. Within minutes of their arrival at the Claiborne's, a host of other guests descended on Aunt Honey's solarium. He had been forced to endure two hours of their mindless prattle while balancing that ridiculous teacup on his knee.

Adelaide followed him into the room, fanning her flushed cheeks. "I declare, but this heat is about to wilt me right down to my bones."

"A nap will fix you right up," he growled.

"You're probably right, dear. But be sure to have Tilde wake me no later than half past six. The Wellingtons and the Turnbulls are coming for dinner at eight. Oh, I shall miss Constance and Davy when they return to Cottonwood."

He nodded absently and reached across the desk for a decanter and a glass.

"Dear, do wear the burgundy coat tonight. You look so handsome in it. Your father always favored the color. And, son, you are going to be very surprised how Marylove Turnbull has blossomed in the past year. Such a charming girl. Well, I'm off. Don't forget, now."

He groaned and helped himself to a bracing shot of bourbon.

Paul toyed absently with the food on his plate, painfully conscious of the girl in yards of saffron eyelet sitting next to him. Marylove had indeed blossomed from a plump, ill-favored adolescent to a more robust version of her brother, Percy, and her father, Thurston Turnbull. He shifted nervously beneath the disconcerting gaze she trained upon him.

"Doctor Paul, do you think I am too young to consider marriage?" she whispered abruptly. His fork clattered loudly onto his plate.

"You see," she edged closer, "Johnny Tredaway declared his affections for me at your Aunt Honey's soiree this afternoon. He's going to ask Papa for permission to call on me when we return to Three Fountains next week."

Paul stifled a grin and the sudden urge to whisk the giddy creature from her chair and whirl her about the room

Adelaide surveyed the pair with smug satisfaction and nodded in their direction to her daughter. Marylove was clearly besotted. Surely, Constance could find no fault with a match between her brother and Margaret and Thurston's only daughter.

After the Turnbulls departed later that evening, Paul walked out onto the verandah. The sound of his brother-in-law's hearty laughter followed him into the night. He sensed a presence behind him and turned as Connie slipped her arm through his.

"Mother was in rare form tonight." She smothered a laugh against his sleeve.

"Let's walk." Paul grasped her hand without waiting for a reply and led her down the steps to the street.

The Wellington townhouse stood silent and dark but for a single lamp at the downstairs parlor window. The sisters, Iretta and Maybelle, had reopened the house only a few months after their niece's death. Yet, a haunting stillness lingered about it even now.

In a few days, Connie and Dan would take Davy and return to Cottonwood. But for a while, at least, he and his sister could push back the harsh realities of their lives and remember how it had been before the man she loved had rejected her, and she had given her broken heart to Dan Wellington. And before Emma had died.

"I think we should go back, Paul," she whispered. "Mother and Dan will wonder what's become of us."

He turned, his face a mask of utter despair.

Tears sprang to her eyes. "Time will heal the pain, my dear. And someday there will be another in your life. You must believe that."

"Like Dan?" He expelled a ragged breath, stunned by the anguished look on her face. "I'm sorry, Connie. That was cruel. I had no right."

"My husband is a good man, Paul, and your best friend. He cares for me deeply." Her voice quavered.

But what about passion? He wanted to shout. What about desire? Do you simply endure and dream of Charles Eden still? His shoulders slumped. "Dan is a fine man, and I am a selfish, insensitive fool. Come, let's go back."

They retreated in silence, each conscious of old wounds that had been recklessly laid open.

Dan was waiting by the gate as they approached the house. "Hello, you two."

Connie rushed into her husband's embrace. Her face burned. Paul had happened upon the truth too easily. Dan absently kissed the top of her head and threw a heavy arm about Paul's shoulders.

"We were wondering where you had gotten off to."

Paul forced a smile. Dan was solid, and he loved Connie beyond reason. If he suspected that she loved him any less, it did not matter. And how could Davy not love this gentle bear of a man? Connie was right. There was no finer or more honorable man than Daniel Wellington.

Eight

Eden's Gate Plantation, north of Charleston
September 21, 1828

"**D**amned abolitionist bastard!"

China and silver clattered the length of the table. Victor Eden rubbed a hand through a thick shock of white hair, glowered at each of his dinner guests, and finally settled on his son seated to his left. His scowl deepened. Charles's pretended indifference only fueled his drunken rage.

His neighbor, Thurston Turnbull, signaled to the servant standing behind his chair and nodded toward his empty glass. "Damn shame. Seems like somebody would have caught the sonofabitch and strung him up long before now." He reached across the table and speared a thick slice of ham onto his dinner plate. "We lost two of the household help a week ago and two prime field hands the month before that."

Victor grunted. Plantations along the river road had all lost slaves. But, in recent months, the man they knew only as the 'Shepherd' appeared to have singled out Eden's Gate and the Turnbull place, Three Fountains, for liberation. The two properties were separated by a rutted track that led east from the river road and followed a labyrinth of blackened, viper-infested waterways that emptied onto the salt flats and the ocean beyond. It was into this hell's pit that runners willingly risked the dangers of water moccasins and wildcats rather than suffer bondage to either of them.

Two nights past, the abolitionists had attempted to rescue three field hands from Eden's Gate, but the runners had been caught before they reached the swamp. One had been torn to pieces by the dogs, another shot, and the survivor whipped so soundly he would not return to the fields for a week.

Charles Eden felt his father's eyes boring into him. He would not be baited this time, not with a roomful of guests sitting down to Sunday dinner. He raised his glass and drank the last of the wine with forced calm.

Percy Turnbull kept his eyes trained on his plate in a desperate bid to escape his host's attention. Victor Eden was a drunkard whose cruelty toward his slaves, and his wife and son, was legendary.

Victor's sullen glare shifted to the younger Turnbull. "And what say you, young Percival? Do you believe this Shepherd fellow can be caught?"

Percy gave a start and eyed his host warily. Victor's question caught him off guard. "Uh, indeed I do, sir. Once he's captured, and he surely will be, peace will be restored along the river."

Victor gave a mocking laugh. "Oh, we will catch 'im all right, and when we do, we will castrate the sonofabitch."

Augusta Eden paled and turned, seeking reassurance from the servant positioned behind her chair. "Zina?"

The medicine woman gripped her mistress's hand. "It's awright, Miz Augusta," she whispered.

"Perhaps the ladies would like to retire to the parlor, Father." Charles pushed himself away from the table and rose to his feet.

Margaret Turnbull rewarded him with a grateful smile. Charles always managed to rescue them when these abominable dinners turned ugly. Goodness knows, one had only to endure a single sitting at the Edens' table to understand why Victor Eden's wife had long ago retreated behind an opiate veil.

Victor gave a grudging snarl of assent.

The majordomo held Margaret's chair and then assisted her daughter to her feet. Charles kept his eyes trained on his mother's halting progress.

"Charles?" Augusta's hands fluttered erratically. He moved quickly to her side and lifted her trembling hand into the crook of his arm while Zina grasped the other. "I would like to go to my room now." Charles cast an apologetic smile at the Turnbull women, ignoring his father's sneer of disgust.

"Of course, you should go up and rest, Augusta dear," Margaret said, seizing the chance to escape. "It's time we were getting back home. We will do this again soon, when you are feeling better. Colombo, fetch our wraps."

Thurston clapped a hairy hand on Victor's shoulder. "Better let Zina give you something for that leg. It's bound to be paining you pretty bad by now."

Victor nodded miserably and watched his guests prepare to depart.

"Thurston!"

"Coming, Margaret, coming."

Margaret walked briskly toward the vestibule, eager to put the evening behind them. Victor's injury had only fueled his usual nastiness. The stallion that had thrown him was from Three Fountains's stock, and they would never hear the end of it. Her husband only pretended to befriend Victor Eden, but he didn't fool her for a minute. It was more land Thurston was after. Sooner or later, Victor would be forced to sell another parcel if the rumors about his losses at that Perrault woman's gaming tables proved to be true.

"Percy!"

"Yes, Mama." Percy sighed and ambled down the steps. Marylove hurried after her brother.

Thurston heaved himself into the coach with the women, leaving Percy to follow on his own mount.

Victor scanned the abandoned dinner table and sagged in his chair. A pained scowl twisted his features.

"Colombo."

The majordomo turned away from the door. "Yes, sir, Mastah Victor?"

"Get upstairs and tell my son and that Zina to get back down to the library."

"But what about Miz Augusta?"

"You can stay with her. And tell Zina to bring her medicine box."

The front door burst open, and heavy steps strode purposely down the hall.

"Why, if it isn't *Mister* Taylor. What took you so long?" Victor sneered at his overseer.

Grier Taylor's eyes darted angrily around the room. Being the old man's bastard son had some privileges, but they didn't include a place at Augusta Eden's dinner table.

"Help me to the library." Victor gave a yelp as Grier pulled him to his feet and drew his arm about his powerful shoulders.

Victor sank against the leather cushions of his chair and watched Grier retrieve a bottle of whiskey from the sideboard, pour a full glass and hand it to him. He gulped it down and grunted.

"How's your leg?" Grier frowned. "Looks swelled up bad."

"Hurts like hell. Zina's coming. She'll give me something to take care of it."

Grier let his breath out slowly. Damn, he wouldn't have a chance to convince the old man that he needed to go to town for a day or two. He had not been off the place in a while, and his urges were getting mighty desperate.

"Father?" Charles paused in the doorway, pointedly ignoring the overseer. "Colombo said you wanted to see me."

Victor waved Charles toward a chair. "Where's Zina?" he snarled.

"Right heah, Mastah Victor." Augusta's keeper eased past the overseer and knelt before him. "I brung you somethin'."

Grier's gaze traveled the full length of Zina's body. The glow from the lamps played off her ebony skin, tracing the curves of her breasts through the worn bodice. Zina was as sleek as a cat, tall as most men on the place, and strong, too. He licked his lips as she took the empty whiskey glass from Victor's hand and opened her medicine box on the sideboard.

"That ain't the poison you give Miz Augusta, is it?" He eyed the vial in her hand suspiciously.

She turned slowly without acknowledging his question and returned the glass, half-filled with amber liquid, to Victor. "You drink this heah medicine, Mastah Victor. I mix you up somethin' special. Gonna make you feel good real soon." She sank to her knees and gently eased the offending boot from his swollen leg.

Grier's fists curled at his side. She dared turn her back on him, the black bitch! "You didn' answer me."

"Leave her be, Taylor." Charles's expression remained stoic, yet there was an unmistakable warning in his voice. Zina turned slightly and gave him a telling glance. There was no need to stir the overseer up. He would just make trouble later.

Victor sighed as she massaged the purple mass of flesh above his ankle. Zina might be lacking as a breeder, but she had eased too many aches and pains to think of selling her off the place. He was inclined, as he rarely did, to agree with Charles. He would not think too kindly of Grier messing around with this one. No, not kindly at all. In fact, he had plans for Augusta's keeper. He turned to Charles. "Want you to go to Charleston, boy. Got word that Sam Gunnells has a Mandinka he's gonna auction off. I want him for Eden's Gate. Think you can handle that?" His voice was laced with sarcasm.

"Me?"

Charles's startled response caused Grier to utter an involuntary oath. Charles didn't know a cussed thing about judging the worth of a prime field hand and even less about bargaining for the right price.

"Grier, need you to round up a coffle to take to Savannah next week. Cull out about two dozen. Half good stock and fancy the rest of 'em up the best you can. I don't want anybody claiming he didn't get a fair deal from Victor Eden."

"Why Savannah?"

"The market's too slow to sell stock in Charleston right now. Sam Gunnells isn't offering top dollar, and he won't be expecting to get it either. We can sell higher in Savannah to cover the cost of the Mandinka here in Charleston and have some left over."

Grier turned away to hide his anger. The old man needed more money to pay off his gambling debts to that whore, Kate Perrault. It didn't make a damn bit of difference that she was dead. Franklin Miller meant to collect every cent owed to her especially now that her daughter had showed up in Charleston.

"The boy, here, hasn't got the experience to turn a whole coffle. There's not much chance he can do a whole lot of damage with just one slave to worry about."

Charles stiffened at Victor's rebuke. "We have a Mandinka, Father."

"We have a smithy. I want a *breeder!* And Juno's no breeder. He and Zina here been paired up better than fifteen years, and he hasn't managed to get a whelp off of her in all that time."

Charles gripped the arm of his chair.

Grier gave a coarse laugh. "You hear that, Zina? Master Victor's gonna find you a real man. Old Juno done had his chance."

Charles sensed Zina's struggle to keep her features passive while she continued to massage the old man's leg. He stood abruptly.

"When do I leave?"

Victor's shaggy brows raised a notch. He tipped his head and looked up into his son's eyes.

"The auction's in two days. I expect you back by the time Grier's ready to leave for Savannah. Ask Grady Forbes over to Cutler's Landing to ferry you back upriver. Don't want that buck jumping the traces on you and heading out overland. Water's your best bet."

Charles glanced down at Zina. "I'll keep it in mind." He turned and strode from the room.

Grier returned to the sideboard. "You know I coulda—"

Victor threw up his hands to silence his protests. "It's time the boy learns a thing or two about managing this place. As long as he hangs on to his mama's skirts and thinks about nothing but horseracing and that stallion of his, he's not going to be fit for much."

Zina sank back on her haunches. "You be needin' anythin' else, Mastah Victor?"

"No. Get out of here and see to Miz Augusta." He gave a careless wave dismissing her. She rose and gathered up her medicine box and followed Charles from the room.

Victor reached for the glass of whiskey in Grier's hand. "How's that Hugo doing?"

"He died this morning."

"Damn!"

"He was a runner. Maybe it'll teach them others a thing or two."

"Seems to me your lessons are getting mighty costly here lately. Can't afford to keep losing valuable hands like that." Victor cursed and hurled the glass against the hearth. "We got to find out how they make their way through the swamp to the salt flats."

Grier frowned. No white man had ever gone in search of the elusive trail through the swamp and survived to tell about it, and he didn't figure on being the next one to try. "We can hire more patrollers down by the canals and along the road. Any of them bastards make a break for it will be caught for sure. Maybe next time, we can snare that 'Shepherd' feller, too."

Victor forced a wry smile. "I would find that mighty pleasing. Yes, sir, mighty pleasing. And just so you know, mister, I see the way you look at Zina. You keep your distance, you hear. I don't aim to have a passel of troublesome mixed bloods here at Eden's Gate. Don't want to see your mark on any whelps about the place."

Early the next morning, Charles walked down the hallway to his mother's room. Zina drew a brush through Augusta's faded hair, but stopped when he knocked on the door and entered. There would be time to fix her up after he said goodbye.

He knelt beside the chair and frowned when Augusta shrank against the cushions, twisting a bit of crumpled lace in her fingers. When he took her hand gently in his own, her face brightened with a childlike innocence.

"Stephen?"

"No, Mama. It's me, Charles." He hurried on before the veil descended over her eyes once more. "I have to go to the city for a few days. I'll be staying with Cousin Stephen and Miz Grace. Shall I give them your regards?"

"No, no you must not. Father will be very angry. He does not approve of Stephen, you know." Her hands fluttered helplessly, her eyes filled with tears. Charles sighed. His grandfather had been dead for twenty years.

"Don't worry. Grandpa won't ever know." He rose and kissed her cheek, nodded to Zina, and strode from the room. Zina watched from the window as he hurried down the front steps moments later.

He seized Belezar's reins from the stablehand. The stallion shied nervously, then settled under his touch. It would not do to leave the animal on the place. As soon as the old man was able to get about, he was apt to shoot the spirited mount. Charles glanced up at the windows of his mother's room. Zina raised her hand. He nodded. They both knew where he was going and why. He swung into the saddle and raced down the avenue and through the gates.

Nine

The Reverend Stephen Flynn drew deeply on his pipe. A lazy trail of smoke curled toward the roof of the downstairs porch. He felt a momentary pang of guilt knowing how much his wife detested the foul practice. Grace would scold and he would repent, and their comfortable charade would continue. He smiled to himself and settled back in his favorite rocking chair. The voices of the choir practicing for Sunday's service drifted toward the parsonage from the church next door.

A lone rider progressed along the street at a measured pace, unrecognized until he passed the church. Stephen squinted against the afternoon sun. A grin suddenly split his face. "Grace, come quick. We are about to have company. It's Charles."

His wife bustled through the door tucking a stray curl beneath her knitted snood.

Her shoes clicked down the steps as she hurried to keep pace with Stephen's long strides.

"Charles." Stephen reached the gate and clasped their visitor's hand as he dismounted.

"Cousin Stephen. It's good to see you, sir."

Grace gave a happy cry and clasped him about the waist. "Oh, Charles, what a pleasant surprise. You look well, dear. And your mother, how is she?"

"She's fine, Miz Grace. She sends her love." The lie came easily. His pleasure at seeing them both was so genuine, he felt no guilt in offering it.

"Grace, you're smothering the lad." Stephen laughed and clapped

Charles on the shoulder. The Flynn bloodlines were thankfully evident in Augusta's son. Sunlight enhanced the burnished auburn hair that lay softly against his collar. His gray eyes were honest and quick to humor. Stephen sighed inwardly.

The door burst open and a girl in a blur of gingham rushed down the steps. "Charlie!"

Charles grinned and planted an affectionate peck on Ginny Flynn's brow. There was not another smile in the city as bright as hers. She grasped his arm with comfortable familiarity.

Grace hurried back up the walkway. "Cassie," she called out to the servant standing just inside the doorway, "fetch brandy for our guest, and don't forget Reverend Flynn's tobacco. We can air the parlor later. Charles, you will be staying the night with us, won't you?"

"A couple of days, if it's no trouble."

"Charlie, you just made Mama's day. If you had said 'no,' she would never have forgiven the slight," Ginny giggled.

"What a scandalous thing to say." Grace's protest fooled no one. "I will have Cassie set another place at the table." She swept through the front door and disappeared in the direction of the kitchen.

At dinner, the conversation was interspersed with frequent bursts of laughter. The warmth of the small dining room contrasted sharply with the stagnant grandeur of Eden's Gate.

"Oh, Charlie," Ginny's eyes brightened, "Miz Iretta and Miz Maybelle reopened the Wellington townhouse this past spring. Paul is back from Boston, and he has decided to stay with Miz Adelaide. I suppose no one can blame him. And Connie and Dan are here in the city with Davy. We saw them ride by in the carriage yesterday."

Stephen shot his daughter a warning glance, and her words trailed off. She blushed, mortified at her thoughtlessness. None of them missed the sudden pain in Charles's eyes at the mention of Connie's name.

"More dessert, Stephen? Charles?" Grace hurriedly attempted to cover the awkward silence.

Charles smiled. "No, thank you, Miz Grace. But Cassie did a fine job on that pie."

After dinner Stephen ushered Charles into his study. Throughout the evening, his shrewd gaze had seldom strayed from his young cousin's face. He walked to his desk and retrieved a bottle from the drawer. "Grace and Ginny are delighted to have you here." He poured a shot of liquor into two small glasses and offered one to his guest.

Charles accepted the whiskey and nodded. "To Miz Grace and Ginny."

Their glasses touched with a pleasant clink.

Stephen smiled to himself. It had been almost thirty years since he and Augusta had cloaked their young love for one another behind a façade of easy banter between cousins. He had been determined to establish himself before asking Allard Flynn's permission to court her and then making a proper offer for her hand. A year at the seminary was all that he had asked. She had begged him not to go.

Augusta's last letter reached him as the first snows of winter blanketed Philadelphia. Her father had gambled away the last of a modest fortune, and deliverance had come with her marriage to one of the wealthiest planters in the region. By the time the letter arrived, Victor Eden had married her and taken her from Charleston to dwell in his great country house, Eden's Gate. Within a year, she had borne him a son.

Two more years passed before Stephen summoned the will to return to Charleston. Grace Pickering, Augusta's closest friend, cast aside her pride and accepted his offer of marriage knowing in her lonely heart that he still loved another.

Stephen sank into the chair across the room. "What brings you to the city?"

"Sam Gunnells sent word he has a prime field hand for sale, likely a full blood Mandinka. He's going to auction the fellow off tomorrow night. Father would have come himself, but he suffered a fall from a horse last week and busted his leg up pretty bad," Charles offered a wry smile, "so, he sent me instead."

"I see." Stephen's eyes narrowed, and he stroked his chin thoughtfully.

"We have two Mandinkas on the place now," Charles continued, "the smithy, Juno, and the medicine woman, Zina. Father paired them up when Juno was in his prime and Zina only thirteen. They never produced any young. Father has plans to breed Sam Gunnells's Mandinka to Zina."

Stephen struggled to hide a sudden flash of anger. "Are you acquainted with this Gunnells fellow?"

"I have never had much to do with slavers."

"They are a vile lot of renegades."

Charles understood. Ever since the Congressional edict of 1808 forbade the importation of slaves from Africa, planters had relied upon men like Sam Gunnells to supply them with new breeding stock. "Some argue they provide a needed service to our agrarian society."

"I find that a difficult philosophy to embrace," Stephen protested. His own driver, John Davis, was a gentleman of invaluable worth who suffered only the misfortune of color. Born to a mulatto woman and a white master, few sons of Charleston wrote a finer hand than he or spoke the King's English with the precision of a titled lord. "How many slaves do you have at Eden's Gate?"

"At last count, one hundred sixty three."

Stephen did not bother to hide his disgust. "I cannot understand the need for one more when there are so many, but if Victor is determined to have this Mandinka, perhaps I should accompany you tomorrow night."

Charles's eyes lit up. "I would be grateful if you would, sir."

"Then tomorrow night it is, but now it's late and we should retire."

Grace stirred beneath the bedcovers as Stephen closed the door and sank down upon the bed without bothering to remove his clothing. He locked his hands behind his head and stared up into the darkness.

"One hundred sixty three helpless souls," he whispered. "Merciful Heavenly Father."

The hours passed, and just before dawn, a gentle rain began to patter softly upon the roof. Still, he tossed until Grace groaned and turned toward him, her protest barely audible. "For goodness sakes, Stephen, must you thrash so?"

He swung his legs over the side of the bed and walked to the window. Had Charles suspected? Had he been too forceful? Lately, he seemed to toss caution aside. There was so much to do, and he sensed there was little time. How much longer could he conceal the double life he led?

"Stephen," Grace whispered, "please come back to bed."

"Charles is here for the Mandinka. I am not sure I can go through with the rescue now."

"You will do what you must, Stephen."

"The boy will do his best to please that swine, Eden, by outbidding all of the others. I cannot let that happen."

"Come back to bed, dear. You're exhausted."

For weeks Stephen and his men had known the Mandinka was in the city, brought in with a coffle from the Delmar farm near Georgetown. According to Gunnells's man, Enos Kemp, this Rameses fellow possessed a keen intelligence. Once he was rescued, he would be recruited to help free his brothers and sisters in bondage, but now, by the strangest irony, the one person who might stand in the way of their plan slept in the room across the hall.

Stephen returned to the bed. Poor Grace. The years had not been kind, yet she stood beside him through the hardships, the soul wrenching fears and deprivations. He reached for her hand and gave it a gentle squeeze. He could sense her smile in the darkness. She moved against his shoulder and fell instantly back to sleep. He closed his eyes and forced himself to remain still.

Charles opened the door that led from his bedroom onto the upper side porch. He stared into the rainswept blackness remembering a similar night when the drawing room at Eden's Gate teemed with guests too long denied its hospitality. The ball to formally announce his coming marriage to Connie had brought forth society's best. Tables groaned beneath the bounty from Pansy's kitchen, and liquor flowed too freely.

Victor Eden had looked on with unabashed pride at the young woman who would soon become his daughter-in-law and preside over a house too long left to neglect. The wedding was to have taken place when Paul DuPre returned from his studies in Edinburgh. Charles had chafed with impatience, but Connie loved her brother almost as much as she loved him. He had relented, knowing it would be all the sweeter between them for having waited.

Dan Wellington had appeared late in the evening to claim a waltz and swept Connie from his side. He looked on as Dan led her into the whirling crowd of dancers and laughed down into her shining eyes. Connie reached up and impulsively kissed Dan's cheek, and in a haze of whiskey, he had misjudged her kindly gesture toward her brother's best friend.

Later in the library, his accusations had been vile. Her denial had been incredulous, disbelieving, and pained. Dan Wellington was a family friend. Nothing more! He had turned his back on her then, and tonight, the one he still loved slept safely in her husband's arms across town. His heart ached with a terrible, burning jealousy.

Ten

The slave compound

Footsteps echoed along the wooden corridor that led from the auction hall to a stockade directly behind it. Three men approached a pair of cells at the far end of the stifling enclosure. Sam Gunnells lifted his lantern and squinted through the gloom.

The mute raised her head from a bed of straw as the arc of light swung toward her. For an instant, her golden eyes caught the fire of the lantern's flame. She closed them again and folded her small frame into the same position she had laid in for five weeks, since she and the Mandinka had been brought to the stockade. She was nearly white, and according to the Widow Delmar's overseer she had not uttered a single word in the seventeen years since old man Delmar brought her up from the quarters to the main house the night she was born.

Gunnells turned and stared hard at the giant in the adjoining cell. His name was Rameses and he was a formidable specimen, coal black with corded muscles that gleamed in the flickering light. He showed no signs of the malaise that affected the mute, and he had struggled like a savage beast when they first attempted to drag him into his cell. The stockade had echoed with his rage until Dobbs felled him with a blow from the butt of his pistol.

Gunnells turned toward his men and motioned the older one forward. "Clean 'em up tomorrow," he glanced back toward the cells and dropped his voice, "and, Kemp, keep an eye on the girl. Dobbs has got a mean hankerin'."

"Shore will, Mistah Gunnells."

The stockade had been quiet for hours. Rameses braced his back against the rough planking and clasped his powerful arms about his knees. A few steps away, the mute crawled toward a bucket of fetid water by the cage door. She sagged against the iron bars and reached for the gourd dipper, oblivious to others who slept fitfully in their cells nearby.

Rameses slipped his hand beneath his own bed of straw and grasped a piece of broken wire he had wrenched from a bucket of slops. The edge had been scraped to razor sharpness against the stone floor. He rose to a crouch and moved silently across the narrow space. "Pearl." His voice was purposely gentle and coaxing in the dark and frightening place. She stared at the hand that beckoned to her through the bars that separated them.

"Come!" he whispered more forcefully this time.

A glimmer of recognition flashed in her eyes before the veil drifted over them once more. Rameses's breath quickened with renewed urgency. Gunnells was auctioning them off soon. With her affliction, and old Mastah Delmar no longer around to protect her, she would suffer unspeakable tortures at the hands of strangers. Afterward, a quick, fatal slash to his own throat would end the torment for both of them.

"Give me yore hand."

She reached out. He clamped his fingers about her wrist and dragged her toward him. As soon as she was within reach, he grasped the back of her head and pressed the sharpened wire against her neck. She mouthed a silent scream and kicked the bucket causing it to clatter loudly across the floor. Rameses scrambled back against the wall and shoved his weapon beneath the straw. In the distance, a door burst open and footsteps pounded down the hallway. The guards swung their lanterns aloft. Pearl had crawled back to the far corner of her cell and lay shivering on the wet straw.

Enos Kemp glanced at Rameses. He had not moved from where Kemp had last seen him. "C'mon," he motioned to Dobb, "let's git some sleep."

"You go on. I can stay and clean this here mess up. Mist' Gunnells would want—"

"Dobbs!"

"Comin'."

Rameses expelled his breath slowly. Pearl would not venture within his reach again.

Another hour passed. Unable to sleep, Rameses heard a hinge creak down the hallway. He rose to his feet and pressed himself against the wall. A shadow hurried through the darkness, paused, and looked about before making his way toward his cell. A hat was pulled down across his eyes. A bandana covered the lower portion of his face.

"You." The intruder's voice was muffled. "Git over here. Ain't got much time."

Rameses advanced cautiously and gripped the bars. He was certain the voice belonged to the man Gunnells called Kemp.

"You and her are gonna be sold tomorrow night, but me and some others gonna git you away from here before yore new master can take you out of the city. You understand whut I'm tellin' you, boy? You and her gonna be free!" The shadow turned abruptly and hurried away.

Rameses's heart gave a wild leap. Slowly, he sank to his knees. *Free.* And he had almost ended both their lives.

Eleven

"So, you're leaving after all!"

Georgette glared at the tear-stained pages on the dressing table. That damn letter was the reason Lily barricaded her door the day before, refusing to admit anyone until she threatened to summon Xavier to break it down.

"The girls said you wouldn't stay, but I reminded them you were Kate's daughter. 'Made of strong stuff, just like her ma,' I said. Well, I was wrong." Georgette scowled at the dejected figure standing by the window, watching the afternoon shadows lengthen across the lawn.

Lily turned, choking back her tears. "I know that I said I would stay, and I have tried to accustom myself to Swan House, but I don't belong here, Georgette. Please try to understand. I am *not* Kate."

And she had tried, until Reverend Mother's letter arrived. Sister Agatha's death had come a week after she and Thaddeus sailed for Charleston. How could she not have known the frail little nun was so ill? Her thoughts had been only of the journey ahead, and to what end? Virtual imprisonment in a house where the most sinful acts were commonplace. Reverend Mother would surely allow her to return to the convent. She must.

Georgette shook her head to dispel the sense of defeat that settled over her. Once Lily left for New Orleans, it would mean the end of Swan House and everything they risked their lives for.

"I'll send word to Franklin and tell the others in the morning."

"I'm sorry, Georgette."

"So am I, Lily. We had hoped you would come to think of this as your home. Your mother would have liked that." She wrenched open the door and fled from the room.

Lily walked over to the dressing table, sank down on the vanity chair and buried her face in her hands.

Polly emerged from behind the screen where she had listened to the exchange between the two women. "Child, you gonna make yoreself sick if you keep carryin' on like this."

"What am I to do, Polly? Mister Miller said that Swan House would be sold should I ever leave. But I cannot stay."

Polly's expression softened for a moment. She laid a hand on the girl's shoulder. "Miz Georgette's just upset."

Lily shook her head. "She will never forgive me. And what will happen to you and Xavier and the others?"

"You ain't to worry 'bout that. Miz Georgette and Mistah Franklin, they see after us. We gonna be just fine. Don't want you to think unkind of Miz Georgette neither. Yore mam put a lot of store by her. Just remember, some things ain't always what they looks to be."

"I don't understand."

Polly reached down and drew her up, holding her at arm's length. "Time you was gittin' some rest." She walked over to the bed and drew back the covers.

Lily slipped between the sheets and closed her eyes though she knew she could not sleep. She would tell Jack first thing in the morning and then ask Franklin Miller to arrange her passage on the next vessel to New Orleans.

The door closed softly as Polly left the room.

Thaddeus leaned against the windowsill, his arms crossed over his chest. Georgette paced the length of the room, wringing her hands.

"Georgette, sit down. You're wearing out the rug, for God's sakes!"

"I cannot believe it's over. It's too much to take in. Oh, Thaddeus, why did you ever let me talk you into bringing that girl here?"

He reached out and pulled her up against his chest and heaved a deep sigh. "You know why, Georgette."

"If Jack can't convince her to stay, what will we do?"

"I don't know, sweetheart. I guess we all hoped she would take to the place after a spell."

"Ha!" Georgette's anger surged again.

"Hold on, now." He pulled her back into his arms and stifled her protest with a kiss, and another, until all thoughts of Lily vanished from their minds. Three months apart was a long time, and they were still making up for it.

Twelve

That evening, Sam Gunnells's Auction House

Stephen and Charles shouldered their way through the milling crowd to the front of the hall. As the sale commenced, Charles cast a worried look around. The building was filled with planters and agents from Charleston, Beaufort, the rice islands, and as far away as Savannah. Garnering the Mandinka for Eden's Gate would not be easy.

Stephen's anger mounted as the hours wore on. He glanced at Charles. The lad had discarded his coat. Sweat beaded his brow, and his lips were drawn in a taut line. Stephen felt a grim sense of satisfaction that Victor Eden's son had no stomach for this wretched business.

At last, Sam Gunnells signaled for the Mandinka to be brought from the stockade. The crowd pressed closer to the dais as Rameses mounted the block. A collective murmur of appreciation spread throughout the hall as bidders turned toward one another and nodded. There was strength in the brute and, they suspected, danger. But a heavy hand with the lash could tame a savage nature. Gunnells was forced to shout to be heard above the crowd.

Stephen sighted his collaborator near the side door. Enos Kemp gave a slight nod. All the preacher's men had to do now was wait. As the last bids were called out, Stephen prayed that Charles would concede to the rice planter from St. Helena. The gavel crashed down upon the podium.

"Sold to Mister Charles Eden of Eden's Gate Plantation!"

Stephen's heart sank. Charles expelled a ragged breath.

Rameses's defiant glare sought out the man who had bid so fiercely to claim him. Their eyes locked. Charles struggled to quell the appre-hension that coursed through him. The Mandinka would run the first chance he got. The old man was right. It would be best to transport him by water. He watched a pair of armed guards lead Rameses from the block and disappear in the direction of the stockade.

Sam Gunnells leveled a critical eye at the crowd. Their faces were flushed with excitement and too much free whiskey. He turned toward the side door and gave a nod.

"And now, gentlemen, a *fancy* like none any of you have ever seen. Little Pearl is gentle-bred and damn near as fair skinned as you and me. And she's easily worth as much as the Mandinka, 'specially since she's never been broke in."

An impulsive bid from the back of the room prompted a burst of laughter. Gunnells grinned good-naturedly and motioned to Dobbs to bring the girl forward. A sudden hush descended over the crowd. Stephen's anger turned to anguish. He had seen others similar to this, unwanted by-blows carelessly bred at the pleasure of their white sires and their light-skinned mistresses, but he had never before seen one who could stun a room to silence. He glanced about nervously. In an-other minute, the place would erupt into pandemonium.

Charles felt his breath catch in his throat. His father's hatred of mixed bloods fled from his mind as he gauged the excitement that ig-nited the room. The girl's terrified gaze darted across the raucous crowd until she spied him silently staring up at her, his eyes filled with pity.

Gunnells demanded silence and then called for an opening bid. The bidding grew heated and reckless once more. Almost as abruptly as it commenced, it was over. The gavel descended. The fancy, like the Mandinka, was destined for Eden's Gate. Charles watched anxiously as Gunnells's men rushed her from the hall. He was conscious of the mutterings around him.

What the hell's he gonna do with her? Everybody knows Victor Eden don't allow mixed bloods at Eden's Gate.

Stephen backed away toward the side door. The plan to free Ra-meses, and now the girl, had become infinitely more dangerous. Only he and John Davis would attempt the rescue. No harm must come to Charles. Fearful they might be recognized, the men who followed him could get it in their minds to kill his young cousin.

Charles searched the crowd and saw Stephen emerge from the shadows and glance about before walking toward him. Later, they rode through the deserted streets in silence. Grace greeted them at the door and watched as Stephen wearily mounted the stairs. A few minutes later, she extinguished the lamp beside their bed and slipped beneath the covers. She laid her head against her husband's shoulder and felt his lips brush her hair. There was no arguing with him. She knew what he must do, and her heart ached for the benign treachery that would rob him of sleep this night.

Across the hall, Charles tossed restlessly upon the bed. The fancy was his, bought with his own money. Let the old man rage. And then, a cold sense of dread settled about his heart. In his determination to save the helpless girl from those lusting bastards at the auction hall, he had not given a thought to Grier Taylor and the danger that awaited her at Eden's Gate.

The next morning, Grace stood at the window and gazed out at the street. Stephen had slipped away from the house before first light. It would be late before he returned. Her husband was not a young man. How much longer could he continue this double life, a man of the church by day and a reviled abolitionist who rode the river road by night?

The rescue of the Mandinka and the fancy would be the most perilous one he and John Davis had ever attempted. *White, Grace!* He had whispered with soul-wrenching despair as they lay together in the hours just before dawn. God knows what bestiality and degradation the girl would be forced to endure at the hands of Victor Eden. Curse the man's despicable soul and all others like him.

She blinked to dispel the tears that gathered behind her lashes. It shamed her that jealousy rivaled her worries for her husband's safety. Had she only imagined that Stephen searched Charles's features too intently? Perhaps it wasn't just Victor's cruelty that drove him to liberate Eden's Gate slaves, but that Victor Eden had stolen the only woman her husband truly loved.

"Miz Grace?"

"Oh, Cassie. I didn't hear you come in."

The cook's hands twisted in the folds of her apron. "I heard Mistah Charles movin' about in his room. You want me to start fixin' breakfast?"

"Yes, do. Ginny will be down soon, too."

"What do I say if Mistah Charles asks after Reverend Flynn?"

"Just tell him that Stephen had to take care of some church business and leave the rest to me." Grace managed a wan smile and sighed. Not even Ginny suspected her father's double life. So many lies. So many sleepless nights waiting, praying, and listening for Stephen's footsteps on the stairs, and weeping silently into her pillow as he slipped into bed and patted her on the shoulder with a whisper, *I'm home, Grace.*

John Davis's and Cassie's risks were as great as their own. They only pretended to be bonded to her and Stephen. It was a charade that had kept them safe ever since they left Philadelphia and followed Stephen to Charleston. The four of them were bound together for a purpose that could end with a chance recognition—or a bullet. The danger had been there from the beginning, and the fear of discovery had not lessened with time.

"Heah they come." Cassie turned and fled in the direction of the kitchen.

"Mornin', Mama. Look who I bumped into. What a sleepyhead you are, Charlie."

He grinned, but Grace detected traces of weariness in his features. Charles had slept no more soundly than she or Stephen.

"Good morning, Miz Grace." He brushed her cheek with a light kiss, and she felt a sudden lump constrict her throat. Tonight, while the city slept Stephen and John Davis would be about their sinister business, returning home before Charles awakened and prepared to leave for Eden's Gate. Pray God that Enos Kemp did his part well. Sam Gunnells and his guards would shoot at the first suspicion of intruders. She gave an involuntary shudder and swayed.

"Miz Grace, are you all right?" Charles reached out to steady her, his eyes filled with concern.

"I'm just a little tired. Now, you two have a seat and Cassie will bring your breakfast out in a shake."

A half-hour later, Ginny sank against the back of her chair and held up her hands. "Oh, I am just stuffed. No one can make hotcakes as good as our Cassie. Now, if I could only loosen this corset a tad."

"Virginia Althea Flynn," Grace gasped.

Charles laughed at the mischief that twinkled in the girl's eyes.

"Yoo-hoo, is anybody home?"

Grace rose from her chair as the visitor bustled into the room and stopped abruptly. "I beg your pardon, Grace. I had no idea you had company."

"Gussie, how nice to see you. And what lovely roses."

"Yes, they are pretty," Ginny quickly interceded. "Charlie, Miz Putnam always brings flowers for the church."

Gussie Putnam fixed the Flynn's guest with a cold, unwavering stare.

"Gussie, I don't believe you have been introduced to Stephen's cousin, Charles Eden?"

"I've heard the name, to be sure."

Charles pushed away from the table and gave a slight bow. Everyone in the city had heard of his broken engagement to Constance DuPre. Judging from the old harridan's malevolent stare, she pegged him for a scoundrel of the first order.

"A pleasure, ma'am," he murmured.

"Indeed. Now, Grace, don't forget to put the roses in fresh water with just a pinch of sugar. By Sunday, they should be in full bloom. They are my best pinks, you know."

"Of course. Let me fetch a vase. Won't you stay for a cup of tea?"

"No, thank you. I really must be going. Ginny, I will see you at services come Sunday."

"Bye, Miz Gussie." Ginny glanced across the table and rolled her eyes as her mother escorted their guest to the door. "La," she whispered, "but she is a trial. She comes every week reminding us to put her flowers in fresh water with just a pinch of sugar. I can't understand how Mama puts up with her," she giggled.

"Your mother is a fine woman, Ginny."

"Oh, Charlie, indeed she is. I wonder how she manages sometimes. Why, we hardly see Papa at all, living right here in the same house. Somebody always wants him to perform a marriage, or preach a funeral, or he's out visiting sick folks. Just last week, Miz Dovie Hamilton was feeling poorly, and he was away for two days. Mama just smiles and says it's all the Lord's work."

"And *you* would not want to be a preacher's wife?" He stifled a grin at the pretty grimace.

"Lordy, no. Now, Mama has her heart set on me marrying Cousin Rupert Pickering down in Savannah. I like him well enough, but he's a lot like Papa, what with him studying to be a doctor. They are both so dedicated to their callings. Papa's a real shepherd to his flock, and Rupert—" A tray of dishes crashed to the floor and Ginny gave a startled cry. "Oh, my goodness!"

Cassie's eyes locked fearfully on the girl's astonished face as she dropped to her knees to gather up the broken crockery.

Grace stood frozen in the doorway, her fingers clutching the sill.

"Cassie, are you hurt?" Ginny flew from the table and knelt beside the servant. "Charlie, quick, hand me that napkin." She quickly swaddled the bleeding cut with the linen cloth.

"It's all right, Miss Ginny," Cassie whispered and flinched from the pressure of her touch. "Ain't nothin' but a scratch."

"I'll fetch Mama's medicine chest."

Grace moved toward the pair. "Here, let me have a look. Ginny, aren't you going to the market with the Cromartie girls this morning? Look at the time. They will be calling for you any minute. Hurry along now. I'll see to Cassie."

"Well, if you're sure?" Ginny shot a doubtful look at her companion. "Charlie, you're welcome to accompany us if you like."

"I have to see Sam Gunnells this morning. Miz Grace, is there anything I can do?"

"It's nothing serious, Charles. Now, you go on along. We'll look for you back here come suppertime." She watched as Ginny and Charles hurried up the back stairs.

"Miz Grace, that child gave me a terrible fright. You don't reckon Mistah Charles thinks—?"

"No, of course not." Grace's reassurance was unconvincing.

"I hope you right, and I am real sorry 'bout the dishes. Just couldn't think of no other way to keep Miss Ginny from goin' on 'bout Reverend Flynn."

"Don't fret about a few broken plates. Goodness knows, we have enough real trouble to worry about." Grace gave her friend's arm a squeeze. "Now, let me get the medicine chest."

Charles glanced about the small room he occupied. It was sparsely furnished with white cotton curtains tied back at the windows and a colorful quilt on the bed. Stephen's meager stipend did not allow for luxuries, yet Grace had managed to create a real home out of the modest parsonage. He felt a curious reluctance to leave.

He walked out onto the upper porch and braced his hands upon the railing. The front door slammed below. Grace hurried along the stone path in the direction of the church next door.

Papa's a real shepherd to his flock . . . gone for two days to the Hamilton place . . . don't know how Mama manages . . . the Hamilton place . . . a shepherd

Charles felt the flesh prickle on the back of his neck. The Hamiltons had traveled to Columbia for a wedding more than a month past. And their place was less than two miles upriver from Three Fountains and Eden's Gate.

Lost two of the household help and two prime field hands the month before. Thurston Turnbull's voice echoed beyond Ginny's mindless patter. Charles's pulse quickened. No, it couldn't be! Cousin Stephen, the leader of a pack of reckless zealots? Was that the reason he had offered to accompany him to the auction the night before? Was there a plan even now to rescue the Mandinka?

Grim-faced, he strode back into the room and tossed his belongings into his saddlebags. He had to leave the city before Stephen realized that he suspected his secret. He slipped down the back stairs and hurried toward the stable. Moments later, he swung into the saddle and urged Belezar down the narrow alley at a reckless gallop, unaware of a carriage passing the church.

The woman screamed and clutched the child to her as the skittish horses reared, nearly unseating her driver. Charles leapt from his mount and grasped the team's harnesses while Belezar danced nervously away from their flailing hooves. After he coaxed the animals to a standstill, he turned to the passenger huddled fearfully against the cushions.

"Connie?" The tension in his face suddenly vanished. Without thinking he reached out and then jerked his hand away. "Are you hurt?"

"No, no, we're fine." She relaxed her frantic grip on the protesting child, unable to take her eyes from Charles's face. The sunlight glinted upon his hair, and his eyes were as clear and gray as ever. Yet, there was no hint of the humor she remembered, only pain and regret.

He shook his head. "I apologize. I was careless, and Belezar is mighty skittish yet."

"Belezar? He is magnificent." She cast a nervous glance at the stallion.

Charles gave a soft whistle, grateful the beast condescended to respond. He grasped the reins and mounted with an easy grace that belied the trembling in his limbs. He gazed down at her, struck by the uncertainty in her eyes.

"You're looking well." Beautiful, his heart cried. More beautiful than he remembered.

She blushed and smiled self-consciously.

"That's a handsome lad."

"Davy is the image of his father. Daniel and I have been caring for him while Paul has been in Boston."

"I heard that your brother returned to Charleston recently."

"Yes. He's staying with Mother for a while. We're on our way to the house for a visit." Her voice trailed off awkwardly.

"Then I must not detain you."

"Miz Augusta and your father, how are they?"

He smiled. "They're both well. I'll tell them you asked about them."

"Yes," she whispered, "do."

"It's good to see you again, Connie."

"Goodbye, Charles," she called after him as he dug his heels into Belezar's sides.

He turned when he reached the end of the street and watched the Wellington carriage continue on its way. A familiar pain splintered his heart with renewed fury.

Thirteen

Water oaks and palmetto thickets guarded the steep embankment overlooking the river. Towering cypresses grew among the shallows, shading a wooden dock and a weathered steamer tied to the pilings. On the ridge overlooking Cutler's Landing, a thin trail of smoke rose from the chimney of the ferryman's cabin. A mulatto appeared in the open doorway and rubbed her hands on her soiled apron. She barked a terse command at the albino sprawled across the stoop. The youth pushed himself away from the steps and trudged down the path leading to the water. His bare feet made no sound as he dropped onto the deck of the boat and sank down upon the coils of hemp next to the bridgehouse. He trained his colorless eyes on his pa and the stranger who paced back and forth across the deck.

Grady Forbes turned his leathery features toward the middle of the river and squinted into the setting sun. The swift midstream currents caught the blaze of the fiery orb. Along the bank, dusk had begun to settle upon the swampy undergrowth. The evening rang with a chorus of crickets and bullfrogs. The ferryman walked to the opposite side of the steamer, spat a stream of tobacco over the rail, and studied the tangled roots just below the water's surface. "Current's too tricky on up around the bend to navigate this here river at night. We gonna have to wait fer first light. Won't have no trouble then." Forbes pursed his lips and shook his head. "That's mighty fine hoss you got there, Mist' Eden. Wouldn't want to take a chance on somethin' happening to 'im if he wuz mine."

Charles cursed under his breath. By now the Flynns knew he had fled from the parsonage. How long would Stephen and his collaborators lay in wait along the river road before they realized he intended to return to Eden's Gate by water? They knew every inlet and bog from Savannah to Portsmouth. Cutler's Landing was bound to come to mind. Charles reached into his coat and touched the leather holster beneath his arm.

The albino scrambled to his feet and pointed toward the embankment. "Wagon a'comin."

"Git up to the road and lead them animals down here, boy. That there track can be mighty dangerous if you ain't used to it." Forbes's curious progeny sprinted up the steep rise and grasped the harnesses and guided the team down the slippery descent. Charles and the ferryman strode across the deck and hurried down the plank.

"Sorry to be so late, gennelmen. Mister Gunnells woulda' come hisself 'cept there wuz some commotion over to the stockade." The driver jumped agilely from the wheel. "Name's Enos Kemp."

Charles ignored his outstretched hand, not bothering to conceal his irritation. "I had hoped to be upriver by now, Mister Kemp. As it is, we will not be able to leave before daylight."

Forbes circled the wagon and gave a soft whistle. "Ain't never seen a buck as fine as this one. And whut you got here?" He reached over the side of the wagon and grasped a fistful of the girl's hair and pushed it away from her face. "Damn, she's most near white."

Charles shoved him aside and approached the back of the wagon. "It's all right, Pearl. No one is going to hurt you."

Forbes stared at her curiously. "Whut's the matter with her? Cain't she speak?"

Charles felt a stirring of apprehension in the pit of his belly. He climbed onto the bed of straw and knelt inches from where she crouched. Slowly, he reached out and gently captured her small face in his hands and forced her to meet his gaze. There was nothing in her expression, not even the desperation he had seen the night before.

"A mute," he whispered. A cold dampness formed on his brow. A scarred face or a twisted limb might offer her some protection, but the inability to speak would render her defenseless. Grier Taylor's image flashed through his mind.

He motioned to Enos Kemp. "Unchain her." The driver dropped

to his knees and unlocked the tether that bound her to the wagon. "Now him." He scrambled to the other side and removed the second restraint. For a moment, Rameses's eyes searched Kemp's face.

Charles withdrew his pistol from the holster inside his coat and offered it to the ferryman. "Take him aboard and secure him to the railing."

Forbes grasped the weapon, involuntarily stepping back as Rameses leapt to the ground and stretched himself to his full height. "Shore don't want this bastid gittin' loose," he muttered, and clutched the weapon tighter.

Charles turned and lifted Pearl in his arms and felt the dreadful gauntness of her body through the coarse shift. Once they reached Eden's Gate, he would give her over to Pansy and Zina. The cook and the medicine woman would know what to do.

Enos Kemp watched intently as Charles carried the girl into the bridgehouse and Forbes secured Rameses's leg chains to the railing. "Guess I'd best be gittin' on back seeing as how you gennelmen got things in hand here. Pleasure doing business with you, Mister Eden. Mister Sam sends his respects to yore pa."

Charles nodded and silently watched Kemp climb into the wagon and urge the team back up the steep incline.

Forbes's eyes shifted expectantly in the direction of the bridge-house. "Spect you'll be wanting to bed down fer the night. Janie will fix you a pallet in the cabin. I kin camp out here on deck and keep a eye on things."

Charles trained a cold stare upon him. He had seen the fire in the man's eyes when he looked at Pearl. "We'll fare well enough, Mister Forbes, and, I'm willing to pay for whatever food you can spare for the three of us."

The ferryman nodded. "The woman kin stir up some vittles fer you."

"I would be obliged if we can get an early start in the morning."

Forbes shrugged and started up the embankment.

The moon laid a silvery path across the black water. A trace of light spilled through the small window of the bridgehouse. Charles rubbed his eyes and shifted stiffly in the wooden chair by the door. The gun lay on the table beside him. The girl had not moved or uttered a sound since he had taken the untouched food away from her. He didn't know if she slept, and if she did, God only knew what horrors haunted her dreams. He closed his eyes. In a few hours, they would be on their way upriver.

Outside, the stallion pricked his ears and jerked against the tether. Rameses rolled onto his side. He had heard it too, muffled footsteps along the dock. He forced himself to remain still as two cloaked and hooded apparitions materialized out of the blackness and crept silently across the deck. The rescuers had come like Kemp said they would. His heart pounded wildly as they made their way to his side.

The taller of the two tested the chain that bound him to the railing. "The others?"

Rameses nodded in the direction of the cabin on the ridge and turned toward the bridgehouse. The other man slipped across the deck and pressed himself against the wall next to the doorway. Inside, Charles gripped the arms of the chair as the door slowly swung open to reveal a silhouette framed in the narrow opening.

"We have come for the Mandinka and the girl." The growl was menacing, smothered beneath the disguise. There was no way to identity the intruder by his voice, yet Charles recognized his cousin's familiar stance. He glanced at the weapon just beyond his reach. If he could frighten Stephen, force him to flee—he lunged and grasped the pistol.

Stephen's body struck him full force sending them both crashing to the floor. The gun discharged with a muffled crack. With a hoarse cry, Charles pushed himself to his knees and stripped away the hood that concealed his cousin's features.

Stephen gripped the arm of his bloody garment and groaned

Charles spun around and grabbed the gun as Stephen's accomplice burst through the doorway. Only Stephen's cry stopped his driver from hurling himself upon his cousin. John Davis shoved Charles aside and pulled Stephen to his feet drawing his uninjured arm about his shoulders.

"Wait." Charles motioned them away from the doorway.

"Mist' Eden, Mist' Eden!" Grady Forbes's lantern swung wildly as he scrambled down the path and onto the dock. "Heard a shot. You awright down there?"

Charles paused and then stepped out onto the deck. "Nothing to worry about. Just a water moccasin." He deliberately shoved the gun into his belt and waited until Forbes disappeared behind the closed door of the shanty before motioning the two men from the shadows.

"Don't take them, Charles," Stephen rasped in pain. "You're not like the others. Let them go."

"You know I can't."

"Then God forgive you. You have condemned them both to hell."

Rameses jerked savagely on the chain as Stephen and John Davis descended the ladder and made their way along the dock. He felt the touch of cold metal against his temple.

Charles knelt, keeping the weapon trained upon him as he refitted the lock John Davis had partially dislodged. He rose and retraced his steps to the bridgehouse and sank down upon the cot, dropping his clenched fists between his knees to still their violent trembling. Grace would hate him for what he had done. He buried his face in his hands and felt a movement behind him. Although Pearl made no sound he knew that she sensed his torment, just as he felt the terror that made her draw closer. He turned and stared intently into her eyes.

"Stephen's wrong," he whispered. "Nothing will happen to you, Pearl. No one will hurt you, I promise." There was the briefest flicker of light there before she retreated from him once more.

Outside, the faint sound of hoofbeats faded in the distance. Rameses's desperate bellow of rage echoed across the silent river.

Fourteen

"Miz Georgette, Mist' Thad! Wake up!"

They both groaned.

"I swear, I am going to strangle that Sauchie one of these days," Georgette mumbled, reaching for her dressing gown.

The insistent whisper turned shrill. "You all hurry up, and let me in!"

"We're coming." Georgette lurched for the door and wrenched it open.

Sauchie stumbled into the room. "Mist' Thad, Xavier say for you to come down to the cellar quick. Mist' Stephen been shot!"

"Oh, no!" Georgette's fingers flew to her lips. "I knew this would happen one day. Oh, hurry, Thaddeus." She reached for the bellcord beside her bed and gave it several frantic jerks. "Sauchie, fetch the medicine chest from the pantry, and bring towels and clean linen."

"And send Xavier to fetch Miz Grace," Thaddeus barked, pulling on his trousers.

The servant nodded and flew from the room, relieved to see the coachman hurrying up the stairs. "Mist' Thad say to git over to the parsonage and fetch Miz Grace." Sauchie grasped his arm and pro-pelled him back down the stairs. "Don' let nobody see you."

Moments later, Thaddeus and Georgette reached the dimly lighted ballroom and turned toward a hidden passage beneath the staircase. Georgette reached for a globed light on a nearby table. Thaddeus shoved a potted fern aside and pressed the trip latch concealed beneath a carved rosette. A small door moved silently on its hinges revealing steps that led down into the cellar.

〜

Lily sat up in her bed, awakened by the sound of footsteps hurrying along the gallery. She tossed aside the bedcover and opened her door in time to see Thaddeus and Georgette reach the ballroom and suddenly disappear into the shadows. She stepped back from the banister as Sauchie and Polly emerged from the direction of the kitchen, carrying towels and a medicine chest.

"He ain't dead, is he, girl? Lordy, please don't let nothin' happen to Mist' Stephen." Polly's whispered plea carried across the cavernous room.

Confused, Lily watched them approach the staircase and then disappear as quickly as Thaddeus and Georgette. A shiver of fear rippled through her. Summoning her courage, she crept along the gallery and hurried down the stairs in time to hear a door close with a soft click nearby. Spying the potted fern Thaddeus had moved, she approached a shallow alcove beneath the staircase. A towel lay on the floor, dropped there by one of the servants. It was not unlike the entrance to a secret passage in the old orphanage. She had played there with the other children when the weather kept them confined indoors. Her fingers searched the smooth surface of the wall. Instinctively, she reached for the rosette and tripped the latch. The door swung open.

Guided by a faint light from below, Lily grasped the handrail and inched forward, stifling a gasp when a man's voice cried out.

Georgette knelt beside Stephen and worked frantically to cut away his bloody sleeve. His lips tightened with pain as she gently probed the wound. She settled back on her haunches and gave a relieved sigh. The bullet had passed cleanly through his arm.

"It's only a flesh wound."

"Thank God," John Davis whispered. Stephen would not die. Grace would be spared her grief and the scandal that would have followed. And Ginny would be spared the loss of a father who vowed never to reveal his dangerous secret to his only child. He shook his head. If Stephen had not stopped him, he would have killed Charles Eden tonight. Each foray along the river, and each secret meeting with one of the conductors embedded in the slave populations, tested their mettle. On nights when the dogs and patrollers came too close, it was Stephen's fierce resolve and cunning that bolstered John Davis's courage and forged their escape. That, and the grace of the Almighty.

"Oh, Stephen," Georgette whispered, "you gave us such a fright. Polly, go upstairs and get some water to boiling. We have to clean this wound and get some fresh bandages on Reverend Flynn before Miz Grace gets here. It's not as bad as it looks, but she wouldn't be knowing that to see these bloody rags about the floor."

Polly sprang from her crouch. Her shriek strangled in her throat. "Miss Lily!"

Georgette froze. Thaddeus looked beyond her to the apparition poised on the stairs in her nightrail. Lily stepped down onto the stone floor and moved quickly to Stephen's side.

Stephen struggled to focus on the hauntingly familiar features that wavered above him. *Kate's girl.* She couldn't be anyone else.

Georgette slowly rose to her feet and backed away.

Lily gave her only a glance and turned back to the wounded man. Who was he, and what was he doing here? But there wasn't time to worry about that now. "Polly, fetch hot water. Sauchie, tear off some strips of that linen. Georgette, bring the medicine chest closer. Raise the lantern, Mister Parks."

The commands were rapid and sure. Her movements were quick, yet gentle. Stephen closed his eyes. It was almost as if Kate knelt beside him, with one glaring difference. Kate would never have attempted the bloody task herself. The minutes crept by. A fine sheen of perspiration covered Lily's face by the time the last strip of linen had been tied. Stephen opened his eyes and attempted a weak smile. He was rewarded with a slight uplifting of her lips.

"My thanks, young lady," he whispered.

"Stephen!"

Grace Flynn rushed through a hidden door that concealed a tunnel to the coach house above. Xavier burst through the door on her heels and stopped short, retreating back into the shadows.

"It's all right, Xavier." There was a resigned weariness in Georgette's pronouncement.

Stephen reached for his wife's hands as she sank to her knees beside him. "Now, now, Grace, don't cry," he whispered. "It's only a scratch. Miss Lily did a fine job of patching me up."

Lily studied the small woman. Hers was an unremarkable face

filled with fear and gratitude. Grace Flynn clutched her husband's hand against her pale cheek. "Thank you for taking care of my Stephen," she whispered.

John Davis cleared his throat. "Uh, Miz Grace, we need to get the reverend home as quick as we can. I don't think we were followed, but you never can tell. There's been quite a stir up and down the river lately."

"You're right. Xavier, help John Davis get my husband up to the coach house. He has to deliver his Sunday sermon in a few hours. We will take the gig. It's faster, and we aren't likely to be recognized."

Lily's protest was instinctive. "No! The wound could start to bleed again."

"He cannot stay here." Georgette's voice was firm.

"It wouldn't do for Stephen to be found here," Thaddeus interjected. "Best he makes it to his own place as fast as he can. If he was followed, they will be here soon."

"They?" Lily looked from one to another. "Who are 'they'?"

"Patrollers," Stephen winced. "Georgette's right. You could never explain why I happened to be here."

"Who shot you, Stephen?" Georgette knelt beside Grace Flynn.

"I don't know. We were ambushed. It was dark." His eyes shifted to John Davis.

Grace turned away. *Charles.* She had only to see the unspoken warning in Stephen's eyes to know. She turned to Georgette. "We have to hurry."

Georgette watched them disappear through the hidden tunnel. When she turned, Lily was no longer there.

Georgette approached the door and glanced back at Thaddeus. She took a deep breath and knocked. Polly gave her a warning look before admitting her into the room.

Lily did not acknowledge her presence at first, but remained at the window staring out at the gray dawn. The girl had not faltered once. The sight of Stephen's bloody wound had not reduced her to predictable hysteria. Kate would have been proud.

"Thank you, Lily, for taking care of Reverend Flynn."

When Lily turned her expression was genuinely perplexed. "What is a man of God doing in a place like Swan House? And why would anyone want to kill him?"

Georgette sighed inwardly. They had not been honest with Kate's daughter, not even when she announced that she was returning to New Orleans. They needed more time to prepare her for the role she would have played, but time had run out.

"Mister Parks didn't bring me to Charleston just to give away my mother's fortune, did he? Does my coming here have anything to do with that man in the cellar?" There was a tremor in Lily's voice.

"Yes," Georgette nodded.

"Does Jack know about this?"

"No, Jack knows nothing. He is exactly what he appears to be."

Lily's relief was evident. "Then what is Reverend Flynn's connection to this house, and to you and Kate?"

Georgette glanced toward Polly, sending her from the room with a nod. She studied Lily for a moment. The stubborn tilt of her chin almost coaxed a smile to Georgette's lips. How like Kate she seemed at times. She walked to the settee and patted the cushion next to her. Lily walked toward her, almost reluctantly it seemed. Georgette squared her shoulders. There was no need to mince words now. The girl had seen too much to be fooled. There was nothing to do but tell the truth, and be done with it.

"Swan House is a secret station of the Underground Railroad, a place to help slaves escape from people like Victor Eden, Thurston Turnbull and Lemuel Hamilton. We hide them here until a ship comes to take them north. Other than those who are directly involved, only a few trusted people know about our work. Folks hereabouts would not hesitate to burn us out if they ever discovered what this place really is.

"Sauchie, Mohab, and Xavier are all freedmen, brought down from Philadelphia years ago by Stephen Flynn's driver, John Davis, to aid in the cause. Polly is Ezra Swan's half-sister. She was born here. She has remained safe by pretending to belong to Kate—and now to you. Franklin and Thaddeus see to the welfare and protection of this household, and nothing more."

Lily's eyes widened in disbelief.

"As the owner of Swan House, your mother was the shield that protected us all," Georgette continued. "After she died, we needed someone with her incredible courage to take her place and maintain her masquerade."

"But how did the two of you become involved in something so dangerous? I don't understand."

"We were both forced to leave New Orleans over twenty years ago. As luck would have it, we found ourselves on the same ship bound for Charleston."

Georgette hurried on, "My ma had been the finest seamstress in the city before she died. I was going to use the money she left me to open a dress shop of my own. But my step-pa wanted it all for himself. When I refused to turn it over to him, he threatened to kill me. Our old housekeeper, Bella, stabbed Ben LeBlanc with a pair of scissors. She was afraid the law would think I did it, and she sent me away. I learned later that she was hanged for the crime.

"I hid out for weeks until I was able to secure passage on a ship to Charleston. Captain Ezra Swan sensed that I was in terrible trouble, so he put me in his own cabin and told me to keep out of sight."

Confused, Lily shook her head. "But what about Kate?"

"The night before we were to sail, the captain asked if I would be willing to share quarters with another woman who had just come aboard. He said she was sick, and he offered me free passage if I would look after her until we got to Charleston. After we were safely away from New Orleans, Kate told me that she had given birth to a daughter just two weeks earlier."

"That was me," Lily whispered. "But why did she leave me behind?"

Georgette sighed. "I don't think she had a choice. At least, she thought that you would be safe from whatever she was running from."

"What was she like back then?" Lily asked wistfully.

Georgette ventured a smile at the first sign of warmth from the girl. "She was young and scared. She looked a whole lot like you in those early days. But she never talked much about herself. There was a part of Kate that no one could reach, and I learned not to pry."

"What was Captain Swan to Kate?"

"He had been a wild one in his youth. Society didn't want much to do with him after his family passed on. Kate wasn't in love with him, but she needed his protection. It wasn't long after we reached

Charleston that she became his mistress."

Lily closed her eyes. "Oh."

"Ezra was never home much. No one came to call except strange folks that he met with in private. One night, after we had been here about a year, his crew brought him home on a litter. He died from lung fever two weeks later."

"What happened to you and Kate after that?"

"Your ma seemed to shake off her fear. She declared that she was going back to New Orleans to find you. Whatever scared her enough to make her leave you behind did not seem to matter anymore. Maybe she had acquired a bit of spunk from the captain. Once she found you, the three of us were to go on to Saint Louis. I would finally get to open that dress shop that I had always wanted."

"But why didn't she come for me?" Lily's voice sank to a whisper. Tears blurred her eyes.

Georgette grasped her hands. "That was the worst of it. Two days before we were to leave for New Orleans, Ezra's banker, Franklin Miller, came to Swan House with his will. The captain had left everything to Kate, but there were conditions. Unless she agreed to continue his work, she would forfeit everything. We had no idea that Ezra was one of the abolitionists operating here in the city. Kate wanted no part of it. But the very next day, a letter came for her here in care of the captain. The person who wrote it claimed that you had died of yellow fever. It was unsigned, and there was no mention of where you had been buried."

"But Mister Parks found a grave," Lily protested.

Georgette nodded. "He made a few inquiries before the two of you left New Orleans. The plantation had belonged to a family in the city, but it was sold after the house was destroyed by fire. No one remembered a woman named Kate Perrault, or a child, who had ever lived there. Thaddeus didn't pursue it any further. He had found you, and that was all that was important."

"But the person who sent the letter had to know the truth about us," Lily insisted.

"I always suspected that Kate knew who it was from. She locked herself in her room for days. When she came out, it was as if the life had gone right out of her. There was no longer any reason to leave. We would stay here. She would do what Ezra wanted. But she would do it her way. She used his money to make this house over into a gaming palace. Stephen Flynn and his followers continued their work and recruited me to the cause. I joined willingly. Finally, I had found a way to make up for Bella's sacrifice."

Georgette paused. "There's something else you should know about Kate. There was a man in her life for a brief time. His name was Gaston DuPre. He was a doctor here in Charleston, married with a son and a daughter. He died here at Swan House fifteen years ago. No doubt his widow, Adelaide DuPre, was fit to be tied when she heard you had arrived in town."

"Georgette, did Kate ever tell you anything about my father?"

"No, she never talked about him, never mentioned his name. I always figured he was the reason she left New Orleans in such a hurry, and alone."

Georgette pushed herself wearily to her feet. "Just before she died, Kate told us that you were alive. I cannot explain it, but she just seemed to know. If it proved to be true, we thought that you would be the one who could protect us. All Thaddeus had to do was find you and bring you here. And though you look so much like your mother, we needed time to make you like her in other ways." Georgette's laugh sounded more like a sob. "Imagine our surprise when we found out where you had been all those years." Her voice dropped to a whisper, "We don't want you to go, Lily. It will be like losing Kate all over again."

She laid a hand on Lily's shoulder then hurried from the room without waiting for a response.

Fifteen

Eden's Gate Plantation

Rameses's gaze swept the crowded compound and settled on the pair standing apart from the others. The smithy's expression was resigned. Zina drew closer to clutch Juno's arm. Resentment smoldered in her eyes.

Victor gave a nod of approval as he and Grier emerged from the back door of the main house and made their way toward Rameses and Pearl. They had watched from the study as Charles and the two slaves made their way up the path from the boat landing. Charles had cradled the girl on the saddle before him and allowed Belezar to set his own pace. Rameses trotted along behind, tethered by a rope tied to the pommel of the saddle. From a distance, it was obvious the Mandinka was everything Sam Gunnells claimed him to be.

Victor ignored his son and circled around Rameses, noting his muscled limbs and the unscarred flesh on his back. "You gonna do just fine, just fine," he said. "Grier, take this boy over to the forge and have Zina fetch 'im some food. I expect he's hungry." He turned and appraised the small figure huddled in the doorway of the cookhouse and fixed Charles with a disgusted sneer.

Charles pulled Pearl to her feet. Rameses made an involuntary move toward her and felt the bite of the overseer's crop on his arm.

"Here, now. You best fergit about that li'l gal. Looks to me like she's spoke fer."

Charles swung around at Grier's taunt. His fingers tightened protectively about Pearl's arm. Anger compressed his lips in a hard line.

The overseer's eyes burned with the same lust he had seen on a hundred faces the night of the auction.

Sixteen

Swan House

Lily retrieved her worn valise from the back of the armoire and slipped into the faded homespun gown and hooded cloak hidden inside. A pair of scuffed brogans completed her disguise. When she opened the door leading from her bedroom onto the outside gallery, the early morning sky was heavy with clouds, the air steamy from a recent rain shower. A distant rumble of thunder warned of another approaching downpour. She hurried down the back stairway to the side portico and the carriage house beyond. If she could reach Saint Bartholomew's Church and return before the household awakened, no one would suspect she had ventured into the streets alone.

It was after the discovery of Stephen Flynn in the cellar that she understood why Georgette and Franklin Miller had kept her hidden behind the gates of Swan House since she arrived. Her startling resemblance to Kate made recognition almost a certainty. They had hoped for time to prepare her for the role she would have played had she agreed to stay. But in less than a fortnight, she would be on her way back to New Orleans. The sooner she put Charleston behind her, the better for everyone. She possessed neither the courage nor the heart to make their impossible scheme succeed. Swan House would be sold, and the threat to Georgette and the others would vanish. In time, Kate's best friend would understand there could be only one Kate. Anything less could put all of their lives in jeopardy, but, there was one last thing she had to do in spite of the risk.

By the time she reached the carriage house, young Micah had hitched the mare to the market gig. He eagerly took the piece of rock candy she had promised and held the reins as she climbed into the small conveyance. Rain began to patter softly on the roof of the buggy as she guided the mare down the avenue and onto the cobbled street.

Other than an occasional street vendor beginning their early morning rounds, there were few people about. She kept her sight fixed on the soaring spire of Saint Bartholomew's until she reached the church. She climbed down and secured the buggy to the branch of a sweet gum tree and approached the entrance to the cemetery. The gate creaked loudly in the early morning stillness.

A stone pathway led to the church on a nearby rise. Near the top, she spied the marble crypt Polly had described. She approached slowly and removed her glove, letting her fingers trace the name carved into the stone.

Kate had never intended to stay in Charleston, but fate had robbed her of any reason to leave. She had made a life for herself and created a family from a strange assortment of wanderers and misfits fleeing from their own demons. Providence, it seemed, had brought her mother here for a purpose greater than herself.

What if her own journey was to end here? Could she resign herself to a life she could never have imagined? Georgette had offered no clue to the identity of the man who had fathered her. Was he, too, forever lost somewhere in her distant past? Could it be that his death was the reason Kate fled from New Orleans, or had the reality of the man himself created such terror in her heart that she was forced to abandon her child to save them both? Lily felt the first stirrings of a bond with the young woman who had given birth to her. Tears stung her eyes as she recalled Georgette's plea. *We don't want you to go, Lily. It will be like losing Kate all over again.*

She backed away from the crypt as a strong gust of wind sent a cold shower raining down upon her. Covering her head with the hood of her cloak, she turned and rushed toward the path, and collided with a man hurrying to escape the sudden downpour himself.

She cried out. Strong hands seized her arms to keep her from tumbling down the slope.

"You foolish girl, what are you doing out in such weather? Can't Father Jonathan keep you urchins contained?"

Lily struggled to free herself from her captor's painful grip.

"Hurry along." His voice was harsh and impatient. "Blast, we're getting soaked!"

She was forced to keep pace with his long strides as he made for a shelter midway down the path. Suddenly, she found herself spun around and abruptly deposited upon a stone bench.

"I'm sorry, I didn't see you!" she protested, rubbing her arms.

"Be still." He drew a handkerchief from his vest pocket and pressed it to her forehead.

She angrily pushed his hand away and fumbled with her specs. When she glanced up her eyes widened. He was younger than he sounded, not more than three, maybe four years older than her. She drew a sharp breath as Paul DuPre's dark and piercing eyes mirrored her own surprise.

"You're not a child," he exclaimed.

"Of course not." For an instant, fire ignited in her eyes.

He thrust the soaked handkerchief at her, pointing to the smudge above her brow. "There."

She snatched the handkerchief from his fingers and gingerly applied it to her forehead.

"My apologies." He sensed he had offended her. "I just assumed that you were one of Father Jonathan's orphans."

"No, I am not a foundling." Her voice was scarcely more than a whisper, her expression pained.

He eyed her sodden cloak and the ill-fitting spectacles and frowned. "Then you must be one of the helpers that care for his brood?"

"No, I am new to the city." She hesitated. Polly had returned to her room after Georgette departed two nights before. One glance told the servant that Georgette had revealed their secret. Her warning flashed through Lily's mind. *Don' tell nothing 'bout yoreself to strangers. Most anything you say could make a heap of trouble for all of us.*

Paul sat down on the bench beside her. "Well then, what do you do? Do you have a trade?" He glanced down at her scuffed shoes. She appeared to be a menial of some sort, perhaps a shop girl. He resisted the urge to reach out and adjust the unsightly specs perched at a precarious angle upon her nose.

She averted her eyes. His stare was unsettling. "I care for the sick." Her hand trembled visibly as she returned his handkerchief. "My name is Lil . . .Lettie Brown."

His expression appeared to change as he slipped the linen into his vest pocket.

She stood abruptly and pulled her cloak closer about her. "I have to go home now. I'll be missed."

"You can't wander about in the rain," he protested. "At least let me provide you with a ride." Without waiting for her to reply, he seized her arm once more and propelled her down the path toward the gate.

"No, please. I live just a short distance away."

"Nonsense. My trap is across the street." Her feet flew off of the curb as he wrenched open the gate and steered her to the opposite side of the street. Without a word, he pushed her into a smartly polished conveyance and jumped in beside her.

"Where do you live, Miss Brown?"

"Who . . .What? I don't know. I mean, I lost my way. That's how I happened to be in the cemetery," she finished lamely.

"Who are you staying with?" His voice hinted at impatience. "I'm familiar with most of the places here in town."

"A yellow house, with green shutters. I have a room there." Her cheeks flamed at the absurdity of the lie. She bit down hard on her lip.

"Piero's Boarding House?"

Did she only imagine the dismay in his voice? Lily shrank against the cushion. What were the chances such a place really existed? "I don't want to take you out of your way. I can walk from here. It cannot be far."

"Actually, you have managed to wander quite a distance." He dismissed her protest and urged the horse in the direction of the waterfront.

Several minutes later, they stopped in front of a two-story dwelling with weathered yellow paint and sagging green shutters. A faded sign proclaiming the proprietor's name swung to and fro above the front gate.

Lily cast an uncertain glance at the dilapidated structure. "It was kind of you to bring me here."

He nodded, struck by the vulnerability of her gaze. Little wonder he had mistaken her for a child. He reached across and opened the door for her.

"Perhaps we will meet again under more favorable circumstances.

If you're looking for work there's a clinic nearby. Miz Piero can direct you. Go there and ask for Doctor Hadley Baker. Tell him that Paul DuPre recommended him to you."

She gasped and scrambled from the trap. Paul DuPre? Of all the people in the city to have happened upon, Adelaide DuPre's son had delivered her to a strange address halfway across town. Had he known who she really was, no doubt he would have snubbed her shamefully.

Paul shrugged and urged the animal on through the downpour. He looked back once to see the drenched figure staring after him.

An hour later, Lily found her way back to the cemetery. The rain had ceased, and sunlight bathed the hillside. Pedestrians turned to stare as she ran for the gig. She jerked frantically at the reins, climbed in, and gave a fearful shriek.

"Micah! What are you doing here?" she stared in disbelief at the small figure huddled on the wooden seat.

"Don' be mad, Miss," he pleaded, his eyes wide with fear. "I followed just to see that you wuz awright. Paw say we got to look after you 'cause you family."

"Xavier is going to be very angry with you. He must be frantic by now. And where is Joseph?"

"He wuz still sleepin' when I lef' the house."

She sighed and snapped the reins across the mare's back trying, not to imagine the switching the boy was likely to receive when they returned.

Thaddeus and Jack waited on the steps as she guided the gig beneath the side portico. Their expressions were stern and disapproving. Not waiting for assistance, she climbed down and hurried past them as Micah scampered out the other side and dashed for the safety of the stable.

"Lily?" Jack pushed past Thaddeus and raced up the steps after her.

"Miz Georgette," Sauchie shrieked as she entered the house, "Miss Lily back home."

Georgette rushed from her room and leaned over the banister. "Where have you been? You had us worried to death. Thaddeus and Jack have been looking everywhere for you."

Exhausted, Lily moved slowly toward the staircase. Anger was beginning to replace the familiar uncertainty in her features. Georgette felt a shiver of apprehension race along her spine. It was an expression she knew only too well.

"Please come downstairs, Georgette, and ask the ladies to come down as well."

Georgette huffed impatiently and shrieked her summons, storming ahead of the grumbling women who stumbled from their rooms in various stages of undress.

"Disappearing without a word to anyone and coming back drenched to the skin," she muttered, shaking her head.

Polly watched from the gallery as the querulous parade headed for the stairs.

Lily barely glanced at Mohab who hobbled across the room and removed the dripping cloak from her shoulders. Instead, she trained a curious gaze upon the disheveled assembly. Fanny yawned broadly and abruptly clamped her jaw shut at Georgette's unspoken warning. Gradually, the mutterings ceased, and the women appeared to instinctively tighten their ranks.

"Well, we are all here." Georgette fixed Lily with a questioning look.

"Have Xavier and the stablehands bring the carriages and wagons to the front of the house first thing tomorrow morning to transport trunks and wardrobes to the docks."

Georgette's fingers flew to her lips. "Oh, Lily, please say you are not leaving so soon!"

"They are not for me." Her gaze traveled past Georgette, whose eyes widened in disbelief.

"*The girls?*"

Polly expelled a deep sigh. "Bout time."

Lily ignored the swell of denials directed at Georgette. She approached the stairs, forcing the women to give way and allow her to pass.

"But you can't just send them away." Georgette raised her voice to be heard above the outburst of wails and protests.

Lily turned and leveled a determined look at Kate's best friend. "Give each of them enough money to pay for their passage to any destination they choose, and make sure they are all ready to leave first thing in the morning."

Jack shot a disbelieving glance at Thaddeus. "What just happened?" he muttered under his breath. Thaddeus shrugged, as confused as Jack.

"Thaddeus?" Georgette wailed as the two men retreated toward the vestibule, intent upon escaping the melee that was about to ensue.

Lily turned and glanced up at the figure on the landing. "Polly, I think that I would like a cup of my mother's tea. You know how we like it."

"I shore do."

The next morning

Franklin gazed out at the sunlit street as his coach traveled at a brisk clip along the battery. Yesterday's rain had cleansed the stagnant air, bringing a cool morning breeze and the first hint of fall to the city. It was days like this that Charleston displayed her proud beauty best.

Georgette's message two days earlier had come as no surprise. Swan House had enjoyed astonishing prosperity for years, but it was obvious now that it could never be the same without Kate. With Lily returning to New Orleans, perhaps it was time to remove the threat of danger from Georgette and the others, and to silence the wrathful demands of Adelaide DuPre and her flock of harpies once and for all.

As his coach approached the gates of Swan House, the groan of twisting metal and cracking stone caused the team of horses to rear and lunge. Franklin clutched the leather handstrap while his driver struggled to control the frightened team.

"Sylvester?" he shouted. "What's going on out there?"

"Don' know, Mastah Franklin," the driver called back genuinely perplexed. "Looks like they tearin' the place down."

Franklin peered out of the window and gasped. Kate's marble nymphs lay in a heap of crushed rubble at the base of the two pillars.

"To the house! Hurry, man!"

Moments later, the coachman brought the coach to a halt behind a procession of conveyances waiting at the front steps. A mountainous barricade of baggage littered the verandah. Ten angry viragos shrieked at the hapless drivers to have a care with their belongings. Georgette stared at the pandemonium in helpless confusion, beseeching Thaddeus and Jack to restore some semblance of order to the pending exodus. The banker pushed his way through the crush of trunks and hatboxes.

"Oh, Franklin, thank God you are here." Georgette's fingers bit into his arm.

"Where's Lily?"

The threesome turned toward the door. He didn't wait for a reply, but broke free of Georgette's grip and dashed through the vestibule into the silent ballroom.

"Mohab!"

The majordomo looked down from the landing and signaled his helpers to continue with their task.

"Mornin', Mistah Franklin."

"Where are you taking that?" Franklin pointed his cane at the portrait balanced between two workmen on ladders."

"Movin' Miz Kate to the attic, sir."

"The attic?" he gasped. "Who told you to take that portrait down?"

"I did."

He spun around to find Lily standing a few paces behind him. He flushed and snatched off his hat, crushing it in his hands. She could have been Kate herself dressed in one of the gowns Polly had selected from the armoire that morning. Only the spectacles marked a difference between the girl and the portrait destined for the attic.

"Please come into the study, Franklin. There are things we need to talk about." Before the president of the Farmers and Merchants Bank exited through those doors again, there would be no doubt who was now in control of Kate's empire.

One week later

Georgette stood at the top of the stairs and surveyed the empty ballroom below. Since Lily had decided to stay, she had not ventured out alone again, but seemed content to spend hours each day in the study with Franklin going over the changes that were to come. A week before, Xavier had been dispatched to deliver discreet messages throughout the city announcing the temporary closing of Swan House. They would need time to restore the place and to transform Kate's daughter from a simple convent girl to a lady worthy of her mother's legacy.

Seventeen

Adelaide DuPre balanced the silver teapot with an unsteady hand and poured the hot brew into one of her finest china cups. Frances Pardee smiled sweetly at her hostess's solicitude.

"Addie, I declare, these quince tarts are just divine. Tilde must give my Becky the recipe."

"Of course, Frances," Adelaide responded with an anxious smile. "Do have another."

Honora Claiborne gave an audible sigh, hoping her twin would stop dilly-dallying and get to the real reason she suffered Frances Pardee's presence at all. It had been almost two months since Kate Perrault's daughter had arrived in Charleston, and no one had caught so much as a glimpse of her. That is, not until Frances paid an unexpected evening visit to Madame Gerow's dress shop and happened upon her and that horrid woman, Georgette LeBlanc, examining Madame's finest silks.

Word of the encounter spread quickly, but Madame remained mute to her customers' questions, and unmoved by their threats to withdraw their patronage. Vowing they would never stoop to frequent a shop that catered to those vile women, business had, in fact, increased tenfold.

"Oh my, I cannot eat another bite."

Adelaide smiled indulgently. "Now, Frances, what is this we hear about your recent trip to the dressmaker?"

"Oh, *that?*" her guest fairly simpered. "Well, my Clarissa ordered a morning frock a fortnight ago, and Madame promised it would be finished by Thursday. As it happened, we were on our way home after dining with the Ballards Wednesday evening and saw a light in the shop window. Clarissa insisted we stop and inquire if her gown was ready." Frances and Adelaide unconsciously leaned closer to one another. To Honora's disgust, she felt her own back leave her chair as well.

Adelaide settled the pot onto the tray with a nervous clatter. "And?"

Frances laid aside the spoon and lifted her cup to her lips once more. "Well, you can imagine our surprise to find Madame buzzing about those two creatures from Swan House as friendly as you please. She did not realize that we were standing there for quite the longest time. Finally, she turned and, I declare, she all but shoved them into a fitting room."

"And the younger one, oh, whatever is her name? Did you see her?"

Honora heard the telltale quaver in her sister's voice and rolled her eyes. Addie's pretended indifference did not fool her for a minute.

"Why, let me think. Did Madame address her as 'Lula'? No, I have it. She called her 'Lily'." Frances crowed.

Adelaide sighed. "But, what does she look like? Oh, do tell, Frances."

Frances shifted her gaze knowingly from one twin to the other. Addie flushed and reached for the teapot.

"More tea, Honey?"

Honora shook her head. She wanted to reach out and shake her sister, anything to stop this foolish charade. Addie's determination to drive Kate Perrault out of Charleston had never been prompted by a sense of propriety, but to lance a wound that had festered in her heart ever since her husband had died in the whore's bed all those years ago. News of Gaston's shocking indiscretion had found its way into every drawing room in the city scarcely before Nathan and his friends could spirit his brother-in-law's body down the back stairs of Swan House.

Frances's eyes glittered with malicious glee. The blade had found its mark. All she had to do was twist it just the slightest bit. Her voice dropped to a conspiratorial whisper. "Why, you would not believe it. It's quite the most astonishing resemblance. The girl is the spitting image of her mother. The very image!"

Adelaide wilted visibly. It was too much to bear. It had been fifteen years since her husband's scandalous betrayal, but time had not lessened the heartbreak or the jealousy.

"Addie?" Honora laid a hand on her sister's arm.

"Honora, she looks positively ill," Frances gasped.

"Tilde, fetch Miz Addie's salts! Frances, I am sorry to end this delightful visit, but sister has not been well lately. She should retire. You understand, of course?"

"Well, yes." Their guest eyed the last tart regretfully. "I really should be getting home. Fennemore will be worried." Frances gathered up her reticule and smoothed her skirt. "Addie dear, you must take care of yourself."

"Let me show you out." Honora grasped the woman's elbow and guided her toward the door. If she were less than a lady, she would have propelled Frances Pardee headlong down the front steps. Instead, she placed a peck on her cheek, remembering to smile as she slammed the door behind her.

She stalked back into the sun parlor, snatched the vial of salts from the servant's hand, and angrily waved it beneath her sister's nose. "Addie, whatever were you thinking? You know that Frances Pardee is a spiteful witch and that no good would come of this. It serves you right. You deserved to be put in your place. Such questions, I never would have imagined. And Frances was not unmindful of your reasons for asking."

"Honey, please." Adelaide choked and flailed weakly at the acrid odor.

"No, I will not shush. Everyone in the city knows about your husband's affair with that Perrault woman."

"Honora!" Her twin bolted upright. "Do be quiet!"

Honora stiffened in disbelief, then turned on her heel and stormed from the room. "Tilde, my parasol, if you please."

"Honey? Oh, sister, please stay."

The front door slammed shut once again.

Paul handed the reins of his mount to the stablehand and started up the walkway as his aunt rushed down the steps past him.

"Aunt Honey?"

"Impossible!" she spat. "You mother is just impossible. Oh, never mind. Goodbye, dear."

He hurried to open the coach door for her and shook his head as the brougham sped away. By tomorrow, the two sisters would be sitting down to tea together. All would be forgiven. Thankfully, some things never changed.

⌣

After Adelaide retired for the evening, Paul retreated to the study and reached for the newspaper, then laid it aside. His mother had said little at dinner. The altercation with Honora had upset her more than she would admit. Ever since she learned that Kate Perrault's daughter had arrived in Charleston, she had been unusually preoccupied. Frances Pardee's revelation that she had actually encountered Lily Perrault only heightened her distress. According to Tilde, it was Aunt Honey's reminder of his father's affair with Kate Perrault that launched the twins into one of their infamous spats. He started to rise when a soft knock sounded at the door. He waved the coachman into the room.

"I come by to give you this glove. Found it in the trap. Tilde say it ain't Miz Addie's." Caleb deposited the soiled article on the desk.

Paul recognized it immediately. It belonged to the girl he had met at the cemetery. The image of Lettie Brown standing in front of Piero's Boarding House in her sodden cloak and unmanageable specs flashed through his mind with surprising clarity. He picked up the glove. There were signs of mending. It was obvious that her circumstances were meager, and it was probably the only pair she owned.

Paul glanced up. "You should be getting some sleep. I think Mother plans to call on Aunt Honey first thing tomorrow morning."

"Yes, sir. G'night, doctah."

Doctor. Had it been a slip of the tongue, or had that crafty old fellow intended to address him that way? Even Adelaide had taken extraordinary pains to avoid the question they all wanted to ask, but didn't. Would he practice medicine again? How could such a casual reminder of the past still cause so much pain? The pilgrimage to Emma's grave the week before had proven how deeply old wounds could hurt. The visit to the Wellington townhouse afterward had offered no comfort. Davy clung desperately to Connie or Daniel whenever he approached. There was no trust to be found in the tearful eyes of his son.

I care for the sick. Lettie Brown's revelation had come as another unexpected reminder of the calling he had once planned to devote his life to. He had chosen to ignore it at the time. In fact, he had been unaccountably harsh, even offensive, judging by the confused look she directed at him after he had deposited her at the Piero's front gate. Maybe there was a way to make amends for his gruffness, some assistance he might offer the girl should he encounter her again.

He had not given any thought to engaging a nurse to care for Davy when the boy returned from the country. Perhaps Miss Lettie Brown would consider such a post. She had denied that she was a foundling, but her features had softened when he mentioned Father Jonathan's orphans.

He studied the small glove. *Perhaps we will meet again under more favorable circumstances.* The desire to see Lettie Brown again seemed to take on a curious urgency. He would return her glove to Piero's boarding house himself.

The next day

Esperanza Piero stood on her front porch and watched the young gentleman retrace his steps and fumble impatiently with the broken latch on the gate. She planted her work roughened hands on her wide hips and shrugged. The rank smell of fish and soiled laundry drifted through the doorway.

Paul DuPre's expression had darkened to a scowl when she denied the woman he was looking for occupied one of the rooms advertised on the crude sign over the front door. She had dared to laugh when he insisted he had deposited Lettie Brown at the gate scarcely a week past. "Look about you, laddie. You kin see fer yerself this ain't no place fer a lady. Only menfolk, mostly fishermen and the like, bunk down here."

Paul's frown turned to confusion as he hurried toward the trap and climbed in. Impoverished or not, no self-respecting young woman would ever seek shelter in such a place. Lettie Brown had purposely misled him, or had she? She had admitted to being lost when he asked for an address. Could she have been referring to another yellow house and been on her way there when he insisted on driving her here in spite of her protests? The dismay on her face supported the notion that it was he who had been mistaken. A feeling of apprehension changed his anger to worry. What if she had met with some misfortune, and the fault was his?

Perhaps she had taken his suggestion and gone directly to see Hadley Baker. Hadley could have taken pity on the poor girl and offered her shelter at the clinic. There were pallets to spare, and he often provided temporary refuge for those who had no means to pay for a bed or a meal elsewhere. Paul snapped the reins and set out in the direction of the waterfront clinic.

"Who?" Hadley Baker appeared as perplexed as Esperanza Piero.

Paul's frustration was evident. "Lettie Brown, a young woman I lent assistance to a week ago. She's young and stands about so high." His hand bobbed to a level just beneath his chin. "She wears spectacles. She claimed to be trained to minister to the sick. I recommended the clinic to her. It occurred to me that you might be in need of help."

Hadley stroked his chin thoughtfully. "No, I don't recall meeting anyone of that description. And I'm reasonably certain I would have remembered the lady."

Paul nodded and turned to leave.

"If she comes here, should I send word to you?"

"Thank you." Paul started for the door anxious to escape his friend's questioning stare.

"Paul?"

He turned slowly. His shoulders stiffened.

"It *is* good to see you again. Some of us were wondering when you might come by or even if you would."

"I'm sorry, Hadley. I've been busy."

"It's all right. You don't have to explain." The young doctor approached and extended his hand. He let it drop when Paul pointedly ignored the friendly gesture.

"We are all sorry for your loss, Paul. Father never got over the shock of Emma's death. He died soon after you went to Boston."

Paul turned away for a moment remembering the pain in the old doctor's eyes when he emerged from Emma's room holding the mewling newborn in his arms.

"He should have warned *me* about the risk. Either of you could have said something yet you kept her condition a secret, and she died!"

"What could we have done, Paul? Emma was father's patient. She begged him not to tell you that she should never attempt to have a child. My God, he brought her into the world. Don't you think it frightened him when he found out that she had ignored his advice? She was so determined to give you a son that she was willing to risk her life to do it."

The anger and pain in Paul's heart was evident in his anguished expression. He started for the door once more. It had been a mistake to come here, one that would never happen again.

"You have a place here at the clinic, Paul, if you ever want to come back. We could use another doctor." Hadley's voice trailed off as the door closed shut.

Eighteen

Lily and Georgette exchanged puzzled glances as Polly ushered the caller into the solarium. The light from the windows lent fire to the copper curls that cascaded from beneath a tired straw bonnet. She rivaled the height of an average man, yet her movements were graceful, and her high angular cheekbones surprisingly delicate. Generous lips ventured a curiously timid smile, and her eyes, as green as seawater, were filled with uncertainty.

Lily gave a quick push to her specs. "You asked to speak with me, miss?"

Fiona O'Flarety realized with a start that she was staring. Christ's sweet eyes, that slip of a girl couldn't be Lily Perrault, the woman all Charleston was talking about!

"M'name's Fiona O'Flarety." She bobbed an awkward curtsy.

Georgette motioned the young woman to a chair. Her appraisal was blatant and open as Fiona settled herself and smoothed her dusty skirt. "What can we do for you, Miss O'Flarety?"

"I have been in the city for a week, mum, over to the Town Theatre. The troupe's packing up to move on to Savannah tomorrow. I'm thinking I might like to stay in Charleston."

"You are an actress, then?" Georgette brightened. Everything about their visitor seemed suited to the stage, yet her discomfort did not lend itself to a seasoned performer.

"I need work. I hear ye'll be opening soon." Fiona twisted the small bit of tapestry in her lap. Her face was unnaturally pale.

"Miss O'Flarety, do you know what sort of establishment Swan

House is?"

Fiona blushed. "A gaming house, mum. The whole town's talking of nothing else."

Georgette employed her most persuasive smile. "Tell us, my dear, what, ah, experience do you have, other than the stage of course." The other ladies she had personally selected could command the admiration of their most jaded patrons, but none could compare with this one. With the proper gowns and Sauchie's skill with the curling rods, Fiona O'Flarety could raise the dead.

Fiona's eyes widened. "Oh, mum," she whispered, "it seems I have misled ye, but not a'purpose. Tis real work that I'm after."

Georgette's smile began to wilt. "Whatever do you mean by *real* work?"

"I was a household maid back home in Ireland." She leaned forward. "I can cook, and I sew as fine a stitch as ye'd ever hope to see."

Georgette's senses reeled. "Maid, cook?" she wheezed.

Lily broke in. "Miss O'Flarety, we have servants to take care of the wardrobes, and there are four cooks in the kitchen already. I am sorry."

Fiona ducked her head and sighed. "I see. Well, I need not take up any more of your time."

Lily nodded, while Georgette continued to train a pained look upon a treasure lost.

"I thank ye both for your time, ladies." Fiona rose to her feet abruptly, spilling the contents of her reticule onto the floor. "Oh no, would ye just look at that." She dropped to her knees and reached for a worn deck of cards strewn across the rug. "These belonged to me Da. He was a gambling man. I carry them for luck." She swiftly whipped them into order and stuffed them into the pocket of her rumpled skirt.

Lily's eyes softened. "You're alone, then?"

Fiona rose to her feet. "Da died when I was twelve. None of me brothers could match 'im at the tables, so he taught me the game. It was just a wee bit of sport in the beginning. He would outfit me like a lad and we would go down to the pubs in the neighboring villages where nobody knew us. He'd wager me hand against any man there. When he passed on, I went alone. They was hard times after Da died." She noted the pain in Lily's eyes. "Oh, it's all right, miss. It kept food on the table for the boys and me. I was good at it, ye see, 'til I stopped looking so much like a lad anymore."

"Where are your brothers now?"

Fiona swallowed hard. "Back in Ireland. The two older ones went to the mines. Da would have hated that. The younger two are in a place for foundlings. Maybe someday I can bring them all together again. Well, now, I should not be troubling ye with me foolishness. I have to get back to the boarding house to help with the packing."

"Wait." Lily turned to Georgette. "Send someone to find Jack."

"Jack?" Georgette's eyes narrowed suspiciously. "What are you up to?" she whispered.

"I am not sure, yet."

Georgette glanced from one to the other. There was a familiar set to Lily's chin and the same shrewd glint she had seen in Kate's eyes many times.

Fiona gasped when Jack sauntered into the room a few minutes later. His green frockcoat was open to reveal a ruffled shirt and a gold vest of striped satin. Fawn-colored breeches fit snugly into his polished boots, and the silk ascot at his throat had cost more than a month's worth of her own wages, but it was his hair and that magnificent moustache that hinted at his true heritage. He was a fine figure of a man and Irish to his toes.

Lily rose and tucked her arm in his. "Jack, allow me to introduce Miss Fiona O'Flarety. She's looking for work."

Fiona felt a surge of hope. She had not been dismissed after all, but why? She rose from her chair. "Surrah." The Irish lilt rolled softly off her tongue.

Jack's eyes widened appreciatively. He reached for her hand and guided it to his lips. "Miss O'Flarety," he murmured, casting a speculative look in Georgette's direction. Her lips curled in a sneer.

"Both of you, please be seated." Lily nodded toward a table by the window. "Georgette and I will take the settee." She walked to the sideboard and withdrew a sealed deck of cards from the top drawer. They were new, with golden swans embossed on a field of ebony. The design had been Jack's idea. Her smile deepened as she placed the unbroken deck between the gambler and his opponent.

"What's this?"

"Miss O'Flarety says she has some skill with cards, Jack. We would like to see how good she really is, and who better than you to challenge her claim?"

"What?" he exploded.

Fiona paled.

Lily returned to the settee, ignoring the flush that radiated above Jack's collar.

"But she's a *woman*."

Georgette arched a brow and fixed the gambler with a smirk. Jack Faro had just made his first mistake. Fiona's Irish ire was rising visibly. Her eyes glittered. One hand drummed impatiently next to the cards.

Jack's fingers reluctantly closed over the deck. "Very well, but I warn ye all not to make y'selves too comfortable." He turned to Fiona with a taunting smile. "This won't take long."

Before he could break the seal, she snatched the cards from his hand and snapped the wax that bound the paper band. With barely a flick of her wrists, the cards separated into two equal stacks and sliced unseen into one another. She returned Jack's challenge with a calculating stare.

"No mercy, Jack." Georgette pressed her fingers to her lips to hide her smile. If Fiona O'Flarety could best Jack Faro, Swan House stood to gain handsomely. She would lure patrons to the gaming tables in droves, just as Kate had done once. Georgette glanced about the room and sighed. It was a house full of strangers now, but with a new spirit. She felt Lily's hand cover her own and give it a gentle squeeze. Lily smiled and nodded toward the doorway.

The household had begun to slip into the room. Georgette's face brightened when she spied Thaddeus among the onlookers. Trust him to watch Jack's humiliating defeat at the hands of a woman.

Jack's coat lay across the arm of the settee. His cuffs were turned up, and his ruffled shirt was open at the throat. The crumpled ascot lay on the table, stained with sweat. He stared hard at the cards in his hand and spread his miserable sacrifice across the polished surface. Fiona covered the lot with her clutch of royal ladies. She had beaten him.

He gave her a lazy smile and pushed away from the table. "Lily, if I might have a word with ye?" He nodded toward the doorway.

"Of course."

Fiona sighed as the two of them left the room together. So that was the way of things. Not Lily Perrault, but Jack Faro would have the final say as to whether she would go or stay. She pushed aside the cards and reached for her reticule once more. It was a long walk back to the boarding house, and she was bone weary.

Georgette jumped to her feet. "Here now, where do you think you are going?"

Bewildered, Fiona sank down on her chair and tried to ignore the crowd of bystanders casting curious glances in her direction. She sucked in her breath when Lily entered the room moments later.

"Welcome to Swan House, Fiona."

Fiona stared down at Lily's outstretched hand.

"Ye mean . . . ," she stammered.

Georgette gave a delighted cry that sounded oddly like a cheer. The onlookers burst into applause.

Jack pushed his way through the crowd balancing two glasses of champagne. "Miss O'Flarety, Fiona, if I may, allow me to congratulate ye on an amazing win. Your talents will serve Swan House well." Her hand trembled as their glasses touched. She blinked rapidly.

"We will be spending a lot of time together," he whispered, intending that only she should hear, "teaching ye to play an *honest* hand." He turned on his heel and left the room. She stared dumbfounded after his retreating figure.

"I do not know what to say, miss!" She waved the fragile glass absently in the air. Lily rescued the delicate crystal and smiled.

"Georgette will help you get settled."

"Thank ye, thank ye, Miss."

Georgette grasped Fiona's elbow and propelled her toward the stairs. "Come along, dear. Xavier will take you to fetch your things from the boarding house. You will have the room at the end of the hall. We open in three weeks and there's so much to do. Jack will acquaint you with the tables tomorrow. And there's the dressmaker and your hair. We simply must do something with all of that." Georgette waved her hands absently, at a loss to do justice to the girl's most abundant asset.

Fiona's senses swam. Who would have believed that she would walk into the most elegant establishment in the city and find herself a home, thanks to the curious honor of a man who had suffered a dishonest and humiliating defeat at her hands? Her heart fluttered erratically. There was something quite extraordinary about Gentleman Jack Faro.

Nineteen

L ily sat at her dressing table rigid with fear. In less than one hour, Swan House would reopen its doors, and she would descend the grand staircase for the first time as the heir to Kate Perrault's empire. By morning, those who crowded into the ballroom below would proclaim her the toast of Charleston or ridicule her as an imposter unworthy of her legacy. And those who depended upon her to continue Kate's masquerade could soon be fleeing for their lives.

She stared at her reflection in the mirror and nervously picked at the lace ruffle on the sleeve of her dressing gown. Jeweled combs secured the braided crown Sauchie had fashioned atop her head. They were costly enough to feed the nuns and their charges for an entire winter.

Ever since she agreed to stay, preparations for this night had been grueling. As a legion of workers labored to transform the house and gardens, Georgette had coached her relentlessly, shrilling her displeasure whenever she missed a simple dance step or selected the wrong piece of silver at the private meals they shared in Kate's parlor. There were secret fittings with the seamstresses, the hat maker, and the tortures of Sauchie's curling rods. Every evening, Franklin came to dinner and stayed to deliver another lecture on the principles of business and finance.

At night, when all of their demands ceased and she took to her bed, the image of the stranger with pain and anger smoldering in his dark eyes came to her in her dreams. She had told no one but Polly of her encounter with Adelaide DuPre's son. Would he be among the crowd eager to greet Lily Perrault as she descended into their midst tonight? He would brand her a fraud, if he remembered her at all.

Her hand trembled as she picked up the plumed fan. Had Kate ever known such fear? No, surely not. For twenty years, her mother had so perfectly played the role demanded of her that she had become the very person she had pretended to be. Lily shivered. How could Georgette and Franklin ever have imagined she could take Kate's place?

Two doors away, the servants flew from one charge to another, tucking a stray ringlet beneath a golden net, fixing a stubborn clasp for one, and producing a jeweled comb for another. Georgette moaned. It was opening night, and the ladies she had carefully chosen for their grace and beauty were tripping over one another like sheep. The procession down the grand staircase would be a disaster!

"The gloves, where are the gloves? Claire, your lip rouge is smudged. Fiona, not that gown. Have you forgotten?" she hissed. "Only Lily wears white tonight." The girl would be swaddled from her chin to her toes, and not a hint of bare flesh showing. It was Jack's insane idea. The fool was mad!

Fiona felt thirty buttons bite into her spine through the shimmering silk. It had taken Sauchie the better part of an hour to lace her corset, seal her into the gown, and secure three snowy plumes in her hair. Now, it was all to do over again.

Downstairs, Jack paused before one of the gilt mirrors to adjust the gold studs at his wrists, and eye the flawless cut of his attire. Beyond his own reflection, his gaze swept across the ballroom. The transformation was a hundred miracles encompassed into one. Gone were the garish trappings, the worn damask, and brass banisters. Instead, walls painted the color of rich cream accentuated the white balustrades and mahogany banisters. Sparkling chandeliers glittered above the polished ballroom floor and captured the firelight from the marble fireplace at the far end of the room. On the landing, the portrait of Lily waited to be unveiled. The musicians softly tested their instruments behind a discreet bank of palms and ferns.

In the private dining rooms, intimate tables were laid with linen cloth, silver, and fine crystal. Outside, white columns gleamed in the moonlight, and the reflecting pool sparkled with glimmering splashes of light from the lanterns staked out along the avenue.

Jack glanced at his timepiece, hurried up the staircase, and made for the outside gallery. His face split into a huge grin. A procession of coaches and riders on horseback were making their way along the avenue toward the house. He turned and charged in the direction of the wardrobe room. He could hear excited cries before he burst through the door.

Georgette was slumped in a chair fanning herself furiously. Jack pulled her to her feet and whirled her about the room.

"Georgette, they are coming, half the men in Charleston from the looks of it!"

"Of course they are. Out with you, you rascal." She gave him a shove and laughed as he stumbled from the room.

"Mohab!"

The majordomo stared up at him expectantly from the ballroom below. Behind him a dozen servants waited for his orders.

"Open the doors. The rest of you fetch the champagne. Swan House is back in business!" He waited to see the first guests file into the ballroom. His grin broadened at their looks of astonishment.

The Swan had soared into a new era.

Lily stroked the soft white silk that enveloped her from her neck to her wrists and hugged a miniscule waist before flaring below her knees to cover the dainty slippers on her feet. Polly gently lifted Kate's diamond necklace from its satin bed and settled it about her neck, giving the clasp a decisive snap. Lily managed a smile as the servant placed her hands on her shoulders and gave a reassuring squeeze.

"Polly," a blush warmed her cheek, "do you think Doctor DuPre will be here tonight?"

"Miz Adelaide would just as soon have her boy wade through a pond full of water moccasins than show his fine self heah at Swan House. The last time anybody named DuPre set foot in this place was when Doctah Gaston . . ."

Lily raised her hand defensively. "Georgette told me about my mother's affair with Miz DuPre's husband."

"Well, you ain't to worry. It's gonna be a night you won't never forgit. And it was most likely a good thing you didn't tell Miz Georgette 'bout running into Doctah Paul. She and Miz Adelaide never had much liking for one another. Now, stand up and let me have a look at you. Miz Kate shore woulda' been proud of her girl. Just don't you never forget who you are, and hold yore head high."

As the ballroom filled with guests, Preston Hamilton nudged his brother's arm. "What did you tell Maryanne?"

"That we're attending a grange meeting tonight," George grinned sheepishly.

Preston surveyed his rakish attire, and burst out laughing. He nodded toward a portly gentleman engaged in conversation with Franklin Miller. "No doubt your future father-in-law will swear that you were there."

He glanced beyond the two men at a tall figure standing apart from the crowd. Perhaps it had been a mistake to insist that Paul accompany them tonight. There would be hell to pay if Aunt Adelaide ever suspected his and George's hands in this. And their mother would hold them accountable as well. Ever since Uncle Gaston had committed the unpardonable act of expiring in this very house, Charmaine DuPre Hamilton had fiercely championed her sister-in-law's quest to send Kate Perrault and her establishment straight to perdition.

Paul had returned to Charleston to a round of social events unrivaled in recent memory. Every female of marriageable age in the city had attempted to breach the wall their cousin had erected about himself. He and George didn't have a clue what bedeviled the man until the three of them had escaped from a Claiborne soiree a month past and embarked upon a night of drinking at Crystabelle's Alehouse.

Whoever Nurse Lettie Brown was, she had somehow managed to crack that brittle shell a little. But Paul's search for the elusive young woman had yielded no clues to her whereabouts. His humor had suffered with each attempt to track her down. Finally, he and George had thrown up their hands in desperation. 'Forget her!' they demanded.

At that moment, the orchestra executed a flawless fanfare, drawing the guests' attention to the man who sauntered jauntily down the stairs and stopped midway between the ballroom and the landing above.

"Gentlemen, 'tis a pleasure to welcome ye back to Swan House." Jack smiled hugely in response to the enthusiastic applause. "In keep-

ing with tradition, allow me to present to you the most beautiful ladies in our fair city."

And down they came, one by one, exquisitely gowned in the lat-
est fashions, a demure smile behind each fan. Claire . . . Marie . . .
Caroline . . . Blanche . . . Suzette . . . Elise . . . Jeanette . . . Claudia .
. . Rose . . . and finally, the incomparable Fiona.

Jack felt his pulse race as Georgette's protégée paused and surveyed
the crowd below. Her emerald satin gown accentuated her bare shoulders and complimented the fiery curls nestled against her cheek. Victor Eden lowered his glass and stared numbly as Fiona turned toward
him. *Augusta had hair like that once.* Thurston Turnbull nudged him
on the arm and nodded appreciatively in her direction.

Jack drew in a deep breath. And now, what they had all been
waiting for. "And to officially welcome ye back to Swan House, I ask
ye to raise your glasses to Miss Lily Perrault." He turned toward the
landing and signaled to two attendants to remove the velvet drape
that concealed Lily's portrait at the top of the stairs.

"Miss Lily!" a roomful of voices chorused in unison behind him.

The hem of her gown whispered along the gallery above. When
she emerged into view those who remembered a young Kate gazed
upward in astonishment. Her descent was greeted by a growing swell
of applause. Each movement was a studied sensual turn. Only a momentary misstep revealed her desperate need for the spectacles on her
dressing table.

Georgette stood in the shadows next to Polly and felt tears sting
her eyes. All they had worked for, hoped for, was reaffirmed by the
welcoming cries from below.

Franklin Miller reached for a glass of champagne from Mohab's
tray and lifted it in silent tribute toward Georgette. A satisfied smile
worked beneath his mustache. The girl was everything they could
have imagined, and more. After tonight, Kate's daughter would never
disappear behind her mother's shadow again.

Paul felt the breath explode from his lungs. It couldn't be! The
woman making her way down the staircase was breathtaking, a con-
summate exhibitionist, while the other had been . . . ? He shouldered
his way toward the front of the crowd.

Lily gave a sudden cry as he seized her wrist and pulled her through a crush of admirers all eager for a first introduction.

Jack spun around as the guests surged forward. "Lily?" He glanced about frantically and collided with Mohab. "Where's Miss Lily?"

The majordomo waved his empty tray, and shrugged. Thaddeus sprang from his position by the fireplace and made for the vestibule, his expression grim. He raced down the hallway and reached the door of the study only to have it slammed in his face and locked from inside.

Lily pressed herself against the wall as Paul DuPre strode toward the window and turned on his heel. He crossed the room, bringing his face within inches of hers.

"Lettie Brown, I presume?" His whisper sent a shiver along her spine.

"Please." She raised her hands to stop his advance. "It's not what you think."

His harsh laughter echoed about the room. "Not what I think? What the hell am I suppose to think? The last time we met you were clothed no better than a scullery maid." He gestured helplessly, conscious of the way her gown clung to every delectable curve of her body. He shook his head. "Once Miz Piero convinced me she had no knowledge of you, I went to the waterfront clinic. And need I mention that Hadley Baker never heard of you either? After that, I searched everywhere, went to every church thinking you might have taken ill or sought refuge at one of them." He gave an incredulous bark of laughter.

Lily felt a flush warm her cheeks. He did remember her. "I was never at any of those places."

"That became increasingly obvious. My God, *you* are Kate Perrault's daughter? And what else have you taken such pains to hide?"

She pressed closer to the wall, frightened by the sudden anger in his eyes.

Without warning, he seized her and drew her against him. "You aren't the innocent you pretended to be, are you?" he whispered. "Come, there's no need for lies between old acquaintances."

"No, please." She could feel the warmth of his breath upon her cheek. She averted her face, only to have him capture it and force her back against his arm.

"For old time's sake, Beauty?" he murmured as his lips descended to claim hers. After a moment, he drew back and stared at her curiously. If he didn't know better, he would swear she had never been kissed before.

She wrenched free of his embrace just as the door crashed inward. Paul's lips twisted into a mocking smile. "You are well attended, my dear."

"Thaddeus, no!"

Jack's eyes blazed with hell's own fury as he burst into the room and shoved Thaddeus aside.

"Jack, wait," Lily cried. "Thaddeus, stop him." But the gambler was too swift. Paul closed his eyes, refusing to yield to the unexpected pain of the attack. In the next instant, Jack found himself lifted off his feet and slammed against Thaddeus's broad chest. Both of them tumbled through the open door into the hallway.

Lily stood silent and unable to move as Paul turned and stalked past his attackers. Thaddeus gained his feet and hauled Jack up from the floor.

Jack flushed miserably to see the tears that gathered on Lily's lashes.

She blinked rapidly, and with more pride than they could have believed possible, she walked past the two of them into the glittering ballroom.

"Paul!" Preston hurried after the figure hurrying down the front steps. "Wait, where are you going?"

"I will not be wasting any more of my time looking for Lettie Brown."

"What do you mean?" Preston's face was a mask of genuine confusion.

Paul's scowl deepened. "Nurse Brown has a vocation she neglected to mention. She is Lily Perrault." With that, he turned on his heel and started down the avenue toward the gates.

"She what—who? Wait, you can't walk home, you fool." Preston dashed back into the house to collect his brother.

Stephen Flynn emerged through the trap door into the dark carriage house. The sounds of revelry coming from the house had muffled his footsteps and those of the five runners who followed him through the cellar tunnel. With luck, they would reach the outskirts of the city before first light.

Come morning, Josiah Pickering, Fennemore Pardee, and Rufus Tate would awaken to discover their households had been inconveniently reduced, again.

Twenty

The Claiborne coach traveled briskly through the morning chill toward King Street. A merchant ship had arrived in Charleston two days before with a prized cargo of gloves, perfumes, plumed bonnets from Paris; laces, silks and damasks from Belgium and Spain; and elegant china from England.

In her excitement to view the wares at Madame Gerow's shop, Adelaide had forgotten her lap robe. She shivered and clutched her cloak closer about her. Her irritation mounted as her sister sighed and snuggled beneath a thick blanket of fringed English plaid with no apparent concern for her discomfort.

But it was Honora's defection to the English sector that accounted for most of her regrettable shortcomings, the most grievous being her marriage to Nathan Claiborne. No matter that he was the most influential judge in the city, it was the bloodlines that separated the aristocrat from the pretender, the wheat from the chaff, the diamond from the paste . . .

Honora's sudden cry sliced through Adelaide's mounting fury. Their dimpled chins dropped in dismay at the sight of Georgette LeBlanc's coach pulling away from the dressmaker's shop. Doubtless, that woman had already captured the most desirable fabrics and absconded with a shocking number of those embroidered gloves that were the fashion rage of Paris. Identical frowns deepened at the imagined losses.

Honora's driver maneuvered the coach to the curb and climbed down from his seat. He lent a gloved hand to assist his mistress before turning to her sister.

"Those people should be run out of the city! I declare, their kind has no place in civilized society." Honora adjusted the folds of her cloak knowing her barbed remarks pierced Adelaide's pride. That dreadful altercation at Swan House between Paul and those two thugs had been the gossip of Charleston for weeks.

Adelaide stiffened and swept into the shop ahead of her twin. Honora sighed and followed. As they entered, their eyes devoured the bounty. Breathing deeply of the rare and exotic scents and the crisp smell of fabrics and leathers, their acrid temperaments mellowed.

"Addie, dear, Nathan tells me that Brewster Armstrong has just returned from London."

"Oh?" Adelaide cast a suspicious glance over her shoulder. Brewster Armstrong was one of her brother-in-law's cronies and the wealthiest factor in the city.

"He fetched his daughter home. You remember Sarah, don't you? She has been living with her mother's relations over there since the poor lady's demise. It's even rumored the girl was betrothed to a baron. Can you imagine?"

Adelaide fingered a bolt of fine Scottish wool. "A baron?"

Honora smiled smugly. "Apparently, the dear child had second thoughts and could not bear to be parted from her father any longer. She is, after all, Brewster's only heir. I'm told that he spoils her outrageously."

"That *is* interesting."

Honora fairly gloated. "Nathan says they are still unpacking. However, once word is out that they have settled in, you can be sure they will be deluged with invitations to every social event in the city."

Adelaide paled. More than once, she was certain Paul had been on the verge of declaring for one of the city's heiresses, and each time he had managed to elude entrapment. Her fingers trembled upon her sister's arm. "Honora, do you think it's too soon to invite the Armstrongs to dinner?" she whispered.

"Oh Addie, you must be the first." Honora patted the hand that gripped her arm. Only a fool would have discouraged it. Since Paul's return from Boston, Adelaide had become a woman consumed by a single ambition, to find her son a wife who had no desire to leave Charleston, ever.

"You are so good, Honey. I don't deserve such kindness."

Honora gently disengaged her grip and placed an affectionate arm about her waist, wincing as her sister blew delicately into her linen handkerchief. What a vexing creature she could be.

Later that afternoon, Adelaide jabbed her quill into the inkwell and dashed a bit of sand across the last invitation. The near encounter with Georgette had only fueled her determination to silence those terrible rumors about Paul and Kate Perrault's daughter once and for all. She gave an angry pull on the bellcord.

"Yes'm, Miz Addie?" Caleb was growing old. The quickness was gone from his step. In fact, they were growing old together. She felt an overwhelming rush of self-pity and thrust the sealed envelopes toward him.

"I want you to deliver these invitations to Miz Honora, the Turnbulls, the Pardees, the Pickerings, and this one to Mister Brewster Armstrong's residence. You tell Miz Minerva we would be especially pleased to entertain her family at dinner next Sunday."

His face filled with agonized confusion. "I think the Turnbulls done gone back to Three Fountains. Saw the wagons a'leavin' yestiddy."

"Well, you will just have to ride out to their place first thing tomorrow morning."

"But that a good five, six miles away!"

"Caleb!" She was not of a mind to entertain a refusal when so much was at stake. Thurston Turnbull was a boor, but one of the most prosperous planters along the river. The Armstrongs would find no fault with the guests she could seat at her table. And her son was going to pay court to Miss Sarah Armstrong whether he wanted to or not.

Caleb stalked out of the room and headed in the direction of the back stairs. Miz Addie was becoming a real trial. Yet, the thought of disobedience did not occur to him. Old Pierre Beauchamp had purchased him and his brother, Simon, as companion servants to the twins before their birth, never considering the possibility that Madame Beauchamp would dare to present him with daughters rather than sons.

Adelaide emitted a sigh of relief when Tilde finally released the laces of her cincher and helped her into a silk dressing gown.

"Now, Tilde, check the sideboard again. Come Sunday there must be bourbon for the gentlemen, except for Josiah Pickering. He prefers a dark rum. Peach brandy will do nicely for the ladies and, of course, sarsaparilla for the girls."

Tilde sighed as she turned to the armoire. "Don' you worry none, Miz Addie. I know just what to do. You rest now. Things gonna be fine."

"Oh, I do hope you're right. Sometimes I wish Paul was more like Connie's Daniel, settled and content with his lot."

Tilde shook her head and turned back the bedcover to the end of the bed. Paul was his mother's heart, and for all her protests, she wouldn't want him to be any different than the way he was.

The Armstrong house, days later

"I am not going, and that's final!"

The screech reverberated from the floor above—angry, defiant, and alas, predictable. Brewster Armstrong planted himself at the foot of the stairs, his hands clenched at his side.

"I am warning you for the last time, Sarah. I will not tolerate disobedience. You will dress and be downstairs in ten minutes." He felt the sweat break out on his forehead. An invitation to one of Adelaide DuPre's dinners at last, and this slip of a girl dared to refuse the hospitality of one of the most important hostesses in the city. A family's social standing could be destroyed for such a perceived slight, particularly if the offended party happened to be Adelaide DuPre or her twin, Honora Claiborne.

Uptairs in Sarah's room, the maidservant glanced fearfully toward the doorway and back to the girl seated at the dressing table. "Miss Sarah, you best do like yore papa say."

Sarah's face was set in a stubborn frown. "I will not set one foot outside of this house. He cannot make me." She picked up her hairbrush and dragged it through her dark brown hair, frowning at the lack of a single curl.

Lord Spencer Bronough had assured her it was her finest asset, and his thick fingers had caressed it more times than she could remember. In fact, everything had been just fine in London until her father had arrived unannounced at Uncle Edmond's townhouse in Mayfair and dragged her back to this backwater hell.

The rustle of silk caused her to turn. "Heah's yore purtiest gown, Miss Sarah. Why, every head gonna turn when you walk into that room. Shore gonna make Mastah Brewster mighty proud." Desperation crept into the servant's voice. Appealing to the girl's vanity had never failed to sway her before.

Sarah eyed the frock with distaste. It was one of several that her father had hurriedly commissioned before sailing for home. A bodice of soft green satin and more than a dozen yards of gossamer silk in the skirt had cost him a handsome sum. The dressmaker had declared that she was a vision, an angel. Just like those simpering pretenders who would be clustered around Paul DuPre tonight.

Downstairs, Minerva Armstrong bustled into the parlor. "Brewster, what is all the commotion about?"

He scowled at the diminutive figure of his sister. "Your niece is being stubborn, as usual. She says she has no intention of accompanying us to dinner at the DuPre's tonight."

"Oh, my!"

"I curse the day I ever agreed to send her to her mother's people. Those heathens corrupted her completely." His features twisted with frustration. A secret dispatch from his own London solicitor had warned him of the scandalous affair between Sarah and Spencer Bronough, a married man with daughters older than Sarah herself. It had been the talk of London, and it was only a matter of time before English relations spread their vicious gossip to their Charleston cousins. Once these stiff-necked fools got wind of it, the girl would be ostracized, and God forbid, consigned to spinsterhood in his house forever.

Adelaide DuPre's invitation was an omen, a godsend. The woman was hell-bent on finding her son a wife. If rumors could be believed, none of her choices had caught the young doctor's eye, until Sarah, one could only hope.

"The chit will present herself at Adelaide DuPre's dinner tonight if I have to break down her door and dress her myself."

"You wouldn't!" Minerva's silver curls bobbed indignantly beneath her lace cap.

"I dragged her backside all the way home from London, didn't I?"

"And she has scarcely spoken a civil word to you since."

"Miss Sarah, please. You gonna have a fine time."

She was homesick for London and thoroughly miserable. Her father meant to keep her in this horrid place without hope of a reprieve. *Like it or not* he had declared, *she was home to stay.* Well, if he would not let her go willingly she would have to do something to force him to change his mind, something truly outrageous.

"Sarah!" Clearly, his patience had come to an end.

She stared at her reflection in the mirror. A wicked smile teased the corners of her lips. "Bernice, tell father that I will be down in a wink."

The servant eyed her suspiciously and carefully placed the gown she had chosen upon the bed. "I be right back to do yore hooks."

Sarah jumped up from her chair and flung open the doors of the armoire. Her laughter floated across the room.

"Mastah Brewster, Miss Sarah say she comin' right down."

"Thank God." He sagged against the newel post and mopped his brow. Minerva pierced him with an accusing glance.

"See there, you just need to be patient with the child." She turned to the majordomo. "Linus, fetch my cloak." She began to pull on her lace mittens.

Brewster extracted his gold watch from his waistcoat and sighed deeply. They would be unforgivably late, but the girl had come to her senses and relented.

Sarah surveyed her image in the mirror, a satisfied smirk on her lips. Beneath a velvet overskirt of scarlet, a satin gown of the same color sheathed her supple form; the neckline plunged scandalously between the soft swell of her breasts. It was the latest fashion in London and Paris. Bronough had commissioned this one himself. Everyone who was anyone coveted the style. After tonight, her return to London would be all but assured.

Bernice dashed into the room and gasped. "It ain't fittin', Miss Sarah! Young ladies don't wear them kind of clothes 'round heah. 'Sides, I heard Mastah Brewster tell you to git rid of that shameful rag."

"Oh, shush, and help me with these hooks."

Bernice shook her head. "Yore papa's gonna skin both of us alive."

"Now, fetch my cloak. No, not that one. The gray velvet."

"But, yore hair, we got to set you some curls, Miss Sarah."

"Oh, blast! I forgot about that. Hand me my combs, hurry." Sarah worked furiously and sat back to survey the results. "There."

The servant eyed her uncertainly. "Young ladies don' go to socials with they hair hanging halfway down they backs, neither. It ain't proper." But, nothing about Sarah Minerva Armstrong was going to be remembered as proper this night. Bernice sighed and placed the cloak about her shoulders.

Sarah hurriedly pulled on her gloves, and adjusted the hood to conceal her handiwork. "Wait up for me. This shouldn't take long." Her laughter floated behind her as she swept from the room. Brewster stared up at the vision coming down the stairs toward him. The velvet cloak whispered across the floor as Sarah brushed past him to plant an affectionate kiss upon her aunt's cheek.

"Aunt Minnie."

"Sarah, my dear, you are the prettiest thing. Don't you think so, Brewster? Why, when Paul DuPre claps eyes on our darlin' girl . . ."

Her brother shot her a warning glance. "Come, ladies, hurry along now." He fidgeted impatiently as Linus adjusted his cloak about his shoulders and rushed to open the door.

"Froncie's got yore shirt ready, Mastah Paul." Caleb hurried into the room carrying the freshly pressed garment.

Paul applied the razor to his face. In a few minutes, he would be in the midst of that melee downstairs, forced to endure another offering of sacrificial maidens handpicked by his mother. She didn't seem to understand that he felt nothing for the women she deemed suitable or for any others that he chanced to meet.

He reached for a towel and paused. But that wasn't altogether true. More than once, in the silence of the night, a vision in a white silk gown, with eyes as blue as a summer sky, appeared in his dreams. Lettie Brown's transformation had been shocking. Yet, he had seen tears when there should have been rage, a silent sense of pride when indignation would have done better. Who the hell was she? An innocent who knelt at prayer beside her silken bed at night or a brazen beauty who could drive a man mad with longing? Angel or witch, she was still an imposter.

He jerked on the shirt and picked up a patterned silk ascot. It was new. His mother possessed a passion for ascots. He frowned at his image in the mirror.

"You gonna wear the burgundy coat tonight, Mastah Paul? It's Miz Addie's favorite. She say it remind her . . ."

"Of my father?"

"Yes, sir. She say you the spittin' image of yore paw."

He dug his fingers into the offending piece of silk and jerked it from his neck. Caleb stared in bewilderment as it fell to the floor.

"The black will do well enough."

"But that yore funeral coat. I don' think Miz Addie gonna like that."

"The black, if you please, Caleb." Paul heaved an exasperated sigh.

Caleb retrieved the black coat and a plain ascot from the armoire and shot him a troubled glance. "You git on down there, boy. Don't keep yore mam's company a'waitin."

Paul pulled on the coat and walked unhurriedly toward the door.

Adelaide sailed across the room and clutched her twin's arm. "The Armstrongs are here, and where is my son? Oh, I declare, I just don't know what has gotten into him lately. Honey, you and Nathan must help me receive. Tilde, Tilde," she hissed. "Go upstairs and see what's keeping Paul. Hurry."

Honora Claiborne captured her husband's arm and propelled him toward the vestibule.

"Mister Armstrong!" Adelaide cried as the harried man ushered his sister and daughter through the door. "Minerva, it's so good to see you again. And this lovely young lady must be Sarah? My dear, allow me to present my sister, Miz Honora Claiborne, and her husband, Judge Nathan Claiborne."

"How do you do, Miz Claiborne, Judge." Sarah briefly touched their fingers, rewarding Adelaide's effusive greeting with a demure smile.

"Tilde will take your wraps, and if you will follow me, I will introduce you to our other guests." The servant slipped the gray velvet cloak from the girl's shoulders.

"Oh, my word." Adelaide's gasp was followed by an involuntary oath from Brewster Armstrong.

A smile of feigned innocence curved Sarah's lips as she slipped her hand into the crook of her father's arm. "It's the latest fashion in London and Paris," she murmured, ignoring the growl in her ear.

Adelaide's fingers fluttered at her throat as she glanced toward the drawing room. All eyes were riveted upon the guest of honor.

Paul wrenched open his door and made for the stairs. For the second time in as many minutes, Adelaide's gasp of distress echoed across the room. Whatever was he thinking? Why, he was dressed for a funeral! And where was the ascot she had purchased for him expressly for this evening? Honora reached out to steady her sister. Her disbelieving glare strafed her nephew.

Sarah's gaze traveled the length of the man who paused on the stairs. Her eyes reached his and locked. A smile teased her lips as he slowly resumed his descent, moving with an easy grace. Adelaide Du-Pre's son was most assuredly no backwater bumpkin.

Paul felt his pulse quicken at her brazen appraisal. It was obvious Miss Sarah Armstrong was no saint, no fragile bit of porcelain, but a thoroughly enchanting renegade whose fires could blaze as hotly as his own.

Sarah's fingers tightened upon her father's arm. "That's the man I intend to marry," she whispered.

Brewster mopped his brow and stuffed the crumpled handkerchief into his pocket.

Adelaide stared dumbstruck as Sarah swept from her father's side and claimed her son's arm.

"Uh, ma'am, if I may?"

"What?" Adelaide stared at Brewster Armstrong's extended arm. "Oh, of course Mister Armstrong." She laid her fingers lightly upon his sleeve.

"I would be especially pleased if you would call me 'Brewster', Miz Addie."

She winced at the familiarity.

Twenty-One

The river road, March 20, 1829

"Looks like we got a busted wheel, Miz Wellington. The Eden place is just up the road. I 'spect we can git a brace of some sort to do us until we git back to Cottonwood. You can wait up to the house while I talk to those folks."

Connie's look of distress heightened Elzy Parrish's anxiety. Ever since he had hired on as Daniel Wellington's overseer, the Wellingtons had never paid a call on the Edens that he could recollect. And no one from Eden's Gate ever visited Cottonwood except the overseer who came to buy seed corn last spring.

She nodded. "Go fetch a wagon, and come back for us."

Parrish glanced around at the deserted road. Folks were might jumpy lately with runners busting loose up and down the river. It wouldn't do to leave the women unguarded for long. He untied the horse tethered to the back of the coach and swung into the saddle.

"Be back soon as I can, ma'am."

"We will be fine, Mister Parrish, but do hurry." She watched him race toward the house in the distance and disappear around the bend. How strange they should find themselves stranded here. Seeing Charles in the city all those months ago had unsettled her more than she dared admit, even to herself. She had pleaded homesickness when she returned to the townhouse later that afternoon and persuaded Dan to leave for home the following day. She had not been back to the city until her mother's visit to Cottonwood a week ago.

Come back to the city with me, Constance. Davy must get to know his father, Adelaide had insisted.

But Davy had resisted Paul's awkward advances and recoiled at the cloying sweetness of Sarah Armstrong. A worried frown creased Connie's brow. Her nephew's instincts about the woman in his father's life seemed far more astute than Paul's. She was glad when Elzy Parrish arrived the day before to fetch them home.

As they approached Eden's Gate an hour later, Connie felt a tightness form in her throat. The scene was achingly familiar. This was to have been her home once. The house stood a hundred yards back from the river road, partially concealed by a canopy of massive oaks that lead from the main gates. Twelve pillars supported an upper and lower gallery that spanned the length of the house. Trees and flower gardens were beginning to leaf out and bloom. Soon banks of azaleas and wild honeysuckles would lend their sweet fragrances to Augusta Eden's gardens. Only servants tended the grounds now, with no direction from their mistress. Closed draperies in two of the upper windows disguised a painful secret and hinted at the unhappiness that permeated the grand old house.

It had been three years since she and Charles had announced their betrothal here, but there had been a senseless quarrel. Less than a year later, she had married Daniel Wellington. She felt tears gather behind her lashes and struggled to hold them back. Why had she ever agreed to wait here at the house? The wagon came to a stop at the front steps. Elzy Parrish climbed from the seat and helped her down. She walked to the back of the wagon, and took Davy from his nurse, and glanced nervously toward the front door.

"Won't be long, ma'am," Elzy Parrish called back over his shoulder.

She nodded and led the nurse up the steps. Before she could raise her hand to knock, the front door swung open.

"Miz Connie! Ain't you a sight fo' these tired old eyes! Done sent yore overseer on to the forge. Juno's a'fixin' 'im right up."

"Colombo!" Her eyes brightened with genuine delight. "It's so good to see you again. You haven't changed a bit."

He scrubbed his hand self-consciously through a silver mat of hair. "Thankee, ma'am. Come on in the house and warm yoreself by the fire. Now, would you look a'heah?"

"This is my nephew, Davy. It's been a long trip from the city and he's tired. I wonder if he might have a drink of water?"

"Yes'm. The girl kin follow me to the cookhouse. Just laid a fire in Miz Augusta's mornin' parlor. You go along and make yoreself comfortable. Remember how you always favored that room. Miz Augusta, she doin' porely. Ain't up to company these days."

Connie turned, walked across the hallway, and pushed open the door. A crackling fire blazed in the hearth. White lace curtains complemented walls of soft yellow damask. Charles had proposed in this room by the piano that had once been Augusta's pride. Connie started to remove her cloak as the door burst open. "Pansy!"

A huge grin spread across the cook's face. "Miz Connie, just set yoreself down on that settee. I put on the kettle soon as I heard you was comin' up to the house. Pearl's a'bringing tea and some of my spice cake. Knowed how much you always liked it."

"Indeed, I did." Connie laughed softly. "How have you been, Pansy, you and Dancer?"

"Just fine, Miz Connie. Me and my man doin' just fine." She turned as her helper backed through the door, balancing one of Augusta's fine silver trays. "Come over heah, Pearl, and set that tea on the table."

The girl moved unsteadily and deposited the tray onto the table with a clatter. Her golden eyes widened fearfully as she glanced at Connie.

"That's fine, Pearl. You go on back to the kitchen now. I help Miz Wellington with her tea."

Pansy's helper nodded and hurried back the way she had come.

"Pansy, who is that child? She looks so frail. I don't remember her."

Pansy poured the steaming tea into one of Augusta's best china cups. "Pearl's full-growed, a mixed blood, a fancy. 'Bout six months ago, Mastah Charles fetched her home from that auction place in the city. Why, I thought Mastah Victor was gonna take a buggy whip to that boy on the spot!"

"Oh?" Connie lifted the cup to her lips. So, that was why he had been in the city, to purchase more hands for Eden's Gate. But a fancy? Whatever possessed him? Victor Eden hated mixed bloods, and that girl was almost as white as she.

"Mastah Victor sent Mastah Charles to buy a Mandinka, and he up and comes back with her, too. Said he bought her with his own money. Shore upset things 'round heah, I can tell you!"

"And how is Charles?"

"Oh, he fine, Miz Connie." Pansy's smile didn't reach her eyes. "He and Mastah Victor be at odds with one another most of the time. One goes one way, and t'other one goes someplace else. Right now, Mastah Charles is over to the Turnbull place looking at another hoss he thinking 'bout buying. He be back soon, if'n you want to wait."

Connie turned to conceal the sudden flush that burned her cheeks. She deposited the cup carefully onto the tray. "No, we have to be getting home, Pansy. In fact, I would like to get back before dark. I am sure that Mister Parrish has what he needs to repair the wheel by now. Perhaps Colombo could inquire?"

"Colombo!"

The majordomo shuffled through the door.

"Miz Connie say to find out if'n her man is ready to head for Cottonwood. She and the boy need to be gittin' on home." Pansy turned and smiled. "Shore been good to see you, Miz Connie. You always did b'long heah, you know." She fixed her with a knowing stare. "Heah, now, let me help you with yore cloak. I go and get yore girl and the boy."

"Thank you, Pansy. Please, give my regards to Mister and Miz Eden, and to Charles."

Pansy placed the cloak about her shoulders and patted her arm.

Connie gave a sigh of relief as Elzy Parrish guided the coach through the gates of Cottonwood at sundown.

"Here comes Mister Dan!" he called from the seat above.

"Stop!" Connie pushed against the door and alighted before the overseer could climb down to assist her. Dan reined in hard, leapt from the saddle, and clasped her in a smothering embrace. It pleased him that she seemed eager for the reunion.

"Lord, but I've missed you, sweetheart." He laughed and was rewarded by her tremulous smile.

She glanced up into her husband's eyes and marveled, as she always did, at the unconditional love reflected there. Dan was her sanctuary and her strength. He would never allow any harm to come to her. She pushed the image of Pansy and Colombo standing on the steps of Eden's Gate from her mind as his lips claimed hers.

Eden's Gate Plantation

Charles picked absently at his food. His features were drawn into a sullen mask. Across the table Victor scowled after the angry outburst between the two of them minutes before. Pansy's announcement that Connie had been in the house that afternoon had rekindled old resentments. The harsh words that followed were all too familiar. The cook picked up a steaming tureen and left the room, shaking her head and muttering. "Fussin' and a'fighting, all them two ever do, if'n they talk a'tall. Shoulda' kept quiet 'bout Miz Connie's visit."

"Colombo." Victor pushed himself away from the table.

"Yes, sir?"

"Tell Maxie to bring the coach around. I feel like going into town. Company's better there." Now that the fair Fiona reigned over the gaming tables, Swan House beckoned stronger than ever. He shot a disgusted look at his son as he left the room. Charles rose, captured a bottle of bourbon from the sideboard, and made his way down the hall.

He entered his mother's morning parlor and sank into a chair by the hearth. Colombo had extinguished the lamps, but embers still glowed faintly beneath a layer of ash in the fireplace. Connie had been in this room. He could feel her presence and imagined he could smell the scent of her perfume. The bourbon slid easily down his throat. He closed his eyes and drifted into a troubled sleep.

"Mastah Charles!" Zina's desperate cry echoed from the back of the house.

He lunged from the chair as she burst into the room.

"Mastah Charles, you got to come quick! Mistah Grier gonna whup Juno! Done took 'im to the shed," she sobbed, frantically clutching at his arms.

"Why? What happened?"

"Patrollers caught runners down by the dikes. Them boys told Mistah Grier that Juno was gonna help 'em find the way through the swamp. He gonna kill my man, I know he is."

Charles swore under his breath as they raced for the back door and headed toward the seed shed behind the forge. Christ, more runners, and the whole damn countryside already up in arms over their losses. Stephen must be mad. The fierce howls of the dogs echoed across the compound.

"Grier, open the door!" He pounded on the rough planking, then ran back to the forge and grabbed up an axe.

"I don' heah nothing in there. He done killed 'im!" Zina wailed.

A crowd began to emerge out of the darkness. Charles swung a desperate blow and then another. Rameses shoved his way through the onlookers and threw his shoulder against the stubborn barrier. The wood splintered and gave way with a loud crack.

Zina screamed at the sight of the smithy suspended by a thick rope from a beam overhead. His feet scrubbed against the blood-spattered floor, his head sagged onto his massive chest. The three young accusers cowered in a corner. Drawing into their threadbare coats, they shivered more from terror than the chill of the night.

Grier flung the whip across the floor, reached for a jug, and took a deep swallow. "Yer too late, Charlie," he slurred. "I took care of 'im. Gonna take care of them others, too. Yes, sir, gonna show 'em whut it means to run from Eden's Gate."

"Rameses, get Juno down." Charles advanced slowly, his fists clenched at his side.

Zina fell to her knees and gathered Juno's head onto her lap. She glanced about frantically.

"Cleo, fetch my medicine box and a quilt, hurry." The girl bolted from the edge of the crowd and ran to do her bidding.

The overseer swayed and raised the jug to his lips once again. "You damn coward," he leered at Charles. "You ain't fit to run this here place." The swill spewed from his mouth as Charles lunged and sent them both sprawling across the floor.

The two men struggled to their feet. Charles aimed another blow at the overseer's jaw and swung with all the power he could muster. He collapsed to his knees beside Grier's motionless body. Strong arms reached down and pulled him to his feet. He saw a momentary flash of approval in the Mandinka's eyes. Charles nodded and wiped his bloody mouth on his sleeve.

"Prince, you and Georgie, take Taylor back to his cabin."

The two drivers approached cautiously and shouldered the overseer's weight between them. Charles turned and pushed his way through the crowd.

Pansy gave a startled cry as he stumbled into the cookhouse and slumped onto the bench by the hearth. She rushed toward him. "Pearl, fetch me a clean rag from the pantry and brang that jug of whiskey and a cup over heah. Miz Augusta gonna have another one of her spells if'n she see her boy like this."

Charles watched Pearl's slender hands pour the potent brew into the cup and raise it to his lips. The fiery liquid scalded his throat. Her fingers trailed against his bruised flesh. Her eyes were confused and frightened. "It's all right, little girl. It's all right." He attempted a painful smile to reassure her.

Juno moaned as Zina applied the pungent salve to his back. Neither was aware that Rameses had slipped back into the shed and crouched a few feet away.

"Zina?" Juno whispered hoarsely.

"Hush, now. Gonna take care of you." She lifted her eyes and glared at the three runners cowering in the corner. The oldest had not yet reached manhood. The youngest whimpered fearfully. Zina gave a start as Rameses rose slowly and approached Juno's accusers. They stared up at him, speechless with fright. He jerked them to their feet and propelled them toward the smithy forcing them to look upon his torn flesh. With a nod to Zina, he shoved them through the broken door and loosened the ropes that bound their hands. Come morning, Victor Eden would have them whipped, or Zina would have her own revenge at the risk of bringing the old man's wrath down upon herself.

"Run," he growled. They scuttled away from him, hardly daring to believe he was not going to kill them. Rameses shook his head as they struck out across the empty compound and disappeared into the darkness. They likely wouldn't make it through the swamp to the flats beyond, but to stay would mean certain death. He turned and stood in the doorway, watching the medicine woman tend to the smithy's wounds.

Juno closed his eyes. A single tear streaked his battered face. "I was gonna meet up with 'em down by the dikes, Zina," he whispered. "I knowed Mastah Victor was gonna take you away from old Juno and give you to that Rameses. Next thang, them dogs put up a fuss and Mistah Grier come a'runnin' outa the house. Thought he was gonna turn them beasties loose."

"Ain't nobody gonna give me away. Mastah Charles see to that." She grasped the medicine box and struggled to help him to his feet. Rameses suddenly appeared at her side. He reached out to support Juno's sagging form.

Her eyes blazed hotly. "You keep away. Go on now, git!"

He retreated and watched the pair lurch toward their cabin and disappear through the doorway.

Twenty-Two

Victor scowled across his desk at Charles and Grier. What the hell had gotten into those two, fighting like common field hands? Ever since Charles fetched that fancy home from Charleston, the boy had not had a rational thought in his head. And Grier, striping Juno up? A scarred back was the mark of a dissenter, and the damn fool had done a proper job of whipping the smithy to a bloody pulp. Wouldn't be selling him off the place now. Victor pushed himself to his feet, planted his fists on the desk, and leveled a malevolent glare at the overseer.

"I want those dikes along the river shored up again, and this time, *you* can show 'em how it's done proper."

"Dikes?" Grier sputtered. That meant working knee deep in mud and silt, in that bog working alive with snakes and leeches. "That's field-hand work. I ain't gonna—"

"You will do what you are told to do, mister. I don't expect to see you back here before suppertime."

"Yes, sir." Grier flushed angrily.

"And you," he turned to Charles, "get over to the Hamilton place and square up with Miz Dovie for that pair of mules I bought from her last week. You can take Maxie and Dundee to fetch 'em back since *Mister* Taylor will not be requiring their help today. And, mind you, be back here by this afternoon. There's a meeting at the Turnbull place. It's time we figured out how to catch ourselves a slave stealer."

Charles kept his eyes trained over his father's shoulder and his bruised hands fixed behind his back. Stephen was becoming more brazen and reckless. Preacher or not, those damn hotheads would kill him if they could ever catch him. At least the old man had excluded

Grier from the meeting.

"Now, both of you get out of here."

Three Fountains Plantation

"Those ruffians are breaking down my rose trellises!" Margaret Turnbull wailed to her daughter as another pair of riders rode up to the house and tied their mounts to the hitching post alongside a dozen other spirited animals. Throughout the afternoon, neighboring planters continued to arrive at Three Fountains. Shouts and vile curses echoed through the crowded drawing room as the liquor flowed freely. Above it all, Victor Eden could be heard angrily denouncing the man who continued to elude capture in spite of extra patrols positioned at every known point of escape along the river.

Victor paced before the hearth and glared at each guest in turn. For more than an hour he had laid an unrelenting siege to their common sense with his venomous diatribe. Dan Wellington viewed the gathering in troubled silence and felt a momentary pang of guilt for the lie he had told Connie and his aunts. He claimed to have business to discuss with Lemuel Hamilton and promised to be home by nightfall. Connie had smiled and lifted her face for his kiss. Iretta shot him a suspicious look. Connie and Maybelle would never question his explanation, but Iretta was not so easily fooled.

What was he doing here among these hotheads? Given the chance, Victor Eden meant to kill the Shepherd and his followers. But who were these men who could strike with no warning and disappear without a trace? Were any of them present here tonight? No, it wasn't credible. The men who filled this room were all avowed supporters of slavery, too eager to follow that drunken fool Victor Eden's lead. All but one.

Charles's greeting had been stiff and awkward. He sat apart from the others, obviously ill at ease. If today was any indication, he and his father suffered a cold and distant relationship. Dan shifted restlessly and waved aside the servant's offer to refill his glass. Finally, he pushed himself up from his chair.

"Gentlemen, I must bid you all good evening. It's a long ride back to my place, and my wife worries when I am late, especially in these uncertain times."

Parnelle Burke shot him a grateful look and leapt to his feet. "I'll ride along with you, Dan. Ruth's past her time, and I should be at home in case the child decides to come tonight." He edged closer and dropped his voice to a whisper. "Damn fools. Somebody's going to get killed."

Dan nodded grimly and led the way toward the vestibule. They emerged from the house and hurried down the front steps.

Victor's gaze bore into the others, suspicious and calculating. "Did ya'll take notice of how quick Wellington took himself out of here? Mighty strange when a man won't offer to help his neighbors out, especially when he hasn't suffered a single loss of his own stock. Reckon why that is, now? Could it be that Mister Wellington and this Shepherd are acquainted? Maybe related? Or, maybe—?" Victor's unspoken hint hung in the air as others glanced about, seeking affirmation of the notion that Dan Wellington could be the renegade they were after.

"Could be we ought to pay closer attention to our neighbor," Victor's scowl deepened. "Wouldn't hurt none to keep a watch on Mister Wellington's comings and goings for a spell."

Charles's face registered disbelief and disgust. His father was spoiling for trouble. Without realizing it, Dan had committed a serious blunder by leaving so abruptly. *My wife worries . . . my wife.* His words had unwittingly tightened a fist about Charles's heart. If anything should happen to Dan Wellington, Connie would be free. Repulsed by the longing that seized him, Charles bolted from his chair and started for the door.

"Where do you think you're going, boy?" Victor's voice cut him off in midstride.

Slowly, he turned. "Home, Father, where I might find some semblance of reason. The rest of you men would be wise to do the same."

"You come back here!" Victor's jaw clamped shut as the front door slammed with a crash, for the second time.

Charles hurried down the steps and quickly untied Belezar's reins from the hitching post. Moments later, he reached the river road and turned north. No other animal in the county was as fast as the stallion, and he could still catch the two men before they reached Parnelle Burke's place.

Dan set a steady pace through the gathering dusk. Parnelle's excuse to accompany him had been an impulsive ruse. Ruth Burke had produced four sons in rapid succession and her husband had awaited the arrival of each one locked away in his study, drunk as a lord.

Parnelle glanced over his shoulder and signaled the approach of another rider gaining on them. "Over there." He pointed to a copse of trees just ahead.

They bolted from their hiding place as Belezar thundered past. Dan recognized the stallion and called out. Charles hauled on the reins and whirled about as Dan and Parnelle drew abreast.

"You men need to get to your places as quick as you can, and stay put for the night. The old man made sure to point out how fast you left Turnbull's place, Dan. He even hinted there could be a connection between you and the Shepherd. Those fools are liquored up and looking for trouble. Tomorrow they will realize their mistake, but not tonight."

Dan glanced at Parnelle, his distress evident. "We're much obliged for the warning, Charles."

With a nod, Charles turned Belezar in the direction of Eden's Gate. He glanced back at the two men riding hard for the safety of their homes.

Eden's Gate Plantation

Grier strode across the compound from the direction of the stables. The stench of the canals clung to him. The hounds lunged against the side of the pen as he approached his cabin. He pushed open the door, reached for the jug on the table, and sank onto the cot. After a while, he heard the door of the cookhouse slam shut. That would be Pansy making her way across the compound to her cabin. He pushed himself off the narrow bed and walked unsteadily to the window. He could see a faint light in the window of the leanto and felt the heat rise in his loins. Victor had warned him away from the quarters, but the old man didn't pay no mind to Charlie's whore. She was out there all alone, but not for long.

A short time later, Charles handed Belezar over to Rameses and hurried toward the house. He climbed the back stairs to his room, pushed aside the curtains, and stared down at the leanto. It was early, and Pearl would still be awake. Suddenly, he spat out an oath and bolted from the room. A shadow had momentarily blocked the pale light at the window. She was not alone.

Pearl cowered against the wall clutching her torn shift. The overseer cursed and jerked at his breeches. She curled tightly into herself and mouthed a silent scream as he lunged for her.

Grier heard the door crash behind him. The blows came in rapid succession, a brutal attack that left him strangling on his own blood. He stumbled across the kitchen and down the steps. Charles clutched the doorframe and glared down at him.

"You be gone from here by tomorrow, you sonofabitch, or by God, I will kill you!"

He watched Grier stagger away in the darkness before he slammed the door and pushed aside the torn curtain that separated the leanto from the kitchen.

He knelt by the cot. Pearl's shift had been all but stripped from her body, and the marks of Grier's hands had begun to bruise her flesh.

"Little girl?" he whispered and reached out to stroke her hair. For a moment, she did not respond. When she turned, he saw the terror in her eyes. Without thinking he gathered her against his chest. She stiffened and then her arms stole around his neck, clinging to him as he stroked her back. He drew back and gazed down into her eyes. He felt himself drowning in the desperation he saw there. Softly, gently, he pressed his lips to her brow, her face, and finally her lips. He reached over and extinguished the single candle, then lowered himself onto the bed beside her.

He was awakened before dawn to the sound of a sigh so faint he barely heard it. Pearl lay against him, her face next to his. For the briefest time, they had come together with their desperate needs and filled the emptiness of their lonely hearts. He eased himself off the cot, pulled on his clothes, and quietly let himself out of the room.

Later that afternoon

Victor leaned back in his chair and trained a disbelieving scowl on his son. "You want me to put Grier off the place? Who the hell's gonna run Eden's Gate?" The memory of Charles's abrupt departure from Three Fountains the evening before still rankled.

"There are other overseers, responsible men who do not have to resort to violence to run a place."

"Has it ever occurred to you that a strong hand with the lash is exactly what this place needs? No, I don't expect it has seeing as how you have never shown any interest in doing your part around here. Why, I would be a fool to let the best damn overseer in the county go. Hell no, Grier Taylor stays at Eden's Gate, and you had best get accustomed to that fact."

"Then, if you will excuse me, I have some business to take care of."

"Oh, you go ahead, boy. No doubt, it's important," Victor smirked. Charles turned on his heel and left the study.

"Get rid of Grier, bah." The old man tilted his glass and swallowed the contents. "Important business. Can't imagine what could be so pressing."

Charles burst into the cookhouse. "Where's Pearl?"

Pansy nodded in the direction of the leanto.

He pushed aside the makeshift curtain. She looked small and vulnerable sitting on the cot. He knelt beside her and took her hands in his, forcing himself to smile in spite of his anger.

"We're leaving here, Pearl," he whispered. "No one will ever hurt you again. I want you to stay close to Pansy until I come for you tonight." He stroked the gentle sweep of her brow and rose to his feet.

"Pansy."

She turned as he emerged from behind the curtain. "Yes, sir, Mastah Charles?"

"Keep her close to you. I'll come back tonight, after everyone has gone to bed."

"I watch after her like she was my own youngun."

He nodded. By now, Grier knew that his threats were nothing more than empty posturing. There would be no stopping the bastard. He left the cookhouse and made his way toward the stables where Rameses bedded down in the loft above the stalls.

Rameses finished brushing Belezar's coat and released the stallion from his tether. He emerged from the stall to put away his tools and paused, sensing a presence nearby. A shiver of apprehension rippled across the back of his neck as Charles stepped out of the shadows.

Twenty-Three

Victor rose slowly from his desk as the four men filed into the study. His gut tightened at the way they glanced uneasily at one another. Nathan Claiborne cleared his throat. Thurston Turnbull was ominously silent, while Fennemore Pardee and Lemuel Hamilton kept their distance near the door.

"Afternoon, gentlemen. To what do I owe the pleasure? Offer you all a drink?"

"No, thank you." Nathan drew a deep breath and paused for a moment. "Victor, I am afraid we bring bad news."

Victor's knuckles whitened as he clutched the edge of the desk. "Is it about my boy?"

Nathan nodded. "About a week ago, a trader out of Boston spotted a signal fire on one of the barrier islands. A castaway by the name of James Dunning was picked up. He claimed he was aboard a steamer that put into Charleston a little over a month ago. It was bound for Norfolk with a load of gunpowder, and then due to head on to New London. But there was an explosion. *The Pegasus* never reached Virginia. Dunning was the only survivor."

Victor swallowed convulsively. His eyes were hard as flint.

"Sam Cromartie's brother, Maxwell, is the harbormaster in Portsmouth. He sent a messenger to inquire if anyone else from Charleston was on board. There was a single passage and two cargos listed for Charles Eden."

Victor paled. Charles, Pearl, and Rameses had all disappeared the same night.

"Damn sorry, Victor," Thurston muttered.

Victor shook his head. Nathan saw the growing desperation in the man's eyes as reality penetrated the first numbing wave of shock. As Victor began to sway, he rushed to his side and eased him down into his chair. "Whiskey!" he barked. Thurston retrieved a bottle of bourbon from the sideboard and splashed a hefty amount into the glass on the desk.

They departed a half hour later, leaving Victor to the task of mounting the stairs, one terrible step at a time. He opened the door into the curtained gloom. He could not recall the last time he had entered his wife's room or slept in her bed. Years, a lifetime ago.

After she had given birth to Charles, Augusta had barred her door and drawn their only son into her forbidden sanctuary, to the brink of her insanity. But even the boy had not been able to capture the whole of her. There had always been something buried deep within her soul, something she shared with no one. She did not open her eyes as he dragged a chair over to the window beside her. For the briefest moment, the image of her as a bride flashed through his mind. He reached for the lifeless hand in her lap.

"Miz Augusta, I have something to tell you."

When he emerged from the room a few minutes later, she was as he had found her, locked away behind a wall of silence, unresponsive, unaware. He doubted she had even heard his words.

Colombo stood at the bottom of the stairs watching him descend. It was obvious from the pained expression on the majordomo's face that Nathan Claiborne had given him the terrible news. When Victor reached the last step, he clapped a heavy hand on the servant's shoulder.

"Send Maxie to the city to tell Reverend Flynn and his wife. They are Miz Augusta's only relations. And tomorrow, I want you to deliver a personal message from me to Miz Constance Wellington at Cottonwood. My son thought highly of her, you know."

"Yes, sir, Mastah Victor." The majordomo's eyes filled. "I shore do that for you, sir." He watched Victor walk slowly down the hallway.

Charleston, June 13, 1829

Grace paused in the doorway of the parlor. Only the chiming of the clock in the vestibule broke the heavy silence. Stephen had discarded his coat and flung it on the settee before collapsing into his chair. She watched him scrub absently at his brow. It had been four days since Victor's driver had come with the news that Charles was dead.

Stephen's forced calm had been her mainstay when they had arrived at Eden's Gate the next day and confronted Victor's harsh coldness, and again when Zina admitted them into Augusta's shadowed chamber. She detected the first ominous crack in her husband's control as he knelt beside Augusta's chair and whispered her name, and then drew back from the madness reflected in her eyes.

"Stephen?" Augusta's hands had fluttered instinctively to the tangled mass of faded hair that lay in disarray about her shoulders.

"Yes, my dear, it's me, Cousin Stephen. And Grace is here, too." He had drawn her to his side so that Augusta might see her.

"Grace? Who is Grace?"

"She's my wife."

Augusta's eyes closed then. A single tear escaped from beneath her lashes and trailed down her withered cheek. "Why didn't you come for me, Stephen?" she whispered. "I prayed that you would. Oh, why didn't you come back for me?"

He averted his face as Zina administered the tonic that would calm her mistress. "Let's go, Grace." She was hard pressed to keep pace with his strides as they hurried down the stairs. Once outside, he drew in deep gulps of air and then pushed her into the carriage.

In Augusta's confusion, she had unwittingly opened a wound that neither she nor Stephen had ever acknowledged. He had kept to himself since they returned to the city, but no longer. She could not, would not endure another day, not another hour of this silence.

"Stephen."

"Yes, Grace?" A profound weariness crept into his voice.

She advanced slowly into the room and stood behind his chair, letting her fingers trace the worn tapestry, not daring to touch him, not yet. "You have scarcely spoken a word or touched your food. Ginny is beside herself with worry. Can't you at least speak to the child?"

He sighed. "I'm so sorry, Grace, for everything."

She grasped his shoulder only to feel him flinch and pull away. "Stephen," she protested softly, her eyes filling with tears.

"I killed them. Charles came to me asking for my help. I had warned him that terrible things would happen to Pearl and Rameses if he took them to Eden's Gate. I was smug in my own self-righteousness. I condescended to help him. It was my idea for him to take them to New London aboard the *The Pegasus*. The captain was a sympathizer to our cause. Georgette hid the three of them at Swan House until the steamer put in to port. I booked a single passage for Charles and listed the other two only as cargo. John Davis smuggled them on board the same night. I knew the captain would not want to tarry if there was a chance Victor could come looking for his son." He swallowed hard. "Because of me, they're all dead."

"No, no, Stephen." She sank to her knees before him and imprisoned his face in her hands, forcing him to look into her eyes. Miraculously, she felt his arms close about her, pulling her up against him.

"And you, my good and faithful girl, after all that I have forced upon you. Oh, Grace, how brave you have been to have endured it all these years—the worry, the fear, the terrible danger. When I saw the madness in Augusta's eyes I felt ashamed. I never realized how much I love you, depend upon you, that without you . . ."

"Stephen, oh, Stephen, my dearest, please say no more." She held him, her tears mingling with his own. Yet, her heart soared. She was free of the ghost of Augusta Eden. No longer would the doubts rise unbidden in the darkness, in the long hours when Stephen went about his work.

Twenty-Four

G rier stepped up onto the porch of the cookhouse, reached for the bucket suspended over the well, and splashed water into a battered tin basin. His face and arms were burned from the sun and pocked with insect bites. For two weeks, he had driven the crews from first light until dusk, clearing the last of the bottomland that bordered the swamp.

Victor had not ventured from the house since Nathan Claiborne and the others had come about Charles. The house servants whispered that Augusta had spoken not a single word since. And now, there was real trouble brewing. Franklin Miller had arrived unexpectedly the day before. The loans advanced against last year's crops continued to go unpaid. Eden's Gate would be auctioned off in a matter of weeks if the obligations were not satisfied. The old man had ordered the banker off the place, only to have Thurston Turnbull show up two hours later offering to purchase yet another tract of Eden land. Within minutes he, too, had stormed from the house, his face suffused with anger.

It was damn time somebody took things in hand. He tossed the dirty water into the yard and strode down the walkway toward the back door of the main house. Victor raised his head from the desk when he walked into the study. The man's features were ravaged with fatigue and dissipation. His hand trembled as he reached for the whiskey bottle nearby.

"Heard Franklin Miller was here yesterday. And Turnbull. Whut did they want?" Grier asked, but he already knew.

Victor scowled fiercely. Before it would have signaled caution, but no longer. "Sent the bastards packing." He slammed his fist down on the scarred surface. "Coming here like they owned the place. Threatening me, bah. Don't know who the hell they think they are." He squinted at the bottle. "Turnbull wants to buy twenty acres down by the river. Says if I don't sell to him, he'll buy the notes from the bank. I told 'em both to get the hell off my property and be quick about it." He tilted the bottle toward his lips. Grier reached across the desk and jerked it out of his hand.

"Here, now!" Victor tried to rise and fell back in the chair. "What do you think you're doing?"

"You and me need to have a talk."

"Gimme that."

"I said, we got things to talk about."

"Hell, I heard what you said." Victor made another attempt to recapture the whiskey and cursed. "What you bothering me for? You know how to run this place. I taught you good, eh?"

"I reckon you taught me a lot of things." It had been twenty years since Victor first brought him to Eden's Gate. For fifteen years before, that he and his ma had struggled to survive on a few acres of played out soil bordering Eden lands. They had suffered the callous stares of those who passed by in their fine carriages to call at the big house down the road. But Victor never glanced past the rail fence until Annie Taylor's tired heart had given up the struggle. The day she was laid to rest, the old man had ridden up the overgrown path and stared down at him curiously, as if he had never seen him before.

Augusta Eden had stood on the verandah with her arm about Charles's narrow shoulders and watched in silence as he and Victor approached the front steps later that day. She had turned without a word and drawn her son into the house, banishing her husband's by-blow to the quarters out back. But Charles was dead now. There was no one standing in his way but a drunken fool who was about to lose everything.

"Didn't come here to talk about crops."

Victor stared up at him suspiciously. "So, what's on your mind?"

"You gonna lose the whole damn place if you keep on like you going."

Victor gave a mocking laugh. "Seems everybody's interested in my business."

"Miller ain't a man to fool with. He kin take the place if he has a mind to. And Turnbull wants Eden's Gate, all of it."

"Then let the bastards have it!"

"Whut the hell you talking about? This here land's been in the family since yore pa settled here. You cain't just up and throw it away. Cain't do that!"

"Don't you understand? There are no more Edens. My son is dead."

A deathly silence settled about the room. "Whut about me? I ain't so different from Charles."

Victor drew a ragged breath. "So, that's what this is all about."

Grier tossed the bottle aside and gripped the edge of the desk. "I am yer son."

The old man raised his eyes slowly. "I never laid claim to you."

"You fetched me here when Ma died. I got a right."

"I needed your land. Paid you more than it was worth. And you needed work."

"All them years I was growing up, you gave my ma money and took care of us. Why else would you do that if I wuzn't yore blood kin?"

"It was easier to pay her a little something whenever she needed it. I don't know who your pa is. Your ma likely didn't know either. I was just a boy then, not her first, and damn sure not the last to . . ." He cried out as Grier bounded around the desk and hauled him out of the chair, twisting his shirt in his scarred fists.

"My ma wuz a God fearin' woman. She never 'spected you to marry up with her. Said you wuz a gennleman, too fine fer the likes of her. But you knowed the truth, and that's why you brought me here. If it wuzn't fer that crazy old woman upstairs, I woulda' had proper schooling and lived in yer fancy house. 'Stead, I had to make do with a shack out back while Charles never did a damn thing 'cept hang onto his mama's skirts. He hated yer guts. And me, I done ever'thing you wanted. Ever'thing!"

Victor stared up at his accuser whose arms were braced on either side of the chair. Grier's features were twisted into a brutal, jealous mask.

"I am a Eden, same as Charles. Only one left that's got any right to this here place. It's gonna be mine one day. Mine!" He pushed away and stared down at Victor's crumpled form. "You and me going to town tomorrow to see Miller so you kin square things with the bank. Then we gonna pay a call on Judge Claiborne. He's gonna fix you up a new will. I ain't meaning to lose this here place."

Victor sagged in the chair as Grier turned and stalked through the door. He pulled himself to his feet and weaved across the room.

"Colombo."

"Yes, sir?"

"Tell Maxie to get the coach ready. I feel like going to town for a spell."

"Yes, sir."

Swan House, later that night

Fiona glanced up from the cards in her hand, a look of silent desperation in her eyes. Victor Eden had wagered Eden's Gate against the turn of a single card. She forced herself to remain calm, hoping Lily or Georgette would stop the game before it was too late.

The spectacle had begun to draw onlookers, each sensing a scandal in the making. Again Fiona paused, giving the man one last chance to withdraw his wager. Instead, he shook his head to the dismay of those who pressed closer to the table.

It was clear that Victor's opponent did not relish the role she was being forced to play in his macabre performance. The tension had mounted as the bidding became more reckless. It was as if Victor yearned for the chance to lay his terrible burdens upon the table and be done with it.

Georgette glanced at Fiona and placed her hand gently upon his arm. "Victor, please reconsider." Her eyes implored him as if she knew the final card to leave Fiona's hand would destroy the man. He managed a hint of a smile. His eyes were dead, resigned to whatever fate awaited him. Finally, she nodded, and Fiona slowly turned the card. Victor drew a harsh breath.

Nathan Claiborne stepped forward, alarmed at Lily's ghostly pallor and Fiona's stricken eyes. "You all witnessed Miz Georgette's attempt to persuade Mister Eden to withdraw his wager. If any of you gentlemen wish to challenge Miss Lily's claim to Eden's Gate, speak up now."

The spectators looked at one another shaking their heads. Victor had been given every chance to withdraw. None offered the challenge that could still save the man from his own foolhardiness.

"Eden's Gate is in forfeit!"

Lily could not take her eyes from Victor's face as he rose slowly from the table and with surprising dignity, offered a gallant bow to her, and then to Fiona, and finally to Georgette. A sad smile touched his lips. Without a word, he turned and pushed his way through the silent crowd, brushing aside the hat and cane that Mohab held out to him.

He stepped onto the verandah drawing in great gulps of air. It was over, and the pain rushed in upon him. Until that moment, he had not realized that it was Charles, not Grier, who had driven him to plunge headlong into a gamble he knew he could not win. They had been so different from the very beginning. But he loved the son Augusta bore him, the son he had killed with his stubborn pride, the only one meant to be master of Eden's Gate. Better to lose it all to Lily Perrault than to leave it to the monster who waited for him back at the house. She, at least, was kind to a tired old man.

A gentle breeze rustled through the branches overhead as he approached the steps. Moonlight glinted off the barrel of the derringer he withdrew from his pocket and raised to his temple. A shot rang out, momentarily silencing the incredulous voices inside.

Victor lay dead, his blood trickling down the front steps, the weapon next to his outstretched hand. Fiona pushed her way through the crowd that rushed out onto the verandah. She fell to her knees beside Victor's body.

"I killed him, I killed him!" Her frantic cries echoed above the chaotic confusion of those stunned by the brutality of the act. Unseen hands lifted her to her feet, and she found herself in the comforting arms of Jack Faro.

Four days later

Stephen looked out over the mourners crowded into the small country church. Victor Eden had performed few noble deeds in his life to expound upon, and the funeral service had been brief.

Augusta stared straight ahead, the desperation of her plight held at bay by Zina's medicine. Grace and Ginny sat on either side of her, while others appeared to purposely distance themselves from Victor's widow. Even the Turnbulls kept their eyes averted. Word of her husband's wager had traveled with the news of his death. There was not a soul for miles around who did not know that Victor Eden had lost everything to Lily Perrault.

In a few hours, Augusta would travel to the city, consigned to Stephen's and Grace's care, and the spare bedroom at the parsonage.

Twenty-Five

Charleston, July 9, 1829

Franklin Miller leaned back in his chair and glared at his visitor, undaunted by Thurston Turnbull's anger.

"But I am offering her a fair price!"

"Thurston, Eden's Gate is not for sale, at any price."

Thurston's attempt at civility was collapsing visibly. He surged to his feet and braced both hands on the desk. "Tell her, Franklin. Tell her she has to sell to me, or by God . . ." He slammed his fist on the polished surface.

"Sir, I will not be intimidated by you, and if you are foolish enough to attempt it again, I shall take the greatest pleasure in having you ejected from these premises." Fire flashed in the banker's eyes. Victor was barely cold in his grave, and this pompous bastard had the audacity to march into his office demanding to purchase the note that Lily held on Eden's Gate.

Thurston dragged his handkerchief from his vest pocket and mopped his brow. For years he had only pretended to befriend that drunken fool, Eden, waiting for a chance to seize more of his land. And it had been within his grasp until Victor had given it to that Perrault woman.

"Franklin, we have been friends a long time. No sense us getting at odds over this. I need that land."

Franklin closed the ledger in front of him with a decisive snap. "Thurston, take my advice. Go home, and forget about Eden's Gate." He rose and reached for his satchel and cane. "Lily won't sell the place. You see, to her way of thinking, it still belongs to the Edens."

"But Victor lost it. I was at Swan House the night he . . ."

Franklin frowned and shook his head. "If you will excuse me, I am late for an appointment in Nathan Claiborne's office."

"Miller, you come back here!"

Thurston collapsed into the chair as the banker marched through the door without a backward glance.

"Otis," Franklin barked at his clerk, "show Mister Turnbull the way out."

Nathan Claiborne nodded to the three men seated around his desk. Neither Stephen nor Paul suspected the reason they had been summoned to his office. He turned toward Franklin who withdrew a document from his satchel and passed it to him. Nathan cleared his throat and peered over the top of his reading specs.

"Stephen, Paul, I have been retained by Miss Lily Perrault in the matter of the Eden estate. Franklin, here, will be acting on her behalf in this transaction." The banker nodded grimly. Paul shot a questioning glance at Stephen.

"I will be as brief as possible. *Against* Franklin's advice, Miss Lily intends to renounce her immediate claim to Eden's Gate with the provision that the property be placed in trust for Miz Augusta for the remainder of her lifetime." Nathan stifled an urge to smile at his nephew's look of astonishment. "Further, she has requested that the two of you be appointed trustees of the estate, insuring that all existing debts against the property will be paid in full within three years and that no additional obligations will be made against Eden's Gate without the mutual consent of the two of you. Stephen, as Miz Augusta's next of kin, you have a personal interest in this matter. Miss Lily felt your appointment to be a prudent one." He could only imagine what prompted her to name Addie's son as the second trustee.

Stephen's hands trembled as he reached for the document Nathan pushed across the desk. Merciful God, who could have imagined it? Wait until Grace heard the news! The image of his wife's tired features flashed through his mind. Returning Augusta to her home and the care of Zina and Pansy would restore peace to his household once more. "I shall do my best to safeguard Augusta's interests."

"And you, sir?" Franklin fixed Adelaide DuPre's son with a challenging stare.

Paul shrugged helplessly. "I . . . of course."

"Excellent!" Nathan leaned back in his chair with a devilish glint in his eyes. Since the confrontation at Swan House, Paul had become one of Lily Perrault's most outspoken critics. But this would silence his condemnations. Henceforth, the young man would be compelled to keep silent about the lady who presided over Swan House. Nathan could scarcely restrain his glee, imagining Addie's dismay when she learned this bit of news.

"Franklin and I will be calling on Miss Lily this afternoon to complete the final arrangements. The four of us will meet again as soon as Franklin's staff completes their assessment of the plantation accounts. In the meantime, you gentlemen need to hire a new overseer as soon as possible. It seems that Grier Taylor saw fit to leave Eden's Gate before Victor's funeral."

Stephen surged to his feet and thrust out his hand. "Thank you, Nathan. Franklin, thank you!" He hurriedly scrawled his signature on the document and handed it off to Paul.

Nathan watched Paul hesitate and then pen his own signature beneath Stephen's. He smiled. "Nephew, your Aunt Honey and I would like for you and your mother to join us for dinner this evening."

Paul responded with a resigned scowl. "Thank you, Uncle Nathan."

Twenty-Six

Charleston, September 2, 1829

"Who, did you say?"

Nathan trained an incredulous look at his clerk.

"Etienne Cruz," Ferris Judson repeated, taken aback by his employer's unexpected reaction.

"He's *here?*"

"Yes, sir, downstairs. He says the two of you are old friends, and he's asking to see you. Do you know him, Judge? If you like, I can send him on his way."

Nathan pushed himself to his feet and reached for his coat. "Nothing of the sort. Show him up here." It had been three decades since he and Etienne Cruz had shared lodgings at Harvard, but their contacts had dwindled through the years. Strange that the man should suddenly appear with no forewarning. In spite of his feigned indifference, Nathan's face split into a huge grin as he hurried after his clerk.

The visitor drummed his fingers impatiently on the arm of the wooden chair. A crested ring of gold and ebony flashed in the sunlight that filtered through the windows of the courthouse rotunda. He rose to his feet at the sound of footsteps descending the stairs.

The bespectacled younger man with a balding pate and dour expression approached hurriedly. An uncertain smile replaced the condescending annoyance he had exhibited a few minutes earlier. Clearly, Nathan's clerk abhorred any disruption to his precise routine

"Judge Claiborne will see you, Mister Cruz. Kindly follow me, sir."

Nathan stood in the doorway of his office. He watched the tall figure reach the landing, and stride purposely toward him.

"By damn, it really *is* you." He stretched out his arm in genuine welcome.

"Nathan!" Etienne Cruz's strong grip conveyed the power that the very mention of his name evoked. "It's good to see you again."

"I could scarcely believe it when Judson told me you were here." Nathan ushered his guest into the office. "Sit down, sit down." He motioned toward one of the leather chairs positioned in front of his desk. "Offer you a drink?"

Etienne gave a curt nod, assessing his surroundings as he took the chair Nathan indicated. "You have prospered, my friend."

"Investments mostly," Nathan confirmed. "Cotton, northern textiles, and good markets abroad." He poured a double shot of bourbon into two glasses and sized up his friend in turn. Etienne Cruz had been a heartbreaker with the ladies in his youth, and the passing years had not diminished the Creole's considerable charm. Only a hint of silver at the temples marked the black hair that lay against his collar. But there was something unreadable in the man's brooding eyes that didn't fit his disarming smile.

Nathan sank back in his chair and raised his glass. "It's been a long time, 'Tienne. What brings you to Charleston now? Business or pleasure?"

Etienne tossed back the whiskey in a single gulp. "Cruz Shipping opened a London branch twenty years ago. I've divided my time between England and New Orleans ever since. It has been suggested that we transfer our British interests to Charleston. As it happens, I was able to conclude my business in London earlier than I anticipated, and it seemed like a good time to visit your city and assess whether or not such a venture would be mutually beneficial to the company and to the city of Charleston."

"You won't be disappointed. Charleston has become a thriving center of commerce in recent years. In fact, I would estimate the amount and value of cargoes passing in and out of our harbor would rival any major port in the east and New Orleans as well."

Etienne returned his glass to the edge of Nathan's desk. "I've seen the figures, and they're impressive," he admitted. "If it can be arranged, I would like to meet some of your business leaders in the next few days and present our ideas to them."

Nathan templed his fingers across his vest. After the death of his father, Etienne had become the head of the most influential shipping family in Louisiana. Charleston could profit handsomely with the increased trade Cruz Shipping could generate. Promoting his friend's project could prove to be beneficial to his own ambitions as well. Nathan smiled at the prospect.

"Tell me, how is your stepmother? I trust Madame Celine is well."

Etienne smiled. The wariness that emanated from his eyes appeared to soften at the mention of her name. "Mother enjoys good health, and she remembers you with great fondness. I plan to be home in time for her birthday next month. She doesn't expect me until December."

"She doesn't travel with you then?"

Etienne frowned. "Since the deaths of my wife and my brother, and most recently, my father, she prefers to remain close to home. Her nephew, Louis de Fonvielle, maintains a residence nearby. He and his wife, Estelle, keep a close watch on her when I am away."

"I was sorry to hear about your brother, 'Tienne. Of course, your father's passing was reported in all of the papers here. And Woodrow Picard sent word to me of your wife's death some years ago. I wrote to you. I didn't know if you ever received my letters?"

Etienne merely nodded.

Nathan's voice trailed off. He had stumbled into that one without thinking. According to their old schoolmate, there had been whispers that the fire that took the lives of Catherine Cruz and her unborn child had been no accident.

He expelled his breath slowly. "Am I correct in assuming you're not married?"

"I never felt compelled to take another wife." A haunted expression momentarily transformed Etienne's features in the instant before he could turn away. Nathan shook his head and reached for the decanter once again.

As the morning wore on, rapid-fire conversation interspersed with bursts of laughter could be heard through the door. When Etienne rose to leave, Nathan found himself reluctant to end the reunion. He walked around the desk and clapped a hand on Etienne's shoulder.

"Tell you what, you have been at sea long enough to appreciate a solid floor beneath you for a few days. Let me send word to Honora that you'll be staying with us while you're in Charleston."

"That's very kind of you, Nathan, but, I wouldn't want to impose on your wife."

"Nonsense. Honey will be delighted to have company. I can show you around the city and introduce you to some of our leading citizens. Come to think of it, there's a grange meeting next Wednesday night. All of the planters hereabouts come into town for that, especially since they started gathering at Swan House."

"Swan House?"

"The grandest gaming establishment east of the Mississippi. I wager there's none finer in New Orleans. Now, I can't just go barging over there in broad daylight. Honora would have my hide. But we'll just ease over there Wednesday night, and I'll introduce you around." Etienne responded to Nathan's chuckle with a grin.

"I'll send my driver for you around six o'clock. We dine at eight. Judson!" Nathan was certain his clerk had spent the better part of Etienne's visit with his ear pressed against the door.

"Yes, Judge?"

"See Mister Cruz out and send a messenger to Miz Claiborne to expect a guest for a few days. And Judson, have some posies sent over to Swan House. Let Miss Lily and Miz Georgette know that I'll be bringing an old friend around next Wednesday evening."

The clerk didn't bother to conceal a frown of disapproval as he led Etienne from the room.

Nathan sighed. Ferris Judson, for all his remarkable efficiency, could be a stiff-necked pain in the ass. A visit to Swan House might loosen him up, make a real man out of him. He walked to the window and watched Etienne exit from the building and climb into the hired carriage.

"Judson!"

The harried man rushed back into the office. "Yes, Judge?"

"You might also tell Miz Claiborne that I think it will be a fine idea to invite her sister to dine with us tonight."

"Miz Adelaide, sir?" Judson eyed him curiously.

Nathan chuckled and rubbed his hands together. Ever since Adelaide's husband had bellied up between Kate Perrault's silk sheets, Honora's twin had succeeded in instilling one driving ambition in his heart, to find her another husband as far away from Charleston as possible. Etienne Cruz was made to order. He was an aristocrat from the highest level of Louisiana's Creole society, and London and New Orleans were both *weeks* away by the swiftest vessel afloat. Invite her? Hell, he had half a mind to go over to her place and drag the harridan to dinner himself.

The Claiborne house, later that evening

Etienne raised his glass toward the portrait above the mantle. "Your wife is a gracious lady, Nathan. You are to be envied."

Nathan puffed visibly. Indeed, he was. When he arrived home that afternoon, the house had been transformed into a virtual garden of late seasonal blossoms. The aroma of roasting goose and caramelized pudding promised a meal fit for royalty, but nothing compared to Honora herself when she descended the stairs in her finest dinner gown. Her eyes sparkled with excitement. *Etienne Cruz? Oh, Nathan, how exciting! You must be so pleased to see him again.* Trust her to recognize the importance of the man who would be occupying their best guest room for the next several days.

"Honey and I have been married twenty-seven years, and she is as beautiful as she was the day we met."

Etienne smiled. "It appears that you have everything a man could ask for."

Nathan sobered. "Sadly, we have no children of our own, but, we dote on Honey's niece and nephew, Constance and Paul. Her twin sister was widowed at a young age. We took the whole family under our wing."

"Honora has family here in Charleston?"

"Ah, yes. When Adelaide married Gaston DuPre in New Orleans, she insisted that Honora accompany them back to Charleston. Those two ladies have been inseparable all of their lives. Perhaps you knew the family? Beauchamp? Their brother, Jean-Claude, defected to Boston after their father died."

"My father had business dealings with Beauchamp's bank for many years."

"Honey tells me she has invited her sister to join us for dinner this evening. Dear Addie is a frequent guest." Nathan pretended not to notice the hint of suspicion in Etienne's eyes. Well, what if he was a bit obvious? And it was true, his sister-in-law did visit often, whenever she knew he would be absent from the house. If there was one constant he and Honora's twin could lay claim to, it was an abiding dislike for each other's company.

"I look forward to an introduction."

"A kinder soul you will not find in the entire city." Nathan dismissed the annoying prick to his conscience. In his opinion, Adelaide DuPre's waspish tongue rivaled a saw blade, and the witch possessed the warmth customarily attributed to a viper.

A soft knock interrupted their discourse. "Miz Addie has arrived, Judge."

"Good, good." Nathan clapped Etienne on the back and hurried him from the library past the baffled servant.

"Sister, how good of you to join us this evening." Honora swept into the drawing room and greeted her sibling with a peck on each cheek.

Addie noted the unusual flush of excitement that pinked her sister's complexion. She sighed and allowed the maidservant to remove her shawl. "Oh, I don't know if I should have come. I'm certain that Paul is about to propose to dear Sarah. La, but courtship is an exhausting business."

"All the more reason for you to take some time for yourself. We are having a very special dinner tonight." She rushed on before her twin could protest. "A friend of Nathan's will be joining us. In fact, he's our houseguest for a few days."

Adelaide stiffened. "Oh, no, Honey! Not another one of your husband's boorish acquaintances. I simply cannot endure it."

"Addie, please. This unseemly animosity between you and Nathan must cease. And Etienne is such a charming gentleman."

Adelaide pressed her fingers to her temple and grimaced. "I really should not have come tonight. I am not well. Please make my excuses to your guest."

"I will not. You cannot do this to me, Adelaide. Not this time! I forbid such an insult to my husband," Honora hissed.

"Hester, my shawl, please!" Fire flashed in Adelaide's eyes. "Your husband doesn't fool me for a minute. He would like nothing better than to see me wed and carried bodily out of Charleston. Lord knows, he has coerced every eligible male in the city to call on me at least once. But no more. Your guest will have to make do without a dinner partner tonight!"

"Addie, my dear."

Honora winced at the sudden flash of panic in her sister's eyes. Secretly, she was as desperate as Nathan to find a suitable husband for her twin. It had been fifteen years since Gaston's scandalous betrayal. For the sake of Constance and Paul, dear Addie had faced down those who had condemned her husband openly, but, beneath that brave façade, she was a lonely and distrusting woman.

"Sister." Honora moved to Adelaide's side and placed a reassuring hand on her arm. "Allow me to present our guest, Monsieur Etienne *Cruz,* from New Orleans, and London."

Adelaide gave an involuntary gasp. The Cruz name was one of the oldest and most respected ones in New Orleans society. She shot her sister a questioning look. Honora's brow arched knowingly, confirming her suspicion. Nathan stepped aside to allow his sister-in-law an unimpeded view of their guest.

Adelaide's senses swam. That man couldn't possibly be one of Nathan's friends!

Etienne surveyed Addie's confusion with a bemused smile on his face. He reached for her hand and lifted it to his lips. "Madame, I am honored."

Nathan glanced at his wife, his eyes widened with astonishment. Her sister was speechless!

Adelaide blushed at the warmth of Etienne's touch. She glanced down at her gown in dismay. She was still wearing her morning frock. Her eyes narrowed as she glared at Honora's gown of beaded muslin.

Compared to that preening peacock, she was as drab as a sparrow. Her flush deepened beneath Etienne's appraisal. Her doubts were forgotten when he smiled and offered her his arm.

Etienne pulled off his coat and laid it on a chair by the bed. The Claibornes had spared no effort to ensure his comfort. A globed lamp glowed softly at the window; a vase of flowers graced the mantle. It was easy to understand Nathan's unabashed infatuation with his wife. Honora Claiborne and her sister were two of those rare women who bore their ages with remarkable success. Their identical features revealed no telltale lines. Jet black curls set off alabaster complexions that boasted only the slightest blush. Their Creole heritage was exquisitely evident in the way they carried themselves with an indefinable grace that came naturally to few.

A sense of loneliness unexpectedly swept over him. He walked to the window and stared at his own image in the shadowed glass. The genial mask he had maintained throughout the evening had slipped to reveal features that were harsh and pained. He was no longer a young man, and tonight he felt all of his forty-nine years. He turned back to the bed, sank down upon it, and stared up at the ceiling.

There was no doubt that Nathan had been genuinely delighted at his sudden appearance, but Nathan Claiborne was shrewd. He must have secretly questioned the obscure reason he had given for being in the city.

Would his friend think him mad if he dared to reveal the truth; that halfway through the voyage a compulsion he could not explain had forced him to change course for Charleston, that nightmares from the past had returned to plague him night after night, or that accusing voices whispered indecipherable messages to him when he drank too much and waited for exhaustion to claim him?

After all the years that had passed and the torment he had been forced to endure, was he at last succumbing to the same terrible sickness that drove his brother to take his own life?

Against his will, Etienne felt himself drifting toward that netherworld between darkness and dawn, a timeless place where ghosts came to call and images of a raging fire filled him with unspeakable terror.

Twenty-Seven

Several nights later, Nathan studied his wife as she sat at her dressing table and absently plied a brush to the ebony curls that fell shining and abundant to her waist. A perplexed frown played about her face.

"Honora?"

"What? Oh, I am sorry, dear. My thoughts were elsewhere."

"So I noticed. You have hardly spoken a word since dinner. Is something troubling you, sweetheart?"

She gave a soft sigh. "Oh, I don't know. It's just a feeling I get whenever Etienne thinks no one is watching him. There is a distance about him."

"Considering the extent of his holdings and the responsibilities that rest upon his shoulders, I'm sure he has much on his mind. But I like the man, Honey. Old friendships seldom endure, but we have managed to rekindle a genuine regard for one another."

She picked up her brush again. An uncertain smile tugged at her lips. "Well, he has been very attentive to Addie."

"Ah!" Nathan's face lit up. "Would you have ever believed it? Your sister here to dinner every night for a week? Why, just this evening she actually smiled when I offered her another glass of wine. Had I suggested such a thing before, I would have gotten a temperance lecture. I'm delighted that Adelaide finds pleasure in Etienne's company. In fact, the two of them are getting along far better than we could have hoped."

"But do you really think bringing them together so often is wise? I must tell you, Nathan, that I'm having second thoughts about it."

"Good Lord, why?" he sputtered. "They are splendidly well suited to one another."

"Addie has begun to change since she met Etienne. I'm afraid that she may have genuine feelings for him. What if he doesn't care for her in return? What happens when he decides it's time to leave Charleston? Oh, Nathan, she could be hurt badly. She would never let us forget that we introduced them to each other."

"One has only to see them together to realize that he's obviously taken with her. There is nothing to worry about. You will see."

"He has invited her for a tour of the *Saracen* tomorrow."

"Now, that should cause quite a stir among the gossips." Nathan stroked his chin thoughtfully. Ever since the *Saracen* put into Charleston, a crowd gathered at the docks daily to view the impressive flagship of Etienne's fleet. To his knowledge, no one had been invited aboard. Addie would be the first, and the honor would not go unnoticed.

Honora worked furiously with the long braid that bound her hair. "I explained to Frances Pardee just yesterday that it's only because Etienne is our houseguest that Addie agreed to partner him at dinner a few times during his stay. I don't think she believed me, but we've been most discreet, don't you think?"

Nathan smiled indulgently. "Servants talk among themselves. There are no secrets among the households in this city."

"Oh, did I mention that the Pardees lost another one of their people two nights ago? It was their laundress this time."

He ripped out an oath. "I don't understand how this continues to happen. Somebody right here among us is bound to be in league with that Shepherd fellow. Good God, what is this society coming to?"

Honora rose from the dressing table and walked toward him. Nathan felt his throat constrict at the sight of her body through the thin silk. He placed his hands gently upon her shoulders. "That's a mighty fetching gown, Miz Claiborne," he declared huskily.

"I thought you hadn't noticed."

Nathan's heart soared. After all their years together, she could still blush at his frank desire for her. "Reckon it's about time to turn in."

She moved away from his embrace and slipped out of the matching peignoir and laid it across the chair. He extinguished the lamp beside the bed and quickly shed his robe, waiting until she slipped beneath the covers before joining her. His arms closed about her as she snuggled against his shoulder.

"Uh, sweetheart, there's a meeting at the grange hall tomorrow night. I thought I would take Etienne and introduce him around. That is, if you and Addie can spare us for the evening?"

"Of course, dear." She murmured.

He breathed deeply of his wife's perfume, and drew her closer.

The following evening

The Claiborne coach sped along the dark streets toward Swan House. Soft lights shone through curtained windows along the way. Moonlight laid a silver path across the harbor. Etienne could make out the silhouette of the *Saracen* in the distance. Soon he must leave for New Orleans, and the prospect disturbed him. Whatever force had led him to this city had not yet revealed itself.

The image of Adelaide flashed through his mind. Could she be the reason he was here? No, surely not. The voices that invaded his dreams were becoming more threatening and insistent, drawing him deeper into his past than ever before. The journey he had embarked upon began long before Adelaide DuPre offered him a brief glimpse at a way of life he had vowed never to embrace again.

Only that morning, he had escorted her aboard the *Saracen* and felt a sense of genuine pleasure as she stood beside him on the bridge, gazing out across the harbor. Ebony curls peeped from beneath a red velvet bonnet and lay against the delicate curve of her face. She had looked up at him with a delighted smile. He felt his pulse unexpectedly quicken as he placed her hand in the crook of his arm and led her across the deck.

When he had looked down at her again, the happiness seemed to have disappeared from her eyes. Had she been frightened by what she saw in his features, or had he only imagined it? His frown deepened. No matter how strong the temptation, there was no place for such a woman in the life of a madman.

Nathan leaned forward in anticipation as they passed through the gates and traveled along the shell-packed avenue that led to the house. "We're here." He exited the coach and hailed the figure hurrying down the steps toward them.

"Mohab, looks like a sizable crowd tonight."

"Evenin', Judge. Yes, sir, business is right good."

Nathan grasped Etienne's elbow and hurried him up the wide steps.

"The ladies thanks you for the posies, Judge." Mohab scurried past them to open the door.

The sounds of laughter greeted them as they made their way through the vestibule and entered the ballroom. Etienne glanced around. Nathan's description of Swan House had been woefully lacking. If its appointments were any indication, Lily Perrault was a well situated woman indeed.

"Josiah, Thurston. Good to see you both." Nathan clasped each outstretched hand in turn. "Allow me to present an old friend of mine, Etienne Cruz, from New Orleans and London. Etienne, meet Josiah Pickering and Thurston Turnbull."

"Gentlemen."

"And these two young bucks are Addie's nephews, George and Preston Hamilton. Their mother, Miz Charmaine Hamilton, is the sister of Adelaide's late husband."

The younger brother thrust out his hand. "A pleasure, sir."

"George, here, is soon to be married to Josiah's youngest, Maryanne." Nathan gave an approving smile. His eyes searched the crowd. "Pres, I don't see Paul here."

Preston Hamilton grinned. "I believe he's keeping company with the Armstrongs tonight."

Nathan gave an impatient snort and captured two glasses from a silver tray. "It's a tradition here to toast the lady of the house when she comes down the stairs. Now, there is a sight you will not soon forget, my friend."

Etienne accepted the drink. His hand trembled. Nathan's good-natured comment had unleashed a memory that suddenly thundered back with a vengeance.

Once a lifetime ago, he stood at the foot of a staircase much like this one. Catherine descended slowly toward him. Joy illuminated her face as he reached for her hand and drew her into his arms.

He kissed her gently, almost reverently, and then took her hand and

led her toward the window as the first light of day spilled across the floor.
The priest he had summoned from the nearby settlement cleared his throat.
He scarcely heard the man's words until . . .

   'Will you, Etienne Cruz, take Catherine Perry to be your wife?'

"Here they come!" The response of the crowd jolted him back to the present. He watched, oddly detached, as each exquisite woman descended the staircase. Then an expectant hush settled over the room. Nathan gave him a nudge with his elbow.

"Watch this, 'Tienne. In just a minute you will understand why every man in this room is pushing his way to the front of the crowd."

A figure in a scarlet gown materialized from the shadows and appeared at the top of the stairs. Golden curls lay across her shoulder. Diamonds glittered about her slender throat. Lily's eyes swept the crowd, yet she did not appear to take it in, but held herself aloof. Etienne stared transfixed. The vision descending the staircase could not be real.

"*Catherine?*" he whispered.

Twenty-Eight

The Armstrong residence

"Yes, indeed." Brewster Armstrong reached into his coat for a cigar and cast a probing look at their guest. "With the inheritance her mother left her and the dowry I intend to settle on her when she marries, our Sarah is going to be a well-set young lady one of these days." He paused as the servant produced a lucifer from his vest and cradled the flame.

"Oh, Father, please." Sarah feigned a becoming blush and stole a glance at Paul. He had been disturbingly quiet all evening, and it alarmed her.

Brewster exhaled a plume of smoke. Ever since Adelaide DuPre had invited them to dinner, her son had been a frequent caller. Yet, he had not formerly declared his intentions. It wouldn't hurt if the young man understood right up front that Sarah was a fine catch in her own right, unlike those Pickering girls or the Cromartie sisters.

"Mighty lucky man who gets our girl, mighty lucky." Brewster sensed his daughter's nervousness and saw the desperation in her eyes.

"More brandy, sir?"

Paul forced a smile and silently waved the servant away. The evening had stretched interminably long. He found the secretive glances that passed between Sarah and her father troubling.

Minerva deposited her teacup onto the table beside her chair and reached for her embroidery frame. "I'm sure that Paul does not have the slightest interest in Sarah's fortune."

Brewster fixed his sibling with a scathing glare.

Minerva picked up a thread and discarded it in favor of another color. "Why, he's hardly spoken a word all evening," she scolded, turning toward their guest. "Now, dear boy, I happened to see Frances Pardee at the market this morning. She says that Doctor Baker's sister, Felicity, confided to her that he wants you to rejoin his practice. My, such an opportunity."

Sarah stiffened. Paul had not mentioned a word about going back to that dreadful clinic where the vilest afflictions were to be found. She struggled to suppress a shudder.

"Why would Doctor Baker ever think that you would do such a thing? I mean, well, really Paul, you did say that you never intended to practice medicine again." She cast another troubled glance at her father.

"Sarah, I have seen Hadley Baker only once since I returned from Boston. He did mention there was a need for another doctor at the clinic, should I wish to return. I committed to nothing."

"Sarah's right," Brewster interrupted. "Why, a gentleman with your connections must have had many opportunities offered to you since you returned to Charleston." He glanced at his daughter and hurried on before her anger prompted her to say something foolish. "You know, I have entertained the idea of taking on a partner should the right young man come along."

Sarah seized upon her father's impulsive statement eagerly. "Yes, he has mentioned acquiring a partner many times. Why, just the other day Father was saying how good it would be to have someone to . . ."

Paul scrubbed at his brow and allowed Sarah's voice to recede. He felt a sudden urgency to leave. Pres had frowned and had shaken his head when he had refused his invitation for another evening at Swan House. Even George seemed eager for the adventure, knowing his future father-in-law would be there, and no doubt, Uncle Nathan and Etienne Cruz. He rose abruptly from his chair.

"Sarah, Miss Minerva, please accept my apology, but I'm feeling unwell tonight. I think it best if I beg off the remainder of the evening."

"Oh, my goodness." Minerva hurriedly rose from her chair spilling her embroidery onto the floor. "Of course, you should go home and rest. We do hope it's nothing serious." She pressed her fingertips to his brow and propelled him toward the vestibule. "Linus, fetch the doctor's hat and cane. Sarah, darling, say goodnight to Paul."

"But he promised to accompany me to Clarissa Pardee's recital tonight." she wailed.

He turned and gave her a peck on the cheek. "I am sorry, Sarah. Perhaps your father can serve as your escort. The two of you will have a fine time." He almost smiled at the crestfallen look that transformed Brewster Armstrong's face.

"But—!" she sputtered as he hurried toward the door.

"Sarah?" Brewster gasped as she stormed past him and rushed up the stairs. He winced as the door slammed overhead. Paul DuPre was slipping through his daughter's fingers, and him the finest catch in Charleston. "Blast the girl" he growled. "I should have left her in England."

"Brewster, you cannot mean that." Minerva's lip quivered.

He sighed heavily.

The following morning

Honora glared at her husband across the breakfast table. Nathan was inclined to offer a conciliatory smile, but quickly dismissed the idea. The woman was angry, disbelieving.

"Nathan Claiborne, how could you? Whatever possessed you to take Etienne to that horrid place? Can you imagine what will happen if Addie ever finds out?"

"I offered to introduce him around, especially to the grange members. They have taken to holding their meetings at Swan House. It seemed like the most expedient thing to do." He flushed and shook his head. "It would be good to have Etienne relocate his London operation to Charleston, Honey. I am enjoying having him here with us. You won't tell the other ladies about their menfolk meeting over at Swan House, will you?"

Nathan planted his elbows on the table and rubbed his hand across his brow. Etienne had borrowed the gig and left the house before breakfast. He had mentioned something about looking at land that Lemuel Hamilton had for sale out on the river road. Honey had readily accepted his hurried explanation, but Nathan suspected he had other things on his mind that had nothing to do with land sales of any sort. The image of Lily Perrault dancing in Etienne's arms most of the evening before flashed through his mind. Whatever possessed him to confess to Honey that they had been to Swan House when a plausible story would have done just as well? Damnit, he could not lie to the woman. He never had.

Honora's gaze softened in spite of her anger. "Oh, Nathan, you are impossible at times." He seized her hand and pressed it to his lips. Honey's temperament could be fearsome when she was riled, but she had a kind and good heart.

"Honey? Honey, are you here?"

"It's Addie! Oh, Nathan, what if she's already heard? What are we going to tell her?"

His features sagged as his sister-in-law swept into the room.

"Addie, dear, do sit." Honora motioned her twin to a chair. "Hester, fetch Miz Adelaide a cup and saucer, and one of those warm croissants. They are delicious this morning, sister. You must try one."

Adelaide's eyes darted from one to the other. Nathan looked unwell. Honey's hand trembled visibly as she lifted the silver teapot. She glanced at the empty chair across the table.

"Where is Etienne?"

"Etienne?" Honey offered an uncertain smile. "Oh, Lemuel Hamilton sent word that he has some property he wants to sell. Etienne left early this morning to see it and talk with him about it. We expect he will be gone upriver most of the day, perhaps until tomorrow. You know how hospitable the Hamiltons are. Butter? Some blackberry jam, perhaps?"

Nathan pushed away from the table, darting a grateful look in his wife's direction. "If you ladies will excuse me, I have a busy schedule today." He planted a quick kiss on Honora's cheek and rushed down the hallway.

"Simon, bring the carriage around. Hurry, man!"

Twenty-Nine

Thaddeus entered the study and paused. No lamps had been lighted to relieve the late afternoon shadows. Georgette stood silhouetted against the window watching the couple in the garden.

"Georgette, what are you doing in here all by yourself?" Thaddeus crossed the room and peered over her shoulder. "What's going on out there?"

"I have no idea," she replied irritably, and shrugged. Etienne Cruz had been a constant and decidedly annoying presence ever since the first night Nathan Claiborne brought him to Swan House. For more than a week, he had arrived at midmorning to take Lily for picnics in the country and stayed for afternoon tea when they returned. At night he reappeared, after having dinner with the Claibornes. It was as if he had laid a personal claim to the girl, allowing no one to intrude upon their time together. And, strangely enough, Lily appeared to welcome his attentions.

"He has scarcely let her out of his sight since the Judge first brought him here."

"I hear he's a mighty rich man."

Georgette shrugged. "Many rich men come through here, but none as demanding and arrogant as this one. The first time he came, I told him Lily was not available to see him. He saw Sauchie coming from the kitchen and ordered her to deliver his calling card to her mistress immediately. Almost scared poor Sauchie out of her wits." Georgette's eyes flashed angrily. "What could I do, but allow it?"

Thaddeus tweaked a curl at the back of her neck. "Well, I don't think there's anything to worry about. He'll be gone soon."

"Not soon enough." She frowned. "Lily says he's asking a lot of questions, especially about Kate."

"Kate?" Thaddeus asked, genuinely perplexed. "What sort of questions?"

"Oh, like where did she come from? Was she from Charleston? Who were her folks? Those kinds of questions. Why, he even asked her about our friendship. I warned Lily to be very careful about what she tells him. He is no fool," she sighed. "I don't like it, Thaddeus. There's something frightening about that man!"

"Well, maybe we better ask Franklin to have a talk with the Judge about his friend."

"We cannot risk having him find out what goes on here. It will be someone like Mister Cruz who will not be fooled for long by the façade we have created."

Georgette gave a soft gasp. Etienne Cruz had turned away from Lily. She could see the flash of anger in his face and the sudden reversal when Lily slipped her hand into the crook of his arm, but, his smile seemed forced as he covered her hand protectively.

"Look, they are coming back this way." Georgette grasped Thaddeus's arm and pulled him away from the window. "Light the lamp by the door. It won't do for Lily to think we are spying on her."

The flame sputtered in the globed lamp just as Lily and Etienne entered the room. Clad in a modest shirtwaist and skirt, her hair held back by a simple grosgrain ribbon, Lily appeared childlike alongside the powerful presence of her companion.

Georgette felt a ripple of uncertainty travel down her spine. Good Lord, but the man was unsettling. "Good afternoon, Mister Cruz. May I assume that we will have the pleasure of your company later this evening?"

"Unfortunately, no." His eyes seemed to bore through her. "I'm leaving for New Orleans the day after tomorrow. I plan to spend the remainder of my time here with the Claibornes."

"How disappointing. Perhaps you will visit Swan House again, the next time you are in our city." Georgette knew her attempt at civility didn't fool him. Her distrust of him was palpable. "If the two of you will excuse us, Mister Parks and I have things to attend to before we open tonight." She pushed Thaddeus from the room and scurried down the hallway on his heels.

"Thank goodness!" she whispered. "The sooner that man is gone, the better."

Etienne's departure should sweeten Jack's sour disposition. For days, he had sulked like a scorned lover. Well, no more. Tonight, it would be business as usual.

That night, Lily sat at her dressing table, oblivious to the faint sounds of revelry coming from downstairs. She did not turn when Georgette rushed into the room.

"Lily, the guests are arriving. Polly, she's not dressed."

"She say she ain't goin' downstairs tonight."

"But she must! Everyone is asking for her."

Lily drew her dressing gown closer about her. "Not tonight, Georgette."

Alarmed, Georgette hurried across the room and laid a practiced hand on her forehead. "Polly, send for Doctor Baker. She feels feverish."

"No." Lily's protest was barely more than a whisper. "I'm very tired. I just need some time to rest. I will feel better tomorrow."

Georgette searched her face. "Very well. Fiona can take your place in the procession tonight." She turned toward the door then paused. It was Etienne Cruz's departure that upset the girl. She was certain of it. She glanced at Polly, her concern clearly evident in her expression. Rather than reassuring her, Polly merely shrugged and shook her head.

Georgette sighed. "We'll look in on you later. Come, Polly. Let's leave our girl to her sleep tonight. I can use your help with the wardrobes." She ushered the servant from the room and hurried off in search of Fiona.

Lily walked out onto the gallery and gazed up at the stars. For more than a week, Etienne Cruz had transported her beyond the loneliness and isolation of Swan House. He was kind, his interest in her life genuine. No detail was too insignificant to escape his attention. He asked endless questions. In the time she had spent with him, she had told him of her years at the convent and of Thaddeus's discovery of her at the Charity Hospital. There was a deep sadness in his eyes when she revealed her longing for the father no one claimed to know anything about. And there was his strange preoccupation with Kate.

She walked back into the room and reached for the carved box beside the bed. The letter that Kate had read each night before she slept was no longer there. She suddenly felt a fearful sense of dread. What had possessed her to give it to Etienne? His eyes were bleak as he read the message from the anonymous writer, telling of her death.

I am not without influence in New Orleans, Lily, he had said. *I have connections to secure information not readily available to everyone. I'll find the person who wrote this heinous lie to your mother. And perhaps, I'll discover the identity of your father as well.*

In that instant, a feeling of hope had transformed her features. If anyone could make such a promise and deliver upon it, it would be Etienne Cruz. He had turned away from her then, but not before she glimpsed the anger in his eyes, and it frightened her. She had slipped her hand in the crook of his arm, and he had closed his hand over hers. When he turned, all traces of anger had vanished.

Promise me, he reminded her as he prepared to take his leave for the last time, *that you will send word through Nathan Claiborne if you need me for any reason.* He had taken her hands in his for the briefest moment before hurrying down the steps to the waiting coach.

The following evening

Nathan glanced over at his guest and poured a glass of brandy. Etienne's demeanor had been noticeably subdued at dinner, and Addie had been conspicuously absent again. Even Honey had excused herself as soon as courtesy would allow and hurried up to their room.

Addie was in a state, his wife had confided as soon as he had arrived home that afternoon. Frances Pardee was spreading spiteful rumors that Etienne had been seen arriving at Swan House at all hours for the past week. It was a lie, of course, but Addie was so vulnerable that she had readily accepted the gossip as truth. In fact, when Etienne attempted to call on her earlier, he had returned to report Addie was unwell and not receiving callers. Just wait until she saw Frances Pardee, Honey had threatened. She intended to give her a proper scolding! Nathan had shaken his head, gathered her hands in his, and wisely prevented his wife from committing an act she would only regret later. For once, Frances was right. Etienne had acted with reckless indiscretion and presented himself at Swan House several times.

If Honey's shock and dismay were any measure of her twin's anger, his hopes of wedding his sister-in-law to his friend had been irrevocably dashed.

Etienne accepted the brandy he offered, but didn't raise it to his lips. Nathan downed the contents of his glass and reached for the decanter again. Etienne's silence didn't bode well, and intuition dictated that Nathan brace himself for whatever might be on the man's mind.

"Nathan, I have something to show you."

"Oh?"

Etienne slipped his hand into his coat, withdrew a gold watch, and held it out to him.

Nathan placed his glass on the sideboard and opened the embossed case to reveal a miniature portrait inside. He didn't try to conceal his dismay. Christ, what was Etienne doing with this? He had known Lily Perrault only a short time. Was he about to announce their betrothal? Images of the twins flashed through his mind. Perspiration beaded his brow.

"Lily is an extraordinarily handsome young woman." He arched a brow and leveled a questioning look at his friend.

"The lady you see there is not Lily Perrault. I have carried that portrait for twenty-five years." Etienne met Nathan's gaze. His eyes were haunted.

Nathan pursed his lips and frowned. Honey's suspicions were right. There was indeed more to Etienne Cruz than he had revealed since he had been in Charleston.

"If this woman is *not* Lily, then who the hell is she?"

"My wife, Catherine."

Nathan glanced at the portrait and back to Etienne. His eyes widened. "Your wife? I don't understand."

"Nor do I. There is much to tell, if you are willing to hear me out."

"The evening is yours. I think you know that anything you share with me will be kept in absolute confidence." Nathan returned to his chair across from Etienne, prepared to give the man all the time it would take to tell his story.

Thirty

The next morning, Nathan followed his guest down the front steps to the waiting coach. The secrets Etienne has shared in the privacy of his study the night before had left him speechless. Was it possible there was a connection between Kate Perrault and Catherine Cruz? Etienne had said nothing to Lily of his suspicions, but she may have unknowingly provided him with the identity of the only person who knew the truth about Kate, and the deaths of Etienne's wife and their child.

"I can never repay your kindness, Nathan." Fatigue was evident in Etienne's features. Neither of them had slept well the night before.

Nathan clapped a hand on his shoulder. "Take care of yourself, my friend. I will be waiting to hear from you."

Etienne climbed into the coach. "Say goodbye to Honora for me?"

"She's sorry to see you go, Etienne. It's been a real pleasure for us to have you as our guest."

Etienne's invasion of their household had proven to be a nightmare she never expected to recover from, Honora had declared in the privacy of their bedroom. Addie was stubbornly refusing to respond to her messages, and her own patience was hanging by a thread. The twins' infamous tempers were about to propel them headlong into a spat of dreadful proportions!

Etienne called up to the driver. "To Miz Addie's house, Simon."

Nathan attempted an encouraging smile. Etienne had called at the DuPre house the day before, and his efforts to see Addie had been rebuffed. He was unlikely to meet with success this time.

Tilde peered through the lace curtains of her mistress's bedroom window and watched the Claiborne coach come to a halt at the front gate. "He's back, Miz Addie."

Adelaide lifted the cloth from her forehead, her eyes flashing with renewed anger. Mister Cruz was proving to be most persistent, but her answer would be the same. She was indisposed and unable to receive callers.

"You know what to tell him, Tilde."

"But, Miz Addie . . ."

"You will not allow that man to enter my house, do you understand? Go along now." Adelaide sank back on her pillows and listened as Tilde scurried down the stairs and stammered the message. The front door slammed with a decisive crash. She bolted upright at the sound of determined footsteps stalking up the stairs.

"He wouldn't dare!" She gave a shriek as Etienne's powerful frame filled the doorway. The anger in his face dissolved at the sight of her in her dressing gown, a tumble of black curls falling about her shoulders.

"How dare you come into my room," she sputtered. "Caleb, come up here at once and throw this ruffian into the street!"

Etienne continued to stare at her. He closed the door, muffling her enraged cry.

Caleb pretended not to hear her next demand to fetch the constable. Instead, he turned and scurried down the hallway in the direction of the back door.

Etienne approached the bed and planted his arms on either side of his captive. "Adelaide, I have suffered your 'indisposition,' whatever the hell *that* is, for two days. Now you threaten to have me forcibly ejected from the premises. Why am I suddenly unwelcome in this house?" He grasped her chin forcing her to meet his eyes.

Her own snapped with fire. "I will have you arrested if you do not leave a once!"

"Oh? And what transgression will you accuse me of that will not compromise your own reputation?" A mocking smile warned that his anger was beginning to rise.

"Do you think that I care?" she whispered hoarsely.

"Yes, my dear," he replied tersely. "Your kind always cares."

"Oh, you insufferable—get out!" Her words were lost as his arms suddenly closed about her, and his lips stifled her condemnations. Her fists flailed helplessly against his chest and suddenly stilled.

Without warning, he released her and stepped back. "Forgive me. I had no right to do that."

"How dare you touch me after that whore!" she hissed.

He gaped at her, stunned by the fury in her voice. "What are you talking about?"

She clutched her gown closer, pushed herself from the bed, and stood before him, trembling with anger. "I know about your *visits* to Swan House. Everyone knows. Don't you dare deny that you were consorting with that vile creature."

"Lily?"

"You went there several times!"

"I don't deny it. But I had good reason. There are things I cannot tell you now, Addie. I can only ask that you trust me until I—"

"Trust you?" She emitted a shrill, unconvincing laugh. "You insult me, sir."

He stepped back as if she had struck him, anger suffusing his face. "It was not intended, I assure you."

"Please, just go," she pleaded, pressing her fingertips to her temples.

He backed away but paused. Then he retraced his steps down the stairs and slammed the front door behind him once again.

With a cry, Adelaide rushed to the window and watched him wrench open the gate and bark an indistinguishable order to Simon. She was jealous. Horribly and shamefully jealous. Never had a man stirred her to such fury. Etienne's reckless kiss burned upon her lips still. And she dared accuse Lily Perrault of wickedness?

Later that afternoon

Paul knocked on the door of his mother's room. She had not appeared downstairs all day. Tilde opened the door and attempted to brush past him carrying a tray of untouched food.

"What's going on here?" he demanded.

"Uh, well, Miz Addie had a caller this mornin'."

"And?"

She glanced over her shoulder. "Maybe, you best ask yore mam 'bout that."

Paul pushed the door open. Adelaide's eyes were red from weeping. He grasped her hand, alarmed. "Mother, what's wrong?"

Adelaide sniffed and dabbed at her eyes.

"What has happened to upset you so?"

"Etienne Cruz!" She buried her face in her handkerchief and gave way to a fresh burst of tears.

"What did he do?"

"He's been consorting with that harlot from Swan House. Everyone is talking about it," she gulped and hurried on, "and he embraced me in a most ungentlemanly manner."

"He did *what?*"

"Oh, Paul, do go away."

He stared at her helplessly and then turned and strode from the room. Moments later the front door crashed shut for the third time that day.

Nathan started to rise as Paul burst unannounced into the Claiborne's solarium.

"Where's Etienne?"

"He left hours ago. What's wrong, nephew?"

Honora laid her stitchery aside. "Dear boy, you look so angry."

"There was an altercation between Mother and Etienne. She's so upset she won't discuss it, but I intend to get to the bottom of it."

Honora fell back upon the settee with a cry. "Oh!"

"Where is he, Uncle Nathan?"

"Well, I should think that he's aboard the *Saracen* by now. When he left this morning, he mentioned that he planned to call on your mother to say goodbye. They seemed to take pleasure in each other's company for the time that he was here. Paul, wait."

Nathan turned and paled. "Honora!" His wife lay across the settee, insensible to their nephew's abrupt departure. "Hester, fetch Miz Claiborne's salts." The servant thrust the vial into Nathan's hand and watched anxiously as her mistress coughed and sputtered.

"Nathan, is it true? Addie has been assaulted by that man?"

He rolled his eyes. Etienne was a force to be reckoned with, but a gentleman. If he had acted inappropriately, he had been driven to it. Whatever Adelaide's spiteful tongue had provoked, he had apparently delivered in full measure. Nathan found the prospect almost pleasurable. Damn time that woman was put in her place. With great effort, he pulled his features into a stern mask.

"Now, Honey. Let's not judge too hastily. After all, you know your sister tends to over-react. You have been subjected to her unstable temperament only recently."

"You are right, dear. Addie does upset easily, but one has to make allowances. Have Simon bring the coach around. I must go to her at once."

Minutes later, Nathan handed his wife into the brougham. "Please give Addie my best, my dear." He patted her hand and stood back as Simon urged the team forward. Once the coach disappeared from sight, he turned and walked up the steps rubbing his hands together. Yes, indeed. Miz Adelaide DuPre had finally encountered a real man for the first time in her life. He chuckled as he sauntered into the house.

Xavier guided the coach onto the dock and brought it to a halt within sight of the *Saracen's* berth. He climbed down from his seat and walked back to the window to speak to the lone passenger.

"Want I should take you the rest of the way, Miss Lily?" He peered at her anxiously. She didn't respond at once, but watched the hurried activities of Etienne's crew for several minutes. Come morning, the *Saracen* would be gone and, with it, her last chance to escape from the rejection and loneliness that had become her life.

She glanced down at the battered valise beside her and grasped the handle. Etienne would not refuse her passage to New Orleans. She had only to ask. Yet, where would she go? She could never again return to the convent. She glanced up at Xavier. A worried frown furrowed his brow. Georgette would blame him for this, no matter that in a moment of desperation she had ordered him to bring her here. Inside the valise was a hastily written letter to Georgette. The image of Kate's best friend flashed through her mind. She brushed away a tear that slipped down her cheek. Franklin was right. Georgette and Thaddeus, and even Jack, were becoming the first real family she had ever known. To leave them now would be the ultimate betrayal. She fumbled for her handkerchief and signaled to Xavier.

"Take me home," she whispered.

A look of relief transformed his features as he climbed back onto the seat and took up the reins once more.

The rider on horseback spied the familiar coach approaching from the direction of the dock and urged his mount into an alley.

As the brougham passed, Paul saw the anguish in Lily's face. She stared ahead, unaware of his presence.

His eyes narrowed. So, the rumors were true. Miss Lily Perrault and Nathan's friend had developed more than a passing interest in one another in the brief time Etienne Cruz had been in the city. An unexpected rush of jealousy caused him to jerk on the reins, and set off at a gallop in the direction of the Armstrong house.

Late that evening, Adelaide paced the drawing room nervously. It had been hours since Paul left home. She should never have told him about Etienne's visit. What if there had been a confrontation between the two of them? She gave a sigh of relief as the front door opened.

"Paul?"

He crossed the room to the sideboard. The decanter clinked forcibly against the glasses. He turned, cradling a glass of brandy in each hand. She looked at him curiously and accepted the one he offered to her.

"A toast, Mother, to my coming marriage. I have asked Sarah to be my wife, and she has accepted."

Adelaide gasped in astonishment and gave a delighted cry. "Oh, darling, what wonderful news!" She set the glass aside and hurried to embrace him. "Imagine how surprised Constance will be. My dear, I am so happy!"

Paul gathered her gently in his arms, his chin resting upon the crown her head.

"I thought you would be." He smiled, yet his eyes were bleak. He had left the Armstrongs to their frantic plans. They scarcely noticed when he walked out of the house.

Thirty-One

New Orleans, October 10, 1829

The house on Rue Royale rose three stories behind its stone wall, the first floor visible only through a pair of iron gates that guarded the entrance to the courtyard. On the street, a hired hack discharged a passenger who pushed open one of the gates and approached the house with urgent strides.

A maidservant watched from an upper window as Etienne hurried up the broad stone steps to the main entrance. "It's Mastah 'Tienne," Odette whispered then rushed toward the stairs, calling for her mistress, "Miz Celine, Miz Celine!"

Etienne paused and glanced up at the uppermost gallery. From the time they were children, Catherine had waited for him there after the household retired for the night. They had watched the moonlight dance off the fountain below and vainly attempted to count the stars that littered the night skies. Years later, it was Phillipe who stood there alone and watched silently as he and Catherine climbed the stairs arm-in-arm to confess their secret marriage to Andre and Celine. The anger in his brother's eyes had troubled him then, but it was the grisly horror of Catherine's death a year later that continued to haunt him over twenty years later.

He entered the house unannounced and crossed the vestibule. The afternoon sun penetrated the windows in the drawing room and cast prisms of light across the carpets from the chandelier suspended overhead. Celine's portrait gazed down at him from the mantle as he made his way toward the solarium at the back of the house. It was his stepmother's sanctuary, a place where she read, tended to her correspondence, and received her closest friends. It was from there that she had watched her sons at play in the gardens when he and Phillipe were boys.

Good morning, Mother!

Good morning, Mother! On good days Phillipe's piping voice had echoed his own greeting.

She had smiled down at them from her window and blew kisses, relieved that for a time, however brief, the demons that tormented her younger son were silent.

Good morning, my darlings!

Unlike their father, she had never showed a preference between himself and Phillipe, the son she bore Andre Cruz three years after their marriage. Frail and burdened with a withered limb at birth, Phillipe's afflictions had denied their father a second strong son to carry on his name.

You will make a weakling of the boy, Celine. Andre had scorned her attentions as Phillipe struggled with his cane and later with his anger. But she had remained devoted to her son and shielded him from her husband's disdain as best she could.

Etienne tensed at the sound of footsteps hurrying along the hallway.

"Etienne? Etienne!"

He turned, but did not hurry to sweep her up in his arms as he always did when he came home after a long absence. Celine rushed into the room and threw her arms about him. "Oh, darling, what a wonderful surprise! We didn't expect you for another month," she laughed delightedly. When he made no move to return her embrace or to speak, she drew back and saw the anger in his eyes. Bewildered, she reached up to gently stroke his unshaven face. "'Tienne, what's wrong?"

"Who is Kate Perrault?"

The menacing tone of his voice caused Celine to clutch at her throat and back away.

He advanced toward her, never taking his eyes from her face. "Would it matter to you if I told you that she's dead?"

"How do you know that name?" she whispered.

He knew in that instant that his suspicions were true. He turned abruptly to the window and gripped the sill. "A few months ago, for no apparent reason that I could understand, the old nightmares returned, more horrifying than anything I remembered. Again, it was the fire and voices crying out to me. I thought I was going mad, like Phillipe. I felt a great urgency to return to New Orleans. But midway through the voyage I was seized by a premonition to sail directly to Charleston. I ordered Raoul Mendoza to change course for that city, and as soon as we arrived, I set out to find Nathan Claiborne. I had convinced myself that this irrational compulsion was somehow connected to him. He was genuinely glad to see me, but I quickly realized that whatever force had drawn me there had nothing to do with him."

Etienne paused and drew a deep breath. "Having no plausible explanation for being in his city, I told him that I was thinking of relocating a part of the English fleet there. He offered to introduce me to some of the town's leading citizens and took me to a gaming house where these men congregate regularly."

He turned to see Celine clutching the chair beside her. She forced herself to look into his eyes, and he saw her fear.

"I met a young woman there, and suddenly I knew why I had been *summoned*. When I saw Lily Perrault for the first time I had the insane thought in my mind that she was Catherine coming down that staircase toward me. But we both know that could not have been possible since Catherine died more than twenty years ago—or did she?"

Celine pressed her fingers to her lips. She appeared to fold inward as if to shield herself.

Etienne would not relent. "The resemblance is remarkable. Lily looks exactly as Catherine did twenty-five years ago. I insisted that Nathan introduce me to her at once. For the next several days, I monopolized every minute of time she would allow me to spend in her company, trying to discern if there could be a connection.

"When we were together it was as if I had known the girl all of her life. She felt the bond, too. I'm certain that she told me things about herself that she would not have revealed to just any stranger. She never knew her mother, Kate, or the name of her father. She even shared an unsigned letter that had been written to her mother years ago claiming that Lily, herself, had died of yellow fever as a very young child, *here* in New Orleans!"

Etienne reached into the pocket of his coat. "I promised if she would entrust it to me, I would use every resource I had to expose the person who had written that heinous lie to Kate." He drew a ragged breath. "I had to have it. The instant I saw it I recognized the handwriting." He reached out and grasped her arm then pressed the faded parchment into her hand.

Celine cried out and tried to wrench free of his grip.

"You wrote that letter, didn't you? You have known all along that my wife and our child didn't die in the fire at Heron's Point. You kept the truth from all of us. In God's name, why did you commit such an act?"

The anguish in Etienne's voice caused tears to stream down Celine's face and spill onto the letter. Her hands shook violently. She tried to speak, but no words came from her throat, only a mewling cry. She swayed and crumpled to the floor, the letter still clutched in her hand.

Etienne dropped to one knee and swept her motionless form up in his arms. "Odette!" he shouted.

Celine's maidservant rushed to the stairs and peered down from the landing above. "Miz Celine!"

"Send for the doctor and for Louis and Estelle!"

Estelle and Louis leapt to their feet as Celine's physician entered the room.

The doctor reached for the cloak Estelle retrieved for him. "I have given her something to help her rest. I'll return tomorrow morning. Should you need me before then, send for me regardless of the hour."

Louis pulled his wife to his side. "How is she?" he asked.

The doctor frowned. "Etienne doesn't know the condition of her heart, does he?"

Estelle sighed. "She forbade either of us to tell him. She thinks that he has too much worry and too many responsibilities on his shoulders as it is."

"Well, she obviously suffered a severe shock. Do either of you know what brought about the attack?" The doctor eyed them sternly.

"Odette said she heard Etienne raise his voice," Louis replied. "Can you imagine? There has never been a harsh word spoken between those two. Now, if it had been Phillipe . . ."

"Hush, Louis," Estelle admonished gently. "Do not speak unkindly of the dead."

"Well, it's true," he growled. "That wretched cripple took his anger out on Aunt Celine at every opportunity. Etienne always treated her with the greatest respect. Uncle Andre was proud of Etienne and rightfully so."

"And like his uncle, my husband has always been partial to Etienne." Estelle offered an apologetic smile to the doctor.

"He's my best friend," Louis protested. "I know that he would never intentionally do anything to hurt Aunt Celine."

"Very well, Louis, but, keep a close watch on your aunt." The doctor turned to go, but paused. "And Etienne as well. He is too much like his father not to be concerned."

Louis nodded. Andre Cruz's unexpected death in the prime of his life had come as a shock to those who knew him. Many speculated that it was his guilt over his younger son's suicide that made a widow of Celine Cruz far too soon.

Celine's eyes were sunken and dark. Her auburn hair, unbound and spread across her pillow, was shot with more silver than Etienne remembered. He pulled a chair close to the bed, but did not grasp the hand she reached out to him.

"'Tienne?" she whispered.

"You shouldn't try to talk now," his voice was gruff. "The doctor wants you to rest."

She turned her eyes away from him toward the window. When she spoke again, her voice had lost its fear and resonated with a resigned weariness instead.

"When your father asked me to become his wife a year after my sister died, I felt that I was the most fortunate of women. As a child, I had given my heart to Andre Cruz long before he married Lizette. And, when we married I gained a son that I have always loved as dearly as if you were my own," tears gathered in her eyes. "The only blight on mine and your father's marriage was the son I bore him. Phillipe's infirmities repulsed him. Andre always loved you best, and no one knew it better than your brother."

Celine sighed. "There were no companions for Phillipe in those early years. It was only when Andre brought Jay Perry and his little daughter to Heron's Point to be the overseer there, that Phillipe got his dearest wish. Catherine could always silence the demons that plagued him. When she came to live with us after Mister Perry was killed in that hunting accident, she and Phillipe were inseparable. It was only as the three of you grew older that we realized Catherine had given her heart to you and not to your brother. When the two of you wed in secret at Heron's Point, it was the ultimate betrayal in his eyes. It was then that the sickness took hold of him so violently."

"Months later, when your father asked you to travel with him to Natchez to appraise some cotton consignments, you asked him to take Phillipe instead. He laughed, and I saw the hurt and anger in your brother's eyes. Your first child was coming soon, and you didn't want to leave but your father insisted. The day the two of you left the city, Phillipe persuaded Catherine to go on a last outing before her confinement. He promised to have her home early. I never suspected that he meant to take her back to the plantation."

Celine gasped and pressed her fingers against her breast. Etienne reached for her hand then. "Mother, please," he whispered. "It can wait until you're better."

"No, no, I must tell you everything. When they didn't return by nightfall, I sent two of the stablehands to look for them. The carriage was found outside the city. Phillipe was badly injured, but he was able to tell us that Heron's Point had burned, and Catherine had been trapped in the fire.

"Around midnight, Odette came to tell me that the smithy from Heron's Point was hiding in the stable. Emil begged me to return with him to the plantation at once. He said that Catherine was alive and that the child was coming."

Etienne closed his eyes and forced back the rage that thundered in his chest.

"He said that Phillipe had a gun and that he forced Catherine into the house all the while shouting that the two of you would pay for betraying him. Emil forced open the back door and heard a gunshot. He found Catherine lying on the floor near the stairs. The bullet had only grazed her shoulder, but Phillipe had set fire to the curtains leaving her to die there. Emil rescued her from the flames and took her in his cabin."

Etienne felt the breath rush from his chest.

"By the time we reached Heron's Point Catherine had given birth. I told Emil and his woman to keep her hidden until I returned for her and never to speak of this to anyone. I asked Catherine what she would name her child, and she said 'Lily.' I took a piece of charred wood from the cook fire and scratched that name on the shawl that I was wearing that night. I wrapped the baby in it and hid her in one of Emil's vegetable baskets. He and I took the child and returned to the city just before dawn. I left her on the steps of the convent."

Etienne buried his face in his hands. All those years his own child had been scarcely a stone's throw away. "How was Catherine able to leave New Orleans?"

"As soon as she was well enough, I arranged for passage on a ship to Charleston under the name of Kate Perrault. It was not so very different from her own name. I gave her enough money to take care of her needs, and I promised to send the child to her when it was safe.

"I convinced myself that I did it to protect you and Catherine and your child. But what I did was unforgivable. I ruined your life to save my son and my marriage. I was frantic and irrational in those days before you and your father could reach the city. I knew if you found out what your brother had done you would have killed him, and you would have hanged for it. It would have destroyed your father."

"Why didn't you send Lily to Catherine?" His face was a mask of sick confusion and disbelief. "Why that cursed letter instead?"

"Phillipe grew more despondent over the loss of Catherine as time passed. The sickness festered inside of him more violently than ever. I knew that in time it would destroy his reason completely, and he would harm you. I convinced your father to open the London office and to put you in charge of it. As soon as you were safely away, I wrote that terrible letter. I had to make sure Catherine never returned to New Orleans. So I told her the child had died."

"Did you hear from her after that?"

Celine shivered. "No but I was always afraid she would send someone to find where the child was buried. She knew I couldn't risk a burial in the city. Heron's Point was being sold and was the most obvious place to do what I had to do. I hired workmen from downriver to prepare a grave in the slave cemetery. Whoever happened upon it would have accepted it as proof that Lily was really dead."

Etienne pushed himself away from his chair and walked to the window. "Lily said that her mother read your letter every night until she died."

"I will never forgive myself for the torment she suffered," she whispered, "but I was afraid that once she had the child with her, the temptation to return to New Orleans might have become too great. I could not let you and your father find out what I had done—or have Phillipe discover that Catherine was still alive to bear witness against him. Nothing would have stopped him then. I think that he would have killed us all."

Celine grew quiet. Her eyes closed.

"Mother?"

"When my son took his own life, I refused to leave this house for months. Everyone thought I was grieving myself to death, even your father." A hoarse sob escaped her lips. "They could not have imagined that for the first time since Phillipe's birth, I slept peacefully, and without fear. You have every reason to hate such a mother, Etienne."

Etienne stared out into the growing darkness. "I'm not sure I can ever forgive you, but I will always try to remember that Lily is alive *because* of you. I'm going to bring her home. Her place is here with me. I have to believe that it was Catherine that led me to our daughter and that her spirit is here too."

"I pray that is true . . ."

At the sound of footsteps on the stairs, Louis and Estelle hurried toward the vestibule. Estelle reached for her husband's arm. The pain in Etienne's eyes frightened her.

"How is she?" Louis inquired anxiously.

"She's sleeping. Odette is with her."

"You look as if you could use some rest as well."

Etienne nodded wearily. "But first, there is something that I have to tell both of you."

An hour later they watched Etienne make his way back up the stairs. "We will return tomorrow, cousin," Louis called softly after him. "Come, my love." He reached for his wife's shawl. "Let's go home."

Estelle turned for him to place it about her shoulders. "Shouldn't we stay the night, Louis?" she whispered.

"No." His voice sounded unnaturally harsh. "At this moment, I have an overwhelming need to be at home with our children."

Later that night

"Miz Celine?" Odette's soft whisper echoed across the darkened room as she made her way toward the canopied bed. A globed candle burned low on the mantle.

"Miz Celine?"

The bed was empty. Odette glanced around warily. "Miz Celine, you in heah?"

Down the hallway, Etienne slept restlessly in a chair by the hearth. He bolted to his feet at the sound of footsteps running toward his room. He flung the door open. Odette's eyes were wide and fearful.

"Odette, what's wrong?"

"I went to look in on yore mam. She ain't in her room, Mastah 'Tienne. I cain't find her no place."

He pushed past her and hurried down the hallway. "Mother?" He glanced around Celine's room puzzled. "Wake the others. Search downstairs, and check the galleries."

Odette dashed for the door. He turned toward the staircase leading to the upper floor.

"Odette, wait!"

Midway to the landing lay the silk night shawl Celine had been wearing when he left her hours before. He looked beyond it into the darkness. "Hand me the lamp." He motioned toward a table near Celine's door. "Come with me."

Odette picked up the shawl and glanced about nervously as they made their way up the stairs.

"Why would Miz Celine come up heah? Nobody comes up heah."

"Mother?" His voice echoed in the darkness. A faded carpet muffled their footsteps as they started toward the last room at the end of the hallway.

"Mastah 'Tienne?" Odette's whispered. "Miz Celine ain't gonna be in the nursery. After Mistah Phillipe hang hisself in there, yore pa say nobody go there, ever! She wouldn't do what Mastah Andre told her not to."

He spied a brass key on the floor and reached for the latch. The lamp gave off a wavering light as he pushed against the door and entered the musty room. A candle lay beside Celine's outstretched hand.

"Oh my God!"

Odette peered from behind him and gasped. Etienne thrust the lamp at her, and dropped to his knees. "Mother? Mother!"

The servant backed toward the door, frightened by the way his arms tightened about Celine's limp form as he drew her against his powerful chest. "Mastah 'Tienne, you want I should send for the doctah?"

"No. Send for her priest," he whispered as he lifted his mother and carried her from the room.

Odette stumbled after him. Her wails echoed throughout the house.

Two months later

From the bridge of the *Saracen*, Etienne pulled the collar of his coat closer against the bitter cold and kept his eyes trained on the horizon. They would reach England in three days. It would be spring before he returned to Louisiana to merge his British fleet with the ships of the Cruz Shipping Line of New Orleans. By then, the changes to the house on Rue Royale would be complete.

The day after the funeral, he had returned to the nursery. The full weight of his loss crushed him as he knelt to retrieve a small garment he had overlooked when he carried Celine from there. She had come for the christening gown she had long ago stitched with her own hands. She must have packed it away the first time he sailed for England.

Closing his eyes, he could imagine the sounds of Phillipe's and Catherine's childish laughter as they once played in the nursery together. When he opened them again, there had been only the dusty and faded remnants of a dream, destroyed by the demons who claimed his brother's life in that room.

Spare no expense, he had instructed Louis. When he brought Lily home to stay, there must be no reminders of the tragedies that occurred in the house on Rue Royale.

Thirty-Two

Connie snipped the last thread and smoothed the infant's gown across her lap. She had sent word to Marylove and Johnny that she and Dan would visit the following week to deliver the layette she had prepared for their first child. Her fingers traced the delicate smocking beneath the collar. A sudden ache caused her throat to tighten. It could have been for her own child, hers and Charles's. How was it possible that he was dead? Victor Eden's letter had come four months back.

> *My dear Missus Wellington,*
>> *It is with deepest sorrow that I*
>> *inform you of the death of my son, Charles.'*

Her eyes stung with unshed tears. She stole a glance at Dan. His eyes were closed, and his chin rested upon his chest. He had come in from the fields early and been unusually quiet at dinner. He was pushing himself too hard, but Paul's wedding in three weeks would force him to rest. He would grumble fiercely at the prospect of traveling to the city.

And Davy would leave them soon. The house would echo with a sobering emptiness once again. Sarah had insisted the child remain in the country until she and Paul returned from their wedding trip. When he was old enough, he would be sent away to one of those dreadful boarding schools in the north. Was Paul so blind he couldn't see that his son meant nothing to the woman who was about to become his wife?

She stood, laid the gown aside, and approached Dan's chair. She bent to kiss his cheek then frowned.

"Dan, wake up," she whispered.

He stirred and looked around, dazed and confused. "What? Oh, Connie, I didn't intend to fall asleep."

She rubbed the back of his neck. His flesh felt warm. Normally, he carried Davy upstairs to bed in the evenings, but tonight he didn't protest when Iretta took the cross little man to the nursery and remained upstairs placating his fretful cries.

"Come, off to bed with you, sir."

"Just tired." He patted her hand absently, "but, I think I will go on up, if you don't mind." He rose stiffly and gave her a peck on the forehead.

She smiled. "I'll be along soon."

"Goodnight, sweetheart," he mumbled and walked unsteadily toward the stairs, his steps halting and lethargic.

She turned back to her chair as Maybelle bustled into the room.

"Constance, a game of cribbage before retiring? Oh do, please. I declare, but I believe we are in for more rain." She made straight for the table by the window.

Iretta vowed her younger sibling could converse on a number of subjects within the space of a single utterance, none of which made a particle of sense to anyone but Maybelle herself. *Cribbage, my dear. That's her passion.* Iretta had secretly confided her sister's weakness to Connie soon after her marriage to Dan. *And, don't be fooled by that silly prattle. Maybelle can be utterly ruthless.*

Maybelle slipped into her chair and withdrew a deck of worn cards from her pocket just as a crash sounded overhead. Iretta's cry sent Connie flying toward the stairs with Maybelle at her heels.

Iretta crouched over Dan's sprawled form beside the bed, working frantically to loosen his collar.

"Connie dropped to her knees and grasped her husband's hand, her eyes wide with fear. "Dan? He can't hear me. Daniel!" She pushed Iretta aside and gathered his head upon her lap and bent over him.

Iretta turned to her sister. "Maybelle, send for Mister Parrish. Something is terribly wrong with our boy!"

With a frightened cry, Maybelle hurried to do her bidding.

Minutes later, the overseer and the majordomo burst through the front door and bounded up the stairs. Elzy Parrish ordered the women to stand aside as he and the servant lifted Dan's unconscious form and carried him to his bed.

Connie glanced at the clock on the mantle. It had been hours since Iretta had dispatched Elzy Parrish to Charleston to fetch Paul. Maybelle's plea to send for Hadley Baker had prompted her frightened protest. *No, no, I want my brother. Paul won't let anything happen to Dan.*

Iretta stood at the foot of the bed, her features bleak and stern, her hands trembling beneath the folds of her skirt. Maybelle looked nigh on to fainting each time a moan emanated from the figure on the bed. Connie clasped Dan's hand and held it against her cheek. How could the sickness have come upon him so quickly?

"Connie?" The front door slammed and heavy footsteps bounded up the stairs.

"Paul!" Connie flung herself into her brother's arms as he and Elzy Parrish rushed into the room. "Oh, thank God, you're here."

He turned her gently aside and approached the bed. His heart sank at the sight of Dan's flushed features. He glanced at Elzy Parrish standing near the door and gave an imperceptible shake of his head.

Iretta did not miss the gesture. "What's wrong, Paul?"

Maybelle sprang from her chair and clutched her sister's arm. "Our Daniel is going to be all right, isn't he?"

Paul frowned. At Minerva's invitation, Hadley Baker and his sister had come to dinner at the Armstrongs a few days earlier. He had mentioned a sailor who had been brought to the waterfront clinic with a virulent fever. His two shipmates had left the stricken man by the door before anyone could question them. By the time the authorities reached the docks, the suspect vessel had put back out to sea.

"Have there been any strangers at Cottonwood in the past few days? Anyone from the city?"

Elzy Parrish nodded. "About four days back, a feller showed up 'round sundown asking for something to eat and a place to bed down for the night. Mister Dan said he was welcome to sleep in the barn and told him he could find somethin' to eat at the cookhouse. He claimed he wasn't feelin' too good, but as soon as he got some rest he'd be on his way."

"What happened to him?"

"Don't know. He was gone next mornin'."

Paul felt a sense of dread wash over him. The stranger could have deserted the same vessel Hadley had referred to, and brought the scourge upriver.

At that moment, a fretful cry from the nursery caused Connie to start toward the door. Paul's sharp command stopped her.

"Mister Parrish."

"Yes, sir?"

"I want you to take my son and the women to the city at once!"

"I cannot leave my husband!" Connie's response was indignant, disbelieving.

"Constance, in all likelihood Dan has yellow fever. Think what it will do to Mother if something should happen to you or Davy. There are servants to help here."

"No, I will not go!"

Iretta's stern voice momentarily calmed the terror that permeated the room. "I had the fever as a child, but not Maybelle." She glanced at her sibling. "She and Davy will go with Mister Parrish. I will stay, too. There could be others." She had voiced Paul's worst fear. If the sickness was already in the quarters, Cottonwood could suffer devastating losses.

Paul glanced from Connie to Iretta. He knew he would never persuade either of them to leave, but at least Davy and Maybelle would be safe in the city for now.

"Mister Parrish, take Miss Maybelle and the boy to my mother. We'll send for them when it's safe to return." He could imagine Adelaide's distress when Maybelle Wellington and her grandson arrived at her doorstep alone. Elzy Parrish would be hard pressed to stop her from returning to Cottonwood with him, but stop her he must.

Iretta placed her hands on Maybelle's frail shoulders. "Hurry along, sister, and gather your things." She gave her a swift hug and a gentle push toward the door.

With a whimper Maybelle fled from the room. A half-hour later, Paul stood at the window and watched the Wellington coach race toward the gates.

One day passed, and then another. The lamps on either side of the bed illuminated the jaundiced pallor of Dan's face. Connie bit her lip as she placed a clean compress on his forehead and whispered comforting words he could not hear. Paul reached for his brother-in-law's wrist and felt the rapid beat of his pulse. Suddenly, a choking gurgle brought forth a black and putrid expulsion of bile and blood. Dan slumped back upon his pillows. Connie turned away from the bed with a whimper. Iretta set the basin on the bedside table and gently began to cleanse her nephew's face, ignoring the sickness that gorged her own throat.

"Sweet, sweet boy," she crooned softly.

Paul touched Connie's shoulder, his frown deepening when she did not respond. She had become rigid, unable to comprehend the horror of what had just happened. He lifted her to her feet and wrapped her in his arms, holding her so that she would not shatter.

Iretta turned to the window and stared out into the darkness. In the distance, a great fire blazed near the quarters. Shadowed figures moved about the yard, ghostlike and silent, waiting and watching for a sign. A gentle breeze stirred the curtains, whispering past the tears that coursed down her face.

Charleston, October 28, 1829

The day after Dan's hurried burial in the cemetery at Cottonwood, Paul and his sister and Iretta Wellington returned to Charleston, leaving Elzy Parrish in charge of the quarters and the crops. In the beginning, a few callers came to the DuPre house to offer condolences to Connie and the Wellingtons, but quickly retreated to the safety of their own dwellings. The streets became deserted as the fever escaped the confines of the waterfront and began to advance toward the heart of the city. Casualties mounted each day. There were rumors of quarantine, of neighboring towns and cities barricading their roads against travelers seeking refuge from the pestilence.

The empty drawing room resonated with an uneasy silence. A single lamp cast flickering shadows onto the walls. Black crepe framed the windows and doorways and concealed the mirror above the mantle. Upstairs, the women stirred in fitful slumber. The tension about the house was palpable. Confinement was robbing them of their fragile restraint.

Paul felt restless and agitated as he drained his tumbler of brandy. He set the glass aside and walked out onto the gallery. No lights illuminated the windows of the other houses along the street. A whisper of unseasonably hot wind stirred the branches overhead. The moon laid dappled patterns of light across the floor.

There had been no word from the Armstrongs since a frightened servant delivered a letter from Minerva. The family would not venture out until it was safe once more. The dressmaker had taken sick, and Sarah's wedding gown lay unfinished on the cutting table at Madame Gerow's shop. Curiously, the postponement of the wedding had come as an unexpected relief.

"Paul?"

He turned, surprised by the hoarse whisper behind him. Connie clung to the door clad in her nightrail, her hair tangled about her shoulders. He reached for her hand to steady her. She was trembling as he enfolded her gently in his arms. Her flesh felt cold in spite of the lingering warmth of the night.

"What are you doing down here?" he whispered, laying his cheek against the top of her head. "You should be resting."

"I couldn't sleep."

He felt her fingers bite into his arm.

"Paul, it's my fault. I'm to blame for what happened to Dan."

"That's not true, Connie."

She rushed on in spite of his gentle protest. "The night he was stricken, I had just finished hemming a gown for Marylove's babe. I was wishing that I had made it for mine and Charles's child, and God punished me for my wickedness. He took my husband! Dan was so good, so decent and kind. I didn't realize how much I loved him, Paul, and now I can never tell him."

He felt the cry rising within her before she went limp in his arms. He swept her up and carried her inside. A light appeared at the top of the stairs. Adelaide held a candle aloft, her features mirrored her fright.

"Connie! Paul, what's wrong?"

"She fainted, Mother." He carried his sister into her room and laid her on the bed.

Adelaide placed the candle on a nearby table and knelt clasping her daughter's hand.

"Oh, my poor girl."

Paul walked to the window and flung it open. He stared out into the blackness. He had lost Emma, and now Connie had lost Dan. Would they ever feel whole again?

"Mastah Paul?"

Tilde's insistent whisper penetrated his sleep. He rubbed at his eyes and glanced across the room. Connie had not stirred. Adelaide slept beside her still holding her hand.

Tilde clasped her shawl closer about her and tapped his shoulder again. "Mastah Paul, you got a caller downstairs. It's Doctah Baker."

"What time is it?"

"Not yet first light," she whispered.

He rose stiffly from the chair and ran his fingers through his hair. What was Hadley Baker doing downstairs at this hour? "Ask him to wait in the study. I'll come right down."

"Yes, sir."

Hadley Baker stood at the window, staring into the darkness, his hands clasped behind his back. Paul was shocked at the man's appearance. He looked as if he hadn't slept in days.

"Tilde is bringing coffee."

The doctor nodded gratefully and sank into the chair in front of the desk.

"You look like hell." Paul's frank appraisal brought a hint of a smile to his lips.

"It's bad, Paul, real bad. We've suffered through epidemics before, but nothing to compare with this."

Paul took the chair behind the desk.

"The fever is spreading more quickly than anyone could have imagined. The apothecary's shelves are almost empty. Ships are refusing to put into port, and there's talk of burning the docks. Towns to the north and west of us are said to have barricaded their roads against our people fleeing from the city."

Paul's heart sank. Hadley was not given to exaggeration. The rumors were all true.

Hadley leveled a searching gaze at him. "We need you, Paul."

Their eyes locked, one pleading, the other suddenly wary. A flush of angry guilt suffused Paul's face.

"You don't know what you're asking."

"Asking?" Hadley gasped. "You misunderstand. I am demanding your help, because anything less would mock the seriousness of our plight. You are a damn good doctor who can make a difference to many."

"I couldn't save my own wife or her brother. I didn't make a difference to them. I gave them the best that was in me, and it wasn't enough."

"I understand how it must have hurt you."

"No, you don't. You haven't lost a wife or a brother."

For a moment, Hadley looked away. "My sister, Felicity, died last night. And her Louisa has taken sick."

"My God, Hadley. I am sorry." Hadley's sister had been widowed only the year before, and his niece was his joy. The child's death could destroy a lesser person, but, Hadley Baker was a healer by obsession and a man of unfathomable courage. Paul's shoulders slumped.

Hadley gripped the edge of the desk. "You must help us. These people are a part of you. If you turn your back on them, it will never be forgotten—or forgiven. Make no mistake about it."

Silence stretched between them. Grim-faced, Hadley pushed himself to his feet. He turned and started for the door and then swung about. "None of us can afford the luxury of personal grief. I have long counted you as my friend, admired you, and yes, even envied your skill at times. But the truth is that you have become a self-serving bastard and a coward." He threw up a hand and stalked toward the door. "I'll show myself out."

Tilde clutched the tray of coffee and cups and pressed herself against the wall. "Good day, Doctah," she whispered.

The front door slammed shut.

With an explosive oath, Paul reached for the inkwell on his desk and hurled it across the room.

An hour later, Tilde emerged from the kitchen with a tray of table settings. Adelaide and the others scarcely touched the meals she prepared these days. She sighed and hurried toward the dining room.

"Mastah Paul, where you goin'?" She slipped past him to deposit the tray of dishes onto the table and glanced suspiciously at the leather satchel he carried.

He turned and laid a hand on her shoulder. "Tell Mother I have gone to Hadley Baker's clinic. I don't know when I'll return, but she's not to worry."

"Oh, she ain't gonna like that. You know how she frets 'bout you and Miz Connie."

"Mother will be fine. Send for me if you need me, and do not let the women venture out."

She shook her head. "No, sir."

"Goodbye, Tilde."

"Bye, Mastah Paul. You come home soon."

The front door closed quietly behind him.

Hadley Baker knelt by the pallet and reached for the patient's wrist. Gussie Putnam was one of the lucky ones. He pulled the thin covering over her shoulders and started to rise. The figure standing in the doorway glared at him defiantly. Hadley pushed himself to his feet and walked across the room. Slowly, he offered his hand. He had said some harsh things earlier, things a friend should never utter to another. The hand that closed about his own was strong and assured. The dark eyes that searched his face were no longer filled with anger, but determination.

"Doctor DuPre, thank God."

Thirty-Three

Lily stared down at the figure on the narrow cot. Polly pulled a worn quilt over the scullery maid's body. The two left the attic and made their way downstairs. Polly hurried to the kitchen to break the news to the other servants and arrange for burial of the body in the household cemetery near the back fence.

Lily made her way to her room and stripped away her soiled garments. She slipped into a wrapper and pushed open the doors leading onto the outside gallery. The city lay beneath an acrid blanket of smoke from the fires that burned day and night. But, the number of victims continued to rise daily in spite of the attempt to hold the pestilence at bay.

She had witnessed firsthand what the dreaded yellow jack could do once it invaded a household. The young scullery maid was the first at Swan House to fall victim to the fever. All those who had never previously contracted the disease could still die within days. She turned and rushed back into the house calling for Thaddeus and Jack.

"Leave?" Jack glanced at Thaddeus across the table and eyed the cards in his hand.

"It's the only way you will all be safe," Lily insisted. "Franklin says that all roads leading north and west have been barricaded. Everyone is being turned back. If we can find a boat to transport the household to Savannah, you will be able to leave the city."

Jack gave an exasperated sigh. "The waterfront is under quarantine. And where are we going to find a boat, lass?"

"There has to be a way." Lily turned to Thaddeus. "You must know someone who can help us."

Thaddeus stroked his moustache and frowned. "The Willows, maybe."

"What are ye saying?" Jack eyed him skeptically.

"It's an abandoned rice plantation 'bout three miles south of the city. The house burned several years back, but there's a dock where a steamer can tie up. I know a trader near Cutler's Landing who might be willing to risk it. Kate did him a few good turns through the years. But he will expect to be well paid for his trouble."

"Anything." Lily's eyes flashed with hope. "Just find him, and quickly."

Thaddeus looked at Jack and shrugged. "Guess I'll be back after dark." He pushed himself to his feet and started for the door.

"Jack, have Xavier and the stablehands bring the coach and the carriages around. You will need the wagons for the trunks and provisions. Polly will take charge of the packing. You have to be ready to leave as soon as Thaddeus returns."

Jack followed Thaddeus to the door and turned. His eyes narrowed suspiciously. "Ye keep saying 'you.' Ye've not said 'we'."

"Not all of us will go."

"What do ye mean?"

"I had the fever as a child."

"No!" Jack's eyes flashed angrily. He retraced his steps and grasped her arms. "I'll not leave ye here, woman."

"Jack, please. You and Thaddeus must see after the others." She pulled away and held him at arm's length.

"Georgette will not allow it," he countered, satisfied to have settled the matter.

Lily gave him a push. "Hurry. There isn't much time."

Later that night

Georgette stood on the verandah glaring down at the scowling figure at the bottom of the steps. "I am not going, Thaddeus," she declared. "If Lily refuses to go, don't think that I intend to leave this house either. Kate would expect me to stay here and look after things."

Thaddeus's frown deepened. He glanced past her and arched a thick brow. Lily gave a slight nod. He stalked up the steps, lifted Georgette off her feet, and deposited her across his shoulder. Her muffled shriek echoed through the darkness as he pushed her into the coach and climbed in after her.

Jack hurried across the vestibule toward the front door and stopped short. "Fiona?"

She stepped from the shadows and placed a cautioning finger to her lips. "Shhh, be quiet. I'm staying too, Jack. Now, go on with ye before someone thinks to ask after me."

He stared at her curiously. "You're a brave lass. Take care of Lily for me?"

She nodded and watched him hurry down the steps and climb into one of the carriages. Within minutes, the night had swallowed up the caravan. She waited for Lily to enter the house.

"Fiona, what are you doing here?"

"Now, don't ye be angry. Jack said I was to look after ye."

Lily gave her friend's arm a gentle squeeze. "I am glad you stayed," she admitted and brushed away the tears that welled up in her eyes.

Two days later

Fiona glanced at the food that remained untouched on Lily's breakfast plate. She laid her napkin aside.

"I know what you're thinking, and 'tis a foolish notion. The waterfront is no place for ye."

"I was not . . ." Lily gestured helplessly, knowing her protest was dismissed before she uttered it.

"They will turn ye away."

"But, I can help. I'm a good nurse"

Fiona sighed and pushed away from the table. "I'll have the gig brought 'round."

"I'll be right down." Lily darted past her and hurried from the room.

Fiona shook her head. Jack would never forgive her if anything happened to Lily. She felt a familiar stab of jealousy pierce her heart.

A few minutes later, Lily emerged from the house and stopped abruptly. Fiona held the reins lightly in her hands.

"Well, ye didn't think I would let ye go by y'self, did ye?"

The two rode in silence through the deserted streets. Their eyes stung from the fires that burned behind every house. Infected bedding and clothing had been left to smolder while fearful occupants barricaded themselves behind their shuttered windows. Fiona urged the mare down a narrow alley. Lily clutched her medicine box tightly as they approached the waterfront clinic. Lone riders, carriages filled with the sick, and wagons used to carry away the dead, all surged toward the waterfront from every direction. Cries and curses rang out as panic threatened to overtake the crowd. On either side of the doorway, leantos had been hastily erected to shelter those who were forced to wait their turn outside. About it all was the choking stench of sickness, fear, and death.

Lily climbed down from the gig.

Fiona shot her a doubtful look.

Stephen Flynn spied the two of them and shouldered his way through the crowd. "What are you ladies doing here?"

"We came to offer our help." Fiona glanced about nervously.

Lily reached for the medicine box. "Georgette and most of the household left for Savannah yesterday. Those of us who have had the fever stayed behind."

"You will be a blessing to Hadley and the others, for sure. Only a few volunteers are still able to come. Most are sick or keeping bedside vigils themselves. Three doctors arrived from Norfolk yesterday, and a Godsend they have been, too. Hadley and Paul are exhausted."

"Doctor DuPre is here?" Lily's eyes widened in surprise.

Stephen nodded. "He came two days ago, and he has hardly slept since."

"Oh," she murmured.

Stephen grasped both of them by the arm and propelled them through a side door into the clinic. "You can't imagine how relieved they are going to be to see the two of you. You wait here. I'll just go and fetch Hadley."

"What are you two doing here?" Paul stared at Lily and Fiona in disbelief. Fiona's temper flared beneath his unspoken rebuke. Only Hadley's and Stephen's hurried approach silenced her scathing retort.

"Ladies, Stephen says you are here to offer your help." Hadley grasped each of their hands in turn. "God knows, we need every able body. We scarcely have enough medicines or pallets to accommodate the patients who are here, and more arrive by the hour."

Lily emitted a sigh of relief at the man's obvious gratitude, while Fiona fixed Paul with a glare. He turned abruptly and started across the room.

"Hadley, a word with you!" he called over his shoulder.

"He looks angry," Lily whispered.

Stephen shook his head. "Both men have pushed themselves beyond their limits, I'm afraid. Now, if you will excuse me, I have to get home to Grace. She hasn't felt well since last night. God bless you both."

Hadley was incredulous. "You cannot be serious! You are actually suggesting that we refuse the help of two perfectly capable women when our need is so critical?"

"Do you know who they are?" Paul's voice took on a suspicious hint of desperation.

"I wager that everyone in this room recognizes Kate Perrault's daughter, and I am equally certain none are of a mind to refuse her help."

Paul's shoulders slumped. Hadley was right. If Lily Perrault had once been a nurse as she claimed that day at Saint Bartholomew's, there was much good that she could do. And that Titan with her looked equally capable and determined.

For hours, the grim procession continued to make its way toward the clinic. Lily wiped her face on an apron one of the volunteers had provided. Hadley Baker would soon have to find another place to house his patients. She made her way to the opposite side of the room, knelt beside Fiona, and whispered her plan.

Fiona's eyes widened. "Swan House? Ah, Lily, I'm not at all certain that's a good idea. What would Georgette say?"

By the time Fiona followed her into Hadley's cluttered office, Lily had offered Swan House as a second refuge for the patients who could no longer crowd into the clinic. Fiona groaned inwardly. Relief transformed Hadley Baker's haggard features. Paul made no effort to conceal his irritation.

"Hadley, perhaps the ladies should reconsider. Swan House is, after all, their home."

Hadley's patience began to give way visibly. He turned to Lily and Fiona. "Doctor Oliver Creighton arrived with the volunteers from Norfolk yesterday. I'll ask him to accompany you back to Swan House. I think we can spare one of his nurses as well. We will start collecting what supplies that we can spare and preparing the patients for transport."

Lily clutched the hand he extended to her. "We will do our best, Doctor. Xavier and the stablehands will return with the wagons." As she and Fiona hurried toward the door, she turned to see the two men arguing.

"No one will permit their people to be taken there. Damnit, Hadley, it's a gaming house, not a hospital. Those women are not prepared."

A cold veil dropped over Hadley's features. "They will go, Paul, when they learn that I have entrusted my niece to Miss Perrault's care."

"Louisa? But, why?" Miraculously, the child had taken a turn for the better. To move her now could jeopardize her recovery.

"By giving her over to Lily Perrault and Fiona O'Flarety, I'm letting these prideful fools know that it's all right to go to Swan House. God knows, they will all be better off for it." Hadley rubbed his hand across his brow. "Now, if you will excuse me, I need to have a word with Oliver Creighton."

The DuPre house, November 9, 1829

Paul picked absently at the food on his plate. It had been a week since he had joined Hadley at the clinic. The arrival of two additional doctors from Boston that morning had allowed him to return home for a few hours.

With the help of Lily Perrault and Fiona O'Flarety, Oliver Creighton continued to accomplish small miracles at Swan House. *Saints!* Creighton had stoutly declared their worth to Stephen, and bade him relate their good progress to Hadley and his staff.

Word of Lily's generosity and compassion swept through the city with an urgency equal to the fever itself. Adelaide greeted the news with shock and dismay. Connie frowned with each denouncement her mother uttered, and cast embarrassed glances at Iretta Wellington across the dinner table.

"It's shameful," Adelaide jabbed her fork viciously at her food, "that any self-respecting person would allow themselves to be taken to that horrible place!"

Connie kept her eyes trained on her plate and struggled to hide the pain her mother's words inflicted upon her heart.

"Imagine, going to Hadley Baker and forcing him to accept her help. Well, what was he to do, I ask you? Nothing but the most desperate need would ever have prompted him to send God fearing people to a gaming house. Why, I would not be at all surprised if his reputation is sullied after this. It's disgraceful!"

"Mother, please," Connie whispered and twisted the linen napkin in her lap.

"I'm sorry, Constance, but some things cannot be condoned. Tomorrow, I intend to personally go down to that clinic and demand—"

"You will do no such thing!" Paul threw his napkin onto the table and pushed himself to his feet.

"I beg your pardon?"

"You heard me, Mother. You will not burden Hadley Baker or his staff with your petty grievances. None of you will leave this house until I tell you it's safe to do so. Do I make myself clear?"

"Oh, absolutely, dear," Maybelle chirped, grateful that Paul had effectively silenced his mother's tiresome diatribe.

Iretta gave a tight smile and rose, beckoning to Davy. "You are right, Paul, and I am about to take your son upstairs for the night. Say goodnight to your papa, Davy."

The boy scampered behind her skirt. Paul did not attempt to coax him to his side. He nodded as Iretta grasped Davy's hand and ushered him from the room.

Paul turned back to the others, noting the stubborn tilt of his mother's chin, and the anger that burned in her eyes. "I think I'll go up to bed," he said. "I have to be back at the clinic tomorrow morning."

Connie nodded. Her anger mounted as she listened to his halting steps on the stairs.

"Mother, how could you?"

"Whatever do you mean? I declare, Constance, but you are acting very strange this evening."

"Paul has been away for days. None of us can imagine what he has endured. He's exhausted. Do you think it matters to him that Lily Perrault—?"

"Of course, it matters."

"Well, I am sorry to disagree with you, Mother, but I think that Miss Perrault has done a very noble thing."

"I don't believe what I'm hearing," Adelaide gasped and rose. "After all that's happened there—your own father, and then Etienne. Oh!" She fumbled for the linen tucked into her sleeve and pressed it against her lips. "I'm sorry. I don't know what came over me."

"So, that's what this is *really* all about."

Adelaide sniffed and struggled to compose herself. "I think I should retire as well. Are you coming?"

"In a little while."

"Very well. Good night, dear." Adelaide touched her daughter's shoulder and frowned. Constance should never wear black. She turned and hurried toward the stairs.

Connie closed her eyes, grateful for the solitude. What had compelled Lily Perrault to sacrifice herself and all that she possessed to care for those who openly scorned her? And why did the mention of her name affect Paul so?

Connie pushed away from the table and hurried toward the hallway. "Tilde!" Her whisper echoed down the silent corridor. The servant materialized out of the shadows.

"What you want, child?"

"Tell Caleb to bring the coach around."

"Where you goin' at this hour? You know what Mastah Paul done told you!"

"My brother has no say over what I do, or where I go. Only my husband had that right. I am going to Swan House. I have to do this for Dan. Do you understand, Tilde?"

Tilde heard the desperation in her voice and gathered her close for a moment. She stood back and nodded.

"Constance?"

Iretta made her way down the stairs. "Where are you going?" She eyed Connie suspiciously. "What do you have to do for Daniel?"

Connie's shoulders stiffened. "I am going to Swan House to offer my help to Lily Perrault, and no one is going to stop me."

"Feel that way about it, do you?"

Connie nodded, waiting for the reproach that was sure to come. Iretta could be formidable in her convictions, and she was about to forbid her to go.

"Then, I'm going with you. Tilde, go find Caleb."

Swan House

"Miss Lily?" The servant made her way along the narrow path between the pallets to where Lily knelt.

"What is it, Sauchie?"

"Two ladies heah. Say they want to see you."

"Where is Fiona? See if she can help them. We don't have room for two more, but . . ."

"They ain't sick."

"Then why are they here?"

"Don' know, just say they have to see you."

Lily set the basin aside and rose to her feet. "Very well. You stay here and keep an eye on Miz Hamilton, and, try not to disturb her son. He needs all the rest he can get before she wakes up again."

Sauchie nodded and knelt beside the pallet of Charmaine Hamilton as Lily made her way toward the dimly lit vestibule.

The two women turned as she approached. One was older than the other, and both were garbed in black. Lily sighed. There were so many in mourning now.

"I'm Lily Perrault." She right her specs and clasped her hands at her waist, refusing to lower her eyes beneath the older woman's stern appraisal. Iretta Wellington smiled inwardly. Honest and forthright, this girl. She liked that.

Connie thrust out her hand. "I'm Constance Wellington, Miss Perrault, and, this is my aunt, Iretta Wellington."

Paul DuPre's sister! Whatever was she doing here? "What can I do for you, Miz Wellington? When Sauchie said there were two ladies here, I just assumed . . ."

Connie offered a wan smile. "We would like to offer our help, if there is any way you can make use of us. We are willing to do anything."

"Help? Oh, yes. I hardly know how to thank you."

"No thanks are necessary, Miss Perrault." Iretta grasped Lily's outstretched hand in hers. "You just tell us what you want us to do."

"Please, do not think me too forward but it might be easier if you just called me Lily."

"And you can call me Iretta."

"And Connie."

Lily smiled at that and nodded. "Iretta and Connie, it is."

Thirty-Four

"They did *what?*"

Adelaide paled. She had never seen her son so angry.

Maybelle peered fearfully over her shoulder. "Oh, I'm sure they will be quite all right, dear. After all, Iretta is very capable. She would never allow any harm to come to dear Constance."

Paul leveled a disbelieving glare upon the two women. He had gone upstairs the evening before desperate for sleep only to awaken to the news that Connie and Iretta had slipped away in the night, intent upon offering their services to none other than Lily Perrault! What did it matter that her bravery and compassion for the citizens of Charleston had elevated her above the taint of Kate Perrault's tawdry reputation? Or that opening Swan House to the sick and dying had transformed the jezebel into a heroine throughout the city? Constance had no business in such a place. And Iretta, for God's sake, what had possessed her to become part of such a scheme?

"Caleb!" His summons reverberated off the walls.

"Comin', Doctah Paul." Adelaide's driver hurried into the room and glanced nervously from mother to son.

"We have to fetch my sister and Miz Iretta home. Bring the coach."

"Figgered you was gonna go afta' the ladies. Coach is a'waitin' at the gate."

Adelaide emitted a sigh of relief. "Constance should never have put herself in jeopardy or involved poor Iretta. I can't imagine what she was thinking." She and Maybelle followed Paul and the driver from the room.

"Do hurry back, dear. I'll have Tilde prepare a nice breakfast for all of us, and—"

Maybelle flinched as the front door slammed shut. The confusion in the DuPre household unnerved her. Once this dreadful quarantine ended, she and Iretta and Constance must return at once to the peace and quiet of the country.

Swan House

Iretta handed a basin of clean water to her niece and arched her aching back. Connie nodded her thanks and turned back to her patient. Grace Flynn thrashed against the hands that attempted to restrain her. Reverend Flynn had left his wife's side to post a letter on the chance it would reach the Pickerings in Savannah. Fearing quarantine early on, they had sent Ginny to Grace's relations. Cousin Rupert must not allow their daughter to return to Charleston until the fever had disappeared from the city.

Iretta glanced toward the door and gasped. "Constance, Paul is here, and he's coming this way! He looks very angry."

They watched him cross the room with purposeful strides. "Connie, I have come to take you and Iretta home." He grasped his sister's arm and pulled her to her feet. "You're not strong enough for this."

Connie shot a pleading look at Iretta. "No, I can't go. I won't."

"Constance, you have given Mother a terrible fright."

"Please." Connie swayed suddenly and clutched at his arms. Iretta reached for her, alarmed at her sudden pallor.

"Perhaps Paul is right, my dear. Go along home. I will stay with Lily and the others."

Lily? Paul was struck by the unexpected familiarity. Not a month before, Iretta Wellington would have crossed to the opposite side of the street to avoid sharing a walkway with Lily Perrault. Even she had fallen under the witch's spell.

"Neither of you are staying," he gritted. "This is not a hospital. It's a gaming house."

Connie's eyes flashed with a familiar fire. "What does it matter where we are? Look around you. These people are our friends and family. Aunt Charmaine and Clarissa Pardee came last night. And Miz Grace Flynn just this morning." She fought back tears. "Go home, Paul. Tell mother that we are fine."

"Connie, I—"

"Excuse me," she whispered. "I have to see to Miz Grace."

Paul's lips compressed into a tight line. He turned on his heel and started for the door.

"Doctor DuPre?" Oliver Creighton hurried toward him. "Thank goodness Doctor Baker was able to send help. We desperately need another pair of hands."

Paul scowled at the man who blocked his escape and ignored his outstretched hand. "I am not staying, Creighton. I came for my sister, but she refuses to leave," he snapped.

"I see. Then I won't detain you. Mohab can show you out."

Paul bristled with anger at the dismissal, but before he could reply, another voice silenced his retort.

"If you will wait in the vestibule, I will send Connie and Iretta to you." Lily reached up to right the small spectacles on her nose and shifted a basket of linens against her hip. Dark circles ringed her eyes.

His gaze traveled the length of her plain homespun gown and back to her face. No practiced smile relieved the grim set of her jaw. Her features were pale with fatigue, her hands red and swollen. This was not the strumpet who had sobbed into her lace handkerchief as her driver hurried her away from the *Saracen*, but the woman he had first met at Saint Bartholomew's. She brushed past him, handing off the laundered sheets to one of the servants. When she approached the two women who hovered over Grace Flynn, Iretta shook her head, clearly unwilling to leave. Connie rose to her feet and turned. Paul could sense his sister's grief rushing in upon her.

She had come to Swan House seeking some measure of solace, and he was about to rob her of that small bit of comfort. Against his will, he met Lily's straightforward gaze. There was no condemnation there, only a slight frown that signaled the end of her patience. His shoulders slumped, and he inwardly branded himself a fool.

"Mohab."

The majordomo approached cautiously. "Sir?"

"Tell my driver that he is to return home without us. We will all be staying for a while. Send word to Doctor Baker at the Waterfront Clinic that I'll be assisting Oliver Creighton for a few days." He turned back to the three women. They watched silently as he removed his coat and laid it across his arm. "Creighton says he can use another pair of hands."

"Oh, Paul," Connie smiled through her tears and walked into his arms.

Iretta cleared her throat. "I have to help Fiona," She declared gruffly.

Lily's lips curved into a hint of a smile that disappeared instantly. "Stephen!"

Paul spun around catching Stephen Flynn as he crumpled toward the floor. Lily sank to her knees beside him calling his name.

"Grace?" He closed his eyes, his plea unspoken.

"Sauchie, Polly, fetch blankets and place them next to Miz Grace."

Swan House, November 15, 1829

Paul walked to the study at the end of the hallway. It was a place to briefly escape the horrors that lay beyond the door. Lily was there, staring out the window, silent and unmoving. She did not turn as he approached, but he knew she sensed his presence. He reached out to touch her and let his hand drop, afraid that any gesture would shatter the fragile veneer that cloaked her grief.

"The Flynns were fine people. You did everything you could. Don't blame yourself for something you couldn't help." He finished awkwardly.

She had labored tirelessly over Grace and Stephen, almost obsessively. It was curious how familiar they were with each another. Yet, it seemed an unlikely friendship. Grace had preceded Stephen in death by only a few hours, and Lily had fought for the man's life until the end.

Lily turned slowly and crossed the room, letting her fingers trail across the desk. Stephen and Georgette had often met here in secret, and she had left them to their work. They had decided it was best if she knew nothing of their plans, and she had been grateful for the reprieve. What a cruel blow the news would be to Georgette and Ginny Flynn when her letters reached them in Savannah.

"Can I get you anything?"

She shook her head, surprised at his concern.

"Paul!" Connie stood silhouetted in the doorway. "Mother sent Caleb to fetch us home. It's Davy. He has the fever. Iretta is waiting outside." She gestured helplessly, her voice broke.

Paul felt a chill wash over him. Paralyzing fear held him fast until Lily grasped his arm and pushed him toward the door.

"Go! We will send Xavier with supplies, everything that you will need." She watched the two of them hurry down the hallway and then dashed off to find Fiona.

Thirty-Five

Paul gently lifted his son so that Connie could strip the soiled gown from the boy's body and replace it with a clean one. His sister's fear was as palpable as his own. Davy was sinking deeper into a shadowed world where few survived. Paul laid him back onto his bed. He walked unsteadily to the window and pushed it open. Outside, wisps of wood smoke lingered in the gathering twilight. Many of the fires that had burned across the city for weeks were being extinguished as the fever continued to abate.

He shook his head to clear the distorted images that wavered in front of him and felt the first signs of sickness rising in his throat.

Connie glanced up and circled the bed, alarmed. Her brother's face was flushed, and his hand trembled as he turned and reached out to her.

"Paul?"

"Send for Iretta," he whispered, collapsing onto the chair next to his son's bed.

"Oh, no!" She turned and dashed into the hallway. "Iretta!"

At the sound of her cry, Adelaide and Iretta sprang from the settee and rushed to the stairs.

"What is it, Constance?" Iretta gripped the newel post. "What's wrong?"

Adelaide swayed. "It's Davy. He's dead."

"Paul has the fever," Connie cried.

"Stay here, Adelaide. Constance and I will get him into bed. You are not strong enough." Iretta rushed up the stairs and disappeared into Paul's room.

Maybelle shuffled into the vestibule, rubbing her eyes. "My goodness, what's all the commotion about?"

"It's Paul. He's sick." Adelaide sank down onto the steps. "Oh, Maybelle, whatever are we to do now?"

Maybelle glanced about surprised. No one ever asked her for advice. "Tilde! Come quickly. Miz Addie needs you!"

The housekeeper hurried down the hallway, drawn by Maybelle's cry. "What's goin' on heah?"

"It's Paul," Maybelle wailed, and gestured toward Adelaide's crumpled form.

Tilde knelt and grasped her mistress by the hands and pulled her to her feet. "You come with me, Miz Addie. Don' you worry about yore menfolk. They gonna be just fine."

The next day

Connie cradled her nephew in her arms and studied Iretta's haggard features. The older woman slept fitfully in a chair by the hearth. Davy's bed had been moved into Paul's room the night before, and they took turns tending to them both. The child had been less fretful, but Paul's condition continued to worsen throughout the night. She and Iretta were going to need help, and soon.

Iretta stirred and blinked. "Oh, Constance, forgive me. I didn't mean to leave it all to you." She tried to rise and sank back in the chair with a groan.

Connie laid her nephew on his bed, relieved that he had not awakened. "Iretta, I'm going to fetch Sarah. She should be here."

Iretta arched her brow doubtfully. "Do you think she will come?" There had been no messages from the Armstrongs since Minerva's note postponing the wedding.

Connie frowned. "Why wouldn't she? If it hadn't been for the fever, she and Paul would be married now."

"You go along then, and hurry back. I don't want to call on Tilde unless we have to. She's worn plumb to the bone tending to all of us."

"I won't be long." Connie reached for her cloak and rushed toward the stairs.

"Constance, where are you going?" Adelaide emerged from her room and hurried to intercept her daughter.

"To the Armstrongs to fetch Sarah," she whispered. "Paul needs her. You should be resting."

"I can't sleep." Adelaide's eyes were dark, her movements listless, evidence of yet another fitful night.

"Please try." Connie squeezed her arm gently. "I'll be back as soon as I can."

A coach and a wagon waited in front of the Armstrong residence as servants hurried from the house, their arms filled with boxes and trunks. Connie guided the gig alongside the fence and secured the mare's reins to the hitching post.

"Linus?"

Brewster Armstrong's majordomo turned. A worried frown creased his features. He thrust a clutch of hatboxes at one of the passing servants. "Mornin', Miz Wellington."

"Are the Armstrongs leaving?"

"Mastah Brewster and the ladies goin' down to Savannah."

She turned and hurried to the door, colliding with Sarah as she emerged from the house.

"Sarah! Thank goodness I got here in time. Paul and Davy are both sick, and we need your help desperately." Without thinking, she grasped Sarah's arm causing a silver cask to tumble from her hands. With a cry, Sarah fell to her knees and scrambled to collect the jewels scattered across the steps.

"Father has arranged for a boat to take us to Savannah if we can reach Cutler's Landing by midday. I absolutely will not spend another day in this wretched place."

"But what about Paul and Davy?" Connie stared at her in disbelief.

"I can't think about them now. What if I should get sick myself? Bernice, fetch the rest of my hatboxes, all of them, do you hear!"

Brewster Armstrong dashed past the two women, with his sister on his heels. "Sarah, come along," he barked over his shoulder. "We must not be late."

"Coming!" Sarah sprang to her feet clutching her baubles and ran after her father. Connie walked to the gate and watched the two conveyances carrying the Armstrongs and their belongings race down the street. Linus followed her and handed her up into the gig. His shook his head as he placed the reins in her hands.

"Mighty sorry, Miz Wellington."

"Constance?" Honora hurried across the room as her niece entered the house. "Where is Sarah? Addie said you went to fetch her. We came as soon as Caleb brought the news about Paul." Her voice trailed off as she glanced at her twin.

Connie shook her head. "She wouldn't come."

"What do you mean she would not come?" Adelaide demanded.

"The Armstrongs are on their way to Savannah. Sarah said she would not stay in Charleston another day. They left me standing at the gate."

"Why, I have never heard anything so monstrous." Honora bristled.

Adelaide's eyes flashed angrily. "That family is no longer welcome in this house. Or anywhere else in Charleston if I have anything to say about it."

Nathan rolled his eyes. By the time the twins spread the word about the Armstrong's untimely defection, Brewster might just as well keep his womenfolk in Savannah.

Connie rubbed her hands across her eyes. "I have to go up to Iretta," she whispered and turned toward the stairs.

"Can you believe it?" Honora watched her niece make her way up the stairs.

Connie knelt beside Iretta's chair. Davy's eyes were open. His flesh felt damp and cool to the touch. She glanced up hopefully. "The fever's broken?"

Iretta nodded and smiled. "It seems so."

Connie moved to the other bed. She grasped her brother's hand and held it against her cheek. "Oh, please, Paul, please get well soon," she whispered. "Davy needs you. We all do."

"Lily?" His voice was barely a whisper.

Connie felt the slightest pressure in his grasp. Iretta raised her brow and gave Connie a questioning look.

Connie nodded, a flash of hope transforming her features. "It's not Sarah he wants. He's asking for Lily!"

"You wait right here, Constance. I'll be back soon."

"Iretta, where are you going?"

"To Swan House." She deposited Davy on his bed and rushed from the room.

"Addie, with or without your permission, I intend to ask—beg, if necessary—Lily Perrault to return with me to help care for Paul and Davy. That young woman does not possess a self-serving bone in her body. If anyone can bring them through this, she can."

"Iretta Wellington, you will do no such thing. I will not allow that creature in my house, no matter the reason. I forbid it, do you hear me?"

Iretta planted her fists on her waist. "Adelaide, I have never raised my voice in anger to another woman of my station, and it pains me that you are the first, but you cannot put your feelings above the life of your own son. Why, that's the most mean spirited—"

"Enough!" Nathan stepped between the two women and raised his hands for silence. "This is not the time for petty squabbling. Iretta, Simon will drive you to Swan House."

"Thank you, Nathan." Iretta turned on her heel and stalked from the room.

Nathan leveled a stern frown at his sister-in-law. It was time to take matters into his own hands. Paul's life might depend upon it.

Honora's chin trembled. Nathan had never spoken to her sister so harshly. Adelaide grasped her hand and fixed her brother-in-law with a malevolent glare. And wisely kept silent.

Swan House

Lily stirred the meager fare on her plate. Now that all the patients were gone and the fever appeared to be in retreat, a heavy silence had settled about the house. In the ballroom, Polly and Sauchie were gathering up the soiled bedding for the firepit. She sighed, imagining the outcry when Georgette and the others returned to find Swan House stripped of its finery, down to the velvet draperies they had turned into makeshift blankets.

Charmaine Hamilton had been the last to leave. She had impulsively grasped Lily's hands as her sons carried her litter to the door. *You must come to tea, my dear,* she had insisted. But, Lily knew that simple declaration of kindness was nothing more than the words of a woman grateful to be alive. It would be different once they all returned to the normalcy of their lives. She and Fiona would be remanded to their rightful places, no matter the miracles they had performed in this house.

There had been no miracles for some. She brushed angrily at the tears that suddenly sprang to her eyes.

"Miss Lily?"

"What is it, Sauchie?"

"Miz Wellington heah to see you."

Lily turned as Iretta rushed into the room. The fearful look on the older woman's face sent a shiver of dread along her spine. Connie was not with her. Lily gripped the edge of the table and started to rise. "Iretta, what's wrong?"

"Paul has the fever." Iretta caught her hands in a painful grip. "I would not trouble you, my dear, but we need your help desperately. Oh, please say you will return to the house with me."

Lily's heart plummeted, and she sank back upon her chair. "Adelaide DuPre will never permit me to enter her house, not even to help her son."

Iretta's lips tightened in a determined line. "Oh, yes, she will, my girl. Nathan Claiborne will see to it."

"Iretta, you're back!" Fiona hurried across the room.

"I have come for Lily. Paul is dreadfully sick."

"Oh, no. Well, she had best collect her medicine box and be off. We can take care of things here."

Lily glanced from one to the other. "Are you sure?"

Fiona gave her hand a reassuring squeeze. "Go, and send word if ye need anything."

"I'll only be a minute." Lily sprang to her feet and hurried toward the stairs.

Iretta dabbed at her eyes. "You are a saint, Fiona. I was afraid I wouldn't be able to persuade her."

"I told her what she wanted to hear."

Adelaide stiffened at the sound of the Claiborne's coach clattering to a stop at the front gate. She glanced nervously at her sister and then at Nathan's stony countenance. Surely, Iretta had returned alone. That Perrault woman would not presume to—.

Nathan strode toward the vestibule and drew Lily into the room. "Thank you for coming, my dear. We are all very grateful for your help." There was an edge to his voice, a subtle warning to Adelaide that any unseemly lack of courtesy would not be tolerated.

Stung by the forceful tone of her husband's voice earlier, Honora gathered her courage and moved to his side. "Yes, it's very kind of you." She flushed deeply, imagining Adelaide's smoldering eyes boring into her back. Instinctively, she grasped Nathan's arm and sighed with relief as his hand closed protectively over hers.

Lily's heart constricted, remembering Iretta's declaration as they rushed from Swan House to the waiting coach. *Paul needs you. He called your name. I heard him myself, and so did Constance.*

"Lily!" Connie hurried down the stairs and impulsively clasped her friend in a fierce hug. "I knew you would come."

"How are they?" Lily drew back and searched her face anxiously.

Connie reached for her hand. Lily was frightened to be in this house and more frightened of what awaited her upstairs. "Come with me."

"Miss Perrault." Adelaide's voice halted their ascent. They both turned as she approached the stairs. Adelaide searched the features of her unwelcome guest. They were right, all those who had seen her. Her resemblance to Kate was uncanny. Yet, there was a refinement about her that hinted at a heritage far above her station. Even now, devoid of jewels and clad in the plainest of gowns, the gossips had failed to do her justice.

"Sister?"

Adelaide felt Honora's hand on her arm. She was conscious of the awkward silence that filled the room. "Please," her voice trembled. "help my son."

"I will do all that I can," Lily replied softly and followed Connie up the stairs, not waiting to see Honora Claiborne enfold her sister in her arms or to hear Adelaide's sobs.

Thirty-Six

Lily approached Paul's bed and gently smoothed the bedcovers, never taking her eyes from his face. Though he slept, he seemed to sense that she was there. His restless movements ceased beneath her touch.

"Paul seems better."

Lily snatched her hand away from the quilt. "Yes, and Davy, too." Her smile softened as she turned toward the small bed near the window.

Connie responded with a weary sigh. "I think I'll go to my room for a while. I don't have your strength, Lily. Wake me if you need me?"

Lily nodded and closed the door after her. Connie had seldom left her side since she arrived. Paul's sister seemed determined to prevent a chance encounter between herself and Adelaide, and there had been none. Paul and his son were getting stronger each day. Soon there would be no reason for her to stay.

She started across the room and looked up to find Davy watching her intently. He held out his small arms and smiled. His features were his father's in miniature, but innocent and trusting. She lifted him in her arms and settled into the rocking chair beside his bed. After he drifted off to sleep, she did not return him to the bed right away, but gently stroked the curls from his brow and kissed the top of his head, unaware that Paul lay quietly watching the two of them in the soft glow of the lamp.

Just before dawn, Adelaide pushed her bedcovers aside. Her bare feet made no sound as she crossed the room to the window. In the distance, a street vendor's cart clattered down the cobbled street, another sign the city was coming back to life. In a few minutes, Tilde would hurry out to the gate and make her purchase of butter and eggs for the day.

She pressed her forehead against the windowpane. Dark circles marked her eyes and fatigue creased her features. Sleep had eluded her again, and Etienne's words mocked her in the darkness.

There are things I cannot tell you now, Addie. I can only ask that you trust me . . .

He had asked for understanding and patience, but she had stubbornly refused to give it. Her foolish pride had driven him out of her life forever.

Lily laid the sleeping child gently on his own bed and moved to the other. Paul's features were peaceful in the muted candlelight, his brow felt cool to her touch. Her fingers traced the strong curve of his jaw. His eyes opened. She gasped and attempted to snatch her hand away only to find it captured and held fast.

"I didn't mean to wake you," she whispered.

"I wasn't sleeping."

"Davy is much better."

"I don't know how to thank you for all that you have done for my son and me."

She smiled nervously.

Paul studied her features intently. "Lily, I'm sorry for the way I treated you in the past, all the times I presumed to judge you. I've been a fool, too often."

Her heart gave a sudden leap as his fingers tightened around her own. She blushed furiously, bewildered by the way her head swam and how she trembled inside.

"Forgive me, Beauty?" His dark eyes bore into hers, capturing her so utterly that she could not bring herself to look away. He had called her by that name once before in a voice filled with anger and mockery. But this was different, gentle and kind. He smiled. "I kissed you once. Do you remember?"

She nodded, scarcely able to breathe as he drew her to him, his kiss so light it might not have happened at all.

"I've fallen in love with you," he whispered.

Without thinking, she reached out and touched his face.

Adelaide reached for her dressing gown. The silence of the house seemed strange. It had been a week since the hallway echoed with footsteps scurrying from room to room. She made her way down the hall toward her son's room quietly and pushed open the door. She stifled a gasp and hurriedly retreated to her own room.

Lily stared down into Paul's eyes and saw the tenderness there. A sense of joy coursed through her. For a moment, the world beyond that door ceased to exist. She frowned. She was sure it had been closed a moment ago.

She pushed away from the bed and crossed the room in time to see the light from Adelaide's candle disappear as her door closed behind her. Paul's mother had seen them together and heard her son's declaration. Lily felt a sense of dread surge through her. She turned and forced a smile, taking the hand he reached out to her. He would have drawn her to him again, but she resisted.

"What's wrong?" His eyes narrowed. "Did I frighten you?"

"No."

"I would never do anything to hurt you."

"I know," she whispered.

He searched her eyes and tried to discern the doubt she couldn't hide. "Lily, do you think in time that you might come to care for me as much as I—"

"I do care." Suddenly she felt the tears gather behind her specs. She had almost allowed herself to forget that his world openly scorned the woman she pretended to be. But Adelaide DuPre would never forget who she was and where she had come from.

She pulled her hand away and lightly brushed her fingers across his brow. "Rest," she whispered. "Davy will be awake soon."

"There's so much I need to say to you."

She saw the longing in his eyes and swallowed hard. "We will talk later."

He smiled and closed his eyes.

Connie awoke with a start and looked up into Lily's anxious face. She was dressed, her valise clutched in her hand.

"Lily, where are you going? What time is it?"

"I have to leave now. Davy and Paul are asleep. I think it's better if I go before they wake. Fiona needs me, and Georgette and the others will be coming home soon."

Connie rubbed her eyes and frowned at her rumpled gown. She had fallen asleep fully clothed. She crossed the room unsteadily and grasped the bellcord. "Caleb will take you home. What shall I tell Paul and Davy?"

"Just, goodbye."

Swan House, November 27, 1829

Three days later, Sauchie's cries shattered the early morning stillness. "They home, praise be! Miz Georgette and Mist' Thad, they home!"

Lily threw aside the bedcovers knowing that Fiona would be reaching for her dressing gown at the same time. The messenger had come the afternoon before. Thaddeus had sent word by another vessel that they were only a day behind. Xavier and the stablehands had been waiting at the dock with the coach and wagons since before dawn. She wrenched open her door and raced along the gallery, almost colliding with Fiona.

"Jack!" Fiona's voice was shrill with excitement as she flew down the stairs and across the ballroom, straight into his arms. With a herculean effort, he lifted her off her feet and whirled her about.

"Fiona, lass, you're a sight, to be sure!" He set her back and surveyed the full length of her. Few could match O'Flarety in her finery, but clad only in a cotton nightrail, her fiery mane tumbling about her shoulders, she had never looked more beautiful. He swung about as Lily cried his name.

"Lily!"

She felt the breath rush from her body as he caught her to him in a crushing embrace.

"Lily? Fiona? Where are my girls?" Georgette swept into the room, arms outstretched.

Thaddeus grinned at the sound of her joyful cry. The woman had fretted herself plumb crazy down in Savannah. As soon as word came that the quarantine had been lifted, nothing would do but to secure passage for everyone on the next vessel bound for Charleston.

"And Franklin, is he all right?" Georgette glanced around anxiously.

Lily managed to smile, not trusting herself to speak. In fact, the banker had come to dinner the night before.

A hush began to descend over the room as the travelers realized they were standing in the midst of a ruin. Georgette's gaze traveled the length of their once magnificent ballroom. The velvet draperies were gone. The brocade chairs and carved inlaid tables were pushed haphazardly against the walls. The floor was scuffed and stripped of its polish. The giant urns that had once held banks of palms and ferns had been used to boil soiled linens and now sat abandoned behind the stables.

Georgette's stricken gaze fell upon Lily and Fiona. "Upstairs?"

Lily nodded and struggled to find the words to explain the devastation. "So many came down with the fever, and there were not enough beds at the clinic. Doctor Baker and the others couldn't care for them all. So, we brought them here."

"Things was mighty bad, Miz Georgette, mighty bad." Polly glanced at Lily and Fiona.

"So, you turned Swan House into a hospital? And Stephen and Grace were here, too?" Georgette whispered, her eyes filled with tears.

Lily nodded again, unable to hold back her pain. Fiona embraced the two of them. Their tears mingled together in a numbing rush of grief.

Thirty-Seven

The DuPre house, December 2, 1829

Hadley Baker emerged from Paul's room and shook his head. His friend's recovery was proving to be almost as taxing on the DuPre household as his illness had been. Adelaide glanced up from her writing table as the doctor hurried down the stairs. Connie set aside her stitchery. Hadley noted the pallor of her cheeks and sighed inwardly. Constance Wellington was too young to be widowed and alone.

"Your menfolk are coming along well, Adelaide. Paul is a bit ill-tempered, but your grandson is almost completely recovered. I'll stop by again tomorrow. See that Paul gets plenty of rest."

Adelaide rose from her chair and accompanied him to the door. She knew the reason for Paul's quarrelsome state. Lily had slipped away from the house the week before, and there had been no word from her since. Overhead, Davy's exuberant shriek was followed by the sound of Iretta's gentle scolding. Adelaide smiled, amazed that such a simple act humbled her now. She waved goodbye as the doctor climbed into his buggy and set off to see another patient.

She had scarcely returned to her correspondence when Tilde hurried into the room. "Miz Addie, Miss Sarah is a'comin' up the walk!"

Connie darted a questioning look at her mother. Adelaide laid her pen aside and carefully capped the inkwell. Her back stiffened visibly.

"Do not bother to show her into the drawing room, Tilde. Her visit will be brief." Adelaide walked around the desk and placed a firm hand on her daughter's shoulder. "No, Constance. I would like a private word with Miss Armstrong."

Tilde hurried to respond to the knock on the door. Adelaide followed her into the vestibule.

Sarah had taken great care with her appearance, but her plumed hat and matching magenta gown were more suited to an afternoon soiree than a morning social call. Adelaide was conscious of the drab contrast of her own black mourning gown.

"Miz Adelaide, how wonderful to see you again." Sarah would have grasped her hands had she not drawn them back. "We returned from Savannah just yesterday, and I said to Father and Aunt Minnie that I must come right over and see if Paul was, that is, if he and Davy are all right."

"My son and grandson are recovering."

"Oh, thank goodness. I'm sure that Paul has been asking for me. I can hardly wait to see him."

"Actually, he hasn't mentioned your name once, not even in a fit of delirium."

Sarah's jaw dropped with surprise. "Not once?"

"Not a single time."

"Why, I thought that surely . . ." Sarah sputtered. "Miz Adelaide, you cannot imagine how worried I have been. Constance will tell you how upset I was the day we left for Savannah."

"She did mention the unseemly haste of your departure."

"Then, you can understand how frantic we all were? Perhaps she misunderstood some of the things I said, but I can assure you—"

"Constance is not likely to misunderstand. In fact, given her kind nature, she probably cast the most favorable light upon the incident that she could."

Sarah's eyes narrowed. "I really would like to see Paul, now."

"I'm afraid that is not possible. Doctor Baker has ordered him to rest. I don't think a visit from his former fiancée would be especially beneficial at this time."

"I beg your pardon? Our plans have not changed. Paul and I will be married as soon as he has recovered."

"No, Sarah." Paul's abrupt denial startled both women.

"What are you doing downstairs?" Adelaide gasped.

"I heard voices. I thought it might be someone else."

Adelaide knew what he had hoped for. Lily.

"Paul, darling!" Sarah rushed toward him only to be stopped by his piercing stare.

"Mother's right. There will be no wedding. Tilde, show Miss Armstrong to the door."

"Yes, sir, Mastah Paul."

"You don't mean that." A note of hysteria crept into Sarah's voice. She was being dismissed as if she was of no more consequence than that menial who stood ready to eject her from the premises. Angry tears sprang to her eyes. She turned, rushed toward the door, and jerked it open with an angry screech.

Adelaide turned to see Paul grip the banister for support. "Caleb, come quickly." Her cry brought him hurrying down the hallway. "Help my son back to his room. Doctor Baker told him not to leave his bed. Oh, Paul, do stop grumbling." Her unexpected rebuke silenced his protests as Caleb grasped one of his arms and placed it across his shoulders.

Connie smiled at that. The household had almost returned to normal.

Later that afternoon, Adelaide knocked softly on her son's door and stepped inside the room. Paul appeared pale and exhausted in the shadowed light that filtered through the curtains. She reached out to brush the hair from his forehead. Her heart filled as he managed a smile.

"Hadley says you are doing fine, son."

He nodded.

"But you should not have come downstairs."

"I'm all right, Mother. As soon as I'm able to be up and about, I intend to talk to Hadley about the two of us building a hospital together."

"Oh, that would be wonderful."

Paul studied her face. The past several weeks had been hard on her. There was a seriousness about her that had not been there before. "You were very forceful with Sarah."

An angry flush reddened her cheeks. "Indeed. When I think how shabbily she treated Constance, and you and Davy."

Paul frowned. "It's for the best. I don't love her. I doubt that I ever did."

She grasped his hand and gave it a gentle squeeze. "She would not have made you happy, son. And Davy, la, but he would never have taken to her, not like . . ." Adelaide bit her lip and flushed. Lily. She had almost uttered the name aloud.

"Mother, there's something you should know. I'm in love with Lily."

Her heart plummeted. What did it matter that the city spoke of Kate Perrault's daughter in hushed, almost reverent tones, or that Honora praised her with the same enthusiasm that Nathan did. None of it made a difference. One day, they would all forget that Lily Perrault had faced down the fever and displayed her mettle so bravely. What would happen then?

"I see," she whispered.

"I plan to ask her to marry me when I'm well."

"But first you must regain your strength." Did she sound too desperate, too hopeful that he would change his mind?

"I want your blessing, Mother."

Her smile was pained. "When you are better, we will talk about it. You know, Davy can hardly wait until you take him to the docks to see the ships like you promised." Her voice quavered, remembering the morning she had spent with Etienne aboard the *Saracen*.

"I have so much to make up to the boy. I almost lost him."

"He needs you more than ever with Dan gone, and Constance and the Wellingtons leaving in a few days. This house is going to seem so empty."

"But not for long."

His smile was disarming and heartbreaking all at once. How could she give her blessing to a union that would bring shame upon them all?

The Claiborne house, December 3, 1829

Honora stared at her sister in astonishment. "You are going to Swan House to see Lily? But, why?"

"I have to speak with her before my son makes the worst mistake of his life." Adelaide snatched her handkerchief from her reticule and dabbed at her eyes.

"What has this got to do with Paul?"

"He thinks he's in love with her, and he intends to ask her to marry him."

"Oh, my." Honora fanned her flushed cheeks. So that was the

reason for Addie's visit so early in the morning. "What will you say?"

"I will tell her what Paul intends to do and insist that she reject his proposal."

"You cannot be serious! Why, if your son ever suspected you had done such a thing, he would never speak to you again. And Constance would be appalled. She's very fond of Lily, you know."

"What am I to do? Kate Perrault's daughter in my house, married to my son? I cannot bear it!"

"But she saved Paul's life. And, Davy's."

"Paul's feelings are based on gratitude, nothing more. By the time he comes to his senses, it will be too late."

Honora reached across the table and grasped her sister's hand. "I urge you not to interfere, Addie. Please, leave this to Paul. If he truly loves her, and she loves him, nothing else matters."

"Have you forgotten his father's betrayal?" Adelaide's eyes flashed with anger.

"Paul is not Gaston, nor is Lily her mother. And it was such a long time ago."

"Charleston never forgets, or forgives. This would bring it all back, the gossip and the shame. I can't go through that again." Adelaide sprang to her feet and reached for her parasol.

"Addie, please don't go. You're too upset."

"No, I must. Good day, Honora."

She sighed. Addie could be a stubborn woman when she set her mind to something. No good would come of this.

Swan House, December 5, 1829

Two nights later, a coach made its way slowly up the avenue toward Swan House and stopped a short distance from the front door. The driver climbed down from his seat and hurried up the steps. He returned minutes later and opened the door for the lone occupant inside.

Adelaide adjusted her veil, deliberately avoiding Caleb's annoying frown. When he started to utter another protest, she raised her hand and silenced him. He clamped his lips tightly shut and led the way up the steps. She gave a start as Lily Perrault's majordomo materialized out of the shadows and motioned her down the long corridor to the study. "I sent one of the servants to fetch Miss Lily, ma'am. If'n you would care to sit yoreself down on the settee?"

She shook her head.

He gave a stiff bow and exited the room.

Lily paused at the door. The gentlemen who frequented her establishment required nothing of her, but these clandestine calls from their womenfolk had proved to be another matter. Ever since the fever ended, there had been many who came under the cover of darkness in their discrete disguises. They were all grateful, and curious. She sighed and squared her shoulders and pushed against the door.

"Good evening, Miss Perrault."

Adelaide DuPre! Lily watched in astonishment as Paul's mother lifted her veil. "When Mohab said there was a visitor, I never expected that it might be you." She gestured toward the settee.

Adelaide shook her head. "I think I prefer to stand."

Lily moved closer so that they stood within the circle of the lamp light, appraising each other with searching frankness. She clasped her hands together to still their trembling. "Paul and Davy?"

Adelaide nodded. "They are fine, thank God. And Constance returned to Cottonwood just today."

"I see."

"She needs time to come to terms with the loss of her husband." Adelaide emitted a forlorn sigh, conscious of the prick behind her lashes. She mustn't cry, not here in front of this woman. There must be no sign of weakness, no doubt of her intent.

"Miss Perrault."

"Lily, please."

"Very well, *Lily*. I did not have a chance to speak with you before you left my house. But then, how does one thank another for the lives that she holds most dear in the world?" Adelaide gestured helplessly.

"It's not necessary."

"Oh, but it is. Not everyone possesses the courage you displayed so many times during the past several weeks, or the generosity to open their home as you did. Whatever your motives, genuine compassion or crass opportunity, I realize that my son might not be alive if you had not cared for him."

Lily stared at her accuser, stung. "Opportunity? Paul took care of so many without a thought for his own safety. How could I do any less when he was in need?"

Adelaide's eyes hardened. "I saw the two of you together just before you left the house."

"I know," Lily replied softly. "I chose to leave before you asked me to go."

"Paul has ended his engagement to Sarah Armstrong."

Lily heart gave a sudden leap.

"Because of you." Adelaide's words were a condemnation. "But, it was for the best. It would not have been a happy union."

"I don't know what to say."

Adelaide's stare seemed to intensify. "He claims to be in love with you, and he intends to ask you to become his wife."

"Oh." It was Lily's turn to be astonished. The happiness that radiated from her eyes instantly vanished, replaced by confusion and pain. Clearly, Adelaide DuPre did not welcome her son's declaration.

"He has asked for my blessing. I am afraid that I cannot give it."

Lily turned away.

"If you truly care for Paul you will do the right thing for him and his son and refuse his offer of marriage." Adelaide reached for her veil and lowered it about her face.

Lily turned and appraised her silently. The pain in her eyes was unmistakable, but there was an undeniable sense of pride as well. She walked over to the desk and gave a decisive pull on the bellcord. Almost instantly, footsteps hurried down the hallway.

"Goodbye, Miz DuPre. Mohab will show you to the door."

Adelaide responded with a curt nod and followed the majordomo from the room. Mohab reached the vestibule and opened the door. She flew past him down the steps to her coach.

Caleb closed the door after her and climbed up onto the driver's seat. She stared straight ahead and suddenly felt afraid. What if Lily decided to tell Paul about her visit or reveal her treachery in a letter to Constance? She sighed and closed her eyes. Of course, that would not happen. She had seen the pride in the girl's bearing, the way she looked past her when she bade her goodbye. Lily Perrault could be a formidable adversary if she chose to be. Somehow she knew it would not come to that, but the prospect brought her no comfort. Why had she not listened to Honey and left it alone?

Thirty-Eight

Three nights later

Lily crossed the dark room and cautiously opened the door leading to the outside gallery. Moonlight spilled across the grounds below and glimmered off the fountain.

She searched the deep shadows along the avenue and saw the signal light from John Davis's lantern. It was time. She turned and walked back into the room, taking care to close the door softly behind her. The armoire creaked as she opened it to retrieve the cloak and valise she had hidden there earlier.

"Where you think you goin' with that satchel, girl?" Polly emerged from the small anteroom where she slept.

Lily spun around with a startled cry.

"You think to slip out of yore own house like a thief and not tell nobody?" Polly slipped her hand into the pocket of her shift for a lucifer and reached for the lamp by the door. The flame cast a soft light across the room. She frowned at Lily's plain attire and trained a questioning look at her.

Lily sighed and dropped the valise on the floor. "It's over, Polly. I have to leave."

Polly returned the lamp to the table and turned, her expression defiant. "Why? Cause Miz Adelaide DuPre took it upon herself to barge in heah and poison yore mind with her foolishness?"

"How did you know she was here?"

"I see her man, Caleb, when he come to the door. She didn' fool me with that cloak and veil. What did she want?"

"She didn't want anything."

"'Cept to make shore you don' lay claim to her son, I'm thinkin' ."

"How can you say such a thing?" Lily's eyes flashed angrily.

"It's the truth, ain't it?"

"I don't care what Adelaide DuPre thinks. I should never have come here."

"Where you think you goin' now?"

"I will write to Georgette later."

"And what 'bout yore promise to Miz Georgette and Mistah Franklin? What's this gonna do to them folks?"

Lily closed her eyes and shook her head. "Georgette does not need me now that Stephen's gone. Swan House will go on. It will be all right, Polly. This will always be your home."

Polly's eyes softened as Lily angrily brushed a tear from her cheek. She glanced at the valise suspiciously. "You ain't meanin' to leave heah with nothin' but them old clothes you got on yore back, and what's in that satchel?"

Lily's fingers instinctively pressed against the small purse of money concealed in the pocket of her skirt. It was enough to get her to her destination. "I'm taking only what rightfully belongs to me. No one is going to stop me, not this time."

"Then I'm comin' with you. It ain't proper for a lady to travel by herself. I looked after yore mam when she first come heah, and I 'spect that I need to see after you, too."

Lily searched her face. "Oh, Polly, I will miss you terribly, but you belong here." She walked into her arms, and Polly held her fast as she wept. There would be no personal goodbyes to the others. By the time the household discovered the letters she had written, she would be far away from the city.

Come morning, Georgette, Thaddeus and Jack would find themselves richer than they ever dreamed, if they agreed to the terms contained in the letters addressed to each of them, and she sensed that they would. In time, perhaps Paul could forgive this last bit of treachery.

She stepped back and reached for the valise, then turned and fled from the room. Once she left this house, the woman she had pretended to be would no longer exist.

She slipped silently along the gallery and down the stairs. A single lamp guided her across the ballroom and through the vestibule. The door clicked softly as she emerged onto the verandah. A short distance away, John Davis waited by the coach and reached for the valise as she approached.

"Lily!"

She choked back a fearful cry and spun around. "Jack, what are you doing here?" she whispered and glanced back at John Davis.

"Did ye think Polly wouldn't suspect that ye were up to something," he demanded, "the way ye kept to y'self ever since that DuPre woman came to see ye?"

Her stricken expression confirmed his suspicions. It was because of Paul DuPre that she was leaving. The doctor was in love with her, and Adelaide DuPre would have none of it. Lily was running away, and none of them would ever see her again!

"Lily, ye must listen to reason," he pleaded.

"No, Jack." She turned abruptly and climbed into Stephen Flynn's modest coach and stared numbly ahead. Why couldn't Polly have kept her suspicions to herself? She had to know that Jack would try to stop her before she could make her escape.

John Davis pulled himself up onto the driver's seat and reached for the reins. Impulsively, Jack wrenched open the door and jumped into the coach. Lily turned away, confused and angry. They rode in silence until they reached the docks.

"Lily, wait." Jack reached out and grasped her hand. They sat in the darkness, their shoulders touching. An awkward silence stretched between them. Suddenly, he raised her hand to his lips. Her eyes misted with tears.

"See after the others, will you, Jack?"

He drew back in mock horror. "My God, woman, better someone should see after me once Thaddeus and those women find out what ye've done, and them thinking I'm a party to your blasted trickery!"

Her short burst of laughter ended in a sob. "I can't tell you where I'm going, but I promise that I will write to all of you later. Just promise that you will not try to find me."

His arms closed about her, cradling her against his chest. "How can I let ye go? I love ye, Lily. Let me come with ye," he whispered.

She stiffened and pulled away. "No, Jack. You are the best friend

I ever had, but we were never meant for each other. I am not the one you really want, trust me."

He shook his head, unable to speak. Her nearness had rendered him senseless for a moment, making him forget the reason she was leaving Charleston for good. He reached for the latch and watched John Davis hand her down.

She picked up the valise and hurried up the plank. Jack's last words tore through her fragile resolve.

"If DuPre is any sort of a man, he will go after ye, Lily. Ye can't run far enough!"

The next afternoon, Paul stood at the window, watching the carriages and riders that traveled the street beyond the gate. Lily's crumpled letter lay on the table behind him. Why had she run away? Could he have been so wrong about her after all? He would find her, and when he did, he would strangle the truth from her lying heart.

"Caleb!"

"Yes, sir?"

"Have Joshua saddle my horse. I'm going out."

"Yes, sir."

Swan House

Fiona faced her accuser, as rigid and uncompromising as he. Paul had lashed out, threatening and pleading until she had convinced him she knew nothing. Lily had confided in no one—not Georgette who wept behind her locked door, or that wretched sot barricaded in the study with Franklin, determined to drink himself bloody senseless.

At last, Paul turned on his heel and strode angrily from the house.

"Ah, Lily," she sighed. "He really loves ye. Foolish lass." She turned and started for the stairs.

"Fiona?" Jack rushed into the room with Franklin at his heels. "Fiona, where are ye?"

"What is it, Jack?" She grasped the banister, one foot poised on the step above.

He hurried toward her. "Fiona, you are not going to believe this, sweetheart!" He thumped the letter in his hand. "It's right here. Read it for yourself. We're getting married. The two of us. To each other."

She scanned the parchment and paled. Fire ignited in her eyes. After all the months of loneliness and secret tears, Jack Faro was hers, thanks to the generosity of another woman.

"Fiona? Fiona, wait!"

The gambler swayed and slipped to the floor, a bemused smile on his face. He stared at the toes of Fiona's slippers, dispatched to that unseemly position by one deft blow of her fist.

"Never!" she snapped.

He scrambled to gain his footing as she turned on her heel and started up the stairs. "Ye'll marry me by week's end, Fiona O'Flarety," he shouted, rubbing his jaw. "By week's end, ye hussy."

She stopped and turned midway to the landing above. Jack squinted up at her. Christ, she was a beauty. Maybe Lily was right after all. It was the love for a friend that he felt for her, the best friend he ever had. But it was the witch glaring down at him that stirred his blood, and at that moment, infused him with crippling desire.

"Is it me ye be wanting, Jack Faro, or Swan House?" Her voice was halting, wistful.

He recognized her pain and knew that he had seen that look in her eyes before, never suspecting that behind her brassy demeanor Fiona O'Flarety loved him to the depth of her being. He rubbed his jaw and inched up the stairs, never taking his eyes off of her.

"It's y'self I'm mad about, and I mean to prove it to ye, now!" His leer sent her flying up the remaining steps in the direction of her room.

Franklin Miller shook his head and accepted his hat and cane from the majordomo. Fiona and Jack. Now, there was a fitting pair to carry on Swan House's legacy. Somehow, he sensed that Kate would approve. He nodded to Mohab and quietly let himself out the door.

Swan House, January 11, 1830

Fiona Faro stared at her husband in disbelief.

"You heard me right, madam." Jack raised a hand to silence the retort on her lips. "In keeping with the changes we will be making to Swan House, I can't have my wife strutting about the city half naked."

Her hands gripped the arms of her chair, her lips curled in a feral snarl. Franklin instinctively drew back in his chair. Jack's plans to transform Swan House into the finest hotel in the city had evoked near bedlam in the rooms above, and in the study where he had summoned his new bride to reveal his daring scheme.

"Franklin, show her the figures. Look, lass. Two additional wings here and here, a few changes there, and before you know it, Swan House will be set to host every important visitor and social event in Charleston."

"I am not so sure, Jack." She frowned at the paper Franklin handed to her.

Jack rose, walked around the desk, and took her hands in his. "Darlin', this city has survived a great tragedy. The people have changed, and we have changed, too. We're a family now, with responsibilities to the wee ones."

"Wee ones?"

He smiled gently. "Yes, lass. Your brothers, all four of the buggers."

"Me brothers? Jack what are ye saying?"

"We're bringing 'em home, sweetheart."

Fiona sprang from her chair in a flood of happy tears and sobbed into his collar.

"Uh, Sweets, ye wouldn't mind overmuch if, later on, there was just one little lad in the bunch that favored me, would ye?"

"A houseful if ye want, Jack, a houseful!"

He felt his chest expand to bursting. "No need to be over generous, my love. One, maybe two, will do."

Thirty-Nine

Georgette gazed up at the sign above the dress shop bearing her name. Who better than *Madame Georgette's* to outfit society when she had personally gowned the most beautiful women in Charleston for over twenty years? She tucked her hand into Thaddeus's arm and laid her head against her husband's shoulder. Who could have dreamed it would finally come to this? Respectability was a role they had all embraced with surprising ease. *Ah, Kate, if only you could see us now!*

Thaddeus glanced down at her and noted the momentary frown that creased her brow. No one had heard from Lily since she had slipped away months before. Could Franklin be right? Had she fled to England in search of Etienne Cruz?

"Time to go home, Georgette."

She nodded and allowed him to assist her into the open carriage. John Davis glanced back at her from the driver's seat. Their eyes met for a moment before he turned and flicked the reins across the team's backs. He was anxious to reach the house Georgette and Thaddeus had purchased near the river. And tonight, while the city celebrated the grand opening of Jack and Fiona's hotel, he and Cassie would make their way to the root cellar and lead the four runners to a cove where they would be met and taken aboard a ship bound for New London, and freedom.

The home of Franklin Miller

Franklin studied his reflection in the mirror. The years had not been unkind to the sharecropper's son. Of a half-dozen offspring, he had stood apart from his siblings from the very beginning, determined to become more than just another Miller chained to land that belonged to someone else.

His life had been an unrelenting drive to acquire wealth and power. There had been no time for a family of his own, and friends had been chosen from those who possessed the same ambition that became his creed.

Until Kate.

From the first time he encountered her after the death of Ezra Swan, he knew that he would devote the remainder of his life transforming a vulnerable and heartbroken woman into a force to be reckoned with. For two decades, they had worked together to build the empire he had envisioned. But those times were past. It would all end tonight with the unveiling of the Faros' magnificent hotel. Everyone would be there to witness the beginning of a new era that promised to be greater than the one before it. All that would be missing were the two women who had once presided over Swan House, Kate Perrault and the daughter she never knew.

Franklin reached up to straighten his tie, while his servant brushed the shoulders of his coat one last time.

"Sylvester, how long have we been together?"

"Long time, Mastah Franklin. Long time, yes, sir."

"Indeed." Franklin offered a wry smile and reached for his hat and cane. "It's time."

"Yes, sir. I bring the coach 'round."

Franklin followed his driver downstairs and watched him hurry down the hallway in the direction of the carriage house. He nodded at the maidservant standing by the front door before entering his study. She smiled. It was a ritual only recently begun, but one that would endure as long as Franklin Miller lived in this house.

The portrait of Kate gazed down at him from above the mantle. It had been rescued from the attic at Swan House and delivered to him the day he learned that Lily had disappeared from the city. Franklin took a step back. For a moment, he allowed himself to feel the incredible loss of the only woman he had ever given his heart to.

"Good night, my dear," he whispered. He turned and walked into the vestibule. The servant reached up to place his evening cloak about his shoulders.

"No need to wait up, Clara. I have my key."

Swan House, the Hotel

Jack and Fiona surveyed the length of the grand salon, taking in the smallest details. It was opening night. The guests would arrive soon. Everything must be perfect, from the flowers and candles on the dining tables to the shine on the new parquet floors. Sauchie had been placed in charge of the linens and the silver. Mohab inspected each servant's attire down to the last ruffle on their aprons and trained a critical eye on each pair of polished shoes. Xavier studied his reflection in one of the gilt mirrors in the vestibule, adjusting the new silk cravat Fiona had given to him as a peace offering. Endless trips to Georgette's shop to fit the gown she was wearing tonight had driven the man to near distraction.

Months earlier, almost sobbing in despair, Fiona had packed away the daring gowns that enchanted the men of Charleston in favor of new ones guaranteed to garner the approval of their womenfolk. She felt a flutter beneath her corset and smiled. She had promised Jack a houseful of children, and in just a few months, she would present him with their first.

Caleb guided the DuPre coach down the crowded avenue. It appeared that all of society had turned out for the event. Adelaide adjusted her wrap and cast a nervous glance at Paul. His fierce grip on the leather handstrap hinted at the turmoil he must be feeling. Perhaps it had been a mistake to accept Jack and Fiona's invitation. She attempted an encouraging smile when the coach came to a stop.

Mohab opened the door as they reached the entrance. "Evenin', Doctah Paul, ma'am."

Paul paused, taken aback by the spectacle. Only months before, Swan House had been littered with soiled linens and the vile stench of sickness and death. Now, it gleamed with pristine elegance. The ladies of Charleston, resplendent in their finest gowns and jewels, circulated on the arms of their menfolk, all eager for a glimpse of the couple who had created this magnificent tribute to the city's resilience.

"Addie!" Honora sailed toward her sister, her eyes bright with excitement. "Have you seen the Pardees and the Turnbulls? Look, here come the Faros. Oh my, I have never seen a gown quite so elegant."

Jack and Fiona made their way slowly through the crowd. Jack's welcomes were effusive. Fiona seemed content to smile demurely down at her husband until she turned to see Paul slowly mounting the staircase, his eyes riveted on the portrait of Lily. She whispered in Jack's ear and disengaged her arm, careful not to draw attention to herself as she threaded her way among the guests.

"Paul?"

He turned slowly. "Fiona." His acknowledgement was guarded as they stared at one another, remembering the last time they had met. "I apologize. I shouldn't be here. Please forgive me." He turned to go.

"Come with me." She took his arm and guided him along the gallery to the room at the end. "We kept it just like she left it. 'Tis foolish, I suppose, but we thought that maybe she would come back one day." Fiona smiled wistfully.

He followed her into the chamber that had been Lily's. "Have you heard anything?" His calm was forced.

"No. We expected there would have been a letter by now. I would have sent word to ye, Paul."

His expression was grim as he spied the small portrait on the table. "Why did she do it, Fiona? Why did she run away? She said she cared for me. I wanted to marry her."

"She was afraid, I think. Maybe she thought that if ye married her, it would ruin ye in this town. Knowing Lily, she would never stand for that."

"But there was nothing to fear. There's no one in the city who doesn't believe she's a saint. My own sister will tell you quickly enough that I was not good enough for her." He gave a helpless shrug. "I don't understand women."

"There's not a man alive who can honestly lay claim to that skill."

"Jack!" Fiona turned as her husband walked into the room.

Paul felt an immediate stirring of anger tighten his chest and disappear just as quickly. "My congratulations on your success, Jack."

"Ah yes, the hotel."

"And for convincing this remarkable woman to marry you."

Jack's eyes softened as he reached for Fiona's hand. "Indeed, my love is a treasure."

Fiona blushed at the adoration in her husband's eyes.

"Well, if the two of you will excuse me, I'm sure that I have been missed downstairs." Paul turned toward the door.

Impulsively, Fiona swept the small portrait up in her hand. "Paul, we'd like ye to have this."

He cupped the miniature in his palm and nodded wordlessly. He didn't trust himself to speak, but turned and walked swiftly along the gallery toward the staircase.

Fiona sighed and clasped Jack's arm. "How sad."

He nodded and then brightened. "Miz Faro, would ye do me the honor of joining me and our guests at dinner?"

She grinned and patted the small swell of her belly. "Your son and I would be delighted, Mister Faro."

Forty

"There he is!" Estelle exclaimed, pointing toward the familiar figure who appeared at the rail of the *Saracen*.

Louis exited the carriage and shouldered his way through the throng of bystanders that crowded the docks for a closer look at the four English vessels flying the gold and ebony flag of the Cruz Shipping Line. Estelle's eyes misted when Etienne hurried down the plank and threw an arm about her husband's shoulders. Together, they made their way along the wharf in the direction of the carriage. Etienne's sudden burst of laughter at Louis's obvious jest was a good sign. The months he had spent in England preparing to return to New Orleans appeared to have distanced him from the horrors of Celine's confession, and her death.

"Estelle!"

She felt her small hand caught up in his powerful grip and accepted his kiss upon her cheek as he climbed into the carriage and settled himself across from her.

"It's good to have you home at last, Etienne." She patted Louis's knee. "We have so looked forward to this day."

Etienne leaned toward them, his eyes filled with anticipation. "Tell me, is the house ready? Did you receive the sky glass I shipped for the solarium? What about the new fountain in the back garden? Lily will like that. Swan House has a fountain, much larger, but—"

Louis threw his hands up in mock horror. "You have scarcely been gone six months, you tyrant. How could you expect us to accomplish so many miracles in so short a time?"

"Oh, Louis, do stop teasing. We have enjoyed every minute of it," Estelle laughed.

"I expect a great deal, judging from the bills you sent to London. You spent a fortune, you pirate."

Estelle's laughter prompted a grin from both men. "Wait until you see the house, Etienne. You will be so pleased."

Louis squeezed her hand. "And wait until you see the surprise Estelle has prepared for you. We are hosting a dinner in your honor on Saturday evening to celebrate your permanent return to the city. Everyone will be there—family, friends, dignitaries, and possibly an accommodating widow or two."

"Louis, for shame!"

Etienne grinned at her protest and felt a momentary twinge of envy at the love that softened her stern expression. *Perhaps, one day.*

The driver brought the carriage to a stop in front of the house on Rue Royale. Louis descended first and handed his wife down beside him.

"We were afraid the new fountain wouldn't be ready by the time you returned, but as you will see, your drawings have been replicated in every detail. Of course, I had to promise that robber, Albani, that you would pay a shocking bribe for him to refuse all other jobs until this one was completed." Louis grasped Etienne's arm and propelled him toward the steps. "Come. There is still work to be done before you can take up residence. The upholsterers have promised to deliver the settees and chairs in two weeks. Until then, we have rooms ready for you at our house."

Estelle slipped her hand through the crook of her husband's arm. "It's regrettable that Aunt Celine missed this day. Once everything is complete, Etienne, you will host events such as New Orleans has not seen since your father and Aunt Celine were here. Even now, society waits to see who will be invited to your first ball. I have prepared a list of names, of course."

Etienne smiled and grasped the latch. As the door swung inward, the sounds of hammering echoed through the empty rooms upstairs. He walked to the center of the drawing room, taking in the frescoed ceiling, the new chandelier from Venice, the marble mantle from

France, and rugs from Persia.

"Louis, I'm inclined to forgive your extravagances. It's magnificent!"

Estelle squeezed her husband's arm. "I told you he would be pleased," She whispered.

Louis self-consciously cleared his throat. "We took the liberty of moving your furnishings into your father's room, cousin. Wait until you see what Estelle has done to transform your room for Lily."

One week later

Estelle hurried down the hallway at the sound of the front door opening. The men had left the house directly after breakfast. Tonight was Etienne's welcoming dinner, and Louis had been given the task of keeping him away from the house while she hurried to add the finishing touches to the surprise he had hinted at the day Etienne arrived in New Orleans.

"Louis, thank goodness you're back," she cried. The guests will be here in three hours. You two hardly have time to dress and go over the guest list. And there is something the three of us must attend to before they arrive."

"We'll be down within the hour." Louis gave her a quick kiss on the cheek. "Hurry!" he whispered to Etienne as he rushed him up the staircase. "In all the years I have been married to that woman, she has never once exercised her God-given right to be fashionably late, nor has she permitted me to be. Besides, she's eager to show you the gift she has for you."

"Hurry, hurry, both of you!"

"See what I mean?" Louis rolled his eyes in mock exasperation and chuckled softly under his breath.

An hour later, Louis and Estelle escorted Etienne to the library. They smiled conspiratorially. Then Louis disengaged the latches and opened the doors.

Etienne entered the paneled room, followed by his host and hostess. Illuminated by a chandelier overhead, globed lamps accentuated three framed portraits positioned on easels in front of the fireplace. Estelle watched intently as Etienne left them and approached the first one. When he turned, he was clearly moved.

"Who created these? They are perfect in every detail."

Louis glanced at his wife and smiled. "You may recall that Estelle's father, Antoine Arceneaux, painted the earlier portraits of your parents, and then the one of Aunt Celine after she and your father married. Note the signature on each of these. E'Arceneaux is now recognized as one of the finest portrait artists in the country. The creator of these paintings of your family is none other than Estelle herself!"

"Estelle?" Etienne trained an incredulous gaze upon the diminutive figure clinging to Louis's arm. "This is *your* work?"

She nodded and smiled. "My gift to you, Etienne, and to your daughter, to welcome you both home."

Louis walked to the sideboard and retrieved a bottle of brandy. "Our guests will be invited to view the portraits after dinner tonight. Within a week, Estelle will be besieged with commissions. It happens each time she introduces a new showing."

Estelle blushed furiously as Etienne seized her hands and impulsively kissed her soundly on the lips.

"Your appreciation is noted, cousin." Louis handed off a glass of brandy to each of them and arched a wicked brow. "Have a care that it does not become overly effusive."

Etienne chuckled and raised his glass to his host.

Forty-One

May 28, 1830

"Madame is here, sir."

"My wife?" Louis frowned and rose from his chair. Estelle seldom ventured to the offices he kept near the courts.

As the clerk turned toward the door, she burst into the room. Her face was flushed, and she looked frightened. Louis hurried around the desk as she sank into the chair the clerk held for her.

"*Cherie?* What are you doing here? Are you ill?" He knelt beside her and reached for her hand. "Thomas, a brandy."

"It's Etienne! Oh, Louis, I think that I may have upset him terribly."

He reached for the brandy the clerk pressed into his hand. "Here, drink this. It will calm you." He nodded Thomas toward the door. "Now, what's this about Etienne?"

Estelle sighed. "A letter came for him today from Monsieur Claiborne in Charleston. Etienne had just left to inspect a shipment of new furnishings at the house. I knew that he would want to have it at once, so I went there to give the letter to him."

Louis nodded. Etienne had written to Nathan Claiborne before leaving London, informing him that he was returning permanently to New Orleans. He had smiled when he spoke of Claiborne's anticipated reaction to the news that Lily was indeed his daughter, and that he would sail for Charleston as soon as he settled into the house on Rue Royale. And there was a matter regarding Claiborne's sister-in-law. Most curious. Etienne had been looking forward to a response from his friend since he arrived in New Orleans.

"Oh, Louis, he was so excited when he saw the letter. He could scarcely wait to open it. But then the most frightful look came over his face. He flung it to the floor and rushed from the house quite forgetting that I was there. I didn't know what to do, but to bring it to your attention at once."

She fumbled in her reticule for the crumpled pages. "Here, read it for yourself. You are Etienne's solicitor. It's your duty to know his business."

Louis quickly scanned Nathan's letter and then slipped it into the pocket of his coat.

"Most disturbing," he murmured.

"What is it, Louis? What's wrong?"

"Come, my dear. I suspect that Etienne may be packing his things at this very moment." He grasped her elbow and guided her toward the door. "Thomas, I'll be gone for the rest of the afternoon."

"Louis!" Her husband looked almost as distressed as Etienne had earlier. "Please."

"Lily has disappeared from Charleston. No one knows where she is."

"Oh, no."

Etienne stood at the window. His eyes were dark and bleak. According to Nathan's letter, Lily had left the city after the fever epidemic had ravaged Charleston. She told no one that she was leaving or where she was going. At first, Nathan agreed with Franklin Miller's assumption that she had almost certainly sailed to England. But when his last letter reached Nathan and he had made no mention of her, Nathan and Franklin knew they were mistaken.

Kate's fortune could have taken her anywhere, but Lily had renounced her claim to any part of Kate's assets. That could only mean that she was alone somewhere and virtually penniless.

His first reaction had been disbelief, then fear so consuming that he had packed his belongings and dispatched a messenger to the docks. Even now, Raoul Mendoza and his crew were readying the *Saracen* to leave for Charleston on the next tide. He heard a sound on the street and turned to see the deFonvielle's carriage race through the gate and come to a halt beneath the portico. Louis stepped down and hurried into the house, with Estelle at his heels.

"Etienne?"

"In here, Louis." Before Louis could admonish him, Etienne reached for Estelle's hand and lifted it to his lips. "Forgive me, Estelle, for deserting you so thoughtlessly."

Louis reached into his pocket and retrieved Nathan's letter and thrust it at him. "You frightened my wife nearly out of her wits, you wretch! She arrived at my office completely distraught over your reckless behavior."

"I'm sorry, Louis."

Louis felt torn between concern for his wife and his cousin. He gave an absent wave of his hand. "I read Claiborne's letter. We'll find her, Etienne. We employ agents who are trained to locate missing people."

"Lily is *not* missing." Etienne's response was irrational and angry.

"Well, whatever her reason for leaving Charleston, she has contacted no one since. I would surmise that she does not wish to be found."

Estelle heard a hint of irritation in her husband's retort and laid a cautioning hand upon his arm. "Forgive us, Etienne. It's just that we are concerned—"

"—that you plan to do something foolish," Louis interrupted, "like setting off on a search that could take you away for months." He swung his arm toward the trunks the servants had deposited near the door. "And it appears that is your intent."

Etienne expelled a deep breath. "Lily did not follow me to London, Louis. I made promises to her that I have not kept. I should have returned to Charleston as soon as I knew the truth about us. Instead, I went to England. I'm certain she believed that I never intended to keep my word."

"You did what you had to do, 'Tienne. Certain things were expected of you after Aunt Celine died. Even if you had sailed to Charleston, you could not have breached the quarantine Nathan wrote about."

Etienne braced his hands against the window sill and dropped his head. "For more than twenty years, I have had a daughter I didn't know existed. She came very close to being murdered in her mother's womb before she drew her first breath. Then she was abandoned and consigned to a life of unimaginable poverty when I could have given her everything. And all she ever wanted was to know who her mother and father were."

Estelle's eyes glistened with unshed tears as she walked over to Etienne and stroked his arm. He reached for her hand.

"I wanted everything to be perfect for her when she came home."

"Let me send one of our best investigators to Charleston," Louis insisted. "I know just the man. You need to remain in the city should Lily decide to return to New Orleans."

Etienne frowned. "That's not likely, Louis. She would never be able to return to the life she had known here. Swan House made that impossible. But you are right," he conceded. "Hire your agent. I will pay whatever it takes. Just find my daughter!"

Louis expelled a deep breath of relief. "Consider it done."

June 8, 1830

Louis glanced across the table and frowned. Etienne had scarcely touched his food. It had been a week since they had dispatched John Whistler to Charleston aboard the *Celesta,* the swiftest vessel in Etienne's fleet. With any luck, the search for Lily would yield results forthwith. Whistler was a tenacious bulldog of a man, never known to give up the hunt until his subject was found.

Both men turned as Estelle hurried into the dining room.

"Off to the park, my dear?"

She kissed her husband lightly on the cheek and reached for the basket of refreshments the cook had placed on the table. "Hurry, Louis, and bring my easel out to the carriage. I want to take advantage of the best light."

Louis rose and reached for his coat. "She always searches for new subjects to paint. You might ask her to show you her sketches. She has quite a collection."

Etienne pushed away from the table. "I think I'll ride out to the plantation today. Would you care to accompany me?"

"No, no. I'm expected at the office. I'll see you back here tonight." Louis sighed. Each day with no word from Whistler would be a torment for the man, and even though Etienne no longer owned Heron's

Point, his obsession with that charred and overgrown ruin showed no sign of abating.

Later that evening

Etienne walked out onto the side terrace. Across the way, a lamp glowed softly in the window of the summer house. Estelle glanced up from her task and beckoned to him to join her. He set off down the stone path. A humid breeze stirred the wind chimes above the door. Estelle wiped her hands on a towel and removed the pinafore that protected her gown. "Leave the door open, Etienne. It's so warm tonight."

"So, this is where you work." He glanced about the room at the assortment of easels and canvases in various stages of completion. Louis was right. Estelle's talent was in great demand.

She gathered up a handful of freshly cleaned brushes and placed them on a table beside one of the larger easels. "Tomorrow, Madame Francesca Paulot comes for her final sitting. She's old and quite frail, poor thing. Everything must be ready so that we can begin as soon as she arrives."

"May I look?"

"Of course." Estelle stepped back from the canvas.

"She is rather old, isn't she?"

"And the wealthiest woman in Louisiana." Estelle laughed softly at his frown. "There are some preliminary sketches on the table that may be more to your liking. They are not very detailed. The subject is young and lovely, but there is something indefinable about her. Obviously, she is poor, but I suspect gentle breeding in her background. I thought of asking her to sit for a painting that I have in mind. I'm certain she could use the money."

She heard the rustling of papers and then silence. When she turned her smile faded. "Etienne?" She touched his arm.

"How do you know this woman, Estelle?"

"I see her in the park from time to time and sometimes we exchange pleasantries, but I have never asked her name. She appears to be a very private person."

"When did you last see her?" Etienne's voice sounded strained. She drew back.

"Why, just today. She usually sits on a bench close to the promenade, as if she's waiting for someone."

"What do you mean?"

"Do you see the shawl that she's wearing? It was once very fine. In one of our rare exchanges, she mentioned that she had been wrapped in that very garment when she was left on the steps of the convent during one of the epidemics. Children were often abandoned there and never reclaimed by their kin. I think that she believes if she wears this shawl a passerby may recognize it, perhaps an older person who knew the lady it once belonged to."

She gave a startled cry as Etienne's hand clamped about her wrist. "Come with me."

Louis rushed out onto the terrace at the sound of Etienne's voice.

"Louis, summon your driver, and have the carriage brought around. Estelle and I are in a hurry."

"You and Estelle? Where are you taking my wife?" Louis exclaimed, alarmed.

"To Rue Royale. There is something I want her to see."

"At this hour?"

"Damnit, Louis, hurry."

"I'm coming with you." Louis charged into the house while Etienne paced the length of the walkway. Estelle glanced about bewildered. Minutes later, the three of them sped along the cobbled streets, the carriage wheels clattering noisily in the stillness of the night.

The house on Rue Royal

"What is going on?" Louis whispered, listening to the sound of footsteps hurrying up the backstairs.

"I don't know." Estelle shrugged. "One minute, he was looking at my sketches, and the next minute, he grabbed my arm and insisted that we come here."

"Shhh, they're coming back."

Etienne burst through the door and turned to allow the major-domo to deposit his burden upon a settee directly across from where they were sitting.

"Hold the lantern." He handed it off to the servant. "Louis, bring the lamp from the mantle. Estelle, look at this portrait very carefully, and tell me what you see."

"It's Aunt Celine." Louis shrugged, and looked at Etienne questioningly.

Estelle stared at the image for several moments. Suddenly, she pressed her fingers to her lips. Her eyes widened in surprise. There was no mistake. It *was* the same! "The shawl. The girl in the park is wearing Aunt Celine's shawl."

Etienne felt his heart thundering in his chest. "I gave it to Mother for her birthday the year that I returned from my grand tour. I purchased it in Belgium. It must be the one she wrapped Lily in the night she left her at the convent. Louis, I'm certain the girl in Estelle's sketches is Lily. If it is her, she's here in the city, and I think I know where she may be!"

Forty-Two

New Orleans, the Charity Hospital, June 9, 1830

The two robed figures climbed the stairs to the second floor of the hospital leaving their visitor pacing in the courtyard below. The younger one hurried to keep up with the Abbess's purposeful strides. Reverend Mother seldom intruded upon Doctor Bannon's domain, but the gentleman who had accompanied them was on an urgent mission that required immediate attention from the highest authority.

"Wait here, Sister Michael. I would speak with Doctor Bannon alone." The Abbess disappeared into the doctor's office.

Sister Michael glanced about, aware that silence had suddenly descended over the crowded ward. The other nuns stole speculative looks at one another.

"Lily, what is Reverend Mother doing here?" Sister Mathilde whispered. "Do you think she is going to tell Doctor Bannon that you cannot stay any longer?"

Lily smoothed the coarse linen sheet over their patient and shook her head. "I don't know. I have been allowed to remain here when I should have found another place. It wouldn't be fair to the others for me to continue to stay. I'm no longer of the Order, and I have no sponsor or means to pay for my keep," she sighed.

"Here they come. Doctor Bannon looks troubled. Oh, Lily, they're coming straight toward us!"

"Shhh, you will wake Mister Potterford."

"Lily."

"Reverend Mother."

"Doctor Bannon and I would like a word with you." The Abbess noted the slight tremor in Lily's hands as she wiped them on her apron.

It had been five months since the girl had returned to the hospital seeking sanctuary. She had changed in the two years since Thaddeus Parks had taken her to Charleston. Even now, garbed in that faded dress and clasping work-worn hands beneath her apron, there was a worldliness about her that distanced her from the others.

Lily glanced nervously from one to the other. Phineas's frown softened. The Abbess cleared her throat.

"You're going to ask me to leave, aren't you?"

"Not by choice." The older woman smiled wistfully. "We will be sad to see you go, child. You will always be a part of us."

"If Doctor Bannon will allow me to keep my room here at the hospital until I can find lodging . . . ?"

"That won't be necessary. Other arrangements have been made for you."

"I don't understand." A note of panic crept into Lily's voice. "What am I to do? I have nowhere to go, no way to support myself."

Phineas laid a hand upon her shoulder. "Lily, there is a gentleman downstairs asking for you. Perhaps he can best answer your questions."

"A gentleman? I don't know any—"

"Lily." The Abbess clasped her hands tightly and closed her eyes for a moment. How long had they wondered about the child that Sister Agatha had taken under her wing, and now that the truth was known, why did she hesitate? "He says that he is your father, and he has come to take you home."

Lily appeared stunned. "My father?" she whispered.

The Abbess nodded toward the window. "See for yourself."

Lily approached the window fearfully and stared down at the man standing in the courtyard. Her fingers flew to her lips. The others turned at the sound of her cry. The Abbess and Phineas watched her run toward the stairs. They turned back to the window in time to see Etienne Cruz catch his daughter up in his arms.

Forty-Three

Charleston, January 24, 1831

Nathan Claiborne glanced at the three women seated in front of his desk. He spread a sheaf of papers out before them. "Ladies."

Connie, Iretta, and Maybelle smiled and nodded. Seated across the room, Paul and Adelaide cautioned Davy to be silent.

Nathan cleared his throat. "According to the documents we have here, you, Constance, are relinquishing all claims to your late husband's interest in Cottonwood Plantation?"

Connie turned toward the two sisters seated beside her. "Yes, Uncle Nathan."

Adelaide emitted an audible sigh.

He studied the documents for a moment and silently indicated where she should affix her signature. Her hand was sure and steady as she penned her name. Nathan smiled fondly at his niece. Adelaide's consternation was evident, but he had to give her credit. Honey's twin had lost much of her fire since her son's brush with death.

Nathan turned back to the sisters. "Iretta, Maybelle, the estate of your nephew, Daniel Wellington, now reverts to the two of you. According to this document you have stipulated that your great-nephew, David Wellington DuPre, shall inherit your estate to include Cottonwood Plantation and all other assets in your possession upon the demise of the last remaining sibling?"

The two sisters turned to glance fondly at the object of their generosity who rewarded them with a mischievous smile. Maybelle dabbed at her eyes. Iretta gave a satisfied sigh. Emma's son was the last of their bloodline, and who knew what would come after?

"Paul, at the request of Iretta and Maybelle, you will have the responsibility of administering the estate left to your son should he come into his inheritance before he reaches his majority. Once he attains his legal adult age, control shall revert solely to him. Do you understand and accept these conditions freely?"

"I do, sir."

As they all emerged into the morning chill a half hour later, young Davy suddenly disengaged his small hand from his father's grasp and ran toward Iretta and Maybelle. Paul shook his head and smiled. His son was their world. God willing, they would live to see their great-nephew grow to manhood, knowing their devotion had not been misplaced.

The next morning, Connie, Adelaide, and Davy stood on the front steps and watched Paul hand the Wellington sisters into their coach. Since Dan's death, Connie had no heart to remain at Cottonwood. So much had happened to all of them since Paul had come home. There had been triumphs to be sure, but too many tragedies.

Paul opened the gate and started up the walkway when Adelaide turned and rushed into the house. She snatched her parasol from a brass urn by the door and hurried back down the steps.

"Where is Grandmama going, Papa?" Davy tugged on his father's coat. Paul reached down and swung the boy up in his arms.

"I don't know, son."

"Mother, where *are* you going?" Connie called after her and turned to give her brother a puzzled look.

Caleb rushed through the door. "Miz Addie, Miz Addie? Don' you want yore coach? It's cold out heah, and it ain't fittin' for a lady to go walkin' the streets by herself. Miz Addie?"

Adelaide opened her parasol with a decisive snap, ignoring his protests. She had been stubborn, filled with false pride, and lonely, waiting for word from Etienne that would never come. The memory of the door closing after him had haunted her far too long. Well, no more.

Nathan stood at the window, a trail of smoke curling lazily from his pipe. A perplexed frown furrowed his brow.

"Honey?"

"Yes, dear."

"We have a visitor."

"Oh?" She rose from the settee and joined him at the window. "It's Addie."

They watched in astonishment as she burst breathlessly into the room, her hair streaming in disarray about her shoulders, her cheeks pink with cold.

"Nathan," she gasped. "I want to send a letter to Etienne!"

Honora glanced from her twin to her husband. "Addie, I declare, but that would be most unseemly."

"I don't care. Oh, please, Nathan. Where can I write to him?"

He looked from his wife to her sister, one aghast, the other oddly appealing. They stared at him curiously as he walked to his writing desk in the corner of the room and opened the top drawer. "I have received two letters from Etienne. The first one was posted in London, and this one came by messenger from New Orleans a few months ago." He turned and pretended to study the handwriting scrawled on the envelopes. "I'm not sure if I should share their contents with you, Addie, considering the questionable manner of yours and Etienne's parting."

"Nathan!" Honora stared at her husband in disbelief. "You never said that you had heard from Etienne."

Adelaide gave a cry and intercepted her sister's reach. The envelopes ripped in her haste to extract the pages from inside. For several minutes, her gaze devoured the broad masculine script. When she raised her eyes, her expression was disbelieving, stricken, and fearful.

"Oh, Nathan, why didn't you tell me? After Lily nursed Paul and Davy back to health, I went to her and *demanded* that she refuse Paul's proposal of marriage. It's my fault that she left Charleston. When I accused Etienne of the vilest intentions toward her, he asked me to trust him. I was so sure I was right that I ordered him to leave my house. And you knew the truth all along."

"Addie, that is not altogether true," Nathan protested.

"Oh, I was such a fool!"

Honora's eyes darted from her husband's stern frown to the anguished look on her sister's face. "Knew what? Nathan, what is she accusing you of? Adelaide, you have been harsh in your judgment of my husband many times, but—"

"Honey, Addie is partly right. Etienne suspected—"

"What? What did Etienne suspect?" Honora's voice was shrill. "I don't understand."

"Lily is Etienne's *daughter!*" Adelaide moaned. "Here." She thrust the torn pages at her sister. "Read it for yourself."

Honora's eyes widened as she scanned the letters. "Oh, my word. How can this be? Etienne and Kate Perrault, but how? When? Oh, it's not possible, is it Nathan?"

Nathan expelled a deep sigh. "It's true enough. Lily is indeed the daughter of Etienne and his wife, Catherine Cruz, whom we have known these many years as Kate Perrault. Sit down, ladies. Given the situation, I don't think Etienne will consider it a betrayal of his trust if I tell you what he related to me before he left Charleston."

Honora placed her arm about her twin's waist and drew her down on the settee beside her.

Nathan eyed them both for a moment. This was going to take all the tact and diplomacy he could muster.

An hour later, Honora and Nathan stood on the front steps and watched Simon assist Adelaide into their coach, with Etienne's letters clutched in her hand. Honora laid her head against her husband's shoulder and sighed softly.

"Poor Addie."

Nathan nodded in agreement. Adelaide faced the daunting task of confessing her transgressions to her son. Even if Paul found it in his heart to be forgiving, Lily may have already told Etienne the real reason for her desperate flight from Charleston all those months ago.

"I have never seen her so troubled. Oh, Nathan, is there nothing we can do?"

He patted her hand and shook his head. "Perhaps it's best to leave this matter to Addie and her son, my dear."

"But what about the letters? Why did you insist that she keep them?"

"It may be her only defense against Paul's anger. At least, she can tell him where Lily is and that she's safe."

⌣

Charleston Harbor, January 28, 1831

Captain Edgar Knox turned as one of his men hurried across the deck of the *Crescent Queen*. A gentleman with an urgent dispatch for Monsieur Etienne Cruz of New Orleans waited below. Knox followed the mulatto to the railing and watched as Nathan Claiborne stepped down from his coach with a leather pouch in his hand.

"Captain."

The Scotsman returned the greeting and quickly navigated the plank down to the dock.

"Sir, my clerk tells me you are leaving for Louisiana on the next tide. I need to get an urgent message to Etienne Cruz in New Orleans as quickly as possible."

"I know Mister Cruz personally. I can take your message to him."

"Good, good!" Nathan thrust the pouch at him. "You will find remuneration contained in there that should more than compensate you for your trouble."

"Thank you, sir. You can depend on me." Knox tucked the leather pouch under his arm.

"Remember now, as soon as you arrive in the city," Nathan called back over his shoulder, and climbed into the coach. He rapped on the roof and settled back for the ride home.

The deed was done.

There had been no word from Addie since she left their house four days before, and Honora was worried sick. But with an extraordinary amount of good fortune, the matter would be resolved as soon as Captain Knox delivered his letter, and Etienne dispatched Raoul Mendoza and the *Saracen* back to Charleston to collect a very important passenger.

Forty-Four

Etienne returned the ledger to his desk and locked it, slipping the key into his vest pocket. He glanced up at the portrait above the mantle and smiled. Estelle declared it was her best work. Unlike the exquisite painting of Lily that hung in the drawing room, this winsome image of his daughter in a homespun gown, wrapped in her grandmother's faded magenta shawl, was his favorite.

It had been almost a year since he had first brought her home to the house on Rue Royale. Since that time, Catherine Lillian Cruz, the daughter of Etienne Cruz, had claimed her rightful place in Creole society and become a patroness of the orphanage that had sheltered her since birth. Judging by the number of calling cards deposited on a table in the vestibule daily, she had also captured the hearts of far too many eligible men in New Orleans.

The seasons had flown by in a whirlwind of balls, elegant dinners, nights at the opera, and Sunday excursions in the park, with scarcely a moment unaccounted for except when they retired to their rooms at night. But beneath it all, Etienne had sensed heartbreak and things he might never have suspected had it not been for the arrival of Nathan's last letter.

Lily's bravery during the epidemic had earned her the gratitude of Charleston. It was unlike anything he had ever witnessed, Nathan said. And in the midst of the danger and devastation, Lily and Addie's son had found each other, only to be driven apart by Adelaide's desperate attempt to prevent a union between Paul and the daughter of Kate Perrault. After Lily left Charleston, Paul had searched desperately for her, never suspecting his mother was behind her disappearance. Finally, after learning that Lily was his daughter, and tormented by what she had done, Adelaide had confessed her treachery to her son.

When Etienne first read Nathan's letter his anger had been boundless. Adelaide's stubborn pride had cost all of them dearly, but the realization that they both wanted the same thing for Lily and Paul tempered his desire for vengeance. Instead, he did as Nathan asked. He dispatched Mendoza and the *Saracen* to Charleston with a message for the young doctor.

Etienne rose, walked to the window overlooking the gardens, and stared down at the slender figure on the terrace. Lily turned and glanced upward, sensing his presence there. His heart filled when she smiled. He lifted his hand in greeting then turned away. In spite of all that he could give her, she was lonely. But, not much longer, God willing.

He hurried down the long hallway and stepped out onto the second floor gallery. He was certain that he had heard the sound of a coach approaching. For a week, he had waited for word that the *Saracen* had been sighted, and today, the messenger had finally come. It had been a risky thing to do, but if Paul DuPre truly loved Lily, he would be aboard.

When his driver guided the coach through the gates and brought it to a stop, Etienne's face broke into a huge grin. He hurried down the steps, his hand outstretched.

"Welcome to New Orleans, Doctor. I trust you had a pleasant voyage."

"Indeed, sir. The *Saracen* is a magnificent ship."

"And how did you leave your family? Your mother, is she well?"

Paul smiled and stepped aside. "You can ask her yourself."

Etienne's brow shot up in surprise. "Ask her?"

Paul turned and held out his hand. Etienne watched, astonished, as the woman he had once dreamed of stepped down from the coach.

"Addie?" His sudden flash of anger dissolved into confusion at the questioning look in her eyes and the beginning of an uncertain smile that played about her lips.

"Hello, Etienne."

"It's really you!"

"Yes," she whispered and turned toward her son with a desperate look. It had been a mistake, a terrible mistake, coming without Etienne's knowledge. He was angry, and it was too late to turn back!

In the next instant, her startled cry was lost in the sound of Etienne's laughter as he swept her off her feet. Wrapped in his arms, her tiny slippers dangling in midair, he kissed her soundly.

"Addie! It really *is* you!"

"Yes, yes," she sighed as his arms tightened about her again.

Paul grinned at the spectacle. His mother's face glowed with a radiance he had never seen before. He glanced about, suddenly unsure of himself.

"Lily?"

Etienne pulled Adelaide to his side and sheltered her in the curve of his arm. "Follow that path. You will find her in the garden."

Adelaide sighed as her son hurried away. She was where she belonged at last, safe in Etienne's arms.

Lily pulled her shawl closer about her and reached to pick one of the late spring roses that grew next to the fountain. On moonlit nights when she stood at her window and gazed down upon it, the memories of Paul had returned to haunt her—his face, his voice, and the time he had declared his love. Did he remember her still, or had his own memories been as brief as the loving? She let the petals drop from her fingers and continued along the path remembering to smile at the gardeners who greeted her and kept to their tasks.

Paul opened the gate and stared down at the vision below. The late afternoon breeze fanned the hem of her gown. Her face glowed with the golden flush of sun filled days. She reached up to brush aside a wisp of hair that escaped the blue silk ribbon at the nape of her neck. It was truly Lily, more beautiful than he remembered.

Her name came to her faintly. She turned and gave her specs a familiar push, watching as the man hurried down the stone steps toward her. Her eyes widened as he drew closer. Could it be? Was it possible?

Only when he paused, his eyes questioning, did she free herself from the grip of shock and disbelief. She flew toward him, crying his name. Paul caught her up in his arms. Her laughter mingled with tears as time and again their lips met.

New Orleans, May 7, 1831

As he and Lily approached the flower-laden alter, Etienne nodded toward Louis and Estelle with obvious pride. In spite of the hasty preparations, guests filled the chapel next to the orphanage to overflowing. His daughter was about to become the wife of Doctor Paul DuPre of Charleston.

Afterward, Louis would escort Adelaide to his side to be joined with him in marriage. Following a wedding trip to London, he and Addie would return to Charleston for a reunion with Lily and Paul, and the Claibornes.

Lily's gaze swept the gathering and then turned to the man who waited for her at the altar. Tonight, they would board the *Celesta*. Once they reached Charleston, Paul would join Hadley Baker at the new hospital they were building together. But until then, they belonged only to one another.

Her fingers tightened upon her father's arm. She felt his hand close over hers possessively, almost desperately, and then gently, Etienne released his hold and placed her hand in Paul's.

Epilogue

Eden's Gate Plantation, eleven years later
December 30, 1842

Zina rose stiffly from where she knelt and pulled the faded quilt over the body on the bed. The leanto had grown cold during the long hours of the night. She could hear the kitchen help laying a fire in the adjoining room. The clattering of pots penetrated the numbness of her mind. Odd how normal things could go on, unaltered by death.

She clutched her shawl closer about her and opened the door. The crowd outside had swelled throughout the night and milled aimlessly between the quarters and the cookhouse. They waited for a sign, knowing the medicine woman would not leave until it was over. A muffled cry escaped from the bystander nearest the door, followed by another and another until an eerie keening echoed across the compound. They parted to let her pass as she made her way to the main house.

Zina reached for the banister to steady herself before beginning the climb up the back stairs. A single lamp glowed faintly at the top of the landing. Her shadow lengthened along the dimly lighted hallway. She stopped and pressed her forehead against the door, gripped the latch and entered the room.

"Pansy's gone, Miz Connie."

Constance Wellington's face was drawn with exhaustion. For two days, she had stayed by Pansy's side until Zina had forced her to return to her room. She pressed her fingers to her lips to stifle a cry. Zina knelt beside her chair and awkwardly patted her shoulder.

Through the windows, the first crimson streaks of daylight pierced the tree line beyond the fields. The sun would be up soon, erasing the fine etching of frost from the panes and the whiteness from the barren ground.

"I fetch some tea. Be right back." Zina gently settled Connie's hands in her lap and hurried from the room.

Connie watched the feeble flames dance upon the coals in the fireplace. So many had passed on since Victor and Augusta presided over this place. Soon there would be no one left who remembered how it had once been. She pushed herself from the chair, walked to the window, and absently fingered the velvet drape. In the distance, she could make out the wall that surrounded the cemetery. All the Edens were there, except one. She turned abruptly. It was painful to think of Charles, even now.

The door opened quietly. "Heah, drink this."

She took the cup drawing strength from the steaming brew and waved Zina away from the bed. There was no need to turn back the covers. She could not sleep.

"Find Mister Parrish, and tell him to come to Mister Charles's study." She set the cup and saucer on the table beside her chair.

Some found it strange that she continued to defer to Charles Eden as if he were still alive, 'Mister Charles's study,' 'Mister Charles's library.' It was as if she couldn't bring herself to assert the authority that was unquestionably hers ever since Lily and Nathan Claiborne had installed her as the permanent caretaker of Eden's Gate, following the death of Augusta Eden. By way of a strange and convoluted journey, she had found her way home to live out her days surrounded by the memories of a man who would forever claim a secret place in her heart.

Zina gathered up the cup and saucer and went in search of the overseer.

Connie descended the stairs a few minutes later and paused to glance at her reflection in the petticoat checker. Fatigue made her appear older than her thirty-eight years. Her slender figure had become gaunt in the weeks since Pansy had taken sick. She frowned and tucked a stray wisp of hair into the braided coil at the back of her neck, and adjusted her shawl across her shoulders.

"Good morning, Mister Parrish." She entered the study and moved to the hearth, holding out her hands to the warmth of the fire.

Elzy Parrish stroked his gray beard. "Reckon you know whut you a'doin, ma'am, but burying the cook in the family cemetery, well, if you'll pardon me for saying so, it don't seem proper somehow."

She sighed. She had expected as much. "Pansy came to Eden's Gate with Augusta Eden. If anyone belongs with the family, she does."

"I know whut you're saying, ma'am. It's jest that folks 'round here might not take too kindly to . . ."

She stiffened, signaling an end to his protests. "Mister Charles would have wanted it. It's the right thing to do."

Constance Wellington could be as stubborn as a mule when she set her mind to something, and he was not of a mind to get on her bad side. "I'll see to it, if'n you're sure." He eyed her expectantly.

"Quite sure, Mister Parrish."

He clapped his hat on his head and turned on his heel. It was bound to cause a lot of talk hereabouts when word got out that a slave was being laid to rest alongside white folks, but, he knew that she didn't give a tinker's damn what they thought. He shook his head and left the room.

Connie winced as the front door slammed. The overseer stomped down the front steps and headed in the direction of the carpenter's shed. She walked across the room and pulled the bellcord. "Canaan!" The majordomo hastened to answer her summons. She stared at Colombo's grandson curiously. Why had she never noticed his resemblance to his grandfather before? "Fetch a broom. That man has tracked up Mister Charles's rug."

The following morning, a cold mist chilled the throng that shuffled behind the lumbering wagon. Connie walked between Elzy Parrish and the medicine woman, barely conscious of the cold that crept through the heavy folds of her cloak. Her expression remained stoic behind her veil. It was her only concession to weakness. It wouldn't do for anyone to see her grief. Just ahead, the gates of the cemetery stood open to receive the plain pine coffin.

Zina blinked against the tears that burned her eyes. She had allowed no one in the room as she clutched Pansy's gnarled fingers in those last hours just before dawn. *Pansy, Pansy, you just got to try!* But, she knew even as she uttered the plea that the cook had already given up the struggle and only waited for release from her suffering.

When it had finally come, Zina could imagine the years slipping away from Pansy's tired and haggard features. She was at peace now, paying no mind to an old friend who trudged behind a wagon, desperately longing for those who had left her behind.

As the diggers shoveled the last spades of earth across the mound, the overseer clutched Connie's arm to steady her. "It's best we get you back to the house, ma'am. It looks like we're in for some rain. It won't do for you to get sick."

She nodded and clung to Zina's hand as he led them through the crowd. The first drops of rain streaked her veil, mingling with the tears that slipped down her face.

February 9, 1843

Connie pushed aside her dinner plate. She had no appetite and few interests to occupy the days that came and went. It had been almost two months since Pansy died and a fortnight since Paul and Lily and the children had returned from New Orleans. She had already received a letter inviting her to come to the city for a visit. Her resistance wavered at first, but it was short lived. A strange malaise seemed to have her in its grip. She went into the study, sat down at the desk, and took out paper to write a note postponing her visit for a while. Paul would frown as he read it. His next message would be a demand, not a request.

She frowned at the illegible scrawl and swept the paper into the drawer beneath the polished surface. Perhaps she would try again tomorrow.

She rose and walked to the fireplace to stoke the meager flames. It was during the afternoons that she found herself at odds, as darkness began to creep through the house. The sound of voices outside caused her to turn. Elzy Parrish's protests seemed impatient and harsh.

The door swung open and an odd specter, hidden behind an armful of firewood, wavered toward the hearth.

"Hugh, how many times do I have to tell you to let Canaan fetch the kindling? You are scattering trash all about."

"Powerful sorry, Miz Connie, but Mistah Parrish, he done told me to brang—"

"What's going on out there?" She walked to the window and drew aside the curtain and frowned at the lathered animal by the steps. Another peddler most likely. Elzy Parrish had little patience with itinerants who found their way up the long avenue from the road. She let the curtain drop and reached for her cloak. Judging from the overseer's stance, he meant to turn the stranger away. She opened the front door, feeling the frigid air upon her face.

"Mister Parrish?"

He mounted the steps as she crossed the verandah. "Ain't nothin' fer you to be concerned about. This here feller says he used to be from 'round these parts." He dropped his voice conspiratorially. "I'll send him on his way."

"He looks exhausted. Surely we can spare a meal. It's getting late. He can bed down in the stables." She pushed past him and stared down at the man at the bottom of the steps, squinting to discern his features beneath a battered hat. A mat of silver-streaked hair fell about his shoulders. His hands were rough and reddened from the cold.

"Are you hungry, sir?" She jerked back as he suddenly reached out.

"Connie?" he whispered, his incredulous eyes appeared to devour her.

She backed away, suddenly fearful of the familiarity. Elzy Parrish tensed, ready to spring to her rescue. Only the stranger's apparent recognition held him back.

"I'm afraid you have the advantage, sir. I don't believe that we have ever met." Her eyes shifted nervously to the spavined horse that grazed wearily on the grass by the walkway.

He followed her gaze. "He's not Belezar, but he's carried me a mighty long way."

"Belezar?" she whispered. Her eyes searched the face now so close to her own. "What do you know about that animal?"

Tears glistened in his eyes. "Connie, don't you know me?" The plea came from some raw crevice deep inside his soul.

Elzy Parrish gave a start as she suddenly swayed toward the man with a whimper.

"Charles? Oh, my God, Charles!"

A wracking seizure of coughing caused Charles Eden to grasp the banister and slip to his knees.

"Elzy!" Her shriek propelled the overseer to the man's side. Lifting the gaunt figure in his arms, Elzy Parrish followed her up the stairs to the room at the end of the hall. He deposited his burden onto the bed and backed away as she turned and ran from the room to summon help. Whoever the stranger was, he had just put one hell of a scare into her.

For two days, the house was enveloped in a tense silence. The house servants crept about, giving wide berth to the door that Connie had closeted herself behind. The quarters were rife with rumors, tales of the stranger retold and embellished until it appeared their mistress was possessed.

Connie clutched the thin hand, threaded with veins, scarred and callused. Charles did not respond to the pressure of her grasp. Her tears had fallen upon his face when she scraped away the matted beard, and her heart broke as she traced his furrowed features, aged beyond his years. There was little resemblance to the man who had occupied this room so many years ago.

Paul returned his instruments to the leather bag and latched it. "Constance, I insist that you go to your room and get some rest. You cannot continue this unabated vigil, or I'll have two patients to care for."

"He'll be all right, won't he, Paul?"

He sighed. Why the man still lived confounded him. When Elzy Parrish had ridden up to the house and delivered Connie's frantic message, he could scarcely believe it was possible. For twelve years, everyone believed Charles was dead. Yet, here he lay—or what remained of him—starved, scarred from beatings, and battling to live. He shook his head.

"I don't know, Moppet." He gestured helplessly. Connie was on the verge of collapse. He had never known her to give way like this, not even when Daniel had died of the fever. But he had always known that, as deeply as his sister cared for Daniel Wellington, she had never stopped loving Charles Eden to the very depths of her being.

The door opened and Lily slipped quietly into the room. "How is he?" she whispered. Paul shook his head and glanced toward the bed. She turned and placed her hands gently upon her sister-in-law's shoulders. "Connie, dear, won't you please go rest for a little while? Paul and I will be right here." He shot her a grateful look.

"No, Lily. Charles needs me, and I must be here when he wakes up." She turned and gave her an imploring look.

"Constance." Paul's patience was wearing dangerously thin.

"You wouldn't leave if it was Lily lying there." Anger flashed in her eyes.

He glanced at his wife and shrugged. Lily smiled, remembering the night their twins, Jasmine and Rose, were born. Hell's own fury could not have driven Paul from her side, nor would he convince Connie to leave Charles now.

Paul walked across the room and dropped into a chair by the window, prepared to wait for as long as it took Charles Eden to obey his sister's will. Lily offered no protest as her husband and his sister closed ranks against the demons that kept Charles imprisoned in darkness.

"Miz Connie, you got company." Zina stood at the door.

Connie jerked her head up from the counterpane.

"Strangers a'comin up the road."

She sprang from the chair and followed the medicine woman into the hallway. She could hear the animals rearing as their riders jerked on the reins, dismounted, and strode across the verandah. Their fists struck the door with urgent impatience.

There was fear in her eyes. "It's about Charles. I know it is."

They descended the stairs quickly. Zina stood aside as she gripped the latch and opened the front door, staring silently from one man to the other. They pulled their hats from their heads and nodded.

"Begging your pardon, ma'am. Apologize for the intrusion. My name's George Bates, and this here's my partner, Pete Colter. We come down from Richmond. Been tracking a prisoner who escaped from Bensonville prison 'bout two months back. Followed 'im down this far. Folks up the way claim they seen a stranger headed for these parts 'bout two days back. Figgered he could be hiding on the place. Don't suppose you might have seen 'im?" He paused, noting the sudden pallor of her face.

"A prisoner?"

"Yes, ma'am. Goes by the name of James Dunning. Tall feller, thin, and sickly, too. Surprised he coulda' made it this far. He's been at Bensonville nigh on ten years or better. Gray hair, full beard. Ain't had much need of a razor where he's been."

Colter snickered behind his partner. Connie felt an instant revulsion for the pair. Bounty hunters. "Why was he there, at Bensonville?"

"Goddamn abolitionist. Freeing slaves from plantations all the way from Savannah to the Tidewater, and shipping 'em north." Bates spat.

Connie swayed and gripped the sill.

"Mind if we take a look around, ma'am? 'Spect there's lots of places a man could hide here."

"Search if you like, but you will be wasting your time."

"Aw, c'mon, Bates." His partner growled. "While we stand here jawing, Dunning's jest gittin' on further down the road, and that bounty's gittin' away from us."

Bates appeared to hesitate and then relented. "Well, good day to you, ma'am. Keep a watch out now, 'specially if your menfolk ain't about. Dunning's a mean cuss. Ain't the sort you'd want to run up with."

"Thank you for the warning." She waited until the two had mounted up and ridden away before she slammed the door and sagged against it. Zina gathered her in her arms as a dam of tears burst from her.

"Connie, come quick!" Lily's cry sent them racing back up the stairs. Connie reached the bedside, blood pounding in her temples.

"He's awake. Oh, thank God." She clutched at the trembling hand that reached out to her. She would always remember the gentle smile that crossed his lips as Charles fell into a natural sleep, certain that he had only dreamed of an angel with a sprinkling of freckles across her nose.

September 10, 1843

Charles Eden gripped his cane and drew his wife to his side. His gaze swept the grounds. The afternoon sun had begun to settle upon the late summer flowers that surrounded the house. Connie had created a sanctuary from the poisonous evil that once abided here, but, in spite of the happiness they had reclaimed, there was a sadness about it all. So many were gone now, and in the north, there was talk of war. Perhaps it would not come in their lifetimes, but it would come.

She had remained steadfast as he related the horrors he had endured after the destruction of *The Pegasus*, when he had stolen the identity of the unfortunate James Dunning. Vowing to atone for the deaths of Pearl and Rameses, he had devoted himself to the cause Stephen Flynn had embraced so passionately. For two years, he had evaded capture, until his luck ran out, then there was Bensonville, where men lost their identities and their reason. The memories of Connie had sustained him when his own sanity threatened to desert him. And, like her, he had found his way back to Eden's Gate.

All that mattered was that they were together. They wept in each other's arms and loved with a hunger born of lost years and promises renewed. As he healed, her face glowed with a radiance that would not diminish with the passing of time. She had given him back his life and gained fulfillment in return. Nothing would ever come between them again.

Through the years, many journeys had come to an end, but theirs had only begun.

About the author

After retiring from Florida State University, Lynn Braxton returned to her birthplace in the Panhandle of Florida with her two rescue dogs, Snuffy and Sadie.

Raised an only child, her earliest companions were paper dolls cut from mail order catalogs. Today, while she pursues her passion for history and writing, she still finds time to search among old trunks and boxes, looking for a dusty shoebox filled with those characters who became the foundation for a lifetime of stories.

If you enjoyed *Lady of the House*, please tell your friends and consdier posting an online review. Your opinion helps other readers find this novel. Thank you for your support.

www.ingramcontent.com/pod-product-compliance
Lightning Source LLC
Chambersburg PA
CBHW020346180626
46812CB00001B/366